MORAG PRUNTY

DANCING WITH MULES

A Pan
Original

First published 2001 by Pan Books
an imprint of Pan Macmillan Ltd
Pan Macmillan, 20 New Warf Road, London N1 9RR
Basingstoke and Oxford
Associated companies throughout the world
www.panmacmillan.com

ISBN 0 330 48491 5

9

A CIP catalogue record for this book is available from
the British Library.

Typeset by SetSystems Ltd, Saffron Walden, Essex
Printed and bound in Great Britain by
Mackays of Chatham plc, Chatham, Kent

FOR NiALL

ACKOWLEDGEMENTS

At the risk of sounding like a co-dependant, there is no way on God's earth that I could have written this book without the astonishing array of wonderful people that I have in my life. If I haven't thanked you enough already, it gives me great pleasure to acknowledge you in print because this book is as much down to you as it is to me.

My husband Niall, for looking after me in both practical and emotional ways. For policing my lock-ins, coming round with the tea trolley, keeping me updated on *EastEnders*, and always making me feel like a goddess, even when I turned into a hairy, crazed, pyjama mountain. But mostly for creating a quiet haven in our home and in your heart which gives me the peace and freedom I need to write.

My fellow writers who have supported and encouraged me through my whingeing, word counting and weighing of pages; Gai Griffin, whose whimsical attitude to life never fails to inspire me; Suzanne Power for persistently telling me to write humour even when I kept swearing her off; Ailish Connelly for her natural funniness and quintessential Irishness and Marian Keyes for her endless support, generosity and advice. Knowing you, and sharing with you all, has been the most important step I have taken as a writer.

My best friend Dee – for just always being there, no matter what.

My mother, for her loyalty to my dreams, even when they must have seemed foolish and to be carrying me off in precarious directions – you never pulled me back or encouraged me to be sensible. You managed the balance between believing in me and protecting me. That makes you an exceptional person.

My sisters, Christine and Claire – for celebrating my successes and for the feeling that I have that, no matter where we all are in our lives, you are always close by.

My brother Tom – for always turning me back into a child and making me giggle in Mass. For the times when you helped me realize that having a laugh was the Main Thing.

My extended family – for being the funniest and the best. The stock I come from is full of stories and humour and life. I am one lucky plastic Paddy.

Special thanks to Auntie Sheila for her lifetime supply of 'Nolanic Hyperbole' and for being my Instant Bouncing Research Head during the course of writing *Dancing with Mules*.

Marianne Gunne O'Connor – Superagent, Celtic Tigress and All-Round Glamorous Girlfriend. One of these days it will sink in, but to date I still cannot *believe* all you have done for me! You are my dream-maker.

Vicky Satlow – for the 'Go-Girl' emails and All-Round Ass-Kicking agenting work.

Suzanne Baboneau for being such an enthusiastic, kind and careful editor. But mostly thank you for being the first. Your decision, and that of your colleagues, to buy *Dancing with Mules* has literally changed my life.

Trena Keating for her Lets Storm America! attitude and Imogen Taylor for nursing the book – and me – through to publication.

To all at Macmillan, you have taken my manuscript and brought it to an audience. It may only be a job to you, but it's still a miracle for me – so thank you.

I would also like to thank the *real* queen of Dublin PR – Caroline Kennedy – for all her help, and state, for the record, that the character of Lorna Cafferty is *not* her. I made up her – and everyone else in the book – by myself! However, certain inspirations came from unexpected quarters, and top of the Sense of Humour list is Pat O'Brien, the man credited with Bringing the Brazilian to Dublin. Thank you for letting me 'send up' your beautiful salon in the book.

A special thanks to my boss Peter McKenna for both his tolerance and encouragement.

I would also like to thank the collective of all the Irish people I have met along the way. (Actually, I would like to devote an additional 150 pages of this book to thanking you all individually, but my editor won't allow it. Maybe next time!) Some of you have been steadfast friends listening to my problems over endless cups of coffee or put a roof over my head when I was in need.

Some of you have dressed me, done my hair, manicured my nails, kept the taxman off my back, assisted me at work, sold my car, been good neighbours, brought me salsa dancing, taken my picture, distracted me on shopping afternoons, fed me or just been generally generous and encouraging around my success – you know who you are. All of you have helped turn my experience of living in Ireland into a love affair with life. The people I have met here have helped to create a home in which I feel privileged to live and inspired to write about.

Thank you all.

PART ONE

iN DUBLiN TOWN
ONE SATURDAY . . .

1

Lorna's eyes felt like they'd been taken out in the night, dipped in vinegar and put back in sideways. The vodka gremlins must have been at her in the night again. She was still fully dressed and, as she tried to move to see if she was still alive, her Wolford's twisted unmercifully into the crack of her buttocks. Her first waking thought was a mournful regret that the two-hundred-pound Italian nightie she had bought in Brown Thomas that week was still folded respectfully on her pillow, as she'd been too incapacitated to put it on three nights in a row. On the bright side, its proximity meant she was at home in bed, or at least *on* it which was better than she'd done in the last few mornings.

Wednesday – drinks after work with the girls, and a promise to be in bed by ten. She had bumped into Geoff, a retired rock star who was living a life of tweedy humdrummery in Wicklow, and had managed to get away from his dullard of a wife for the night. He had a couple of nobody, back-stage technician types with him, but by midnight the boys were at home cuddling their girlfriends, and Lorna and Geoff were enjoying a champagne nightcap in the penthouse of The Clarence. She had passed out on the sofa, but it hadn't been a completely wasted evening as he'd agreed to open an art exhibition for her on Friday. That was what good PR was all about. Maintaining your contacts.

Thursday, she knew she had to be up early on Friday for a breakfast presentation to a potential new client. Flannery Frozen Foods were not exactly glamour material, but she needed a few 'meat and potato' accounts to keep the business end of things running. Young fashion designers were all very well for keeping the wardrobe up to scratch, and her travel-company clients paid her partly in free flights, but it was the dog-food manufacturers and washing-powder producers that paid for the Ferrari and the mews in Ballsbridge.

Lorna had been good on Thursday, and was home by eight with the intention of an evening devoted to tackling her hair. She had missed her appointment with Gloria and, really, the mop could not go a day longer without some serious attention. Three days without a professional wash and blow and her sleek highlighted bob assumed the colour and consistency of a grubby bath mat. There had been a shower of rain that day and she'd had to hide it under a jaunty Philip Treacy hat which her assistant Sheila had just blown a month's wages on.

'But the rain will ruin it!'

'Don't worry, darling, I'll buy you another one.'

'But it was the last one in the sh-ho-op,' the little strap whinged.

'Oh, grow up!'

It was Lorna's favourite retort and the only advantage of being ten years older than everyone she employed as she could pretend that she knew what it meant. If she could have afforded to, Lorna would have surrounded herself with veiny old-timers who knew what they were doing. But the economics of her champagne lifestyle meant she had to employ children who were cheap, willing to slave and motivated by the occasional hem-brush of Dublin's most glamorous and successful PR person.

By nine thirty the rollers were in. Then the phone had rung. It was some taxi driver she had given her phone number to the previous Saturday.

'Remember me?'

Lorna didn't, but she was glad of the company all the same. He sounded so crestfallen by her confusion that she had spared him five minutes' chat which, given the half bottle of 'wind-down' chilled Chablis that was already inside her, and the husky how'ya roughness of his voice, led to a quick drink in the pub round the corner. The quiet nobody-goes-there local she used when she didn't want to be seen.

The 'quick' drink was followed by ten more – all of them consumed *very* quickly – by which time she had rung Jury's from the ladies' loo and booked a room for the night. She told the deliciously dark and stocky what's-his-name that she was staying there while her house was being redecorated, then made him drive her there in the taxi, while she lounged in the back and reminded him of all the good reasons he was going to have for risking his licence driving through Dublin under the influence.

Lorna went straight to the Flannery Frozen Foods meeting from the hotel, still slightly cut and mossy from the night's excitement. Within ten minutes she had the big hairy aul' fella of an MD in the palm of her hand. He was up from Kerry for the day and had never seen anything quite so glamorous and alluring as Lorna straight after a night of rampant sex with a complete stranger. Of course, he didn't know that, and she didn't tell him. But Dez Flannery was from a farming background and was very sensitive to the subtle nuances of Mother Nature's aromas. On his way out the door, he took her to one side and said, 'Ye have a lovely natural smell about ye.' Lorna would have slapped him, except that she'd met enough like him to know it was a genuine compliment. Four hours later she was glad she hadn't because they got a call to say they had won the account. Four hours and five minutes later, Flannery's secretary rang to arrange a one-on-one meeting with Lorna 'as soon as possible' to discuss strategy. Lorna negotiated 'dinner' down to a 'late lunch' in three weeks' time.

She spent the rest of the day running around town getting herself 'lovely-fied' for that night's gig – the opening of the Arcade Gallery in Temple Bar. It was the hottest invite in town and her phone was rung red-hot all afternoon. It was Lorna's job to make sure that the important people, press and celebrities, turned up, and that there were enough lick-arse liggers there to make the party swing, but not so many that they would hog all the wine and canapés.

She did this by lying committedly and convincingly to all camps. The press were told that it was going to be 'wall-to-wall celebs, darling', so much so that she didn't know if she should squeeze them in. The celebrities were graded Number One (famous actors living in Wicklow; international authors hiding in Clare and tax-evading rock stars) and Number Two (Irish fashion designers, soap-opera actors, and DJs). Number Ones were told that other Number Ones were flying in from London/New York especially: 'Elton's coming – he said he's only *dying* to see you!' and that there would be 'absolutely *no press*, darling. Won't get in the door, I promise!'

The Number Two celebrities could usually be tempted in with promised social proximity to the Number Ones and of course, '*Press*, darling – they'll *all* be there. In fact I was talking to so-and-so only last week about you and they said a profile was *long* overdue ... yes I was, darling ... cross my heart ... *long overdue* ... his exact words, yes ... see you there at seven!'

The liggers and general Dublin wannabe party animals were more difficult to judge. One never knew when today's nobody make-up artist was going to bugger off to Hollywood and become Madonna's best friend. It had happened to her once before, when she had turned away a nasty little freeloading stylist, Biddy McFarlane, from the door of a party in The Clarence only to discover that her four years in New York had turned her into an assistant fashion editor on *Vogue*. She had renamed herself 'Gorgeous' and had Christy and Naomi waiting in a limo outside.

'I'm Gorgeous,' the purple-haired piglet had announced to the doorman.

'You are in your hole,' he replied and the tabloids had had a field day.

The gallery opening was in full swing by nine, and Lorna had got it just right. Parties were Her Thing, and Lorna had managed to get enough drink into everyone so that the Number Twos thought they were Number Ones and, better still, so did the press. The one Number One who had turned up stayed just long enough to get his photo taken, and even believed Lorna when she told him that Elton had missed his flight but said that he would *love* to see him the next time he was over: 'He is such a lovely man and he *adores* you!'

Lorna was a master at diverting social disasters while creating just enough scandal to get everyone talking. Her greatest weapon was her old friend Lynda Laverty. Lynda was an ex-Miss Ireland who was well into her forties, a good five stone heavier than she had been in her heyday and who – on the verge of complete obscurity – was always grateful for the opportunity to reassert her celebrity status at a public event. She generally achieved this by wearing some brightly coloured minuscule frock and pressing her outlandish breasts in the face of anyone who would listen to her. If Lorna was lucky she might whip them out altogether and 'out' a few ageing politicians who had enjoyed her in her 'Lovely Laverty' days. Lynda was old hat but always entertaining. If the Dáil was closed and it was a quiet week news-wise, she might get a half-column on page six.

When Lynda got drunk, she spoke in around-the-house Irish mammy-speak without drawing a breath. At tonight's gallery opening she had it in for Ireland's top DJ, Rory Mac Rory, who had made a show of her on his talk-radio programme during the last Miss World competition, flummoxing her with questions about Sexism and the Objectification of Women. A furious Lynda had gleefully told the housewives and taxi drivers of Ireland that, from her first-hand experience of it, Rory's precious object was in itself 'nothing to write home about', and reminded him that Sexism had surely lost its last three letters if his behaviour at the afters party for the last Miss Ireland competition was anything to go by. Rory and Lynda were both at the opening, and Lynda was the first to get into the ring, sidling up to Lorna and saying, in a voice just loud enough for him to hear, 'Would you come here for a moment, Lorna, and tell me who that gobshite Rory thinks he is with the cut of his big fecky jumper and the aul' family-man bollocks when the world and the Virgin Mother Herself knows –' she paused to take a big swig of vodka and cranberry – 'that he'd get up on a sick hen!'

Rory, who had his new red-haired production assistant pinned up against the wall, ignored the slight. Lorna deftly disappeared to the other side of the room so she wouldn't be directly associated with the barney she knew was coming.

'A cracked plate!' bellowed Lynda.

The bait wasn't taken. Ms Laverty was a lady who would stop at nothing until she was heard. She stood on a chair and raised her glass in the air.

'Ladies and gentleman, I have an announcement to make . . .'

The room had no option but to stop and listen.

'Rory Mac Rory – Mr Person-fucking-ality himself – would eat the arse off a nun through the convent gates and if there's anyone in this room disagrees with me speak now or for ever hold your pe—' Lynda had not chosen the sturdiest chair in the house and the flimsy foldaway collapsed, sending her crashing to the ground. She was rushed to hospital with a fractured foot, and while Lorna was the very picture of concern, swooping around with instructions and asking everyone to move out of the way, she was secretly pleased that the incident had been halted when it had, and yet *not* before the press had their smutty little story. The saddest thing for Lorna was knowing that it worked both ways. Lynda's life depended on one or two press cuttings a year, however much she had to humiliate herself in the process of getting them. Lorna never challenged her on it or pretended to understand. The two women used each other in this way without ever asking themselves or each other if it made them happy. It was the food of life for both of them. Money for one and fame for the other. It was the unspoken deal that made their worlds go round.

As the party was petering out, Lorna did her last working act of the day, taking her mobile out of her bag and snapping it open before she gave herself time to think about what might be on it. There were six messages from her best paying but least favourite client – a big thick from Galway who made Flannery look like James Bond. Paddy Wallop had a nervous up-from-the-country air about him that made Lorna cringe. He was coming to Dublin in the morning and could they meet for lunch, coffee – *anything*? Wallop was the managing director and owner of Medico, which manufactured and sold medical supplies. Except he didn't just manufacture and sell them – he lived, breathed, slept, chewed, swallowed and digested them. Three hours talking about the importance of strong elasticity in the waistband of incontinence pants was not Lorna's idea of a fun lunch date. But Wallop paid her company forty grand a year for press and public-relations services and got exactly zilch in return. Lorna had, in fairness, tried to get him some publicity in the beginning. She had taken ten hand-picked journalists to Ashford Castle for a weekend, wined and dined them to within an inch of their lives, then taken them on a quick whip round the factory, handed them a press release which was as interesting as the limits of her subject matter would allow and hoped for the best. A week later one of the Sundays had done a cruel but hilarious piece featuring a half-page picture of Wallop illustrating the strength of his new incontinence pants by filling a pair with a stone of potatoes. There was a pull-out quote which read 'Paddy says, "It takes a lot of spuds to fill my pants."' Lorna had strongly advised against the photo opportunity at the time, but in the absence of any other press coverage whatsoever, she had to turn the whole ghastly thing around and convince Paddy that there was No Such Thing As Bad Publicity, and that a full page in a Sunday newspaper would have cost him infinitely more than throwing champagne and oysters into Dublin's greediest journos in Ireland's most expensive hotel over a three-day period. He hadn't seemed to mind and had been her most faithful client to date. She made a mental note to call his office in the morning and say she was going on a shoot to Tasmania for six weeks.

The evening had taken a downturn for Lorna when the party was finally over. It was eleven and she had air-kissed her last guest and, the lack of sleep having caught up on her, was on her way home to bed, leaving the minions to clean up the mess. She had smiled enough for one night, and felt like she'd had a coat hanger stuffed in her mouth for ever. The very last thing she needed was a chance meeting with the Queen of Smug, Bridget Wilkin-Walkins.

Bridget and Lorna had been at UCD together. While Lorna had partied her way into a third-class degree and fallen into PR for free drink and the want of anything else to do, Bridget had graduated with first-class honours, done a masters in marketing, married well, and lived a life of subdued elegant abstinence in a feng-shui minimalist paradise in Dalkey. Lorna despised her.

'Darling!' Lorna heard behind her as the wafer-thin soles of her Gucci mules hit the hard cobblestones.

She struggled to rearrange her fed-up, frowning face into an expression of serene joy and ability before whipping around on her heels in an impressive demi-turn.

'Bridget! And *Thomas*! How lovely to see you!'

'Boring Tom' was officially the dullest man in the world. In their first few months at university he had been considered a good catch on account of his good looks. But once word got out that he was a Class A, non-drinking, Dry Protestant Dullard, all the girls backed off. Bridget moved in and they all thought she was mad. Now the rest of them had alcoholic ex-husbands or were scrabbling around at almost forty for Mr He'll Do, and Brainy Bridget was married to some class of an extremely clever bio-chemistry, scientist-type person, who still had all his own teeth and hair and was a full-on devoted husband and father. It took lack of imagination in a man to achieve that type of respectable longevity and Bridget had been smart enough to spot that at twenty-one.

Lorna always flirted overtly with Tom in the hope he might flirt back and annoy Bridget. If truth be known, she'd ride him from here to Malinhead and send Bridget the video if she got the chance, but Tom remained indifferent to her charms. He was officially impervious to sin.

'Lorna – you are looking *fantastic*!'

'Why *thank you*, Bridget – ' Lorna gave Tom a sideways glance, but got nothing back – 'but I would have to say you are looking *only fantastic* yourself!'

It killed Lorna to say it because it was so true. Lorna had long known that the world is divided into Women Like Lauren Hutton Who Can Wear Beige and Women Who Can't. Bridget fell into the first category, but Lorna needed all the help she could get. Black was the closest she could ever get to elegance.

Bridget could have let it end there, and sent Lorna home depressed, but she was going for the full menu tonight.

'On your way home from *another* party?'

'Opening, actually. Fabulous work – new Irish artists . . .' Lorna struggled to remember one of their names and couldn't.

Bridget was straight back with a hard volley: 'Oh *ye-es*, darling, it is *so* important to support the arts in Ireland. I've *just* been appointed to the board of the National Gallery – I only hope that I'll be able to do as much as you do for young artists with your parties and . . . things . . .' She trailed off as if unable to put words on the shallowness of it all.

Lorna just wanted to scream, *I am best friends with Elton John!* But she knew that Bridget would pretend to be too highbrow to have heard of him. She wanted to cry.

'And look at your *gorgeous* dress, I wish I had the courage to wear something as short as that . . .'

Lorna never failed to be astonished at how cutting

Bridget could be. She was annoyed at herself for feeling hurt; it was slowing down her ability to give a catty answer back.

'. . . and I just don't *know* how you keep that fantastic figure with all the partying you have to do!'

There was not a pick on Bridget and she had three children under her belt.

'Really. Doesn't she look amazing, darling?'

They both turned on Boring Tom. Lorna was inwardly pleading for a wink or a mere crumb of lasciviousness. But Tom's eyes moved lovingly across his wife's face as if he was longing to get her home and tear the back off her.

But Bridget was going nowhere until she had scrunched Lorna's self-worth in her fist and scattered it across the pavement.

'I mean, considering the age we are – we haven't done *too* badly now, have we?'

She rounded it off with a tinkling laugh and Lorna joined in, although her own sounded hollow. She knew she was losing. She just wanted to get it over and done with now.

'I mean, here we are, Two Old Ha-ags – ' she opened her eyes wide and glowered pointedly at Lorna over the word 'hag' – 'and we are like opposite ends of the extreme.'

'How do you mean?'

Even as the words came out Lorna knew they were a mistake. An invite for the executioner to kick back the stool.

'Well, I mean here I am – clean-living, bor-ing lifestyle – no smoking – very little drink – ' she sang-a-song over 'bor-ing' so it was clear she didn't mean it – 'and here you are – a high-flyer, drinking, smoking, party girl . . .' and raised her hands up over 'party girl' as if compensating for the fact that it implied 'sad slut'. 'We're like adverts for no drink and lots of drink! Don't drink and at thirty-eight you'll look like me – ' she shrugged modestly then nodded at Lorna – 'or drink lots and you'll get preserved, sort of pickled permanently at twenty-five!'

Vile Bridget then looked up at her husband as if she deserved a pat on the head for being terribly clever.

Pickled! Preserved in vinegar like a fucking onion! Crunchy, bitter and wrinkled. 'Raging alcoholic' felt like an accolade in comparison. Lorna dug her toes into the cobblestones until she thought her heels would snap, struggling through the shock of the insult to find a bitchy but clever retort. But blind rage had blunted her wit. She wanted to pull Bridget's Nicole Farhi mac over her head and kick her down the street before burying one of her stilettos in the back of the bitch's skull. There was going to be no dignified way out of this. Bridget was smiling at her sweetly, waiting to meet the oncoming lorry of abuse.

'Oh fuck off!' was the best she could manage and, as Lorna tried to turn away with a suitably disgusted flounce, one of her heels got caught in the cobblestones and she tripped in an undignified half-fall which made her look like even more of a sad drunk.

Bridget called after her, 'What? What did I say? I said

you looked twenty-five!' Then to her husband but within Lorna's hearing, 'I hope she'll be all right going home on her own in that state!'

Lorna had no decent alternative but to hotfoot it up to Little's. Little's was owned by Little Mike who was, well, little. (Although after he had initiated one of Dublin's models into his free membership 'arrangement', he always insisted they call him Big Mike.) Lorna was one of his few female members for whom he had waived the physical formalities. Little got a good deal of publicity and profile out of Lorna. In return she got a free pass into the most fun place in Dublin to plaster oneself into a state of acute putrefaction.

Sitting up on the bed with her tights still on and at least ten talented rave artists having a disco inside her skull, Lorna tried to remember how she had got home. She remembered meeting Bridget and the geek (sadly that part of the tape had not been wiped), then the contents of her handbag scattering over the dance floor at Little's. Some bastard had stood on her new Prescriptives compact. Oh God – had she punched him? Had a go at him? Had she . . . ?

'Cheery morning, poppet!'

Lorna jumped under the duvet, forgetting she was dressed.

'Only me, sweetheart. Keep your pants on. Oh, I see you're still fully dressed. Makes a change, the state you were in last night!'

It was Nylon. He must have rescued her from Little's and taken her home. Nylon was the only person in the whole world that Lorna felt she could be thoroughly herself with. Although increasingly she was forgetting what that felt like. The river between her public persona and her inner life seemed to be growing increasingly wide. In public she was viciously confident and capable. The last time her inner life had seen the light was in a therapist's chair when she had bawled uncontrollably at the sad singular shallowness of her existence and paid fifty quid for the insight. She thought it best to give that whole area a wide berth and stick to acting full time. Sometimes it became unavoidable and swooped down on her after a particularly heavy session, or if she forgot her ruling against whiskey consumption. Those times, Nylon was usually on hand to help her pick up the pieces and remind her that she was still an alluring and vivacious woman who men were queuing nineteen deep at the bar to meet. He always managed to convince her it was true even though he was a committed homosexual.

The title Homosexual was the only thing that Nylon *was* committed to. He was one of Dublin's Floating Personality Gays, who earned his crust by doing odds and sods of things that required charm, humour and not too much hard work. He worked a day here and there for Lorna, running errands and party organizing, but mostly sitting on the girls' desks talking about skincare and sidling his way into free lunches. On Saturdays he worked in Dublin's trendiest hair salon, Gloria's Gaff, taking coats and, if a male model walked in through the doors, washing hair. About twice a year he managed to get one of his extremely badly written pieces into *Gay Force* magazine in return for sexual blackmail of the editor, but it was enough for him to call himself 'press' at every freebie lunch and party lig going. He lived on canapés, crisps and champagne, 'borrowed' most of his clothes from still-sleeping one-night stands, and tended to camp out in rich friends' houses to avoid the reality of the grim bedsit in Rathmines where he had been living since he dropped out of college seven years ago. Nylon was fond of Lorna, but he was not committed. She was so lost in the whirl of her hard-core party lifestyle that the bit of comfort she got from having him around seemed as close to real friendship as she could get.

'Did I make a complete exhibition of myself last night?'

Nylon handed her a glass of freshly squeezed orange juice. He was always the perfect house guest. He had to be.

'Truth or Hollywood version?'

'Truth.'

'We-ell . . .'

The brain-rave was in full swing and Lorna didn't think she'd be able to make it through the truth.

'No. Hollywood version.'

'You arrived in Little's to an audience of adoring fans, drank pink champagne . . .'

'Whiskey?'

'Lots, I'm afraid, dear – you were in a bit of a condition . . .'

Lorna waved him away through a slug of juice.

'No, no – back to Hollywood.'

'You danced around your handbag with an unqualified display of style and decorum. Tom Cruise came up and asked you out *again*. You turned him down – The End!'

'I hit a man, didn't I?'

Nylon pursed his lips and nodded sagely.

'Yes you did, dearie.'

'After I dropped my bag on the floor and he stepped on my compact?'

'Got it in one.'

'Then you came and took me home.'

'We-ell.'

Nylon looked at the ceiling. Lorna's face contorted with fear.

'No, we weren't . . . we weren't . . .'

'Ejected? Yes, sadly yes. We were indeed chucked out.'

'And up?'

'All over Derek the Doorman's nice new trainers.'

Lorna curled up into a ball under the duvet. 'Oh God, I can never leave the house again. Were we barred – no – don't tell me . . .'

'Don't worry, darling, bunch of flowers to Zoe, a new pair of boots for Del Boy and I think we'd be cleared of our crimes. I'll have it all organized by lunchtime.'

In reality, Nylon had a hot date with a builder in less than an hour and had no intention of doing either errand. Builders and beefcakes in general were kept strictly to the afternoons as they were pure recreational fodder and there was nothing to be gained from knowing them. Apart, that is, from being nailed to the wall of his bedsit and humiliated to within an inch of his life. He was supposed to be at Gloria's Gaff from ten this morning, but she'd forgive him if he turned up at two.

'You are such an angel – what would I do without you?'

'Die a lonely and desperate old woman – here's your post,' he said, thrusting an official-looking envelope into her hand. 'Found it half under the settee, thought it might be important.'

Then Nylon swanned out to the kitchen to prepare their morning medication of espresso and Rothmans.

'Important', thought Lorna, is love letters and postcards. This was just some garbage from the bank. She always left opening ghastly post until she got into her office, but the lady of leisure charm of receiving letters in bed made Lorna open it.

Thirty seconds later she wished she hadn't.

'Yaaaaaa . . . nooooooooh!'

Nylon heard the scream from the kitchen.

By the time he got to her, Lorna was standing with her palms out slicing the air like a politician. The letter was still in one hand and she was talking herself out of her hysteria.

'It's a mistake. It must be a mistake . . .'

Then she looked at Nylon and smiled with her mouth only.

'Not a problem! Crisis over! A mistake has been made, and I'll sort it all out on Monday!'

'What kind of a mistake, hon?'

Maybe someone had died and she'd gone into denial. How ghastly would that be!

'A bill, Nylon, a tax bill – ' she shook her head and pursed her lips – 'for seven hundred and fifty thousand pounds.'

Nylon's face fell.

'But it's okay because it's a mistake. Ha! A stupid mistake. Quite funny, really!'

Desperation was written across Lorna's face. She wanted Nylon to give her a big hug and tell her that it was fine. That she was wealthy and successful as well as beautiful and young. He said nothing. He knew that Lorna was a serious flake, and it had always been a source of extreme puzzlement to him how she made the money that she did. Like most pathologically lazy people, Nylon did not understand the concept of hard work. He just saw people running around being hysteri-cal for no reason and temporarily losing their sense of humour. The fact that Lorna owed lots of money to this taxman, whoever he was, came as no surprise to him whatsoever. After all, he knew somewhere at the back of his mind that champagne wasn't cheap.

'I'll ring the accountant on Monday. I have the best accountant in the whole world. He'll sort it out.'

Nylon wasn't so sure. But there was no point in

deserting the ship before it had sunk. He still had the rest of the weekend to get through, and here was as good a place to spend it as any.

'Sure he will, honey. Sure he will.'

2

Sandy was beginning to feel like she had known her new boss Rory Mac 'Say it again!' Rory for ever. Not because she had formed some sort of spiritual bond with Ireland's best-loved DJ, but because since she had started as his production assistant less than a week ago, he had not let her out of his sight. He had dragged her to a gallery opening the night before, and if it hadn't been for that big blonde one making a show of herself and him, Revolting Rory would have had Sandy pinned up against the wall all night. Or worse. It was beginning to dawn on Sandy that there might be an initiation ceremony into this new job, and feared that it involved the exchange of bodily fluids. Judging by the lunge he had made for her with his big beery gob as she'd got into the taxi on Dame Street last night, Rory was planning on cashing in his chips sooner rather than later.

Now it was eight a.m. on Saturday morning, and the two of them were in the studio recording his programme. The producer had called in sick, and Sandy was left to deal with him on her own. Which meant she got to grips with all of the technical equipment, which was good, but it still left the piece of equipment in the criss-cross golfer's jumper to deal with.

Thankfully there was a thick soundproof screen between them.

'Time to twiddle my knobs, baby,' came through on her headphones.

Sandy's guts lurched as he threw her one of his dirty, lip-licking winks. How in the name of Christ did he get away with being so unspeakably vile in a city the size of Dublin – with his big, blow-dried pouf of a hairstyle and his garish hand-knit jumpers? Lorna put on the polite nun's smile she had been wearing since she got here. As the newest and most junior person on the team, it was her only defence. It clearly wasn't working.

'Rory Mac – say it again, Rory, Mac – say it again, Rory, Mac – say it again . . . The Rory Mac Rory Sha – ho – ho – hoooooow!'

Sandy could not believe the theme jingle when she had first heard it, and during her first ideas meeting on day two had suggested it be changed. It turned out to be an aberration which Rory himself had invented and of which he was extremely proud. The others had twitched around nervously when she had said it, but Rory then stepped in and saved her by saying, 'It's good to have someone on the team with a bit of spunk!' She had been pleased to have made a good impression, but realized now that his use of the noun had been a bad sign. He had not left her alone since.

'Mary Murphy in Bohola sends birthday wishes to her

little boy Joe who is seven today Freddie Fitzpatrick is eight down there in the County of Kerry and a man by the name of Cormac O'Keefe would like to say he still loves his wife Maura after forty-five years of marriage they live in Derry and a big How About Ye to you and your lovely lay-dee and to all of you out there who are enjoying a special day today I would like to say – cue Cliff, Sandy . . .'

The show always started with requests, and Sandy marvelled, with a sort of horrified wonder, at Rory's ability to run through them without drawing breath. Sandy pressed the button and the sound of the jingle rang through her ears like a bad, bad joke . . .

'Con – Grat – Tew – Lay – SHUNS and Cell-ee-bray-SHUNS . . .'

How had this happened to her? Three weeks ago she had been PA to one of London's coolest DJs, the King of Radio Hip – Horace Deaver. The show had been a mishmash of cruel humour, new underground music and quirky reports on events and stories from around London, which were researched and presented by Sandy. Her career was just beginning to break, and a small story on her had been spotted in the review section of *Time Out* by Rory's boss. The Aul' Fella in Charge of Radio was fed up with people whom he turned down for jobs going over to England and becoming famous. Two months ago the TV interviewer and comedian Dandy McNamara had actually named him – live! On British television! – as the man who told Dan at a job interview, 'You are just not funny.' Aul' Fella had decided to try to redress the balance and had vowed that whenever he saw anyone Irish mentioned in any kind of UK media context at all, he would headhunt them back to Mother Éire.

Sandy was given the real hard-sell spin. They must really want me, she thought.

'You'll be a big fish in a small pond,' they said.

'We've got the Celtic Tiger/fastest-growing youth population/trendiest city in Europe,' they said.

'More money, status, national profile,' they said. 'You'll be working for the National Broadcaster. The Irish equivalent of the BBC!' they said. 'Only better!'

Sandy missed her friends and family in Dublin, and her mother had nearly lost her life with excitement when her daughter told her she had been offered a job with Rory Mac – the Housewives' Choice.

'He's "The King of Radio", Sandra, and a lovely person by all accounts. Maisie's sister Clodagh met him once at a charity drive in Cork. Said he was lovely. Katherine lives near him out in Bray. Says the wife shops in the local supermarket, just like a Normal Person.'

Maisie. Clodagh. Katherine. Sandra's mother seemed to know an endless list of women who were experts on everything from curing arthritis ('Patricia says she gave the mother a spoon of cider vinegar every day and it did wonders for her knee!') to spoken obituaries ('She was a lovely woman but Assumpta said the husband had her run ragged after him!') to radio DJs ('He gets the jumpers from a shop in Killiney. Ve-ry expensive.

Hand-knitted, if you don't mind!'). Sandra had no idea who any of these women were, but her mother quoted them as if they were the Oracle.

In a weak moment, missing home, and caught up with her mother's excitement at having her back in her old room 'for a few months anyway – till you find your feet', Sandra handed in her notice and rented out her flat in Notting Hill to a friend. She was moving home.

Except it didn't feel like home any more. Her five years in London had seen many of her old friends move abroad, and most of the ones that were left had husbands and babies. That was fine for them, but at twenty-nine Sandy had little in common with that settling-down stuff. Her married friends lived in houses mirrored by their own parents; suburban squares with fitted kitchens and cots. They started off wanting Phillipe Stark and kilims, but ended up with wipe-clean surfaces and Scotchguard carpets. Sandy just wanted to live her own life, be a success at work, prove herself. She didn't want to settle for some boy from college whose parents knew her parents.

On her first night home, Sandy went to visit the Last Unmarried, her oldest friend Maeve.

Maeve worked in an insurance company and, while she earned a packet, she still lived at home with her parents in Stillorgan, around the corner from Sandy's folks.

'I'm staying here till I get married,' she had told Sandy.

'You're mad!' Sandy said. 'How can you stand it – do

you not want your independence? A groovy pad in town. You can afford it – Jesus, woman, you must have a fortune saved.'

'I need every penny as a dowry.'

'Ah Jesus!' Sandy was worried that Maeve was only half joking.

'Look. If I leave home, it'll mean giving in finally to the spinster life. At first it would be fun – my own space, wrecking the card in Habitat. Then what? Girls coming around and watching the telly complaining that there's no men in Dublin? Then I'll be so comfy, I'll stop going out altogether. It'll be take-away food and telly – three stone later there won't be a party dress in Dublin to fit me, then I'll go and get myself a cat. The cat will be such great company, I'll have to get another. By the time I'm forty it'll be me and twelve cats living in a one-bedroomed apartment in Christchurch, I'll have an arse you could park a bus in and I'll still be wondering why I'm single.'

'Yes, but, well, does it not drive you mad still living at home . . . ?' said Sandy, her inaugural meal of bacon and cabbage still settling in her stomach an hour later. 'Is it not, well – embarrassing?'

'Why?' Maeve was unfazed by the suggestion. 'I've a fantastic wardrobe which, by the way, is all size ten because the Mammy is a Weightwatchers leader and prepares my evening meals. I'm forced out every night of the week because the alternative is just too dreadful, which is the only way I'm going to meet a man. And, when I do meet one, I have to stay at his – which means

I get to sift out the Mr Marrieds and the Losers Who Still Live With Their Mammies.'

The culture gap was wider than Sandy had thought.

'But *you* still live at home with your mammy!'

'*Not* the same thing, Sandy. Now,' she said, opening her wardrobe door on the Skimpy-Saturday side and running her hands across an impressive collection of strappy, spangly goodies, 'which one of these little beauties is coming out to play tonight?'

Sandy did not have the time, even if she had the inclination or ambition, to meet a man. Besides, she had her work cut out for her fending off her new boss.

'. . . blast from the past there, folks, with "Billy, Don't Be a Hero" by Paper Lace – love that tew-hune! – Jingle, Sandy! Jingle! Wake up, girl!'

Sandy duly banged the button. A monkey. I am an over-trained monkey, she thought.

'Rory Mac – say it again, Roar-reee! . . . And that's going out to Billy in Tourmakeady from a lay-dee who loves you, your ladywife Janice. Now it's that time of the week when culture takes over this vulture! Mary? Now what have you got for us this week?'

Sandy woke up. She was interested in this bit. Mary Scanlan did an arts slot on the show every week. She was a middle-aged woman who had been sidelined from daytime TV on account of her expanding girth, and the make-up department complaints that Mary had point-blank refused to tackle her Facial Hair Problem which had started to show up on screen.

Sandy was curious. She had reported on everything

from poetry readings to salsa clubs on Horace's show and was keen to see how it was done here. Ireland was hot on culture and arty things in general. Hopefully this Mary woman would give her something to aim for. She might meet her for coffee later and get a few tips.

'Well now, Rory, I went to see a play there during the week and it was great gas entirely.'

'Is that so, Mary, and what was it called?'

Rory winked over at Sandy again – honestly, would he ever give up.

'It was called Pull Yer Pants Up There Now, Missis by Bernie Gimlet, and I'll tell you something now, Rory, I really enjoyed it, now, I really, really did.'

'And what was it about, Mary?'

'Well, it was set in Dublin – in a flat – and there was this family – and but now, Rory, I don't want to be going giving the game away. You'd have to go and see it yourself.'

Sandy couldn't believe her ears. Was this a skit? With growing horror it dawned on her that they were being deadly serious. Rory wasn't looking at his guest reviewer at all. Granted, she was no oil painting, but Sandy had had enough tongue-swiping winks for one day.

'And it was good, Mary?'

'Oh yes, it was brilliant, Rory. Brilliant, now. Really good.'

Then, realizing she had run out of things to say, Mary leaned toward the mike and reminded anyone who might have just tuned in, 'Really very, very good indeed,' and sat back in her chair as if her day's work was done.

Sandy started to panic. They had to get another four

whole minutes out of this slot before the next ad break was scheduled, and she had no music lined up. Rory didn't look too hot either, and was grimacing wildly at Mary. He managed to stop her short of saying. 'What?' on air with the most stupid question Sandy had ever heard in her seven years of radio experience. He could have asked what actors were in the play, about the costumes, the direction, the set. In the name of God he could have even asked where the wretched play was on! Easy questions that poor Mary would have understood and might (only might, mind you) have been able to answer. Instead he said, *'Gimlet? That's an unusual name.'*

That sent Mary into a kanniption of confused panic. She started to flail her arms wildly at him; radio sign language for 'What the fuck are you doing?'

Rory flailed back and mouthed 'You stupid cow!'

Mary, cool as you like, leaned down on the microphone and said simply, *'It is indeed, Rory.'*

Then she leaned back, folded her arms, making it quite clear that it was 'yes' and 'no' answers from here on in.

'Where is it from now, Mary, do you think?'

'I wouldn't have a clue about that, now, Rory.'

'Isn't a gimlet some class of a tabard or overall or something?'

'Oh, I wouldn't have a clue about that either now, Rory.'

For three and three-quarter minutes Rory chucked his balls into Mary's court and she squeezed them hard before dropping them back disdainfully over the net. It was certainly the longest three and three-quarter minutes of his life, not discounting the *Live With Lynda Laverty* experience.

After Mary's extremely snippy exit, Rory was raging for the rest of the show. He made a couple of politically dodgy remarks on air, one to a priest who was calling to say they weren't all sex-craved child molesters. *'Well now in fairness, Father, there's been a lot of you caught messing around with children in the news there lately.'* Paedophilia was not the Aul' Fella in Charge of Radio's favourite subject, and his PA was on the phone to Sandy like a hot snot bawling and bleating as if it were *her* fault for putting a priest through in the first place. The other was to a woman from Cavan who was commenting on the ridiculous fashions she had seen on the TV catwalk shows this season.

'In all honesty, Rory, now – who'd be seen dead in mad gear like that?'

'Not the women of Cavan anyway. I mean, you're not exactly renowned for your sense of style, now, are you?'

The switchboard went mad. Never mind the priest. There were women from every town and village and outback farmland in Cavan hollering down the phone that *they* had invented the leg warmer back in '81, and who the hell did Rory Mac Rory think he was when they'd been knitting jumpers for generations that were better than anything he'd ever put on his dirty little jackeen back!

Rory was nearly going out of his mind, and Sandy had to save him by finding extra music.

'Here's three in a row to play us out today. It's a blast

from the past from the mega-70s band ELO – that's the Electric Light Orchestra. This is Rory Mac signing off from me to you this Saturday. Have a safe weekend now . . .'

'. . . unless you're from fucking CAVAN!' he yelled into the mike as soon as it had been switched off.

Sandy was nervous as Rory opened the studio door. As first at hand, she was sure to be blamed somehow. The good thing was that he was so preoccupied with the hellish last hour of his show, he was unlikely to try to drop the hand again.

The last thing she was expecting was that it would work to her advantage.

'That bastard bollocks of a hairy, fat bitch Mary Scanlan. I'll have her killed. I fucking will!'

He said it out as if he still had an audience, but there was only Sandy.

'*You!*' he said, pointing at her as if she were someone he had never seen before in his life. 'You're fucking doing it next week. Go and see a play, read a fucking book. Anything! You're our new arts reviewer – and you had better be good!'

You wouldn't know 'good', thought Sandy, if it was strapped to your arse and you were sent sliding down Croagh Patrick on it.

Still, Sandy had her first radio slot and that was, at least, a start.

She got on the bus to Stillorgan after the show with a smile on her face, and couldn't wait to tell Maeve the Rave all about it.

3

Gloria had been rushed off her feet since eight thirty that morning. Sam Cohen, a friend, client and record producer, had a funky American girl band in town to shoot a video for their latest single. They had set up camp – Winnebagos, catering, make-up huts, the lot – in an inner-city housing estate near to where Gloria grew up. Unfortunately, they had not organized enough security. Enough, in the case of this particular estate, being a sizeable percentage of the US Army. They had lost one van entirely, the wheels off two more, and four nine-year-old lads, known to the local Guards, been found both modelling and attempting to sell a fair portion of the band's wardrobe on the dual carriageway that bordered their wasteland terrain. A mistaken motorist, not interested in purchasing second-hand pop-star paraphernalia, had stopped with entirely the wrong idea about these pre-pubescent boys in drag.

'Hey, look, mista,' said the bravest heart, thrusting a pair of hot pants in the stranger's face, 'you can still smella off-of dem.'

This sent the middle-aged pervert right over the edge. The kid shouted, 'Ya dorty bolliksya' at him, then threw his lucky brick (which he carried in his pocket for 'emergencies' – although generally its purpose was to create rather than divert them) in through the open window. It landed, fatefully for all concerned, in the man's lap, putting pay to his grubby fantasies for quite some time.

Gloria was apprised of these happenings at seven thirty a.m. on a Saturday morning. She had not drunk the six cups of strong coffee she needed in order to function prior to nine.

'. . . but that's not the worst of it. The hairdresser has just called from New York to say she's missed her flight and can't make it until tomorrow. We have to start shooting this afternoon. Gloria – if I sent the girls into the salon would you give them a quick going over? Nothing fancy, just tidy them up a bit . . .'

'Sure, sure, honey. Send them in. Nine thirty . . . yeah . . . yeah. No problem . . .'

Sam was a sweetheart. He wouldn't send her anything she couldn't handle. Anyway, she owed him one. Actually, taking into account the financing he had lent her ex-husband Frank to set up that joke of a modelling agency he pretended to run, she owed Sam Cohen plenty more.

Had Gloria had her caffeine fix she would have remembered that Go Girl! was an American singing sextet. She only had four stylists including herself on that day, and two of them had their first fixed appointments at nine. She might also have remembered that Go Girl! were black, and that neither she nor any of her staff were either trained in, or had any experience of, the extremely tricky and highly specialized art of styling Afro hair, never mind sculpting it up into the complicated mathematical styles that these big American stars were into.

Kevin, her best-looking stylist, also held the post Client Liaison, which was another way of saying Apparently Irresistible. Gloria, who needed all the help she could get, put him in charge of the group as a whole, hoping his charm would make up for his lack of expertise. In the area of doing their hair at least.

'Please, God, let one or all of them fancy him,' she prayed, grateful for once that the slim, sex-addicted Kevin seemed to be scoring with the right type of client, and *not* one who would turn up a week later looking for an engagement ring or, worse, a free set of highlights.

By the time the band had been subjected to the rigours of a thorough scrub at the hands of an overly excited Scooter (junior assistant trainee – and their biggest fan), the six ebony princesses were beginning to look worried. One of them whipped their last CD cover out of her purse and instructed Kevin that they wanted the same look. A symmetrical slanting-sideways pyramid of perfect curls. Kevin looked like they might have to call the priest to have him anointed, but Gloria had promised Sam she would do a good job and she wasn't going back on her word.

Scooter had to be promoted on the spot to trainee

team leader (he had been there three years and was utterly talentless; Gloria hadn't the heart to tell him so she kept giving him ever more convoluted titles to make him feel important), and in charge of sending juniors out to every chemist in Dublin to buy, borrow and beg more rollers. Four hours later and every roller in the salon was wrapped in glossy black.

As if the diva quota wasn't high enough, Saturday at Gloria's Gaff was their busiest time. The advantage of being Dublin's chicest salon was that Gloria and her staff were busy every day and could charge through the nose. The downside was that every two-bit-uppity-tart-off-the-telly wanted their hair cut by Gloria. Most of the time for free. Top of her list of People Who Deserve to Lose an Earlobe was Francesca Duffée (christened Fionnuala Duffy), who presented the daytime TV show *Altogether Now!* Fifteen years of clawing her way up through the mound of dinosaur shite that was the Erin National Broadcasting corporate ladder had brought her to the zenith of her success: sharing recipes and magazine reviews with the fifty or so people who had their telly on at three in the afternoon. She had a huge octogenarian following. This was on account of the fact that, having run out of volunteers for a studio audience, some researcher had the bright idea of coaching people in from nursing homes around the country. Francesca seemed oblivious and behaved, at all times, as if she should be under armed protection from autograph-seekers and stalkers. Gloria wasn't in the mood for her client's big TV ego today. The deluded Fran firmly believed that it was of National Importance 'and in the interests of the public' that (a) her hair was done to perfection (not a problem), and (b) she wasn't left sitting around reception with wet hair and tide-marks where she Might Be *Seen* (a very big problem today).

'I don't like being on view like this, Gloria. I shan't go on about it – but it's *different* for me, you see. I'm a – ' she silently mouthed the last word as if there might be someone listening in – 'celeb-ri-ty!'

'What's thirty-foot long and smells of wee?' Scooter said to Kevin after he had bought Fran a cappuccino to calm her down. The answer was 'The front row of *Altogether Now!*' Kevin didn't say it loud, but it unified them in a bit of inner amusement. Laughs had been a bit tight the last week or so since Gloria's ex, Frank, had started dropping in and 'borrowing' from the till.

Gloria had grown up in the Ballymun flats in the 70s. For the first ten years it had been great. The flat was spacious (the only thing that the architects got right about Dublin's first and last attempt at high-rise living), and the young Gloria never tired of gazing out over the city through the high glass windows. Sometimes Gloria felt as if she were flying. She could see the whole world from up there, and having it spread out in front of her somehow made it seem like she owned it.

As the years went on, the flats became run-down. Graffiti started to appear on the wall, the lifts broke and some of the local lads started to deal in heroin, which was still considered a fun, fashionable alternative to drink. But James 'Jamsey' O'Neill brought home every penny he earned as a factory worker, and his wife Eileen ran a clean, comfortable household. At forty-seven Gloria's father was promoted to floor manager. With the extra money he intended to move the family to their own house in Clondalkin, where his kids might have a garden to play in, away from the scavenging slum he saw Ballymun turning into. Within six months of his new job, James O'Neill died suddenly from a massive heart attack. Gloria remembered coming home on the day of the funeral and opening her dead father's post. It was from an estate agent. Details of six three-bedroomed houses in the north county Dublin suburbs. He had not been working for long enough to get a decent pension from the factory. The only legacy he had left behind him was a handful of unfulfilled dreams.

Eileen went into a decline. She gave up her part-time job as a cleaner, then gradually lost interest in the house and kids. The flat started to gather first dust, then dirt. As the eldest, Gloria took it upon herself to police her brothers' and sisters' washing and dressing routines. One day Gloria came home from school and there was no food in the house. She went to her mother's purse to get some money, but there was none. Her mother shrugged, lit a cigarette and continued to gaze blankly out of the window at the grey curtain of sky. Gloria bunked school the following day and got herself a job for fifteen pounds a week washing hair in a local salon. She was fourteen.

Within six months Gloria had learned everything she could about hair from the mean biddy who ran the shop. By fifteen she was a full-time stylist, but because she was underage, she couldn't fight for a pay rise. She supplemented her pitiful income by doing 'nixers' in the evenings, and by her sixteenth birthday Gloria was running a perming and setting racket from her mother's bathroom. She was cheaper and quicker than any of the salons in their area, and the women of Ballymun would pile into the O'Neills' flat on the ninth floor for their weekly 'do'. Eileen gradually came back to life with all the gossip and activity that was going on around her. Her home became full of life and chat again – central headquarters to the women who organized, cleaned, financed, reared and ran what was rapidly becoming Dublin's most run-down area. Having their hair done once a week helped keep them going, united them against the poverty and the problems that plagued their everyday lives.

'I told de liddle bastard if he came round to de fla' again sniffin' after my Sandra I'll tear the bleedin' headoffim . . . Trow us over a towel dere, luff . . .'

'My Sean came home widdan air gun lass week. "Where d'ya ge' tha'?" I says. "Did ya robbi', ya liddle shi'?"'

The women laughed and opened the door to each other as they gathered in the spacious living room, sitting on every available surface – coffee tables and telly stands – taking turns in relay when the sofa became free. They brought their own towels and shampoo with them and, if there was a spare seat after they'd been done, they often stayed on for the 'bit of social'. Eileen got pride back in her home, cleaning and buying new things for the flat with money which Gloria gave her.

'Dem's lovely new curtains, Missis O'Neill. Mustoff cost a few bob wha'?'

When Gloria was eighteen, there was a summit in Bridie Walsh's kitchen. Bridie was the Godmother of the Ballymun Mammy Mafia. Eileen was summoned.

'A few of us haff been putting away, Eileen. Not much, just a few pennies every week – dat what wheef saved from your Gloria been cheaper dan anyone else.'

There was over a thousand pounds. Enough to pay half a year's rent and, with the women bullying their husbands 'off uppa der fat, lazy arses', all the necessary renovations to one of the shop units in the estate. Fifty women had contributed, and Gloria made sure they all had a share in the profits. They christened it 'Gloria's Gaff' and it was such a huge success that Gloria had to take on and train in two more girls.

Then one night Gloria was looking out of the window of the flat. She remembered her father and how he had lifted her up and pointed at each square block, each tiny toy car, each scurrying figure and said to her, 'Whose is that?' Gloria gave him the answer he always wanted. 'Mine, Daddy.'

'That's right, pet. And whose is the sky?'

'It's mine, Daddy.'

'There it is, Gloria. The sky. All you've got to do is reach out there and grab it. You can have anything you want, girl. Remember that. Anything at all. All you have to do is go out there and get it.'

Gloria decided that night to leave the flats. She knew she was a good hairdresser, but part of her still believed that she was being held up by the kindness and loyalty of her neighbours. She needed to prove to herself that she could do it on her own.

By the time she was twenty, Gloria had enough saved to leave Ballymun to take her chances in Dublin 2. She left the salon in the hands of Bridie Walsh's daughter Rose, who renamed it Hairport and made a reasonable stab at it, although she never reached the dizzy heights of a cover story in the *Irish Hairdressers Journal* like her former boss.

Even back then, in the days before sushi bars and crêpe houses (when you could still leave your car outside a pub and drive it home half-manky), Dublin 2 was still an intimidating place for a young woman from 'De Flats'. It was the home of Brown Thomas, where the South-County-Foxrock-Fanny set would mimsy up and down the grand staircase looking for new things to spend their husbands' money on. Gloria's talents and the charming, friendly atmosphere of her salon quickly won her a name with the all powerful FFs. In this part of town, they could make or break you – and they loved Gloria.

'Door-ling – Gloor-ia may be from the rawng side of the tracks – but just look whort she did with my high-lights!'

'I know! But they're on-ly goor-geous!'

Gloria was not so sure about her clientele. They were rich, and that was good. In fact, she had to put her prices up because their competitive spending meant that they had to be paying more than their friends. But they were also terrible snobs, and would regularly sit in front of her and complain about the profligate breeding habits of their cleaning women.

'I mean, I pay her *two pounds* an hour, and she's pregnant a-*gain*! She didn't come at awl on Friday and I had that big dinner party. Ended up *pee*-ling the pot-ate-*toes* my-se-*helf* . . .'

'No-ooo.'

'Yesssss. Hornest to Gord – I'm sending away for a Fillipino. I don't care if it's illegal. Phillipa Denny has one. Says she's *marr*-veh-lors – keeps the place *sport*-less – sleeps in the kitchen . . .'

Gloria had taken a flat above the shop, and what with the salon being so busy, and her working hours being so long, she barely had the time to go home and visit the family in Ballymun. Although Gloria didn't mind paying for her old mates to come into town to play, they felt that her new status, and the trendy new gear she was wearing, had signalled a change in lifestyle. If she wasn't looking down her nose at them, they felt that she should be. In reality, Gloria was starting to feel very isolated and between two worlds when Frank Doyle came into her life.

He was eleven years older than her and extremely dashing with jet-black hair and spangly blue eyes. Brought up in Foxrock, he was the son of one of Gloria's clients and had come to pick his mother up in her red sports car which he pretended was his. He parked it on the pavement outside the salon.

'You could get arrested for that,' Gloria warned him.

'I'd rather get arrested for something more exciting,' he said. Gloria had a wiry beauty, chiselled features set into an expression much older than her years. She was stylish and wore her hair in long glossy curls which tumbled down her back like a fountain. Refreshing at a time when tight Afro perms were all the rage. Frank spotted class in spite of her now carefully modified northside accent. She wasn't yet twenty-one and she thought she knew everything. There was something about the sure way Gloria had about her that made Frank feel safe. They married within four months.

Gloria learned the hard way. She signed over half her business to Frank, imagining that with his university education and his smart middle-class ways, he would nurture it into something huge. She was wrong. Frank spent seven years partying his portion away and living off Gloria. The business managed to survive on half-fuel, but that wasn't enough for Gloria. She came to hate Frank. Her father had told her she could have the sky if she wanted and she had believed him. Frank had cheated her of that dream. Two years ago Frank had wanted to close the salon and use the money to start a modelling agency in Dublin. Gloria had told him to piss off and he had run off with his latest bit of halfwit totty, a nineteen-year-old called Finola O'Driscoll, who was modelling under the name 'Flame'. Frank was not so handsome now, with the still jet-black hair plastered into a precarious comb-over and a belly that would comfortably house twins. He had a bit of charm left and was able to convince a few people that he still had some money. Enough in any case to convince Flame that it was worth pretending to love him. His increasing dependence on coke and the failure of his new business venture meant that Frank was on his uppers again. He still owned half of Gloria's Gaff, and had taken to picking it up, in cash, from the salon, every other day. Half of the profits and more besides when he could get away with it. That was easy enough as he knew what Gloria was like. She was booked out nine to six every day, and would never create a scene in the busy salon. Gloria spat when she did the cashing up every night, but she felt too tired these days to do anything about it. She hated Frank, but it was hard sometimes being on her own with all this. At twenty-nine, Gloria was ready to give up. She felt like she had been on her feet all her life. Having somebody to share the burden seemed like too much even to hope for. A stupid dream. Like thinking you could own the sky.

By four in the afternoon, the salon was still buzzing, but the worst of it was over. The girl band had been pin curled to within an inch of their lives and were currently all made up and ready to shoot but still shivering in the back of a bus waiting for the rain to stop. Francesca was picking through a plate of sushi with a very important

Aul' Fella in Erin Radio who was trying to convince her that he was separated from his wife (which, for that afternoon at least, he was), and Gloria was enjoying her first fag of the day. The EC ban against smoking in hair salons had been hard to enforce. It was the dull day when a diva suffering from Highlights in Progress couldn't be seen furtively pulling on a Silk Cut in the alley at the back of the salon, frantically hiding behind a wheelie bin lest she be spotted sporting a tinfoil head-piece and a snot-green overall with GLORIA'S GAFF emblazoned on the back. It was on the edge of one of these very wheelie bins that Gloria herself was perched when she saw Nylon sweep in through the front door of her salon.

'Cheerio, darlings!' she heard him announce as she stormed in after him.

'What time do you call this?'

Nylon spun around on his Prada loafers and embraced the air in front of her. 'Gloria! Gorgeous Gloria!'

Today had been one of those rare days when she could have *actually done* with this utterly useless but decorative item in the shop. He was of virtually no practical help whatsoever, but the clients loved his ebullient campness – he made them laugh and always looked great. A couple of them had actually tried to book appointments with him just after he'd started coming in on Saturdays. He would certainly have been able to keep the likes of Francesca Duffée off her back with his chat.

Gloria, no wallflower herself, marvelled at Nylon's

ability to speak to these women on their level about things he knew nothing about.

'Property prices! Don't *talk* to me, darling! I've been trying to trade in the D4 apartment for a mews for months! It's a *nightmare!*'

'Schools! Don't *talk* to me, darling! The sister has had the nephew down for Blackrock for years! It's a *nightmare!*'

'Caterers! Don't *talk* to me, darling! Had the Iranian Ambassador round for dinner last week – paid fifty quid a head for slop! It was a *nightmare!*'

All pure fiction, of course, but the women wanted to believe him. Gloria and her staff never contradicted him because they knew that Nylon wanted to believe it about himself. Gloria wished sometimes that she could be more like him in that way. She still struggled with the fact of her background in the rarefied world of the people she spent most of her time with these days. Gloria loved her family, and visited them most weekends. But they rarely came to see her where she worked. She had tried to relocate Eileen to a 'nicer' area, but her mother wouldn't be moved from her friends, and still had her hair done in Hairport. It hurt Gloria that someone else did her mother's hair, but when she tackled her about it Eileen always blushed and said, 'You're too busy, luff.' She suspected that her old neighbours and friends, and even her family, thought she was too grand for them now. Gloria knew she hadn't changed, but some part of her worried that perhaps they were right.

'Glor – before I forget! I booked Lorna in at five, hope that's okay.'

Gloria glowered threateningly at Nylon. He had the cheek to arrive after the battle was well and truly over, and would be expecting, Gloria knew, payment for the entire war.

'Ple-ease, Glor. She's desperate. Found her last night puking over the bouncer's shoes outside Little's and had to take her home – she missed her appointment Thursday and her hair looks like a withered fern.'

Gloria was desperate to finish up for the day. The idea of that neurotic, PR socialite plonked in front of her pleading for less 'honey' in her highlights just about finished her off. Nylon was looking at her doe-eyed and she could not be bothered to argue him out of it. She knew, in any case, that Lorna would come in anyway, whether she said no or not.

'She can have a wash and blow-dry, the colour will have to wait.'

Nylon started, 'Bu—'

'I said *no colour*, Nylon!'

Whoops! She was in a bad mood. If he didn't back off, Nylon suspected he mightn't get paid at all.

PART TWO

O SWEET MOTHER
IRELAND

4

O Sweet Mother Ireland, now where have ye gone?
You've left and abandoned your poor weeping son
You cooked bacon and spuds in your own modest way
We laughed and we cried, oh yes, many's the day

Now you're in the ground and all covered in earth
Your rosary beads, they are wrapped round your girth
Once you were alive wearing diamonds and pearls
At seventy-six, still a helluva girl!

You were Mother Ireland, my own mammy too
There'll ne'er be another will ever match you
With your tidy red hair all tied up in a bun
Oh how I miss you – your desolate son.

Mr Big had wept his way through two monogrammed hankies, and his secretary, Lindy, had been waved to go and get more from the antique bureau in the ante-room outside his office. Toilet paper, or even regular tissues, would not do. Mr Big would only weep for his mother into the best Irish linen.

He was so beside himself with emotion that he could barely speak.

'Skip – that is beau-ti-ful. Really beautiful.'

Liam felt relief flood through him. The richest man in America, GM-food tycoon and all-round Billionaire Big Guy, had set his assistant the task of commissioning a song for his dead Irish mother. Liam, a.k.a. 'Skip' (as in 'Skip-to-it-boy!') had contacted every songwriter in Ireland and America. Each of them had been apprised of the one-million-pound fee to be paid for the chosen song which Mr Big intended to get the famous Irish tenor Gréagóir O'Droighneain to sing at the opening of the Big Paddy Festival he sponsored in Texas each year. His boss had turned down some of the most popular Irish-American songwriters. There was 'I'd Walk from Here to South Alaska for You, Mammy' by the country and western king Flint Shoehorn; 'Crumbs from Your Table' by the sensitive soul singer Ethna; 'Dead Mammy Mambo' by young Irish rock band Dirty Filthy Animals (that did not go down at *all* well) and Liam's own favourite group, The Trembling Celtics, who had submitted a Definite Possible called 'Red Flame of Fermoy'. Other than the fact that Mother Big had never been to Fermoy, it might have made the grade. Mr Big had quite liked some of them but:

'Nothing – *nothing* like this! It captures her perfectly – read that last line again there, Skip . . .'

Reading this crap out once was bad enough, but the fact that Big was actually moved to tears by it made

Liam grimace on the inside. He was burned through with mortification.

'Oh how I miss you – your desolate son.'

'Desolate. Des-o-late – that is a beau-ti-ful word, Skip – beau-ti-ful word . . .'

Lindy the secretary handed him a hankie on cue.

'And that's just how I feel, Skip – ' *sniff* – 'desolate – ' *sniff* – 'lost – ' *sniff sniff* – 'empty . . .'

Then Mr Big leaned back from the vast grandeur of his desk into the soft bouncy leather of his chair and went for it.

'E-heh-heh-heh-mpty and al-ooooo-ne,' he roared, the linen hankies a distant memory as the tears sprouted from his eyes as if they were on a pump.

Lindy went back to her desk and speed-dialled his therapist.

'Better get down here quick,' she muttered down the line.

Mr Big was a bit emotional these days. He had just lost his sixth wife as well as his mother.

'Dead?' Liam's sister Maeve had asked him during one of his gossipy calls home to Dublin.

'No – I regret to say that the Bitch Pricilla is still alive and well and living with Big's plastic surgeon. He's been a complete bollocks since she left – making my life hell. He wants me to organize a contract on yer man. Keeps saying "Your People can handle this . . ." – he thinks I'm in the fecking IRA!'

'God. How romantic . . .'

'Maeve, don't be disgusting!'

'No, really. I think he sounds gorgeous.'

'Maeve, he is a crass, middle-aged philistine, who has had plastic surgery and a hair implant and I just want to say that if that stationery isn't delivered here by tomorrow lunchtime there will be hell to pay! Thank you and goodbye!'

The line went dead and Maeve assumed that Mr Big himself must have walked into the room. She hoped that her idiot brother didn't get himself the sack before she had the chance to meet his boss.

Liam had been working for Big for almost three years. He hadn't intended it to work out this way. After a good degree and a successful career in London working as an advertising copywriter, he had decided to pack it all in and become a Serious Writer. He had enough money saved to get him to America. Once there, he intended to research and write his Great Literary Novel, which, as every young writer knows, is the first step to being Taken Seriously which is essential if you want to become an Important Writer. Being Taken Seriously was very important to Liam. In his years as an advertising copywriter in London he had developed a reputation for quick-witted punchlines, and there was no one who could match his hammy puns. With his hip art-director partner Jez, they had won every award in the business. This was the team that could make scalloped blinds sexy, and double glazing trendy. Their *Too Good for Fido* Desperate Dan Dog Food campaign had created a national news story when they had dressed supermarket food testers up in puppy outfits and got them to persuade dog owners to taste it before purchasing tins by the crateload. At the height of his career, just before he left London, Liam was starting to get work as a television-comedy scriptwriter. It was the kind of work which a lot of young men in Liam's position would have posted their own fingers to the BBC for. But not Liam. It had all come too easy to him, and if Liam had learned one thing from his Good Irish Catholic Upbringing it was that if things came easy, they didn't count.

Liam had always been able to make people laugh, but, frankly, he just didn't see *the point* in it. He knew that somewhere floating around inside him was a brilliant poet – he just had to pin the bugger down. Behind the *'Yule Have a Merry Christmas'* and *'Let Crazee Cornflakes Start Your Day'* was something really, *really* important that he had to say. Something which no writer had ever said before. Something beautiful and profound – melancholy and yet soul-splittingly enlightening. Liam just had to figure out what it was, but he was certain of one thing – it was in there. All he needed was the time and freedom for all this Very Important Stuff that was lurking unexpressed to come out. When it did, he would finally realize his calling as an Important Writer, astonishing and impressing his family in Ireland, the shallow world of advertising and the universe in general with his Profound Insights and Literary Brilliance. So, to the horror of Jez and all the management at Cosmic Advertising, Liam handed in his notice and booked a one-way ticket to America. America was the biggest place he could think of, and Liam figured if he was going to whip the literary establishment's ass, he may as well start at the top.

America was beautiful, and as Liam travelled across the continent by Greyhound bus, he was sure that the stunning landscapes would inspire him into magnificent prose. *'A desolate stretch of desert puts me in mind of . . . Desperate for a Delicious Dessert? Try Dave's Dandy Cream Slices!'*

Day after day, Liam tried to scribble into his notepad, but it just wasn't working. An old woman sat down in front of him one day, and he tried to imagine the fascinating, tragic circumstances of her life. *'The old lady boarded the bus at Minnesota. Frail and lonely . . .'*

Then somebody shouted 'Hey, Pam!' in her direction and Liam lost his concentration.

'There was an old lady called Pam, who had a head shaped like a spam . . .'

Everything he wrote seemed to run into an ad-line or a limerick. As the weeks went by, Liam became frustrated with the elusiveness of his inner muse. As the weeks turned into months, he began to suspect that his muse had deserted him altogether. After almost six months – and as many notebooks filled with half-finished sentences and brutal black lines – Liam finally realized that there was no muse. No inner depths to plunge, no tortured soul, no brow-bashing, breast-beating poet. Just the standard-issue ordinariness that a decent suburban upbringing in Stillorgan, south county Dublin, will afford. But Liam wasn't prepared to leave it at that. He cursed his parents from high hell, abroad and back again. If only he had the drama of an abused childhood to draw on in his time of need. Even a bit of poverty – or they could have reared him in Rural Ireland. Rural Ireland was *full* of melancholy; muddy fields and rain and cow shite was great for writing. Even if they'd reared him a stricter Catholic, that would have been *something*. He'd have loads of guilt and angst. For God's sake, even the Christian Brothers had been nice to him – letting the boys run discos in the school hall instead of beating them with straps like they were supposed to. Now that he thought of it, Liam realized there was a *mountain* of great Irish writing material he had been denied. Alcoholism. An alcoholic father would have been a real asset. Instead he'd been stuck living a life of dull moderation with two nice parents who rarely raised their voices to each other or their children (never mind sent them out to plough the fields with no shoes while they had-at each other in a drunken rage), and thought that they were doing the best they could. Oh how they had failed him!

Disillusioned, but not ready to give up entirely on his dream, Liam thought about what he could do next. Although the agency said they would always have a job there for him, he was not prepared to move back to London. There had been ferocious mickey-taking at his leaving do and his pride would not allow him to face them again until he had scaled the dizzy heights of literary stardom. Perhaps I should move back to Ireland? he thought, and move to one of those really depressing midland towns. That's it! he realized. I'll live in a caravan on the Athlone bypass, grow a beard and become an alcoholic. He'd start an affair with the oldest spinster of the parish, then refuse to make an honest woman of her, and her brothers would come after him with pickaxes and spades and they'd all end up getting mouldy together on poteen in a bog with the rain of Holy God's tears pouring down on their weather-beaten heads. A year of that and he'd definitely be Taken Seriously.

When Liam took his card out in the travel agent's in Boston to try to pay for his ticket home, he found that he had run out of credit, and only had thirty-four dollars left in his wallet.

'Bollocks,' he said to the woman behind the counter, 'big hairy bull bollocks from hell!'

The woman laughed.

'You're *funny!*' she said – and Liam knew he was doomed.

⬮

Liam had met Mr Big only a few days later while, still in a state of shock, he was hitchhiking in the general direction of New York. He had a banker cousin there who he hoped would lend him the fare home without telling a single other person in the whole world about his predicament. He knew it was a long shot, and Liam suspected that his mother's Emigrant Son Returning Antennae were twitching already. She probably had the ham cooked and the kettle on for his return.

He was carrying a card which had DUBLIN – IRELAND

ambitiously emblazoned in it, and the billionaire Paddy-phile pulled over in his stretch limo and waved him in. Liam was so depressed that he hardly noticed the salubrious nature of the vehicle he was getting into, and having spoken to hardly anyone for days, proceeded to tell Big his whole miserable tale. The Richest Man in America had been so moved by the young Irishman's story, and realizing that he could use Liam to help expand his Irish Credentials beyond an Irish Mammy, who was on her last legs, and the world's finest collection of Waterford Crystal, he offered him a job as his PA.

Liam had taken it with the intention of staying until he had his fare back to Ireland. That had been three years ago. To date, Liam had earned and invested enough to go there and back fifty times over, buy half of Athlone and pay for himself and every member of his family to drink themselves into oblivion for evermore, should they desire to do so. Yet he had not even had the front to go home on holiday.

The truth was that Liam was more disillusioned with himself than he cared to admit. Being caretaker to the gargantuan ego of this mad American was hard work, but it meant that he never had the chance to look at the terrified little turd that his own once grand writer's ego had become.

Big bawled his therapist out of it before he had even fully opened the door. Dr 'Call me Dave' Ashman arrived seven minutes after Lindy's emergency phone call, all chubby sincerity with his corduroy pants and well-trimmed beard – the opposite to the disarranged dangerous whiskers that Liam hoped one day to grow.

'That's good, Xavier – let it all out . . .'

Dr Ashman was the only person allowed to call Big by his first name, and that was only because Big was paying him a hundred dollars an hour to help him 'nurture the possibility of becoming closer to his true self'.

Liam always denied Big's therapist the opportunity to say 'Please – call me Dave!' by calling him Dave anyway, which really made the good doctor twitch. He did it on the grounds that he knew the bearded brain-trainer was only a chancer like himself. Three years ago he'd been selling floor coverings door-to-door before having his Spiritual Awakening and writing the bestseller, *Carpet Your Soul With Love*. The 'doctorate' had been awarded him by the South California University of Self and he was vomit-inducingly self-effacing about the title.

Big hated him as much as Liam did, it was just that he had been told that his 'feelings of resentment' were 'just part of the process'. With that in mind, he flung a lead crystal ashtray at the solid mahogany door. Dr Dave closed it just in time and shouted through, 'Anger is good, Xavier. You have to let it out if we're to achieve closure on this!' He then beat his retreat, giving Lindy an already typed invoice for a hundred dollars on his way out.

It was just like the chancy fecker to instruct Big to

'let his anger out' while he still had a roomful of heavy implements and a nervous PA beside him, thought Liam. But Big seemed to have, if not complete 'closure', then at least a sense of calm around him.

'I want to meet the man who wrote that song about my mother, Skip.'

His eyes were closed in an ecstasy of contained emotion.

Liam blushed with fear and shame. He had written the tripe himself five minutes before the meeting out of sheer dread at not having come up with a result for the Mammy Song Project to date. Liam thought desperately about which of his friends in Ireland could be tempted over to masquerade as the author. Was there one who wouldn't lie down on the shagpile and split their hole laughing at him? He would have to come clean.

'It was me.'

He knew he'd have to do better than that.

'It was me, sir.'

Big looked across at him. An expression of disbelief streaked across his face, and for one terrible moment Liam thought he was for the chop.

The opposite was in fact true. Liam knew that many of his jokes were lost on Big, but even he had not banked on the billionaire's complete lack of irony. You do not get to be America's Richest Man by sitting around working on your sense of irony.

Big looked at his young charge and it all came flooding back. Their first meeting and his talk of wanting to be a writer. He had talked about Ireland with such humility, such grace. Big tried to remember – the lad had talked about caravans and alcoholism and things. And what had Big done? Given him a job as a PA – a *PA*! This guy was no PA! He was a genius! A born poet! A master of words! All the time he'd been getting this lad to run around for him doing paperwork and menial stuff like that when the great blood of Joyce! Behan! Binchy! was clearly pumping through his modest little veins. How could he have been so *blind* – such a phillipine. And to top it all, Big thought, this literary giant – this Caravan-Reared Genius – had called *him* sir! It was almost too much to take. For the first time since his second date with the recently departed Pricilla, Big thought that his heart was going to burst. He was (as Dave would have attested if he wasn't busy carpeting the soul of a soon-to-be-famous actress not two blocks away) right on top of his True Self. There was only one course of action open to him. To do what comes naturally to every true American at times like these. Big walked from his desk into the centre of his study floor, raised the vast span of his arms as wide as they would go, and wiggled his fingers in Liam's direction. He was pitching for a hug.

Liam had only ever seen Big do this once before – after a row with Pricilla. It had been once too often, and he had only been watching. Now he had to participate. In Big's currently volatile state, he wasn't going to risk offending him, so he shuffled over with as much dignity as circumstances would permit, and allowed himself to be enveloped in the Armani-sprayed arms of his boss.

Three whole minutes passed, and just as Liam thought he had inhaled enough cashmere to make a pair of gloves, Big finally let him go.

But that was not an end to it. While he was holding the very essence of all that was Irish in his arms, Big had been thinking. You do not become the Richest Man in America by letting three minutes of quality hugging time pass without having a really good think.

'Skip,' he said, 'I've been thinking.'

Liam did not like the sound of that. Big had something mad on his mind. Madder than commissioning a million-pound song for his mammy; madder than wanting to replicate the Statue of Liberty in Waterford Crystal. He could feel it. He recognized the look. He tried to back his way out of it with his emergency tactic. The stuttering 'Ah, Mr Big, now, sir, musha I wouldn't be good enough to organize a big job like that, sir, sure I'm only a poor wee gom from the smallest country in Europe, sir . . .' routine. Big headed him off at the pass.

'Skip,' he said, raising his right hand and closing his eyes, 'I know that it is your destiny to become a Great Irish Writer . . .'

Liam couldn't believe it.

'. . . and I know that working for me, while it's been surely fascinating and rewarding – ' he challenged Liam with a questioning look and he duly pursed his lips and nodded absolute agreement – 'has held you back from fulfilling that destiny you obviously so richly deserve . . .'

If Big had stopped there, Liam would have taken

whatever handout was offered and been happy with that. But the Big Man was only drawing breath.

'. . . so . . . *first* – I am going to make you the Most Famous Writer in America. I wouldn't insult you by offering you money for your work – I know what a poet values the most is for his work to be seen. I am going to have the words to "O Sweet Mother Ireland" bill-boarded across this land, put on every radio station, published in every newspaper until there is not a man, woman or child in America who does not know what true writing is all about . . .'

Liam was gagging at him like a dying fish. He didn't care about the million quid. He'd *rob* a million quid and murder his own mother before putting his name to that monstrosity.

'No, Skip . . . don't thank me yet because I have to confess that I already have something you can do for me . . .'

Liam had to sit down. He almost missed the chair with shock. Big didn't notice. He was on a roll now. He had the certain confidence of a billionaire who wants something entirely unreasonable and won't stop until he gets it.

'All this business with Pricilla, it's really upset me. Some people think with all my money I can buy love but, Skip? *You* know . . .'

He was standing over him now, ruffling his hair. *Ruffling* his hair with his big scary American palms. This was going to be like the longest, most sincere, terrifying hug in the whole world!

'. . . Damn the therapists and the doctors! Skip, *you* know – because you are an Irishman, and a wise man and a *poet*, Skip . . . *You* know that a man cannot buy love!'

Oh suffering sweet mother of Jesus, what was the lunatic American going to ask him to do?

'Skip – I am not asking you this as an employer – or as the Richest, Most Powerful Man in America . . .'

How bad could it be?

'. . . I am asking you this as a friend, Skip, and a fellow Irishman . . .'

Oh very, very bad indeed, Liam realized.

'Skip, I want you to go back to Ireland and – *find me a wife*.'

5

'I saw Lorna at Punchestown Races last weekend, dorling – she looked *dread-fal*!'

'Gerard Mooney told me that the accountant ran orf with the lot. The business is orn the rorks.'

The Monthly Foxrock Fanny Gossip South City Central Lodge was in full session. The location was Gloria's Gaff, and first on the agenda was the Lorna Cafferty Scandal. It had been all over the papers that week. Her accountant had disappeared to South America with several high-profile media celebrities' tax cheques, including Lorna's which had been signed over to him for the past five years.

'Too much hord-living, if you ask me – Jack said he sore her booking into Jury's lorst Thursday week at gorn midnight with a taxi driver. She wors half-cut, didn't recorgnize him.'

'Whort was your husband doing in Jury's at midnight on a Thursday?'

Melanie Mufton shook her bob in a playful oh-it's-all-such-hilarious-fun laugh, although the truth was she didn't know. Of course everyone else knew that Judge Mufton was taking regular 'diving lessons' with Melanie's tennis partner, Tara Flynn, whose husband 'Flinty' had died not six months previously. 'Someone *ort* to tell her. Mel's *gort* a right to *know*.' But the FF coven to which Mrs Mufton belonged were saving that for another day.

'I can't say I'm sorprised. I always *thort* Lorna'd *corm* to a sorey end with that *oreful* mother of whors!'

Sylvia Cafferty had been the first woman in Ireland to get separated For No Good Reason. At least, that was how it had seemed to her ten-year-old daughter Lorna at the time. There were plenty of women who ran away from wife-beating alcoholics, but few that had left their husbands merely on the grounds of having gone off them. Or rather, if they had, they pretended it was otherwise. Leaving Lorna's father, a standard-issue perfectly functional man, was bad enough, but Sylvia did not leave it at that. The trailblazing TV show *The Late Late* got wind of her, and invited her to be an audience guest on their 'DIVORCE – MORTAL OR VENIAL SIN? SPECIAL'. Everyone knew that divorce was a sin, *per se*, but the specific nature of the sin, it was being argued by a panel of high-profile religious, was dependent on circumstances. If your husband beat you, a kind nun from Kildare explained, then obviously that was Good Reason to leave. But what if you married someone in good faith believing them to be a committed Catholic? asked a woman from Mayo, then you find out he's a filthy heathen who demands you cook him steak on

Fridays making you an accessory to his mortal sin? Nothing a few plenary indulgences wouldn't cure, the monsignor assured her and certainly not Good Enough Reason to leave a marriage. The questions came thick and fast that night. Under what circumstances was it all right to marry a Protestant? What if he converted into a Protestant after marrying you? Sexual fondling under the rules of engagement – mortal or venial? Was a wife obliged to fulfil her marital obligations even when the heathen husband was mouldy and obnoxious to her (the poor woman from Mayo again)? Then the issue of annulment came up. Once you got your annulment the slate was wiped clean – everybody knew that. But supposing you were run down by a bus while you were waiting for your annulment to come through. Did that mean that you were in a state of mortal sin and destined to spend for ever in hell? Or did your Good Reason go towards making the sin merely venial, which meant you were going to get away with purgatory?

It was into this atmosphere of religious semantics that the presenter, feeling that the good people in his audience were forgetting what century they were in, introduced Sylvia Cafferty.

'I have a lady here from Dublin, who is recently separated and would like to get a divorce – is that right, Mrs – or should I call you Ms – Cafferty?'

Lorna was at home watching her mother on the television at a neighbour's house. The whole Walsh family were sitting in their respective regular spots, with this quiet little mite they had agreed to babysit at the last minute squashed awkwardly between the teenage son and the father on the sofa. Lorna was mortified to be sitting between two men, and tried not to move so as she wouldn't accidentally touch one of them. She wanted to be with her own dad – tonight and always. But he'd had to go to England for his job. Really, Lorna knew that he'd gone because Sylvia had sent him away.

'Ooooh look! Your mammy's on the telly!' kind Mrs Walsh said, trying to make the little one feel at home as she came in from the kitchen with tea and a glass of red lemonade for Lorna. Lorna preferred white lemonade, but she was too polite to say. She didn't like seeing her mother on television. It was weird, and she looked strangely orange, her lips sort of buzzing with a mad pink colour.

'You can call me anything you like, Gay,' were Sylvia's first words, and the audience erupted as if she had said something funny. Lorna could see from the slidy smile on her mother's face that she was enjoying herself. She got a terrible feeling in the pit of her stomach.

'Frankly, Gay, I don't know what all this nonsense is about Good Reason. My husband and I simply drifted apart and I left him because, well, if you want the truth – I was *bored*! And, I'm sorry, but I think that is Good Enough Reason for any woman!'

The programme erupted after that. Cassocks were quivering as the monsignors tried to get a grip on themselves without effing and blinding that women were the root of all evil, and the kind nun put a good half hour of airtime into trying to convince Sylvia that she must have Good Reason but was too ashamed to admit it.

However, by that stage the issue of why she had left her husband was ancient history to the outgoing Sylvia Cafferty. An altogether more exciting thing was happening. Sylvia was becoming famous – and she liked it.

For three full months after her appearance on the *Late Late*, the Divorce for No Good Reason debate rampaged through the Irish media like a mad bull, and Ms Cafferty was at the centre of it. She appeared on radio saying, 'It's a woman's prerogative to change her mind!' 'I JUST WENT OFF HIM!' read the headline in a full-page interview with a picture of Sylvia in her newly opened underwear 'boutique'. Her flippant attitude towards the Holy Institution of Marriage caused an uproar in the conscience of the Irish public, and while women the length and breadth of the country secretly looked at their dull lumps of husbands and wished they had the guts to do the same, Sylvia became what she realized she had always wanted to be. A Celebrity. A glamorous middle-aged woman who owned an expensive lingerie shop became famous for having an attitude. She was the first Famous For No Good Reason person in Ireland, and she never looked back.

Had she done so, she might have heard the mortified hush that came over her neighbours' living room as she made that first slice into the heart of the Catholic community in which she, and her daughter, lived. She might have wondered how Lorna had felt when Mrs Walsh broke the horrified silence by saying 'I'll put the kettle on' although she had just put the full tray of newly brewed tea down. She might have wondered why the Walshes were always too busy to babysit these days, or how Lorna coped with the teasing and the torment she got at school. But Sylvia Cafferty was too busy being famous. Too busy to wonder why Lorna, at seventeen, had wanted to go to England and find her father, even though she hadn't seen or heard from him in seven years.

Sylvia moved to America when Lorna graduated from UCD. She hooked up with a wealthy man who believed she was in her mid-thirties, and Lorna would have 'given the game away' so was never invited over to meet him. 'Not unless you have surgery and wear pigtails, darling – hope you don't mind.'

Three fat cheques were sent to Lorna for her first car, the deposit on her house, and six months' rent on her new office when she decided to start up her own business. Sylvia told the rich American they were for her daughter's school fees.

Eventually Sylvia Cafferty got the divorce she had always wanted, and, ironically, an annulment. She married the rich American and there was a small piece about it in the *Irish Times*. She was delighted.

Lorna continued to hate any kind of personal publicity. She didn't mind dancing on the rafters for her clients, but she hated to be gossiped about personally. The whole business with the Scumbag Accountant being front-page headlines, and her being named, was a pure nightmare for her. Every journalist that she had ever refused entry to a party went for her blade first, and even those whom she considered to be on her side hardly spared her. It was Lorna's job to be charming to the press however much they went against her, or her clients, and they knew it. Then there was the frustration of trying to get hold of her accountant and being constantly met with an answering machine that said he had gone on holiday, and wouldn't be back for some time. The shock of seeing her face flash up in a little box behind the newsreader Darina Farrell on *News at Six* as the steely, impassive blonde (and best friend of Vile Bridget) stated coolly that, *'A Dublin man and accountant to many of Ireland's most successful business people, including the public relations queen Lorna Cafferty . . . blah . . . blah . . . blah . . .'*

Finally, there was the utter desperation of finding that she could not flirt her way out of three-quarters of a million in back taxes with a low-cut frock and a dramatic sob story. The man in the Sheriff's Office was committedly humourless and unsympathetic to Lorna's insistence that she had paid the accountant her money in all good faith and it wasn't her fault if he hadn't passed it on to them. Wilfred O'Gorman had been taught that, when in doubt, he was always to say 'You are liable' until it finally sank in.

'But I gave him the money!'

'You are liable, I'm afraid.'

'Look! I have the receipts *here*!'

'I'm afraid you are still liable.'

'But surely he can't get away with this!'

'The liability, I'm afraid, lies with you.'

Lorna was unfortunate enough to have been appointed a tax officer who was resourceful enough to find forty-five (she counted) different ways of saying 'You are liable'. He would not negotiate, and eventually ground her down to an appointment in two weeks' time when they could 'come to some sort of an arrangement'. Lorna could only pray that 'an arrangement' meant sex. As it was she would lose the Ferrari and have to remortgage the mews, at the very best, to raise the money. At worst she could lose the lot, and would end up back at square one. How the Vile Bridgets of the world would love that!

In the meantime, though, Lorna would have to front it out. Dearly though she would have loved to have taken to the bed with a quart of gin, she knew that if she didn't get out there and chuck a few smiles around she might never have the courage to leave her house again. She just hoped she could do it without looking too 'brave'. If there was one thing that Lorna had learned from her upbringing it was how to hang tough.

First on the agenda was organizing her hair. If the hair wasn't right, the world would know that Lorna Cafferty was losing.

Once – just *once* in her whole adult life – Lorna had taken a chance and gone out without the full make-up.

It had been on the press weekend for Paddy Wallop's Medico factory tour. Hopelessly hungover, she had crept out, before dawn ('dawn' being before ten a.m. on Lorna's body clock) and crawled down to the local shop for cigarettes. The summer country air had lulled her into a moment of *au naturelle* insanity and she had just thrown a coat on over her nightie. On her way back, the client himself had caught her staggering up to the hotel with make-up-caked sleep clinging to the corners of her eyes, munching greedily on a packet of beef-flavoured Hula-Hoops. She had given him a curt 'Good morning' and kept walking, but she'd been mortified.

From that day on, Lorna vowed never to let slip again. A suitable wardrobe had to be actioned for every occasion – however tragic it might be. The silver lining to the 'Aftermath of Runaway Accountant' disaster (albeit a small greyish nylon patch) was that it gave the 'I Vont to Be Alone' items a much-needed outing. And it was with a pair of huge Gucci shades perched on her nose and a black pashmina wrapped dramatically around her scrappy home-made hairdo that Lorna entered Gloria's Gaff that afternoon.

'Cafferty for three o'clock's in for her highlights wash and blow, Glor!' Scooter hollered across the salon, repeating above the sound of the dryers, 'Glor . . . Cafferty's in for three!' in case there was a Foxrock Fanny on Grafton Street who hadn't heard him the first time.

A dozen half-cooked heads craned to get a sideways look at how the fallen woman was holding up.

Gloria herself was sitting in the tinting dispensary reading the paper. She had the tiny window open and a fag perched on the rim of it, ready to drop it if one of her staff came in and caught her. The tabloids had not been kind to Lorna. One of the more oily columns had repeated a picture they had on file of Lorna staggering out of a party some two years beforehand, and given a list of celebrity boyfriends whom she may or may not have slept with. It had nothing to do with the story and was just the kind of gratuitous media crap that Gloria hated. She knew what it was like to be at the centre of scandal. When she and Frank had separated, they had been one of Dublin's most gossiped-about couples. Two weeks after news broke of their separation in the Clarissa von Biscuit column in *Ireland Today*, Frank had appeared in the same paper with his arm wrapped round 'gorgeous Irish supermodel, Flame' talking about 'What We Do on a Sunday' and photographed in their 'bijoux Sandymount apartment'. Gloria had kept a brave face on it, giving her clients loads of 'It was very amicable' and 'Flame is such a lovely girl. Lovely, *lovely* person.'

In reality, Frank had paid for the flat out of her money six months before she chucked him out, and Flame was a poisonous string of artificial nonsense whom Gloria had been low-lighting and conditioning for the past year (free of charge) on Frank's insistence that his new protégée was a few short months away from the front cover of Italian *Vogue*. *Vogue*, my arse, Gloria had thought at the time. The closest Flame had ever got to a modelling job was draping herself half-naked across the bonnet of a Skoda at the Dublin Car Show. Gloria hadn't wanted to dash her husband's hopes at becoming a model agent completely, and so had played the dutiful wife. She had been repaid with betrayal, but that in itself wouldn't have hurt her without the gloating nudge-nudge gossip-mongering that went along with it.

When she heard Scooter calling that Lorna was in, Gloria folded the paper and dropped it on a workstation before marching up the stairs to reception. She gave Scooter a dig in the back as she passed and he turned the volume up on the awkward atmosphere by saying, 'Wha-at? What did I do?' (Scooter didn't read the newspapers. He was permanently tuned, inside and out, to MTV.)

When Gloria saw Lorna standing as stiff as a post, all wrapped in black and trying to hold it together, she felt a huge wave of empathy. Lorna wasn't her usual brew, but nobody deserved to endure that kind of humiliation.

'Is it the honey highlights again, Lorna?'

Lorna nodded. Something in the kind way Gloria addressed her made her want to cry. She didn't feel as strong today as she thought she would when she left the house. She was grateful for the glasses and the pashmina, but they were inadequate armour for the hot poker sideways stares of the FFs.

'I'll do you myself today, all right?'

Gloria gave her a gown and led Lorna gently downstairs to the quietest corner of the salon.

As Gloria went into the dispensary to prepare her potions, Lorna tentatively picked up the paper that Gloria had left lying there. She was about to put it aside when her eye was caught by a very interesting ad.

6

Sandy was in her old bedroom unpacking her bag when she heard a loud rap on the front door and her mother calling her from downstairs.

'Sandra Louise! Sandra Louise!'

Why didn't the woman just say what she bloody wanted instead of always making her answer *first* – and why, *why* did she call her Sandra Louise? Sandy had told her a thousand times not to.

'What is it?'

'Sandra Loo-heese? Sandra Lou—'

'WHAT *IS* IT?' she shouted.

'It's Maeve. She's come to see you.'

'Send her up.'

'WHA-AT? SHALL I SEND HER UP? SANDRA . . . ?'

Sandy's mother was driving her stone-mad bonkers round the block and back again. And she'd been back home for less than two weeks.

Part of the problem was undoubtedly Sandy's father. He was one of those Husbands Who Never Say Anything. Sandy supposed he must have said something sometimes during the course of his day at work in the bank, but at home he remained silent. Apart from the very basic please and thank-yous and yes-loves, there was not a peep out of him. Sandra loved her dad to bits, and knew that he adored her, but even she had trouble extracting a full sentence from him.

'Did you have a nice day, Dad?'

'Yes, love.'

'Anything interesting happen?'

'No, love.'

'No robberies or hold-ups or anything?'

She might get a small smile out of him then, but he would not be tempted into conversation.

'No, love.'

'Anything interesting in the paper?'

He'd raise an eyebrow and consider telling her about something interesting he'd just read, but then when he realized that it would involve the actual structuring of words in his mouth, he'd decide it wasn't worth it.

'No, love.'

'Cup of tea?'

'Please.'

And that was that.

Sandra feared that her father must have so much held inside him, so many interesting stories from work and from the paper, so many unsaid sentences and unexpressed feelings that he was destined to explode. He might come charging into the house from work some day shouting, 'The FTSE index is up two points and I refused a woman from Glasnevin an extension on her overdraft!' then have about the house with a sledgehammer.

However, the real problem with (and possibly the cause of) her father's silence, was that Sandy's mother was permanently desperate for a chat. It wasn't that she was one of these verbally incontinent types that talks over you and just has to be making a noise all the time. Agnes wanted answers. Feedback. All of her kids were gone and now – Lord be praised – one of them was back and Sandy's mother wanted to be entertained. For the first week, it was fine. Catching up on all the news. But by week two Agnes's incessant questions were starting to grate, big time, on Sandy's nerves.

'Tell me about your day, love.'

'It was fine, Mum.'

'Anything exciting happen?'

'No – not really.'

'How was Mr Mac Rory?'

'Fine.'

'Did he say anything?'

'Of course he did, he's a bloody talk DJ.'

'No, I mean, to *you*?'

'Well, yes, but I work for him.'

'No – I mean, did he say anything, well, you know, *interesting*?'

'No, Mum, he didn't say anything interesting at all.'

'Do you not like him, then?'

And on and on until Sandy would say, 'I've had a tough day, Mum, I'm just going up to my room to rest. Do you mind?'

'No, love, of course. You go and get some rest.'

But Agnes would have a hurt look on her face as if she knew Sandy just wanted to escape her.

Fifteen minutes later the shouting up the stairs would start.

'Colette was on today! Said she saw your boss with his family on Grafton Street last weekend! Said the five-year-old is a dote!'

Lorna would pretend she hadn't heard.

'I SAID COLETTE WAS ON EARLIER TODAY! SHE SAID SHE SAW YOUR BOSS WITH HIS FAMILY ON GRAFTON STREET LAST WEEKEND! THE FIVE-YEAR-OLD IS A DOTE, SHE SAYS! IN THE SAME SCHOOL AS HER FRANKIE! PERHAPS YOU SHOULD MENTION IT TO RORY TOMORROW! I'M SURE HE KNOWS THEM!'

Her mother would be halfway up the stairs by this time, with a tea towel and a cup in her hand. Eventually Sandy, unable to carry the burden of humiliating her mother by making her shout through a locked door, would come back down.

After she had worn herself out with stories for her mother, Sandy would go back to her room. Staring up at the Laura Ashley print wallpaper that she had chosen herself at sixteen, Sandy started to feel like she was sinking back in time. Turning into the gruff, door-locking teenager who was desperate to escape what she saw as the backward drudgery of Ireland in the no-hope recession of the 80s. Universities belching out first-class honours students ten to the dozen, who would end up on the dole or with waitressing jobs before making their reluctant escape to London or America. Spotty eighteen-year-old boys starting the diet of Friday-night stout and chips that would turn them into fat, slobbery forty-year-old boys. Sandy had made her escape, and now she was back, here, in her old room, the ridge of Bluetac that had once held her precious David Bowie poster in place, peeling off the wall above her single bed. It was as if the years in London had never happened.

Her first job was the receptionist in a large advertising agency. Maeve's brother had been working at Cosmic and got her the job. She had only stayed a few months before getting her first break in the media, as a work-experience junior on a teenage magazine. She remembered making the editors endless cups of tea, trying to be noticed; subsidizing her meagre income by working behind the bar in an Irish pub near where she lived in Harrow. The nightmare train, tube and bus journey into town every day. Hospital, then local, radio. Finally, it all came together in her last six months. The job, the fantastic old flat in Notting Hill with its tiled floors and its Art Deco mosaic window above the front door. She had furnished it with second-hand and Habitat sale stuff. Picked up the gold velvet curtains in an Oxfam shop in Camden Town. Every Sunday morning, she threw a coat on over her GAP pyjamas and walked to the Jewish bakery for chocolate croissants, then down to Cullens for the Sunday papers and fresh coffee. Back in the comfort of her single-girl haven, she would scour the papers for new ideas for her slot on the Deaver show.

The only thing that Sandy had really missed about Dublin was her friends.

When she had first moved there, she didn't understand why people called London a lonely place. She was bright and popular, and had no trouble meeting people and making friends. But as the years went on, she realized that the friends she made did not come with a lifetime guarantee. Not like the ones back home. Friends were easy got, but they were easy lost too. For geographical reasons more than anything else. A friend would move to the other side of the vast city, then it would become just too hard to keep in touch. They would call you for a few months and say 'We must meet up soon', but then the strain of getting from Harrow to Clapham on a Saturday night after a busy week at work would become too much. You had to arrange to meet people months in advance, and then, by the time you got round to seeing them, there was so much news to catch up on, and the last train home was leaving in less than two hours – it hardly seemed worth saying anything at all. So, in one month, Sandy's life might be hectic. Full of dinner parties and clubs, then one of her girl gang would get a new boyfriend and another might move flat and suddenly everything would change. The clique would disband, and Sandy would be left on her own again, having to find a new group of friends to play with.

Boyfriends were an even tougher game. A lesson

which Sandy had learned the hard way. In Dublin, everyone knew everyone. If a boy messed you around, the city was so small that he would be bumping into you, your mates, or your family sooner rather than later. That made the Irish lads a bit careful with you. In London, there were no such rules. They could bury you in bullshit and grow flowers on the grave for all you could do about it.

At home, Sandy had been a popular date on account of her lairy attitude as well as her wholesome good looks. Her first encounter in London had been a real shock. An impossibly handsome pop-video director had picked her up at a party while she was on the teenage magazine. She had got quite drunk and gone back to his place.

What he hadn't said to her. He *loved* Irish women. He *loved* her red hair. He *loved* her cute accent. In fact, and this might seem a bit strange, he said, he thought that he had probably fallen *in love* with her – already! Love at first sight – if she believed such a thing was possible.

Of course it was possible. Sandy knew *just* how he felt.

The problem was, he was supposed to be going away the following morning on a three-week shoot. He didn't think he could go until their new and oh-so-precious love was consummated. He would have to cancel the shoot – *naturally* – because a true Irish Goddess would never *dream* of sleeping with a hugely-successful-model-good-looking-his-own-groovy-pad-in-Camden-Town-low-life like him. Would she?

Sandy would and Sandy did.

She waited three weeks for him to get back from the shoot. Then she waited another week for him to call. Nothing. The shoot must have been delayed. How glamorous to have a boyfriend who was on a Delayed Shoot! Ten days later Sandy began to worry that something really awful must have happened to her new love. She didn't have his number (he must have forgotten to give it to her – love makes you forget sometimes), so she rang his work. He was really, *really* busy, the receptionist said, but she seemed only too willing to give Sandy his home number (a former casualty, Sandy later discovered). Sandy rang, lots and lots and *lots* of times, but kept getting his machine. He wasn't dead because he was at work. Perhaps he was embarrassed – or shy – or . . .? No. *That* was inconceivable! She'd call round there in person and remind him about the red hair and the accent. Sandy got on a bus, then a tube, and knocked on his front door at ten a.m. on a Saturday morning with a bag of Danish and two cappuccinos. To surprise him. She discovered then that something awful *had* actually happened – except it wasn't to him, it was to her. Mr Pop Video Man was stripped to the waist and he was, indeed, very surprised. From behind him she could hear the simpering call of a female voice saying 'Who is it?'

'I thought you'd like some breakfast,' Sandy said.

'Thanks,' he said, taking the bag and coffee tray, and slamming the door in her face.

Sandy was so shell-shocked that she actually waited another full week before finally giving up. Perhaps he would ring and say the woman was his mother – or his sister – who had come to stay. When he didn't, Sandy thought she was going to die of mortification. How could she have been so stupid? So naive.

Sandy was young, and she got over it. Enough for similar scenarios to happen to her several times again before she finally gave up on men. In her last couple of years in London if anyone was going to get a date with Sandy Nolan, they would have to give their parents' full name and address so that if they turned out to be a scumbag, she would have recourse to avenge herself on their families. In any case, her career was more important, and she had her beautiful flat and her borderline designer lifestyle. If her London friends had been more established and consistent, Sandy might never have been persuaded to move back to Dublin.

The reality was, though, that she had been. She was here now, and would give it six months, then decide. She was not yet thirty. There was still plenty of time. Maybe, Sandy thought, she might try to persuade Maeve to come back to London with her and share the flat in Notting Hill. Perhaps that was something worth working towards.

Maeve was standing in the doorway of her room, holding up the back page of the *Daily News*.

'Get that miserable look off your face, girl, and get that snazzy London wardrobe of yours pressed and polished because we are about to hit the jackpot!'

Sandy was not in the mood for a party tonight.

'What is it?'

Maeve walked the one foot from the door to the bed and held the paper over Sandy's face.

'Look,' she said, as if all the answers in the world had come together and met in the span of her hands, 'at this!'

'Big Tom back at the Happy Shamrock for one night only . . . ?'

'*No, no, no* – underneath *that*!'

'Irish-American billionaire seeks bright, beautiful, independent, but above all Irish, wife . . . Blah blah . . . ?'

'It's *him*!'

'Who?'

'Him! *Him*! Liam's boss! Mr *Big*!'

Sandy vaguely remembered Maeve telling her that Liam was working for some big shot in America. She had had little interest at the time, and after a week of '*turning those turntables*' as '*your own Rory Mac's gorgeous new assistant, Se-xeeee Sandy*' had even less interest now.

'Maeve, what are you going on about?'

'Liam – the little feck – is only working for the Richest Man in America. Not only that, I saw the Big One himself in an issue of *Hi-There!* magazine which

Karen sent home from America and he is *only gorgeous*. A cross between Pierce Brosnan and . . .'

'George Burns?'

Maeve looked quite offended, as if she were married to him already.

'No, *actually* – a young Donald Trump.'

'Eeeew!'

'Well, more Pierce Brosnan . . .'

'Is he not ancient?'

'Not really – maybe fifty, but he's had loads of cosmetic surgery so it doesn't matter. Jesus! It doesn't matter anyway because he is *pure loaded* and he's MINE.'

'Maeve, will you get a grip.'

'No – I mean it. This is IT, Sandy.'

'You don't even know if it's the same guy.'

'Oh, but I *do*, Dr Watson. Liam says this Mr Big is huge into All Things Irish. A real Paddyphile. That's how my halfwit brother got the job, by Just Being Irish. Apparently, this guy is always bleating on about his dead Irish Mammy and his sixth wife, some American Dolly with Big Hair called Pricilla who has just left him and now he's looking for a *real* woman. That must be him – and, Sandy, it's *me-eeee* he needs!'

And Maeve twirled around the bed holding the paper to her breast saying, in her best *Gone With the Wind* accent, 'We Arish ah qua-ate the latest thang in American soci-aty, you know – and hey! I'm beautiful, I'm independent, I'm sure as hell Irish and I've got an "in" with Liam working for him.'

Sandy had to admit she was amused by her old

friend's enthusiasm for this fantasy, even if she worried that the stone-mad Maeve might take it further.

'So what's the problem? Just go over there and introduce yourself.'

Maeve sat down, curled her bottom lip and gave Sandy her puppy-dog-that's-where-you-come-in look.

'Can't. Liam won't let me. That's where you come—'

'Oh no!'

'*Plee-ase*, Sandy. It's no big deal. I just want you to send your picture in and answer the ad. Liam is his Right-Hand Man, no less, he's sure to be vetting the replies. If he sees me, he'll chuck me straight in the bin and I won't even get through to the first round. If Liam sees you going in for it, he'll be kind of intrigued. He always liked you.'

'No way, Maeve. No way, absolutely! Forget it.'

'It might mean a trip to New Yoick . . .'

'No!'

'I'll come with you . . . it'll be a laugh . . .'

'Maeve, which part of *no* don't you understand? Anyway, Liam will know you've put me up to it.'

'No he won't. He doesn't even know you're back. We can put a London address. Anyway, he always thought you were very sensible.'

'No, I don't think so.'

'It might make a good story for you. I thought you were *supposed* to be an Investigative Journalist? Well – why don't you "investigate" this?'

Maeve was too expert and determined a manipulator

to miss that trick. Sandy could feel herself being ground down.

'I'll think about it.'

Maeve jumped up and down on the bed and nearly sent her crashing to the floor.

'Oooooh, you're an angel. I've got a pic of you all ready, and I'll even write the letter for you. Don't worry! You won't have to do a thing. I'll get it off tomorrow, then we can start *plotting*!' and she headed for the door.

Sandy shouted after her, 'I thought we were going out for a quiet drink?'

'Stuff that, girl. I've got a wardrobe to edit. American billions, here I come!'

After Maeve had left, Sandy wondered at the bizarreness of this latest scenario. Liam in America? Would he be intrigued by her picture? He thought she was sensible? Sandy could hardly remember Maeve's cool older brother. When they were kids he was always up in his room listening to music, or hanging out in the older boys' discos at his school. He had left for London by the time she would have been old enough to be interested in boys, and she had only vague recollections of him being friendly in a polite way towards her when he got her that job in the agency in London. She wondered what had taken him from London to America. How he came to be working for this rich guy. From what little she knew of him, it didn't seem like his scene. Sensible, eh? Oh, how London had changed *that*! At least it was taking her mind temporarily off the Rory Animal and the what-happened-to-my-life? blues.

'SO WHAT DID MAEVE WANT, LOVE? IS EVERY-THING ALL RIGHT? I THOUGHT YOU WERE GOING OUT FOR A DRINK?'

Sandy went to the top of the stairs and looked at her mum standing there with her cup and tea towel.

'Decided not to go.'

'Wanted to stay at home and have a chat with your old mammy, eh? You are such a good girl, Sandy. I'm so glad you're home.'

Sandy's eyes filled with tears. She wasn't sure if she herself was glad or not any more, but somehow tonight, she didn't feel that spending time chatting with her mother would be such a sacrifice.

7

Lorna was the last client to leave Gloria's Gaff that night. She had stayed really quiet for the three hours it took Gloria to weave through the delicate foil highlights, then trim off her scrappy ends and blow-dry the thick wet fuzz into sleek submission with the powerful pull of her bristle brush. Gloria wasn't much in the mood for chat that day herself, but she could sense her last client's weakness in the way her head flopped to her touch. Normally Lorna was as stiff as a board, tense – her head could be moved from side to side and stay there like a Sindy doll's. She would want to be in and out in an hour, and was constantly tutting and giving out if there was any delay. Today was different. She was as quiet as a mouse.

'Keep your head still, Lorna.'

'Sorry.'

Her voice sounded small and scared. Gloria got the feeling that this was the first time Lorna Cafferty had relaxed in days. It was as if she didn't want to leave this corner of the world, the station next to the dispensary in the basement of Gloria's Gaff. The salon was closed and the doors were locked before Lorna's hair was finished. The world and the accountants and all the gossip couldn't get to her in here.

⬭

Lorna lingered at the front door, taking ages to arrange her pashmina over her newly done hair. Gloria suspected that it didn't really matter. Lorna wouldn't be going out anywhere tonight. But she helped her tie the cashmere shawl in place and, on impulse, kissed Lorna gently on both cheeks as she was stepping onto the rain-smeared pavement and said, 'Don't worry, love, it'll all blow over.' For a second, Lorna looked like she might revert to form, and snap back a nasty retort, but she didn't. Her face softened and she just mouthed 'Thanks', putting on her Gucci shades before leaving, although it was already dark outside.

Gloria sat for a few minutes after she had gone. She was glad that she was able to provide a safe haven for her clients when things went wrong. Somewhere that they could be pampered and have their heads massaged by someone who wouldn't judge them. Someone who knew how tough life could be. It was just that Gloria wished sometimes that she had somewhere herself like that to go. That there was some other person that could help buff down her own rough edges, the flinty bits she had chipped off herself to help protect her from the hardship of first poverty, then love. If her relationship with Frank could have ever been described as that. He had hurt and humiliated her so much, she couldn't remember having ever loved him. Sometimes, she felt like little more than the victim of some cruel trick.

She looked round her empire. Four basins and workstations, three more of both downstairs. They were starting to look a bit scraggy and unkempt; the mirrors aged with hairspray glue, the floors scuffed. It needed a refit, really, but she didn't have the money. She did her best by making the juniors scrub it spotless, but tonight the place was in a bit of a state. Scooter had wanted to leave early. He was working part-time as a DJ, and Gloria couldn't in all conscience keep him here sweeping up hair if there was a chance he might make a go at something else. Scooter was never going to make stylist, and she couldn't keep him here slaving for ever. Anyway, she was running out of titles for him.

Gloria picked up her discarded paper to chuck it in the bin and saw that it was folded on an ad from an American billionaire looking for a wife. God! Wouldn't that be the thing. A big shot coming along to sweep her off her feet. Gloria knew that things like that didn't happen in real life. Not to women like her anyway. She'd had to work all her life for everything she'd got. She didn't mind that so much, but she *did* mind working for things that she hadn't got and being rewarded with things that she didn't want – like Frank. She put him to the back of her mind. If she thought about him now she'd be up all night seething. Best to just put it aside for tonight and get on with the cleaning up.

Just as Gloria picked up the broom, there was a rap

on the big shopfront window. She nearly jumped out of her skin. When she turned she saw Sam Cohen with his hands up against the glass, glaring in like a child checking out a closed sweetshop.

'Hey, Cinderella!' he said as she opened the door, broom in hand.

Gloria liked Sam. She had known him as long as she had known Frank. They were old friends, and used to knock around together as boys in Blackrock. When she and Frank had first been going out, Gloria suspected that Sam had liked her himself. This was confirmed one awful night years later when her drunken husband had announced that 'Sam wants a threesome' after his friend had confessed to Frank in confidence that he thought he ought to treat Gloria with 'more respect'.

'"If you don't pull your socks up, Frank – she'll leave you." Isn't that what you said, Sammy-Boy? Well, you can fucking have her. Go-on . . . go-on, ya big cowardly pouf ya – show my wife a bit of respect there, why don't you! I'll just sit here and watch, yeah? I'll join in and give you a hand if you get stuck!'

Sam had made as dignified an exit as Frank's ravings would allow, and if Gloria had ever had any romantic feelings towards this mild-mannered Jewish friend of Frank's, she put them straight back in the file marked DON'T EVEN THINK ABOUT IT. She knew that the two old friends would make it up. If only for history's sake. Sam had remained loyal to Frank through all of his bullshit over the years. Lending him money when Gloria refused, or ran out. Sam had even tried to smooth things over between them when the bollocks had run off with Flame.

'She's only a stupid girl, Gloria. You're ten times the woman she is.'

Frank had always maintained that Sam Cohen was a closet gay. Certainly his gentle manners and sense of style were better than most men of his age. He had had his hair cropped when he started to lose it which Frank, with his big, black comb-over, said was 'a very bad sign'. At the time, transplants were the In Thing with men that could afford it, but if Gloria had learned one thing in her fifteen years' hairdressing experience, it was that a rug is a rug. You can rivet it to the floor but it is *still* a rug, and men's wigs, no matter how expensive and well made they are, fool nobody.

In truth, Gloria had been half relieved when Flame came on the scene. She prayed every night that Frank would make a go of his new venture so that he would leave her alone. Leave her in peace to lead her own life. If he did well, perhaps he'd stop bleeding her dry, and maybe she would be able to put some money back into the business. Start a franchise of 'Gaff's. Perhaps Flame would be the woman to sort Frank out, slow down his drinking, or stop him doing coke. She thought, after he left, that she might meet someone herself. But Gloria could not see how that would ever happen now. Too much life had happened to her already. Her father had died and left her, then Frank had killed something off inside her. She didn't feel that she had enough life in her left over for love.

Sam was all right, but she could do without Frank's friends calling around to see her. For tonight, she just felt like pretending he didn't exist. However decent Sam Cohen was, he was still Frank's friend and confidant, and Gloria knew that she could never fully trust him.

'I just popped in to thank you for doing Go Girl!'s hair for me. You really pulled me out of a hole. Thought I'd stick my head in and settle up.'

Someone she knew *giving* her money. That made a change. Gloria heard the cynical tint in her thoughts. Had she really become this hard?

'No, it's all right, Sam. On the house.'

'Drink, then? Or dinner? I'll take you out for something to eat. You look wrecked.'

Gloria put her hand up to her hair. She was wearing a pair of black jeans that were at least five years old and a basic white shirt from Marks and Spencer's that was streaked down the front with honey-gold tint. Jesus, she probably did look wrecked. All that time spent glamourizing other women, and she hardly bothered with herself these days.

'Oh no – Jesus, I didn't mean . . .'

'No, I don't think so, Sam. Not tonight.'

Sam shoved his hands into the trouser pockets of his beige linen suit and shuffled about a bit. Not wanting to go, but not entirely sure whether he should stay. He was a good bit shorter than Gloria and sometimes, when she looked at the little stout-baldy cut of him, she found it hard to believe that he was the big shot record producer he was. With big American groups clamouring to record in his Wicklow studios, and The Trembling Celtics, whom he also managed, one of the biggest groups ever to come out of Ireland. He was one of the most powerful men in the Irish arts and entertainment world, and yet here he was wearing a little hole in her lino as if he wanted to burrow down to the basement and stay there. Did he not have some other friend he could go and bother tonight?

Finally, when he didn't make a move to go, Gloria caved.

'Oh all right, then. Give me two minutes to get changed.'

Gloria went to the door of her apartment upstairs which was behind reception, and was about to go up until she noticed the Sam was still standing by the glass window of the salon like a shy schoolboy. The eejit was intending to wait there for her in the dark, like a bloody gargoyle.

'Well, are you coming up, then?'

While Gloria got changed, Sam sat on the sofa and waited for her.

He looked around at the mixture of homey nick-nacks and designer art pieces. A cubist lamp with a white cylinder shade; a black and white framed picture of her family standing in front of the grey tower block of their home. Sam picked out little Gloria's face from amongst them – serious and strained as an adult's. She can't have been more than nine or ten. Gloria on her wedding day, in a tasteless wire frame tucked into a messy corner of the sideboard. She had worn real flowers in her hair that day. As best man, Sam had delivered them to her mother's flat that morning. He remembered feeling slightly ashamed by his own middle-class surprise at where she had come from. The lift had been broken and Sam had walked up twelve flights of stairs with a small box of miniature orchids wrapped in tissue paper. The flat had been alive with excitement – women running around with veils, cups of tea and bacon sandwiches – Gloria, calm and beautiful, sitting amidst the laughter and the panic like a cream goddess. Sam had wanted to stay in the warm generous comfort of that home, but had to go back and peel Frank from the bar of their local.

At Sam's feet was the rug Gloria and Frank had brought back from their honeymoon. Its colours were faded and worn. When he had admired it at the time, she had put her hands on his newly shaved head and said playfully, 'Don't you go getting any ideas about rugs now, Sam!' He could still recall the shiver as her soft hands had run across the velvet of his balding head.

Gloria was only gone for a few minutes, and when she emerged from her bedroom her hair was still damp around the hairline from where she had scraped it back to wash her face. She was wearing a simple black dress that he recognized and a pair of high black boots. The only make-up was a speedy slick of lip gloss. She wouldn't have gone to any trouble for Sam. He knew that, and it was just the way he liked it. She had been put through enough already. As he opened the door for her, he gently brushed the small of her back with his hand to lead her down. Even though it would always be 'just dinner' now and again, he knew that he would never tire of being with his best friend's ex.

Sam Cohen was, and always had been, hopelessly in love with Gloria.

8

Ohnow-aha-Sur-wheet Mutha Ireland-ah-
where have-ah-ye-ah-gone
Ah-hewoove-ah-gone-and-aba-handand-
your-ah-poor-ah-wee-ah-ping-ah-son.

Liam thought – no, *knew* – that 'Sweet Mother Ireland'
was the worst song ever written, but now he was having
to endure the unspeakable torture of actually hearing it
being sung. Mr Big had not liked the world-renowned
Irish tenor Gréagóir Ni Droighneain's operatic interpretation of this heart-melting lament and, after a rummage
through Mammy Big's own vast CD and record collection (which was kept in a vault under Big Towers along
with her cryogenically frozen body), decided that the
only person in the world who could sing this song to its
true and most meaningful potential was an old show-
band singer who went by the name of Hairy Heffernan.
'Hairy' (Bernie by birth) was Mammy Big's favourite
'artist'. In his heyday, Bernie was famed for his ability to

add to the smaulch content of old Irish favourites by appending or replacing the lyrics with 'ahs' and 'mushas', and his own legendary interpretation of the word 'the' – 'Yashi'.

Thus went his first line of 'The Rose of Tralee': *'Yashi pale moon was-ree-hising-musha-yasheen-ah-mountains'*, which was Mother Big's favourite song. Her young son had oft times sat at the helm of Mammy's gold-plated four-poster while the old lady cranked it up on the Bang and Olufsen remote and said, 'Never forget where ye came from, son.' Big's eyes had filled up when he had found the song again, and he sent Liam on a mission to find 'the man who filled my childhood years with the music of Ire-Land. I expect he's retired back home – living in a house in Conni-mara or somewhere'.

Liam didn't have to look far. Cursory local investigations revealed that Hairy was to be found propped up against the counter at the Merry Ploughboy in downtown Manhattan, doing turns at the karaoke in return for shorts (the *regulars* paid him not to sing). At about ten every night, Bernie would adjust the waistband on his ever-shrinking trousers, tucking all the extras into where they belonged, then rummage his way through the subway back to his brother's house in Long Island, where he had been staying temporarily for nine years since his last album – *Hairy's Hit Parade* – had plummeted him into the dingy depths of obscurity. At least once a month, he would upset his sister-in-law Patsy to the end of her, already stretched, tether, by trying to get into bed with the two of them. One time she woke in the middle of the night to find she was nose to nose with Bernie's big red face which was glaring at her horribly as he slept with his eyes open.

There was great cause for celebration in Patsy's heart, therefore, when her revolting brother-in-law was moved, by Mr Big (who was horrified at the ill-treatment of 'Ireland's greatest singing talent'), to an apartment which he owned on Seventh Avenue, and paid a vast sum of money to record 'Sweet Mother Ireland'. As yet, the CD had not been inflicted on the ears of the American public, but Big was transmitting it by hidden speaker through his entire office block. In the toilets, the lifts, his private quarters, his own office and the office of every single person that worked for him in the thirty-storey skyscraper in Manhattan. There was not one of the 103 rooms that was not subjected to the crucifying warble of Hairy's 'yashi's and 'ye's.

Already, Liam was in hell. This morning, though, Lucifer himself was taking the red-hot poker to places Liam didn't even know he had. Places a good deal more painful and delicate than his ears.

'Post's in, Skippy . . .'

Lindy had an unusually smug and bitchy look on her face this morning. Lindy was a tall, frighteningly good-looking lipstick lesbian. Although she didn't advertise the fact, the matt red lips and the leather biker jackets were a giveaway. She had been Queen Bee before Big had hired this know-it-all-Irishman, and she took every chance to let him know it.

'. . . and lover? It's *all* yours!'

Liam followed her eyes to six enormous postbags which were sitting in the corner of the ante-room.

'Better move them downstairs, Buddy Boy, before Big gets in. You know how he *hates* to see the place cluttered.' She looked at Liam as if he were a piece of clutter himself, and got on with emailing her coven.

Liam had been against putting an ad in the Irish newspapers, but Big had insisted.

'Give 'em *all* the opportunity, Skip. My mammy was no hoity-toity lady – she was from Humble Origins. Spread the net wide, Skip, and lets see what turns up!'

What turned up was six ton-weight postbags. Liam knew he would have to trail through the lot, and make Big's choice for him. If he ended up with a Rottweiler fake like Pricilla again, it would be Liam's neck on the line. He hoiked the bags down to the postroom and started to haul through them.

There were girls from the back end of Belmullet who looked little more than children, but whose Spice Girl outfits suggested they were willing to trade in Mayo convent life for a bit of New York action. There were a lot, a *lot*, of middle-aged ladies whose soft-focus Model for the Day studio shots were fooling nobody. Some of them sent touching stories of loutish husbands and hopes for divorce. Others put their age at twenty-five. Liam put a couple aside out of desperation. There were two nuns and a seventy-two-year-old artist from Donegal who said that if that was the billionaire she thought it was, son of that crusty old bag who'd bought one of her paintings in '89 and not paid for it, well, he should be ashamed of himself and could he put a cheque in the post immediately or she'd cast a curse upon him and all belonging to him. There was even one aberration in pink sequins and thigh-high boots that Liam was *certain* looked like some class of a man.

By six o'clock that evening, Liam was exhausted. He had picked out one or two possibles, but nothing as streamlined and elegant as the kind of goods he knew his boss was after. Sure, the Big One would go on about cute little ordinary colleens from humble beginnings, but at the end of the day he was dealing with someone who flicked through the fashion pages of *Harper's Bazaar* when he fancied a bit of female company. And not just flicked. Big actually got Liam to ring up the magazines to get the models' names, and then their model agencies. The first time he had asked him to do it, Liam had been horrified. When he realized how easy it was, how amenable the agents and the girls themselves were to a night out with the American King of High Tack, he was more horrified still. Even Liam himself, because of his proximity to Big's Billions, could have dated any one of the girls himself. While he was tempted at times, he had seen enough of them come and go through his boss's life to know that it wasn't really his scene.

Liam had had enough. He was going to go home to his nice airy warehouse in SoHo, call in a take-away from the Thai restaurant around the corner and soak himself in the old iron bath that sat in the centre of his living room and watch wide-screen TV. If truth be told, as the fat salary cheques from Big kept piling up, and his apartment was coming together with all its boy-gadget stereo equipment, Smeg fridge, pinball machine and the like, Becoming a Serious Writer was slipping further down Liam's Stuff To Do list. It was a long way from the New York high life to a caravan on the Athlone bypass. Liam still harboured his fantasies, but he also knew that money was making him soft. He was starting to develop a skincare regime. He knew it was a problem – putting the whole beard thing on hold was a bad sign. If he delved deep enough, Liam would have found that his confidence in himself as a writer – even a copywriter – was all but gone. Running for Big was about all he was good for these days.

One of Big's bodyguards, Chuck, came into the postroom to do his nightly check of the building for bugs and bombs. Chuck was harmless, but didn't look it, which was important. He had a tight blond crop, and an impassive expression – underlined with a bottom lip which was permanently ajar and protruded slightly making it look like a half-open drawerful of teeth.

'Skip.'

'Chuck.'

Does *anyone* in this country have a real name? Liam thought, not for the first time.

Chuck moved about the room stealthily as if, at any moment, a James Bond baddie might leap out from behind the door. When he was finished poking around, he gave Liam the eyebrow to signal that he was off the hook. No bombs or physical evidence of espionage.

'This the wife thing?' he said, his hand idly rummaging at the top of an open sack.

One thing that *was* Irish about this American corporation was that everyone seemed to know what everyone else was doing.

'Yeah.' Liam kept it simple. He wasn't in the mood for a chat. He wanted to get home to a Fresh Pine Body Bath soak. If he was any kind of a Serious Irish Writer at all, he realized, he'd be going to a seedy bar with Chuck now, to shoot pool and talk about Vietnam. The urge to gather stories was gone off him. He was doomed.

'Hey! *She's* a babe.'

Chuck held out a picture and Liam took it. It was a girl, pretty all right, with long red hair tied back, loose curls framing her lightly freckled skin. She was sitting in a cafe and she was leaning back slightly as if she was genuinely laughing at the person taking the shot. She looked familiar somehow.

He lifted the picture and looked at the letter which was double stapled to it.

Sandy Nolan, 29. Radio producer.

Jesus Christ, it couldn't be!

⬭

'Hi! My name is Sandy, and I decided to reply to this advert because, having lived in London, I have always felt a strong pull towards the second-generation Irish Diaspora. It must be so hard to have a strong Irish connection and yet not be able to live here in Ireland with all our beautiful green rolling hills and little whitewashed cottages. I am single, and long to meet somebody' – blah ... blah ... loads of soppy girlie gumf about love.

Hobbies were listed at the end as: *'Churning butter, listening to opera, tending to hens and hosting dinner parties for an eclectic selection of friends which include high-profile academics, politicians, business people and artists.'*

Christ, she was taking no chances! Sandy Nolan, eh? Wait a minute – she was Maeve's friend. Could his scheming hellcat sister have put her up to it? Naah. Maybe? In any case, it was going straight in the bin! Perhaps he'd take it home first and have a good read.

Liam put the reply in his pocket.

'Hey – keeping the leftovers for yourself, eh?' Chuck winked.

'Are you finished?' Liam asked in the snooty voice he used to indicate to others, and himself, that really he was above all this and just killing time before going back to his Writing Career.

'Jumped-up little shit,' Chuck muttered as he lumbered out the door and left Liam to lock up.

Liam didn't care. He wasn't afraid of any of them. Not *much* anyway.

9

Paddy Wallop had the most magnificent house in Bunkelly, county Galway. There were only twelve buildings in Bunkelly itself. Five of them, including the Wallop Medico factory, belonged to Paddy himself, and the other seven to people who worked for him. But his house was magnificent all the same. Everyone agreed. On top of a hill, Wallop Mansion looked down on a picture-postcard landscape, green fields, valleys, streams – all that, and the ugly factory building somewhere behind it over to the left, where the architect said 'It won't be seen'. Paddy had been offended at the time. His medical supplies factory was, to him and the people of Bunkelly, a beautiful thing. It supplied work to the local inhabitants and the people of the surrounding areas, and, as Paddy was wont to assure anyone who would listen, 'gave relief and comfort to thousands of people'. Because, despite its remote location, Wallop Medico was a hugely successful international supplier of pants to thousands – nay, millions – of unfortunate incontinents the world over.

Paddy was also, by far and away, the most popular man in Bunkelly. The truth was, he had so much money, and nothing to do with it. He had to travel a good deal with his job, but was always anxious to get home. He wasn't interested in helicopter pads or houses in Paris and London, or anything like that. So he spent as much of his money as he could close to home. Bunkelly was therefore the most over-resourced townsland in the country. It had a sports centre, swimming pool, state-of-the-art equipped school, an arts and crafts mini-village and a population of one hundred people all told (if you took in the neighbouring villages of Kilbunion and Claretown). Paddy had stopped short of building them a cinema, and instead, every Saturday the local people would come around to Wallop Mansion for 'cocktails and nibbles' (mostly 'minerals', for the people of Bunkelly were not great drinkers, and cheese and pineapple on sticks) prepared by his housekeeper Marjorie, and watch Paddy's enormous TV, which he kept in his enormous TV Room. When the house was built, he had employed a local woman, Clara Fitzcronin, to do his decorating for him. Clara had always wanted to do interior design, and Paddy didn't see the point of getting some big shot down from Dublin, when the Fitzcronins would better benefit from the fee. Clara went into the vast metropolis of Galway City with local grocer and Man With Van, Festy Pointer, and the two of them came back loaded with peach paint and every bit of floral-print fabric available from Spiddle to Clifden. Clara then spent six weeks ruching and splatter-painting every inch of Wallop Mansion, naming each room on its door with a lavish stencil. When it was finished Wallop Mansion looked like 'something out of a magazine!', as Marjorie had exclaimed with delight. Quite what kind of magazine was open to question. With Clara's choice of smoked-glass coffee tables and gaudy gold fitments, it looked more like the set of a DIY porn film shot in the suburbs of Germany than the home of an International Businessman which, despite his humble outlook, was what Paddy Wallop was.

It was in amongst the plastic plants in gold urns and the stand-up whirly ashtrays (he didn't smoke but Clara said they added 'atmosphere') that a lonely and melancholy Paddy Wallop looked out at the rain drizzling hopelessly down his triple-glazed windows. He had everything. Plenty of money and the nicest house in Bunkelly. Yet, although he should have been the happiest man in the world, Wallop Mansion felt like his own personal corner of purgatory. Paddy wanted and needed a wife, but that was old news. All the women in Bunkelly of his own age were long married, and those who weren't had missed the boat waiting for Paddy. Every decent-looking young wan for miles around had trouped in and out of this house with her mother. Of course, *nothing* as obvious as a Formal Arrangement. That would have been Unheard Of. After all, this was the twenty-first century and far be it from the people of the parish of Kilbunion to go falling behind on the Modran Wheys of Tha World! But it just so happened that every Sunday afternoon some wilful mammy would be 'passing by' on her way home from Mass, and would 'drop in' to see how he was doing and 'Oh my God, Paddy – do you know my youngest, Adele? Here she is now, and as good as gold. Seventeen last birthday and a great cook – she has the dinner on for all of us now at home, haven't you, love?' The young girl would blush unmercifully, then look relieved when Paddy just patted her on the head, and didn't carry her off into a nearby field for a 'road test'.

Marjorie came in every Sunday and cooked lunch for him, but it wasn't the same. There was no reason why Paddy couldn't get married. He was a fine-looking lump of a man. He had a great deal of nut-brown hair which he kept neatly combed in a side parting. A good upbringing meant that he was fully conversant with the basic rules of bodily hygiene, although before his dear mother had finally passed away some two years beforehand she had said, 'Don't leave it too long, son,' and pressed a book entitled *Catholic Principles of Grooming for the Unmarried Man* into his hand. He was in good health and had a fit muscular body thanks to his Keeping Fit Room, although he seldom had the chance to show it off.

No. The only reason Paddy Wallop wasn't married was because he was saving himself for the Great Love of his Life. A flaxen-haired goddess who went by the name of Lorna Cafferty.

The whole Falling in Love with Lorna Cafferty thing had gone sideways after the press trip she had organized to his factory. Until then, she had just been a very attractive, but hard-nosed city woman, the like of which

Paddy had come up against before and never had any special truck with. He hadn't become Europe's Largest Supplier of Incontinence Pants by taking nonsense from Hard-Nosed City Women.

Then, the day after the big slap-up (and *very expensive*, he had pointed out to Lorna at the time) meal for the journalists, Paddy had been taking his morning walk down to Pointer's Corner Shop to replenish his diminished rasher supply. It was then that he saw her. A woman with long blonde hair picking her way delicately through the cowpats and thistles in Pointer's Field. Women not wearing wellingtons were a rare sight around Bunkelly at the best of times, and this, this – Angel (for there was no other way to describe her) had little flimsy stringy things on her feet and some class of a floaty garment billowing from under the gap of her coat. Paddy thought he was dreaming. That God had sent him a woman, finally, a stranger from the heavens dropped into the field right there in front of him. By the time she came closer and Paddy saw it was Lorna, it hardly mattered that she was eating beef-flavoured Hula Hoops, or that she gave him no more than a hoarse 'Good morning'. Paddy had been walloped good and proper with God's own powerful love truncheon. His inner journey of tragic loneliness had begun.

Paddy knew that Lorna was way out of his league. A smart, sophisticated city woman like that would never look at a big ludramawn like him. He also knew, deep down, that she didn't like him very much. He saw the way she glazed over when he talked about his pants

('*Call them "the product", Paddy – please*'). But Paddy Wallop was smitten. The more Lorna avoided his phone calls, the more he wanted to be with her. He kept inventing reasons to go and see her in Dublin. Sometimes he would book himself into The Shelbourne for the weekend and trawl around the pubs and nightclubs of Dublin searching for her. Perhaps if she 'accidentally' bumped into him in one of her regular haunts, she might look at him again. He had tried to get into Little's, where he knew she was a member, on his last trip, but had been turned down at the door.

'Who are you, mate?' the newly appointed *EastEnders*-looking bouncer had asked.

'Paddy Wallop,' he had said, handing him his card.

'Naah. Da-an't fink so, mate. Betta luck nestime, eh?'

Paddy had gone home heartbroken. He knew he was being a fool, but he didn't seem able to stop himself. He even knew that Lorna was a terrible PR agent – for him certainly. He paid her forty thousand pounds a year and got nothing in return, except for the occasional lunch date which he knew she did out of duty. But sacking Lorna Cafferty was simply never on the agenda. Whatever slim hope he had of being with her would be gone for ever if he did that.

On his last trip to Paris his client and friend, an allround Impossibly Gorgeous Frenchman called François, had noticed how upset he was. When he found out it was an 'Affair of the 'Art', he took his Irish friend in ''And'.

'You must play eet cool, Padday. Nev-air let 'er knoe 'ow much you love 'air.'

Paddy got some hope from that. He always made a point of never talking to Lorna about anything except work. Paddy was widely travelled and could have told her about his favourite restaurant in Venice, his last trip to Barcelona, why The Plaza was still the best hotel in New York. He could have told her how much it cost him to build the sports centre in Bunkelly, how much he hated the interior of his million-pound mansion and would she come down one weekend and have a look at it for him? But he didn't. Because if he did she would *know how he felt*, and he would be mocked and mortified. So Paddy always stuck, no matter how much Lorna tried to veer him away from it, to the safe subject of incontinence pants.

Next on François' agenda was Paddy's wardrobe.

'Ze men's wardrob must always be better than 'ers.'

Paddy wasn't so sure about that one. Lorna was a pretty slick dresser and anyway, what did clothes matter, it was the person inside who counted!

But he dutifully allowed François to drag him around Paris, and by the time he got out of the taxi from Galway airport, Paddy was six Armani suits, a dozen crisp cotton shirts and four pairs of cufflinks heavier than when he had left Bunkelly.

Hopeful of assaulting Lorna's hormones with his new-improved wardrobe, Paddy had tried her home phone again. Message machine. Office. Message machine. Mobile. Message machine.

He tried all three again to hear the different messages in her own sweet voice.

'Hullo, darling! Not here right now. Leave a message!'

'Darling'. He knew it wasn't specifically for him. That he was part of the broad term 'Darlings' that included all of her clients and most of the world at large. Oh! But how Paddy longed to be Lorna Cafferty's only sweet darling, and have her here, in Wallop Mansion, lounging on the sofa next to him in some class of a flimsy, floaty thing . . . .

Paddy stopped it right there before his mind led him into the Bad Place. His love for Lorna Cafferty was in God's hands now, and the Big One would surely never reward him if he defiled his pure love with scruffy thoughts of See-Through Nighties and the Like.

Paddy decided to distract himself by looking through the newspaper, but there was little comfort there. The first thing he saw was an ad from some American billionaire looking for an Irish wife. If only his own life were that simple. There were thousands of perfectly lovely women in Ireland and they had to feck off to America to find husbands because their own good Irish millionaires were in love with the Lorna Caffertys of this world. Disgusted, Paddy turned the paper around to the front page. There, in black and white, was a two-year-old picture of his Own True Love staggering out of a nightclub with the headline 'DUBLIN PR QUEEN LOSES THE LOT!'

Paddy read the article from start to finish, then backwards.

By the time he had absorbed its contents, Paddy's heroic testosterone levels were rampaging through his fine Galway muscles, and his fevered mind was plotting ways that he could come to his princess's rescue.

10

The fax came through just as Nylon was making an uncharacteristically early entrance into the offices of Cafferty Public Relations. He snatched it off the machine before Lorna was able to get to it.

'Ooooh. America's Top 100 Rich List! What's this, Lorna? Looking for a hubby? Got the idea from a certain advert in the papers, did we?'

Big's ad had not escaped the notice of Nylon, who, in fact, was the gruesome pink-sequinned vision that Liam had discarded.

'If you're not in – you can't win,' he had justified to Scooter whom he had cajoled into styling the grotesque hairpiece for his shot.

'No, actually – looking for new clients,' Lorna snapped back.

'Ouch! Guess we need them now with the tax stuff, so are we all out of a jo . . .'

The office went deadly quiet as Nylon trailed off. He'd gone One Step Beyond. It was the question on everyone's mind, but only a fat mouth like Nylon would actually say it.

'Firstly, it is not *we*, it is *I* – and secondly, *you* do not even work here.'

She grabbed the fax from her finally silenced part-timer.

'Now fuck off out of my office, and don't bother coming back unless you have a round of cappuccinos and a big bag of doughnuts in those filthy little claws of yours . . .'

Nylon knew she wasn't really mad or she wouldn't be sending him for coffee. He opened his mouth, but Lorna knew what was coming;

'. . . and before you even ask – *you're paying!*'

After he had gone, Lorna stood in the centre of the office and made an announcement.

'I expect you all saw the papers and you know what's going on.'

The minions barely nodded.

'Well, I just want you to know that I will be doing everything in my power to keep all of you on. Yes, I *do* owe a lot of money personally, but that should not affect the business.' (She was lying through her teeth but hoping that they were all inexperienced enough to believe her.) 'I am currently hoping that a big account from an American businessman which I am about to pitch for will provide enough profit to get me out of this hole, but in the meantime, it is business as usual.' They were all still sitting and staring at her like sick sheep.

'Sheila – get that press release for Flannery finished by two. Nicky – I want a letter written saying that it's business as usual here, and faxed to all the papers, magazines, radio stations – in fact, I want every wretched two-bit journalist in this country to get one. Jackie – call all our clients and arrange lunch dates with them in the next two weeks . . .'

'Mr Wallop was on looking for you again . . .'

'*Apart* from Paddy Wallop. Then call Betty and get her in here to do my nails, four this afternoon if she can make it. My hands look like a rhino ran over them.'

The girls felt better once they knew Lorna was her old self, and within a few minutes the office was back to its usual hive of activity.

Now, all Lorna had to do was find somebody rich enough and gullible enough to help pay off her tax debts.

The fax from the press agency in America was still snaking through the machine.

For a woman with Lorna's experience of getting people what they wanted, and knowing how to get what she wanted for herself, America's Top 100 Rich List wasn't hard to edit. An American with shedloads of money looking for a colleen wife? Must be second-generation Irish. Probably had a mammy fixation. She wasn't looking for a Hollywood star – they had no need to advertise. The Wannabe Politicians were all married to each other and if they were Irish, well, there were still enough Kennedys knocking around for them to choose from. In any case, America was much like anywhere else in the world. Money had no problem getting itself married. Right at the end she found him.

Big, Xavier. [Jesus – he had an Irish mammy all right with a Christian name like that!] *Born 1951 to Julias Big and Ita Doherty.* [Bingo!] *Developed father's multi-million pound chemicals business to international billion-pound empire through GM research and production of ready-made foods. Married six times, and recently divorced, Big is known for his support of Irish arts with his rival to New York City's St Patrick's Day Celebrations – the Texas Big Paddy Festival – which he launched last year.*

Renowned for his recent outlandish attempt to have the Statue of Liberty torn down and rebuilt in Waterford Crystal, Big runs his empire from Big Towers in Manhattan, New York, New York.

Oh yes – *this* was her man all right. Certainly tacky enough to take out an ad in all the Irish papers looking for a wife.

Lorna got straight on to international directory inquiries.

11

'Sandra Louise Nolan!'

Sandy was at the opening night for *Lonely Death*, a new play by the brilliant young playwright Eamon Weir. Mr Weir's literary reputation for solemn and intense poetic language was enhanced by his seemingly natural ability to grow a solid and indisputably genuine beard at the tender age of twenty-five, an honour usually only granted by God to much older and more established Serious Writers. However, at that moment Eamon, and his magnificent sample of hirsuitness, were backstage chewing the actors into a froth of intense emotional activity, and Sandy was standing in the foyer of Cursai, Dublin's new-wave arts venue, cursing Maeve for not coming with her and chewing frantically on a stale scone – the only food sold here on the grounds that the work should be enough intellectual nourishment in itself. It was the first time she had been out at a review gig since she'd been home, and Sandy knew nobody. In London, that was par for the course. But the crowd here were all standing in cosy little groups broken only when a member of one would lash across the room and grab *'Duncan!'* or *'Carmel!'* over to meet their husband/boyfriend/daughter or group of friends – none of which Sandy had with her. She felt awkward and alone, and was beginning to realize that anonymity was a shameful state of being in her home town when suddenly she was being called herself.

'Sandra Louise Nolan!'

Only one other person in the whole world had ever called her that apart from her parents – no wait – surely not . . .

'I *knew* it was you – what are you doing here?'

It was Gráinne Greely or the Blue Stocking Bitch as Maeve called her.

'Hi, Gráinne. Just here doing . . . ah . . . you know . . . sort of . . . well, a kind of review thingy . . .'

Gráinne had always made Sandy quiver with nerves. The three girls had been to school together and Gráinne had been the swot bucket in the corner – first with the hand up, started working on her application thesis for Trinity at eleven, got a full scholarship and graduated with honours – that type of thing. She was teased unmercifully by everyone, including Sandy and Maeve, for not owning a pair of Day-Glo leg warmers and for having an unhealthy lack of interest in boys. Now she was arts critic on the *Irish Times* – a job for which you had to be so unmercifully clever it hurt – the zenith of all that was worthy and proper in the Irish media. Sandy would have given up a limb to wipe the arse of a junior sub on the *Irish Times* – and Gráinne knew it. And now

here she was, all pointy features and no make-up just
. . . just . . . just being cleverer than Sandy.

'Oh yes – I heard you were back from London.
You're working out at Erin now? On some radio show,
isn't it?'

Women Who Never Wear Make-up made Sandy
nervous. There was some kind of impervious confidence
about them, as if they were too busy worrying about
the situation in the Balkans to be fussing about with
lipstick, which made Sandy feel silly and shallow and
stupid.

'Oh, it's just some show – you know, a daytime thing
really, not like, well – you know yourself . . .' Then she
did something that she only did when she was really
nervous, something which she really hated herself for.
Sandy shrugged her shoulders and started giggling and
snorting like a piglet. Seeing Gráinne unexpectedly like
this, in all her erudite glory, had pressed Sandy's 'Like
me! Like me!' panic button. She was just a few seconds
away from the self-depreciation dive-bomb mantra
'Don't mind me – I'm only a big thick' when the bell
went and they had to take their seats.

'Come and sit with me – I'll mind you,' said the
Greely, taking her arm.

Explain the fecking thing to me more like, thought
Sandy. Curse Maeve from the Holy High Heavens and
all the way back down to the bowels of hell for not
coming with her tonight. At least if the Rave were here,
they'd have had a laugh at Blue Stocking's miserable

pointy, no-make-up face or dowdy grey coat or flat shoes or *something*! With a sense of liver-hardening doom Sandy realized that actually, there was *nothing* about Gráinne she could laugh at any more. The reality was that with her one coat of mascara and the slick of lip gloss, Sandy felt like a shallow dolly bird next to the intellectual *Irish Times* weightiness of the mighty Greely. How could she hate something which she so badly wanted to be herself? Oh Christ! Where was Maeve? Only she could talk sense into her now!

Sandy could not make head nor tail of the play. It was apparently set in contemporary Ireland, but there were constant references to Greek mythology, and some of the cast were wearing togas with their faces daubed in green paint. At one point, a well-known TV soap actor dropped his toga completely during a *'powerful monologue, illustrating the naked vulnerability of a man facing death'*, as Gráinne described it in the review the following day. At the time, this had passed Sandy by, as the monologue was performed in Irish, most of which she had forgotten since school. To her, it was a pure 'Full Monty' moment. As she was in the front row and within sniffing distance of the actor's shrivelled green-daubed mickey, she could not help but splutter out what almost turned into a fit of nervous giggling.

During the interval, she tried to keep up with the comments of Gráinne and her intellectually charged chums.

'I think it lost something in the translation.'

'Was it originally written in Irish, then?'

'And Greek. Eamon finds it easier to write in Greek, then translate . . .'

'Ahhhh . . . that explains the reference to Socrates!'

'Touches of Tolstoy, I thought?'

'Lets hold off on *that* judgement until we see if our Ivan gets reborn at the end!'

Roars of laughter. Why? What the *fuck* were they talking about? Sandy was desperately trying to follow them, but couldn't so just kept her mouth shut. She prayed silently that they would forget she was there.

'So, Sandy. What do you think of it so far?'

Five serious, beardy, pointy, no-make-up faces looked earnestly at her, waiting for a reply. Then it happened. The intelligent, articulate side of Sandy's brain went into complete shutdown. The meaning of all words with more than two syllables flew out of her head, and she opened her mouth to let out what was left over.

'Yer man's mickey looked like a little frog.'

There was a horrible silence which was broken by the bell. Sandy sat through the second half in a trance of silent mortification. Even when the soap actor whipped his kit off again and ran through the audience howling '*I am re-bo-orn! I am re-bo-orn!*', there was not a tit out of her. Her body was literally weakened with embarrassment and it was all she could do to get up from her seat at the end, say 'It was nice to meet you' to the Pointys, thank Gráinne and walk out, alone, onto the crowded streets to hail a taxi home to Stillorgan.

12

Flame had a problem. The botox which she had had injected into her forehead a month ago was starting to wear off. If she furrowed her brow really, *really* hard, she could see the beginnings of a crease start to form – right there! – in the middle of her forehead!

'Fra-a-a-ank.' Her voice was like a foghorn, sirening across the smoked glass and shagpile of their Sandy-mount 'love haven'. That such a thin, delicate-looking creature could make a noise that any pillaging Viking would have hung up his horns for was beginning to make Frank feel tired. The girl collected cuddly toys, for Christ's sake. Hundreds of fluffy, candy-coloured bunnies and bears which she arranged up on frilly pillows every morning. Frank was starting to think he saw their beady eyes watching him as they made love, and to redress the power balance, had taken to keeping his condoms up the arse of a koala bear called 'Aussie' who was originally designed as a child's rucksack. Flame had been really upset, until he invented the 'Mr Aussie Wassie's coming to get yeh-hoow!' game, and she conceded that at least

Frank would stop saying her 'babies' were good for nothing.

Sometimes, Frank thought that perhaps it was the coke making him paranoid – making him see things. But then he figured he was just being paranoid about that. He still had his model babe, his flat, and at least 70 per cent of his hair. Somewhere at the back of his mind, Frank knew that he was in danger of losing control of his relationship, of his life. What he didn't know was that really, he had lost it already. The fluffy bunnies were making plans for world domination.

'Fra-ha-ha-ha-hank!'

Oh Jesus, the bitch was crying again.

'Don't cry – you'll make your eyes puff.'

He peeled Mr Aussie off the top of his semi-erect penis, where the koala had been residing quite comfortably as part of Frank's daily affirmation of his sanity. If the toy's face transmogrified under his stare into one of shock-horror, then it was unsafe to get out of bed. Today, at least, the expression on the stuffed toy's face hadn't changed. No hallucinations today. It was safe to get up.

He wandered into the bathroom. Flame was poking at her forehead with a two-inch acrylic nail.

'Stop fiddling with yourself,' said Frank as he flicked and flapped his nethers, trying to coax the twelve pints he had drunk last night down his urethra and into the toilet bowl.

'It's worn off, Frank – the lines are coming back. I'll have to get it done again.'

More money! Jesus, this woman didn't know when to stop.

'But you've only just had it done.'

Flame threw him one of her icy stares. The cute little bunny girl 'Plea-ease, Uncle Frank' routine had been binned a few months ago. Since Flame had read the chapter on 'How to Love Yourself in a Relationship' in *Carpet Your Soul With Love* by Dr Dave Ashman, she had decided that the best way she could love herself was by being 'honest with her partner'.

'I had it done *one whole month ago* – you fat fuck.'

Frank looked down mournfully at his belly, and realized that he could no longer see his troublesome little lad from this angle. Nor, indeed, the hand that held it. The great beer-holding bag was well and truly blocking his view. What had happened to him? It used to stick out like a great weapon – especially in the mornings. Pissing first thing used to be like firing a cannon. Now it was like trying to give the kiss of life to a sick hamster. Maybe he should cut down on the drink? Beer was a killer. Perhaps he should stick to spirits? Hell, he'd give up drink altogether. Stay with the coke. Everyone knew drugs made you thin. For the time being anyway. That was it. He'd give himself six months on coke only – just until he looked like David Bowie. Then he'd knock it on the head.

Flame was glowering at him angrily. That was, as far as he could tell. Since the botox injections, his twenty-one-year-old girlfriend had lost the ability to frown. Her face had this permanent veil of smooth calm with two big beads of eyes framed in spidery lashes flashing her feelings through to him in a kind of expressionless Morse code. She was starting to look like one of her stuffed toys and Frank was never sure if the flashy eyes meant she was looking for a ride, or pitching for more money. Either way, he never really felt up to it but what was left of his male pride always wrestled his reason to the ground.

'How much do you need?'

'Seventy-five to get the forehead done, and another hundred for that dimple on my chin. Pascal said the fashion editor on *Vogue* told him that dimples were *very* Last Season.'

Pascal was Flame's agent in Paris. She also had Fabrizio in Rome, Louis in New York and Moishe in Israel. Frank, at Flame's insistence, had made contact with subagents abroad in order that she could start putting 'International Model' on her card. The reality was that Moishe was the only one that had backed up her new big title with actual work; a knitwear catalogue, the cover of a small-circulation Israeli woman's weekly magazine, and three days on a catwalk in a car show 'modelling' swimwear. Paris, Milan and New York were places that she visited regularly to harass her agents and try to get castings for the big magazines. They tolerated her because Frank got their local girls jobs in Dublin and took them to parties where he pretended to know U2. As punishment for getting any other model a page in a magazine, Frank had to finance his own pouting harridan's illusions about 'furthering her career abroad'.

However, Pascal, Fabrizio, Louis and Frank knew in their hearts and in their pockets that Flame was never going to make it. She was pretty in that way that other girls at school are jealous about. Sure, she was a bit of a wet dream for men with her standy-up breasts and her force-ten suction lips, and any woman who saw her in a bikini would vow to never-*ever*-eat again, but the truth was that Flame did not have the kind of simple enigmatic something that it took to be an International Supermodel. The only people in the whole world who did not believe this were Moishe – and that was only because he had worked himself up into a frenzy of, as yet, unrequited lust at the bikini/car show – and Flame herself. As far as she was concerned, with the exception of Moishe, none of her other agents were working hard enough for her, and Frank, as she reminded him constantly, was not prepared to make a committed investment in her.

The reality was that Flame was able to model for one reason, and for one reason only. Because she had that rare and terrifying gift that is bestowed on all little princesses who win the crown 'Prettiest Girl in the School' at age thirteen. Self-confidence. Her 100 Per Cent No-Holds Barred I Am IT and I *Know* It! level of arrogant self-belief was impenetrable. Any question of criticism was met with aggressive puzzlement.

'I'm sorry, Pascal? Not "the right look" – ' and she'd flick her talons over the inverted commas as if she were scooping out an eye – 'for *Vogue*? Me? Are they *mad*? Are *you* mad?'

None of her agents had the guts to cross her. She was life-threateningly persistent. So they would prepare for her trips by begging booking editors to see her and sending her home with assurances that if she grew her hair, erased a dimple, lost a quarter-inch off her bottom, etched a few freckles across the bridge of her newly sculpted nose, Karl Lagerfeld would *definitely* book her for autumn/winter. As for Frank, he had his eye on a blue-eyed, raven-haired molly from Mayo in her late teens (although he had yet to check the birth cert) who had been modelling for him for five months. Country-reared, she could cook and cuddle and had a kind, Catholic way about her that Frank felt sure was begging to be sullied, if only he could get rid of the red-haired hellcat at home. But he knew that if the slick, cynical, Guccied figures of his European contemporaries couldn't get Flame off their books, he didn't stand a chance.

'But I like that dimple, darling. I think it looks cute.'

In fairness Frank didn't really know what dimple she was talking about, but he had been belting away at himself for so long trying for a wee that he was getting the suggestion of a hard-on, and it seemed a shame to waste it. With a bit of work, it could go fully fledged and before he knew it, Frank would be top dog again, mounting his woman with his mighty sword . . .

'Don't even think about it.' Flame could read his sad, middle-aged mind. She had a busy day today. The last thing she needed now was fourteen stone of flab banging away at her for forty-five minutes trying to remember how to come.

'I've a hair appointment in half an hour, and Brian has to do some new shots for me.'

'But you had shots done a few weeks ago.'

'*Before* shots, Frank . . . *before* the injections! Jesus, you are such a tight arse . . . you really don't give a shit about my career, do you?'

The career and the tight-arse attack, while a favourite line with Flame, was actually only a decoy today to distract Frank from the real reason for her photo shoot. She had seen an ad in the paper for an American billionaire who was looking for an Irish wife, and as far as Flame was concerned, it was a done deal. She may not have conquered that whole ridiculous *Vogue* thing yet, but she was still Ireland's most popular red-haired model. Her portfolio was crammed with Tourist Board shots of her doing 'Come to Ireland and Meet a Colleen' impersonations, sitting next to an open fire with no-make-up make-up, tossing back a mountain of red curls as she pretended to laugh at the joke of some halfwit male model in a matching Aran sweater without spilling the half of Guinness she held in her french-manicured mitts. If that didn't bring the billions tumbling down on her deserving head – nothing would. To drum the point home, she planned to get a Scarlet Boost rinse done today, whip on the Virgin from Donegal sprig-print floral dress she kept for seducing clients from the country, and get Brian to do a few misty-eyed close-ups. She would Fed-ex them over to Louis in New York, get him to find the billionaire and have them delivered to his office by courier. No point in answering the ad the same as everyone else – writing a stupid letter. That would be like selling herself. Too tacky. This way it was just her agent doing some rich bloke a favour.

Naturally, he would see her, fall in love with her, marry her and give her endless money to pursue her career. She would be truly international then, with apartments in all the fashion capitals of the world. She could rebuild herself with surgery and still be modelling at fifty. All she would have to do in return was let some Sad Old Bloke (she only half-read the ad, but she *assumed* it wasn't Pierce Brosnan) boff her from time to time, and he couldn't possibly be as old or fat or disgusting as Frank. Case closed.

What Flame didn't know was that to New York Louis, even the vaguest smell of the 'Dublin Dog' moving to America and making him her primary agent was enough to make his Jones loafers curl high enough for him to chew them clean off. He would take her application, tear it, shred it, and incinerate the remains in the giant Phillipe Stark ashtray in reception before checking Flame's chart for her next scheduled trip and booking himself out for a two-week holiday.

'Who's doing your hair?' Frank asked.

'The Bitch is out of the salon today – so Kev said to go in at twelve.'

Frank didn't like Flame calling Gloria 'the Bitch', but the mood she was in today he let it go. He would pick her up there at two, and see what was in the till. Kev was easy enough to get around, and in any case, he had no need to apologize. After all, if it wasn't for him, Gloria would just be another common scrubber trying to scrape a living outside Ballymun. She may have started the business without him, but he was the one who gave her the class to succeed. That business was as much his as it was hers. Frank had heard that Gloria had been seen out a few days ago with Sam. His paranoia had kicked in, as Frank thought they might have been up to something. Then he remembered that the Jew was his oldest friend. Surely Sam wouldn't go putting ideas into her head about barring Frank from the business? Frank felt secure that Sam would make sure he wasn't screwed. His loyalty over the years had proven that to him.

In any case, Frank didn't have time to think about it now. He had to get himself shaved and showered for town. He checked his watch. Jesus! Nearly fifteen minutes for a piss and the lad had almost reached manhood.

Perhaps, if Flame left soon, he'd have time for a quick go at the koala.

13

Liam was seeing women in his sleep. Not the usual sort of pneumatic blondes that normal men dream about, nor even the half-penis half-their-mother visions of the deranged mind. These were nightmares of a nature even more insidious than that. In fact, at this stage, Liam would have *welcomed* an oedipal vision of his mother slowly undressing out of her Weightwatchers leader uniform. He could have done something with that. Written a poem about it; gone for a touch of the old Philip Larkins; got in touch with some Important Angst. The kind of angst that makes Great Writing, as opposed to the angst of a mad boss who wants you to find him a wife.

For the fifth time this week, the dream had reoccurred. It had got to fifty-seven tonight before he woke up. Fifty-seven red-haired, freckled women bounding over a cattle gate with alarming agility; Xavier Big, dressed in tweed cap and plus fours – the full Country Gentleman works – frolicking around the field with them singing 'O Sweet Mother Ireland'. Two nights ago he had been woken when his vision had panned to a nearby animal pen which housed a horrible half-pig in a green-sequinned jacket whom he knew to be the Real Hairy Heffernan. Tonight, Number Fifty-Seven had caught her petticoat on a twig and fallen face first into a cowpat, waking him with a start.

Liam didn't know how much more of this he could take.

Things were getting worse.

Firstly, Big was taking an Active Interest. With the whole Statue of Liberty/Waterford Crystal Project, Big had trusted Liam's judgement when, after a few cursory phone enquiries, his assistant has assured him that it was 'not going to happen'. He was disappointed, naturally, but was soon distracted by other things. Ditto with his attempt to recreate the village his mother grew up in, complete with actual inhabitants, in the grounds of his ranch in Texas. Even the St Patrick Theme Park and his Irish fast-food chain, Boxty Burger, the resourceful Liam had been able to put to rest. However, it was not so with the Wife Project. Big was like a child, popping his head around the door every hour saying, 'Didyah fine' me anyone yet? Didyah? Didyah?'

Secondly, Liam had been put 'in charge' of Bernie Heffernan and 'Sweet Mother Ireland' was number thirty-five in the Irish Music Chart. Hairy was just three numerals away from the new Mary Black single, and in the same universe as The Corrs. Virtually overnight, he had turned from a shambling wreck who was apoplectic with joy at the mere threat of a hot meal and a roof over his head, into an obnoxious, spangly-trousered, wig-wearing gremlin. Liam suspected that it would be quite some time before Mr Bernard Heffernan could be persuaded of the personal and career benefits of joining a twelve-step program, and in the meantime, he had been assigned to 'nurture his genius' and 'keep him out of harm's way'.

Since Genius-Nurturing in Hairy's book equated with a daily whiskey consumption that could keep your average Kerry wake going for weeks, Liam could only hope that the filthy aul' bugger's liver would pack up and move back to Ireland without him.

Thirdly, and significantly (although Liam did not know it yet) Big had 'got wind' of Sandy Nolan's application. Bodyguard Chuck, a man of few words, had reached the 'Conversation' module in Dr Ashman's bestselling boxed CD self-help course *The Seven Stairs to Self-Assertion* and decided to practise his newfound skills in the Big Towers lift one day with his mighty charge.

'*Find Some-One who Intimi-Dates you and find a "Meeting Point". A Place – of common ground. A Place – where you can reach Too-gether-ness. A Seed – of Shared Inter-rest from which Friend-ship can grow and flour-rish.*'

Ashman's hypnotic annotation was still wandering through the vast empty space in Chuck's head looking for somewhere to settle, as Chuck struggled to find the right words before saying, 'Say, Skip sure has some good-lookin' ladies up there in those big bags of his.'

It hadn't come out right so he tried again.

'One-a-them's got sandy-coloured hair so long it falls clean down to her . . .'

Arse, thought Big.

Arse, thought Chuck.

Mercifully, he didn't say it, but the fact that his usually mute bodyguard had said anything at all had impressed Big in a sort of upside-down way. This redhead must be something special if she got the great blond hulk talking.

Big was therefore in a state of acute emotional excitement by the time Liam arrived at his office at seven a.m. It was, Liam had discovered these past few sleepless nights, not possible to arrive in the office early and find it blissfully empty. There was always some ambitious bastard who had clocked in earlier than everyone else to prove a point. The city that never sleeps seemed to be filled with people who thought nothing of being washed, shaved, blow-dried, fragranced and besuited with half their day's work done by six a.m. But the Big One? Liam was one of those people whose eyes only start to settle into their sockets after the eleven a.m. doughnut break. He really wasn't up to his boss right now. Not this early in the morning.

Big had the stereo on full volume to an old recording of 'I'll Take You Home Again, Kathleen' and was chewing through a pile of linen hankies. This man seemed to have an insatiable appetite for heightened emotion induced by overexposure to schmaltz. It was a drug to him. A fucking addiction, thought Liam blearily.

Give me Hairy and the whiskey any day, if I don't have to listen to the words of 'The Cliffs of Doneen' again before I die.

Liam hadn't the jacket off before Big started harassing him.

'Ya-hoove been k-eeping something from your Uncle B-hig there, Skippy!'

He sang it out like it was something to celebrate. Liam had been keeping Big's hopes up and his questions at bay by pretending that he was checking out each candidate personally for both beauty and authenticity before whipping them across the Atlantic for a dinner date.

Big believed him, but it had been three weeks now, and despite Ashman's efforts, the billionaire was still not a great man for the old Delayed Gratification. His divorce from Pricilla had come through ten days ago, and he still had nobody lined up. Liam had been in touch with Louis the model agent, to see if he could fix him up an interesting shift to tide Big over, but he was on holiday for two weeks.

The truth was Liam was terrified by the mixed bag of applicants. He had whittled them down to about a hundred and they were filed under RICH DOGS, ATTRACTIVE SEPERATEDS, TV AND EX-MISS IRELANDS, SOFT-FOCUS POSSIBLES, TOPLESS AND UNDERWEAR, TRANVESTITES?, with only ten ACTUAL POSSIBLES sub-headed as WILDCATS AND COLLEENS. In other words Pretty With Make-up and Pretty Without Make-up. Regardless of results or lack of them, Liam was scared of turning any of this into an actual reality. The idea of actually ringing these women, and actually getting them over to New York, actually meeting them himself and then actually, *actually* sending them out on an *actual* date with Big was too, too horribly bizarre. It seemed unpatriotic somehow. Selling the spirited good women of Ireland to this overemotional American twat who was permanently switched to Turbo-Emote. If Liam was honest with himself, he would have realized that in actual fact, he was just scared. Scared that Big wouldn't like any of the women he had selected, that he would sack him and have him deported. Then Liam would have to relinquish his skincare regime, give up his funky SoHo loft, and go back to Ireland to write a Great Literary Novel which he was no longer sure he was capable of writing. It was the very thing he always said he wanted but, actually, in actual, *actual* fact – he didn't.

Liam tried to join in the game. It was seven a.m. and he was not in the mood for games, but it was his job.

'Ah now there, Xavier – you wouldn't want me to go ruining the old surprise there for you now!'

It was a mistake. Using his first name, wagging the finger, the old paddywhackery plaumause.

A big mistake.

Big had been wifeless for too long. He needed a wife. To make a fuss of him, to tell him he was great, to spend his money. Damn it, to be *seen* to be spending his money. This whole, whole, whole not-having-a-wife-business made him look bad. It was all right for your racing-car drivers and your European royalty playboy types – but he was a Big American Businessman god-damnit! He *had* to have a wife! Even that no-hair no-hoper Trump was never seen without one. *And* he was Irish. Whoever heard of a single Irishman? If this went on much longer, the Kennedys would start to doubt his authenticity.

Big's face darkened and the greatness of his billionaire bulk seemed to cast a shadow over the spindly, poety figure of his assistant. Liam's testicles shrank to the size of peanuts.

'You're holding out on me, boy. Chuck said there's a sandy-haired doll in that bag and I want to see her.'

Liam was not a man who had ever had any notion of the Right Stuff. Valour. Bravery. Sticking to your guns. His testosterone levels had largely risen and fallen with his idea of himself as a Hirsute Literary Giant. But at that moment Liam was taken over by some irrepressible blokey instinct. He did not want to show his boss Sandy Nolan's picture. Did not, would not, could not. Liam would die first.

That is, he *would* die – if he really *had* to. But if there was any way of avoiding it, on reflection, he would rather take that route.

'I don't have it here with me. I took it home . . .'

Big drilled a heavy-eyebrowed doubtful glower into the very core of his assistant's soul.

Liam tried on a hopeful smile, but it didn't fit.

'. . . to study. A lot of these Irish girls, well . . .'

So not working. He was about to besmirch the honest

nature of all Irish women – not a good move. In a panicked attempt at back-peddling Liam blurted out, '. . . she knows my sister! My sister knows her! She's my sister's friend! I was going to ring my sister and . . .'

Big's demeanour changed instantly to one of benign gratitude. Liam flinched as he saw the, by now familiar, threat of a Big Hug fluttering through Xavier's tinted lashes.

'You have a *sister*?'

Liam's peanuts got dry roasted and crushed to a powder with the magnitudinal awfulness of what he had just walked himself into. The minuscule squeak of his voice was reflective of same.

'Yes.'

Was there no end to the beauty of this boy's spirit? His humanity? His generosity? His goddamn honest-to-goodness too-good-to-be-true *Irishness*! He just wanted to well up, right there and then, in his office, and give this boy a great Big Big Hugarooni! A sister! But hey – this clearly wasn't easy for the boy. Big knew when to let it go. He'd leave him to it now. Not embarrass him with questions. Sure he'd take a look at the girl. If she was anything as kind-hearted as her brother . . . ? He'd leave him now to muse it over. That's what poets did. Muse. So he'd been told. Strange kid. Beautiful person. Beautiful. He'd let Skip get to it in his own time. Stop hassling him.

'Okay, kid.' Then he patted him on the back as he

was leaving, his hand lingering affectionately on his shoulder as he said, 'I'll take a look at them both first thing in the morning.'

⬭

Liam heard the phone ring through a trance of paralysed panic.

''Lo,' he murmured into the phone.

'Is that the office of Mr Xavier Big?'

'Humm.'

Lorna launched straight into her spiel.

'Well, good afternoon, I wonder if you can help me? I am calling from Cafferty Public Relations, and I understand that Mr Big is currently looking to procure himself an Irish wife. His ad in the papers here came to my attention and as Ireland's most committed PR and event management company, I naturally felt that this would be an ideal opportunity for us to—'

Liam's thumping heart nearly burst through his throat with excitement, and he all but ate the phone.

'Can you find him a wife?'

Lorna didn't like being cut off mid-pitch, but clearly the straightforward approach was the way to go.

'Certainly.'

'Colleen? Red hair? Unspoiled but intelligent? That type of thing?'

'Classic Country Colleens with or without third-level education. You name them – I find 'em.'

⬭

Less than seven minutes later a fax on Big Inc. headed notepaper confirming Lorna on a first-class seat on the seven a.m. flight from Dublin, and a limo from the airport to The Plaza for brunch, was whizzing its way into the Cafferty PR offices.

14

Shirley had been talking about children so much that Gloria's womb hurt. She had been trying to persuade her younger sister to go back to college. Shirley was a bright kid, but she had had her first child at seventeen – and her contraception record seemed to be going downhill. With three kids at twenty-two, she was living in the same block as their mother with a half husband called Terry whom she knew it was a bad idea to marry – so she filled the gap with another baby instead. Looking at Shirley, sitting across from her in the trendy bistro where they had had lunch, broke Gloria's heart. With her stringy blonde hair and her blotchy skin, all dressed up in a cast-off suit of Gloria's that didn't fit her properly, this afternoon in town shopping with her older sister was the highlight of her month. It should have made Gloria feel proud and happy that she was able to take her sister into Mothercare and buy her two hundred quids' worth of gear for the kids. But seeing Shirley's chipped toenails peeking through the toes of her scuffed sandals, she felt an old sadness wash through her as she realized that her own baby sister was still trapped in a life that she had left behind.

'But why should I go to college? What's the *point*?'

Shirley was getting irritated with her older sister's nagging. She thought today was meant to be a fun day out. She'd enjoyed leaving the kids with Mum, then getting dressed up as if she were going somewhere really glamorous and important. Shirley hadn't had a day away from them in ages, and now Glor was turning it into a lecture.

'You're so *bright*, Shirley – you'd do *brilliantly* at college.'

'I know you've got your big business and your big posh life, but *some* of us have children to think about.'

'I know, Shirley, but you could do so much *more* with your life.'

'What are you saying? That my kids aren't important?'

Gloria couldn't answer that. She was the eldest of the family, and had none of her own. When Shirley had fallen pregnant with her second, Gloria had wept alone in her flat after putting the phone down to their mother. She told herself she was crying for the loss of her sister's youth. In truth, she had been crying into the empty space in her own life. The sham of her marriage, the pathetic hopes she'd once had of having it all. Business, husband, family. Being one of those magazine women who Juggles Their Life. Dreams that had hardened into cynicism, but which still lay dormant inside her.

Sometimes they could be triggered into a quiet despair by the sound of a child wailing in the supermarket.

Shirley mumbled something, then got up from the table.

'Fucking forget it. I'm sorry if you don't think I'm "Good Enough" . . .' and stormed out.

She tried to run after her, but Shirley's thin white legs were already clambering up the stairs of the bus by the time she hit Dawson Street.

Gloria took a deep breath and swallowed back her tears. Shirley was just a kid. She was volatile – always had been. She'd call up there this weekend with a bag of stuff for the kids, and everything would be all right.

By the time Gloria got back to the salon, she was fine again. Fine, that is, until she saw Kevin's stammering and blushing demeanour.

'Oh . . . hey . . . Hi . . . I thought you weren't coming in today?'

The till was open. She arched her eyebrow and nodded in its direction.

'I'm sorry, Gloria . . . he started to do a number in reception about being the managing director . . . he was a bit piss—'

'How much?'

'Two hundred . . .'

'Oh Christ!'

'. . . and fifty.'

'For fuck's sake – nearly the morning's takings?'

Kevin looked sheepish, although he knew that the cash he had given Frank wasn't really his problem.

Gloria's ex-husband was still down as managing director on the stationery, and he still owned half of the business. Legally, he was as much Kevin's boss as she was.

No, Kevin's *real* problem was sitting with her head back in a basin waiting to have two tubes of Scarlet Boost rinsed out of her elbow-length curls. Gloria would murder him if she knew he let the Red Cow into her salon, but Flame had promised the gullible Kevin that she would insist on him being flown to Paris for the *Vogue* cover shoot she felt confident was pending.

Gloria caught sight of her out of the corner of her eye and Flame, never one to hide herself away, gave her a big smiley wave. The Bitch would never make a scene in her own salon, and it was quite busy today. Safe enough. What Flame didn't know was that recent proximity to her family always brought out the fishwife in Gloria. She wasn't having this today. She hadn't worked like a dog for the last fifteen years to have some bimbo scum take the piss out of her in her own domain. Not on the same day she'd fallen out with her beloved little sister. The contrast between the spoiled affectation lounging across the leatherette basin-chair, and Shirley's spindly little naked legs hopping onto the bus back to Ballymun, was too much for her.

She marched across the salon and stood in front of Flame.

'Better run along home quick now, sweetheart. If you don't get that goo rinsed out soon you'll be as red as a smacked arse.'

Flame had a plastic bag wrapped around her skull,

with two butterfly clips holding it in place. She looked up at Gloria, fluttered her eyelashes in a puzzled 'Are you addressing *moi*?' type way, then went back to sawing down her talons. She was going nowhere.

Except she was.

Gloria gripped the astonished model with a two-finger shiatsu clamp to the back of her neck, then bent down and hissed in her ear, while smiling around her at onlooking clients.

'You walk out of this salon *now*, on your own pretty little shoes paid for by *me* – or you get wheeled out of here on that perming trolley and dumped on the pavement like a barrow-full of turf. The choice – as the man says – is *all yours*!' And with that she gave Flame's neck a pinch that would have paralysed a pig.

Gloria then walked across to where Melanie Mufton was flicking through the social pages of Irish *Tatler* to try to find evidence of Judge Mufton's indiscretions and started up some small talk, her hand stroking the perming trolley with obvious intent.

Two minutes later a highly discombobulated and slightly tearful Flame was disengaging plastic from scalp and wrapping the red-gunk remains into the best towel turban she could manage under the circumstances.

As Flame walked out of the salon, with her head stuck in the air trying to assure herself that her natural magnificence could carry off a tint-stained towel turban, at least as far as the taxi rank on Stephen's Green, she was almost pushed into a spin by the figure of Dublin's

Best Known PR Queen who was hammering her heels through the door like a woman at the wrong end of a chase.

'I'm not here . . .' she squawked at Gloria as she sped past her into the loo. Melanie Mufton looked up from her magazine, but she lived in a glass house herself these days and besides, Lorna Cafferty was old news.

A waft of Floris meandered through the salon ahead of Bridget Wilkin-Walkins.

Gloria went to greet her in reception. She knew Bridget as one of those most annoying of clients – the Subtle Blonde Bob. She always waved nonchalantly when Gloria asked how she wanted her hair done, as if hair was of No Real Importance to her. Then, more than once, had looked gravely at the finished result as if Gloria were Beyond Cheap to have given her a blonde highlight that was more than two hairs thick and visible to the naked eye. Gloria had been bullied into redoing Walkin's highlights more times than she cared to remember. She was *not* going to be bullied today.

'Oh *no*, Gloria, I haven't got an appointment . . .'

She said it as though Gloria would be disappointed. Like she might give a shit.

'. . . I just thought I saw my friend Lorna come in here.'

Gloria looked at her in mock puzzlement. Bridget wasn't paying today. Gloria could be as facetious as she liked.

'No, I'm afraid not.'

'Lorna Cafferty – you know . . .'

Gloria knew well, and Bridget knew well that she knew well, but she wasn't finished yet.

'. . . the PR girl? The one that was in the paper over all that, that *business*?'

'I know who you mean. She's not here.'

'We're old friends, and the last time we met she lost something and I just wanted to see if she'd found it again.'

WW was clearly *longing* for Gloria to ask what it was that Lorna had lost so that Bridget could say 'Her dignity'. Her head was craning past the reception desk to see if she could catch her old chum cowering behind a dryer. How humiliating would *that* be!

'I was *sure* I saw her come in here.'

But reliable Gloria was having none of it.

'I'm sorry – you must have got it wrong. Lorna hasn't been in at all today.'

Bridget finally put up the flag and left. She knew she'd seen her. That girl must be a friend of hers. Imagine! Lorna Cafferty mixing with hairdressers! Bridget made a point of never socializing with anyone who didn't have a third-level education. One never knew what the undereducated might do or say next. How common of Lorna to be friendly with a Tradesperson. But then – *quelle surprise* there. Still, it didn't seem quite Lorna's bag somehow. Although – Lorna could be a bit of a dark horse. They had shared a plumber once – quite by accident – and he had been *full* of stories. The seed of an idea blew across the neat tidiness of the

Wilkin-Walkins mind and landed in the box marked GOSSIP POSSIBLES. There was no regular man – none that she knew of anyway. Hadn't been for some time. Perhaps Lorna was a lesbian? The seed grew, flourished and was fully fledged poison ivy in seconds. Could this hairdresser be her lesbian lover? Of course! Omigod! *How* revolting! And now Lorna's Bit of Rough was man-handling (pardon the pun) her away from the *genuine* concern of one of her oldest friends. Having cheered herself, and in the face of Gloria's ('*very masculine*') arm-crossed glare, Bridget finally gave up, and headed for the Brown Thomas car park to rush home and tell Tom news of Lorna's new lifestyle.

When Lorna was given the all-clear with a knock on the loo door, she emerged looking shaken. The hunted expression she had come in with was down a couple of notches on the Emergency meter, but her hair looked like a pile of shredded white cabbage.

She smiled pitifully at Gloria. What the hell must this woman think of her rushing into her salon like that?

But the owner was unfazed, and glad of a bit of drama that didn't centre on her for a change.

'You look like a woman in need of some Serious Attention.'

'Call an ambulance.'

Gloria smiled.

'We don't do hair on the medical card here,' she said, '*yet*. But twenty quid will get that mop smoothed out –

and if you give the kid fifty pee – ' she nodded at Scooter – 'he'll make you a coffee that'll put those eyes back in their sockets.'

Lorna kicked back and let Gloria's soothing touch massage and groom her back to some sense of normality. When the job was done, Gloria had no other clients to tend to, and Lorna, for the want of anything better to do, asked if she'd like to go for a drink. Really, Lorna knew she should be at home packing and getting ready for tomorrow's transatlantic trip. But, for some reason, she felt that she didn't want to leave Gloria's company just yet. There was something about this woman that calmed her. Something motherly. As a general rule, Lorna steered clear of her female peers. She had come to view them as competitive, and out to get her in some way. Many of her experiences of late had borne that out.

She had tried to confide her problems once or twice to Nylon, but he appeared more concerned about what was going to happen to The Mews than to Lorna herself. And so the Queen of PR, true to form, had walked through this mini-nightmare alone. As she had done with her mother's selfish pursuit of celebrity. As she had done with her father's abandonment of her.

Her determination to clamber out of this tax hole had brought Lorna's resourcefulness to the surface. In finding out the identity of Mr Big, the mystery millionaire in the ad, chasing him down, and securing a meeting with him in New York, Lorna knew that, if she played it right, she could be back on her way to the top of the food chain.

Business may have been as usual at Cafferty PR, but as a woman, Lorna's edges were starting to fray. She was stitching them together with the only tools she had at her disposal – cynicism and resignation. Lorna couldn't even get angry with the Bastard Accountant any more. Men were for downing the trousers and shitting all over you. Women were for snapping on the rubber gloves and rubbing it in. The world seemed like a very dark and humanless place. The two acts of kindness she had experienced at the hands of her hair-dresser were the most human things that had happened to Lorna in – she couldn't remember how long.

The two women wandered around to The Shel-bourne on Stephen's Green and settled into a corner of the long oak bar. They drank and talked for six hours.

Lorna told Gloria about the Bastard Mother, the Bastard Accountant, and the Bane Bridget.

'Shtuck-up sthring-o-shite!' said Gloria, who was quite drunk at this stage.

Gloria told Lorna about her hopes to open a chain of hair salons, Vile Frank's attempts to piss all over them and chucking Flame out of the salon.

'The Wh-oooooooooooore!' wailed Lorna, drawing the attention of a separated accountant from Dungannon who was up in Dublin for the night looking for a bit of fun.

'Pish off . . .' the two women urged in unison before he had even opened his mouth to ask what they were drinking, then they collapsed into a pile of teenage giggles.

By the time they had staggered, clutching each other, in a clutter of heels and handbags, across the Green to get a taxi for Lorna, the two women were slightly more sober – or at least, *marginally* less drunk than they had been.

'Gloria O'Neill,' Lorna pressed her new friend's elbows down to her sides and held her in a determined sway.

'I am going to New York tomorrow and when I get back I am going to do *loads* of PR for your Gaff – *free-ee of charr-ge!* – and I am going to FECK that dirty Frank – shit – bastard – SCUM from a huge height and get him out of your salon and YOUR LIFE!'

Gloria, who was still drunk, but not quite as bad as Lorna, said, 'And I – I – am going to –' she freed an arm and squalled the sleek hair of Dublin's Best PR Queen affectionately – 'make sure you have nice hair *always* for ever and ever amen!'

With that, the two women taxied and walked back to their respective beds, feeling that little bit happier for the meeting of a new friend.

How disappointed poor Bridget would have been had she known with what innocence their night had ended.

15

'What the *fuck* was that? No, never mind – you're fired!'

Sandy's first radio review on the *Rory Mac (say it again!) Rory Show* had not gone down at all well.

'*I thought it was interesting that it had originally been written in Irish, Rory, and there were lots of references to Socrates which was interesting because—*'

'*Really, Sandy? And I believe there was a bit of –* 'snigger – '*nudity in the show!*'

'*Well, the theme of "Lonely Death" was of course death, Rory, and the nudity was really an illustration of . . .*'

Sandy didn't know what the soap-opera star's green mickey was an illustration of at all, but she knew she had to make up something intelligent. So she threw in a reference to Tolstoy, as she had heard the Hairy Clevers do during the interval. Rory thought she had said *Toy Story*, and the whole thing deteriorated really fast from there. By the end of the item, Sandy had come out sounding like Melvyn Bragg's love child, and Rory like a retarded guest on a game show. He was not amused. Neither was a woman from Clare who rang in to say it was a 'DISGRACE' that one of Ireland's most 'papular actars' who 'HER CHILDREN' watched on television 'EVERY WEEK' was running around Dublin 'IN THE NIP!'

Rory tried to shake her off by saying it was 'all just a bit of fun!' which did not amuse the half-dozen or so No Make-up Hairy Clevers who were listening in. These included the brilliant young playwright himself, Eamon Weir, who was put straight through, despite Rory's frantic air wrestling to the contrary. Eamon was 'anxious to know' if Rory had 'ever read Tolstoy', and suggested that had he done so he might be better qualified to understand not only 'the gift of life itself' but the work that he and other Under-Funded Performance Artists and Poets were doing to bring important issues like Death and Poverty and Depression to the forefront of the minds of the Good People of Ireland with No Thanks from the likes of Populist Arseholes like him! Rory's retort was that perhaps if Eamon wrote his plays in English 'like a normal person' then the Good People of Ireland, in which he included himself (for Rory believed, on air at least, that he was the Voice of the People and no better or worse than the rest of them), might know what the 'frig he was on about!' If Mr Mac Rory's use of the word 'frig' was ill-advised, his reference to the English language as being the verbal domain of 'normal' people was disastrous. Conragh na Gaeilge, the Gaelic League, came down on him with the speed of a brick falling from forty floors up.

Rory was addressed by the Cathaoirleach himself who spoke in the Native Language of We Island People, asking him: *'An tuigeann tú Gaeilge, Ruaidhre?'*

Naturally enough, Rory didn't even have a scrap of school Irish to draw on, and the simplest enquiry after same sent him into a state of confused panic. Padraig O'Muiracheartigh was therefore reduced to using the Tool of the Oppressor for the remaining twelve minutes of the show, during which the terrifyingly erudite Chieftain (who made the Hairy Clevers look like contestants on *Blind Date*) asked Rory all sorts of interesting and very direct questions about history and politics. The kind of direct questions that are always avoided by people who earn their living by being the Voice of the People because there is No Right Answer and whatever answer you give will always upset somebody. The sort of questions where if you don't answer them that is an answer in itself and then everybody will be upset.

By the time Sandy was given the nod to play out with 'It's Hip To Be Square' by Huey Lewis and the News, Rory was as weak as a wet biscuit. His brain hurt, his pride was irreparably punctured, and he was very, very annoyed indeed. Had he enjoyed even – one – measly – grope from that wretched redhead in the last three weeks, perhaps he might have found it in his heart to forgive her. But *nada*. She didn't even have the daily courtesy to admire his jumpers – and now *this*! The leg-warmer-inventing women of Cavan were nothing,

nothing compared to what he had just been put through. Mary and her hairy moles were back on slot, and Sandy was fired, fired, FIRED!

Sandy didn't know quite how to take it. On the one hand, she was delighted to have played a role, albeit a supporting one, in the hideous humiliation of a man who had been making her life a misery for the past three weeks.

On the other hand, (a) she had just got here, (b) she had nowhere else to go, and (c) it would hardly look good on her CV. When Sandy started to take these three facts apart, she began to boil.

(a) She had just got here. After three weeks she was beginning, just beginning, to get used to the idea of being back in Ireland. She had been bludgeoned into coming here in double-quick time, her flat in London was sublet, her job on Horace's show had been filled, and for the time being anyway, there was no going back.

(b) Jobs in the media in Ireland were scarce. She was already completely overqualified to be the Rat Rory's runner, and now even *that* was being taken away from her. She had no chance of getting a job in print media as she was not intelligent enough and wore too much make-up.

(c) She had worked long and hard to get to where she was today. Where she was was lousy, but that wasn't the point. The point was she had been duped into coming here in the first place! The point was this wasn't her fault and the real, the *real* point was this wasn't Rory's fault either.

Suddenly, Sandy saw the Mighty Jumpered One as a mere 'pawn' (although some might have argued 'prawn' as scarlet temper exploded across his face) in all of this. Theirs was always destined to be an unhappy coupling. But *who* had brought them together?

Over ten years of tea-making, copy-checking, caption writing, knob-twiddling menialness had brought Sandy Nolan to the brink of bona fide journalism. The rug of success she had been standing on might have been small, but it was rich and pretty and she had woven it herself. One man and *one man only* had pulled it from under her and left her standing on the vast lino of obscurity once again, and he was going to *pay!*

Sandy pushed past Rory and his astonished production team (who had gathered around to tell him that Padraig O'Muiracheartigh was a *known* Nobody, and that *no-body* in their right mind would have answered those questions), and out of the studio. She slammed through the network of identical corridors, her mules mashing the grey carpet tiles until she reached the office of the Offending Article.

'I would like to see the Head of Radio, please . . .'

'I'm sarry – Miss—'

The secretary hardly looked out from behind her compact before Sandy had swung through the door of his office.

Sandy was ready for a look of surprise, annoyance, authoritative What-is-the-meaning-of-*this?* indignation on the face of the Aul' Fella in Charge of Radio. What she was not ready for was the spectacle of Himself trying to tune in Radio Moscow on the Godgiven Dials of a topless Well-Known Television Presenter by the name of Francesca Duffée.

Ms Duffée leapt from the leatherette desk on which she had been lying lengthways, fully living up to the 'gazelle-like qualities' attributed to her in a recent *Woman's Way* article profiling her as a perfect example of 'Why Fifty Is the New Thirty'. In less than three minutes, Francesca was buttoning frantically in the cubicle of the first-floor toilets, where she stayed for the rest of the afternoon applying and re-applying her lipstick until her lips nearly fell off, for fear of facing the sure-fire sniggers in the studio canteen.

Needless to say, Sandy was slightly surprised by the incident, but ultimately, she had more important things on her mind. Her career. This man had ruined it and now, damn-and-feck-the-old-bastard, he was going to put things right again.

Aul' Fella was thrown by the intrusion for sure, but he was still fully clothed himself, and didn't get to be the Most Important Man in Radio in Ireland by getting all shook up every time he was caught playing Nipple Draughts with a Well-Known Television Presenter.

'How dare you come barging into my office unannounced, young lady!'

Aul' Fella had pointy-up eyebrows that brushed the

edge of his thick, opulent fringe. Hair was power. He was sixty-plus and he had three times as much of it as he had had when he started as a young producer forty years ago. This man didn't *need* a beard for people to take him seriously. He was *that* important.

When Sandy caught the full Elder Statesman Power of the blue beads glowering at her from under the triangular eyebrows (she didn't know he gelled them into place every morning with his wife's Wella Setting Lotion) she was suddenly Not Very Clever Nolan standing in the middle of a desert of mortification with an armed missile marked ERIN trained on her head. It was either tears or try. She remembered she was nearly thirty and pressed 'Try'.

'I'm sorry to disturb you, Mr . . . er . . . Mr . . . er . . . sir.' (Phew! All his underlings referred to him as Aul' Fella, unless in his presence in which case it was 'sir!' – exclamation mark included.) 'It's just that I'm not very happy on the *Rory Mac Rory*, sir' – she didn't mention the fired bit – but it was by the Grace of God – 'and while, of course, I am grateful for the opportunity, sir, I was wondering if it would be at all possible for me to . . .'

Sandy went on, but Aul' Fella was not listening. As she stood there shuffling and babbling, the Head of Radio was rolling the words 'young' and 'lady' around in his head. They were his favourite words. 'Young'. 'Lady'. 'Young!' 'Lady!' Best of all, of course, was when they were used together. 'Young lady.' 'Younglady! Younglady! Young Lay-dee!' He used them, naturally enough, with Francesca all the time, but they just didn't fit somehow. She was no longer young, and really, although it pained him to say it, she didn't really qualify for the full 'lady' thing. She used to, but you know – there's only so many times you can see a hitched skirt walloping up against a studio wall before a woman starts to lose her – what's the word? 'Elegance' – that's it – her Natural Elegance begins to lose its sheen.

This little one now, she was the real thing. A 'young lady', if ever there was one. Look at her standing there in the little trouser-suit thing, with the neat little shoes and the red hair scraped back like butter wouldn't melt. He wondered if she was tuned into Long Wave and if he could pick up Radio Moscow on her . . .

As he had remained silent throughout her speech, Sandy had begun to get her confidence back, and her pleas had gathered speed.

'You see . . . *really* what I want is to be a Serious Journalist. A news journalist, perhaps focusing on Arts Coverage? Sir?'

Aul' Fella was looking at her intently now. Sandy was glad she had said her bit. She really had turned him around. He was impressed with her. She could tell.

'What kind of *experience* do you have?'

That confused Sandy slightly, as she had just given him a somewhat rambling account of her entire résumé.

'As I said, sir, my experience is quite varied but extensive.'

'Is that so, young lady?'

'Yes, sir.'

Aul' Fella's aul' lad was all but boring a hole in the

mahogany underside of his desk. His mind frantically mapping out a plot for *Carry On Young Ladies With Varied and Extensive Experience* with him in the leading role. But he didn't get to be the Most Important Man in Radio in Ireland by giving the game away too soon. This little one (if he said young lady in his head one more time he'd . . .) had Sexual Harassment Charges written all over her assertive little face. Redheads were mighty if you crossed them too soon. He'd give her a break, and two years' grace to get grateful. She'd be worth the wait. Aul' Fella may have been lecherous but he still had all the patience and wisdom that Hair and Importance brings to a man of his age.

'Have you any ideas there . . . ?'

'Sandy.'

Oh! Sandy! Young lady!

'Sandy. Have you any story ideas that you would like to follow through?'

Sandy could hardly believe it.

'What – you mean for the *Rory Mac Rory Show*, only I've been—'

'No, Sandy.'

Sandy! She's young! She's a lady! She's a younglady! Younglady! Younglady!

For reasons almost beyond his control, AF took his hands from his lap then pressed them flat together and tapped them against his chin in a thoughtful sawing motion as if he was weighing up some important option.

'Sandy – I have funding for a One-Off Women's Interest Slot and I'd very much like you to fill it.'

Aul' Fella felt very much like filling it himself at that moment in time, but the crude implication was lost on Sandy whose mind had suddenly gone blank. He had pressed her panic button, but for all the wrong reasons. For poor Sandy believed that if she didn't come up with an idea, she would lose the biggest opportunity of her career.

Sandy sent idea scouts running frantically around the empty fields of her brain, looking under every rock and bush for the Never Been Done Before Story that was going to launch her career as a Serious Journalist. Something smart enough to impress the No Make-Up Hairy Clevers, and something entertaining enough not to get her the sack again.

Nothing. Aul' Fella was looking expectant. Panic. Nothing. Think – something wimminy – Sex Is the New Chocolate. Been done. Aul' Fella tapping chin. Losing interest. Think. Think. Think! Women. Wimmin's Interest – Why Fifty Is the New Thirty? She opened her mouth . . . no. Been done. The Bridget Jones Generation? Done, done, done – dead, resurrected, dead, buried, given the kiss of life and done again! Jesus! She spent her life *dreaming* of this moment, *boring* her friends with ideas, Maeve would murder her when . . . Wait. Maeve. Billionaire. Her picture sent. Story! Story! Story!

'Sir! There's a billionaire in America and he's looking for a wife, so—'

'Great. Run with it. See Moira outside, she'll fix you up with everything. Bye now.'

While Sandy had been standing there gawping at him

like a stuffed fish, Aul' Fella had remembered he had an important phone call to make to a Well-Known Politician regarding an Unfortunate Indiscretion that had been brought to AF's attention by Another Young Lady and for which the Immediate Transfer of Funding was required.

He had done one good deed today (two if he counted the retuning of Francesca) and now it was time for another act of selfless charity. However, he was confident that in time, Sandy would remember his benevolence and reward him.

Days later, Sandy would realize through canteen gossip how she had jumped from your regular household frying pan onto the sizzling surface of a cafeteria hot-plate.

'Rory's the young bull,' Moira, AF's kindly PA told her, delighted at the entertaining way Duffée was ejected from her boss's office on the day of Sandy's visit, 'he sees a field full of cows, gets all excited and *runs* down as fast as he can to ride one. Aul' Fella now, he's the Old Bull. He *walks* down to the field – cool as you like – and rides them *all*!'

But, for the rest of that week at least, Sandy Nolan was delighted with her new position and her first working phone call was to her friend Maeve to find out what she had put in her application to Mr Big.

16

Hot leather. Is there *anything* – in the whole wide world – thought Lorna Cafferty as she slid her Prada-encased bottom along the cream seating of Mr Big's airport courtesy car – quite as lovely as the feel and smell of hot leather in the interior of a large limousine? She had just spent seven hours drinking champagne, waving away canapés and 'spritzing' her face with First-Class Travel Dew and she was as fresh as a daisy. She had been met at the airport by a Huge Ebony Prince in full chauffeur's uniform, who introduced himself as 'Ben' and was scrapingly apologetic that the air conditioning in the car wasn't working.

'Don't worry, darling, where I come from – a little heat is *always* welcome.'

Ben, being not unfamiliar with the extra-curricular needs of your average Prada-clad thirtysomething businesswoman travelling alone, immediately understood the intonation despite Lorna's Irish accent. 'The language of love,' he was fond of boasting to his fellow drivers who always seemed to pull the short straw action-wise with Japanese businessmen and chemical engineers, 'is universal.'

The portion of champagne inside her, the heat of the leather beneath her short tight skirt and the heaving weight of Ben's broad shoulders in front of her conspired to put Lorna in a downright frisky frame of mind. By the time the airport parking attendants were staring open-mouthed at the BIG100 licence plate, Lorna was already thoroughly conscious of the magnificence of her own underwear. It was purple lace La Perla, over two hundred quids' worth, and given the disastrous nature of her current financial situation she felt it would be *immoral* to waste it. Lorna's detailed and painstaking divestment of her outer garments did not slip the notice of her intended audience whose state-of-the-art security camera went from 'on' to 'close-up' before they were three minutes up the freeway. In less than ten, Ben had pulled over and was giving his charge a Welcome to America that she would never forget.

Anonymous sex was so difficult in Dublin. There was always a danger that you would end up with somebody's son, or cousin – or even (and Lorna had come danger-ously close once or twice) a distant cousin of your own. Going outside of the capital was no good either. Every-one in Dublin, no matter how urbane, had someone 'belonging to them' living in the Country, and Country People knew more about what was going on than anyone else. A glamorous blonde in Prada merely eating lunch in a pub (never mind getting a good seeing-to from the landlord's son) was enough to keep them talking for months. Lorna had learned to be careful over the years, and had developed a taste for nameless taxi drivers and plumbers whom she was unlikely to meet again. Even at that, she knew she was taking risks. So this was great. Total anonymity and, frankly, more meat than your average Clonakilty Pudding. She should travel more often.

By the time Lorna had cleaned out the limo's supply of Freshen-Up tissues, toned down the flush with the help of kind Mr Christian Dior, and re-applied her lipstick, her very happy chauffeur was pulling up outside The Plaza Hotel on Central Park, in New York City, in New York State in the Great Big US of A.

Liam had had one helluva job getting Big there. Xavier had been waiting for him at eight a.m. to check out the pictures of Sandy and Maeve, and Liam had tried to distract him with promises of 'a real live one who's coming all the way over here to meet you'.

'D'ya have a picture?'

Shit! Liam hadn't thought of that!

'I left it at home.'

According to himself, Liam's walls must be lined with pictures of pretty Irish girls at this stage. Big would think he was like one of those freaky serial killers, where the police walk in and find the victims stuck to the wall with penknives, daubed with weird script and candles all over the place.

'But she's gorgeous.'

Liam prayed inwardly that Lorna Cafferty wasn't someone he went to college with. Or a friend of his mother's! Mercifully, he was too intent on getting Big to the meeting to invent other testicle-curling scenarios for himself.

Big's interest level raised itself marginally from Fire Dumb Assistant to Possible Opportunity.

'What does she look like?'

'It's a surprise.'

It sure will be if it's one of Mammy's mates from Weightwatchers, thought Liam.

'Is she a redhead?'

'It's a surprise.'

'Bull-*shit*! I don't have time for this. Get a car to take you back home *right now* and pick up those . . .'

Liam knew it was time to come clean.

'Listen, sir. This is one of the best PR women in Dublin' – he knew that much from Lorna's description of herself, he only hoped it was true – 'Of *course*, she wants to marry you herself – who wouldn't, sir – ' Big's face lightened somewhat. He was starting to feel insecure about this whole Irish wife thing: it was all going too slowly – 'but she also says that if she isn't your first choice, she can help you find Miss Right.'

Big had had his heart set on the whole newspaper/ picture/essay thing. He liked to do these things himself. Make it personal. Liam leapt in for this kill while there was half a question hanging.

'Sir. It's eleven at The Plaza. You've got nothing to lose, sir. Anyway, she might be the One.'

Liam was right. As usual. He was lonely. Lonely and wifeless. This Lorna woman might be the One. Maybe it wouldn't hurt so much to go take a look anyway.

'Do we have a manicurist on call today?'

'Yes, sir. Certainly, sir – I'll have her sent up straight away, sir.'

'I'll take a shave as well, and have the car brought round at ten.'

'Yes, sir!'

Big left his office feeling Back in Charge of His World Again and Liam almost wept with relief.

Xavier Big fell instantly in love with Lorna. He also fell instantly in love with the restaurant hostess, the waitress and two women at the next table who were on a shopping holiday from Denver and had five children between them called Percy, Terry, Kerry, Perry and Shane – information gleaned in the ten-minute delay in Lorna's arrival due to Ben's Exclusive Welcome to America Service.

Liam wished that his boss wouldn't try to chat up strange women, but Big's wifeless state was causing him to have doubts about his masculinity, the resultant symptoms of which involved him throwing his weight around even more than usual at work, then being bleatingly, nauseatingly charming to each and every woman he met. From admiring their hair to asking about their children, Big was on Charm Overdrive in search of a shred of returned Dumb Admiration.

Big was rewarded by overhearing the women from Denver calling him 'a lovely man' as he insisted on paying for their cheque and sat down.

'Where the fuck is this woman, then?'

The sooner this Cafferty woman got here and sorted out this whole Irish wife business, the better.

Lorna tripped into the candy-coloured Palm Room at The Plaza on a wafting wave of sweet, heady perfume with the barely disguised undercurrent of rampant sex. It was at these times (as Frozen Food Giant Dez Flannery would still attest) that Lorna was at her most mysteriously appealing to men.

'I am so sorry that I'm late,' she cooed, correctly assuming that the older man with the pull-back face and the dyed hair was the millionaire, and the scrawny worried-looking one was the Liam/assistant person (although he looked suspiciously like one of her neighbour's children).

She held out her hand to Big.

'I am so very, *very* delighted to meet you, Mr Big.'

He took her hand.

'I am delighted to meet *you*,' he said.

And he was. Okay, she didn't have red hair, but she was a babe and she was Irish and hey! She had *great* nails! He thought all Irish women bit their nails, wore grey underwear and had veiny white skin due to lack of exposure to sunbeds. At least, that's what Pricilla had told him. He had been half-prepared to make such sacrifices in honour of his dead mammy. Now it looked like he didn't have to. Wait till that poisonous little turd of a latest ex-wife found out about this! She'd be – what was that expression he'd heard Liam use? Oh yes – 'Sickened to the Very Hem of Her Hole'. One day he'd figure out what it meant.

'Oh no – the *pleasure* is all mine, Mr Big.'

Lorna was playing eyelash badminton as if her life depended on it. Which, in a way, it did.

'Xavier – please call me Xavier.'

'Xavier. It was *so* generous of you to arrange this trip –' *flap, flap, flicker* – 'and at *such* short notice!'

'Ah – hur – hur – hur.' Big looked pleadingly at Liam not to give the game away. His laugh was gurgly and fake like a bucket of water dribbling down a drain.

'Not at all! It was nothing . . . really . . .'

'But really –' *flap, flicker, flap – flap –* 'first-class! Why, I'm just a simple Irish girl, sure, lookit – I'm not used to this kind of aul' special treatment at all . . .'

Liam was getting irritated at this stage. Lorna's shameless eyelash flap-flirting suck-up-paddywhackery was getting on his nerves. He had resorted to it too many times himself. Why didn't she end the sentence with 'at all, at all', and be done with it? He flicked his napkin on his lap pointedly, but the lovebirds didn't notice.

'Well really, Miss . . . ?'

'Cafferty.'

Such an Irish name!

'Miss Caffrey – I *always insist* my ladies travel in style.'

He raised Lorna's hand to his lips and gave it a Big Kiss.

'Ladies?' she simpered. 'Why, how many *ladies* do you have, Xavier?'

'Ah – hur – hur – hur.' Big was all but sprouting wings at this stage. He hadn't flirted this good in ages!

'Well now – *that* would be telling, Miss Caffrey, ah – hur – hur – hur.'

Liam had had enough of their display of shameless schmoozing. He could see right away the type that Lorna was, and, quickly, that she was not the type Big was looking for – even if the stupid bollocks couldn't see it himself right now. She could give Big all the 'Musha' and 'Yashi' plaumausing he liked, but her Butter Wouldn't Melt shite wasn't fooling *him*. This woman was a long way from the mantilla of modesty card she was playing. Lorna was a Player, in the style of Pricilla – Queen of the Cheque Book. Only worse, because she was probably educated by nuns, and those convent girls had all sorts of tricks that the likes of this American Ape could never dream of. If Lorna made Big walk the full mile, and he ended up with her, Liam's life wouldn't be worth tuppence.

'Shall we get on?'

Lorna and Big looked at Liam as if he were a pimple on the nose of humanity – but they took the hint. The billionaire reluctantly let go of Lorna's hand, and elbowed the hovering concierge out of the way while he pulled back her seat himself, just like his mammy had always told him to.

As he sat down, Liam immediately recognized the

moony-sheep's-eye expression his boss wore as being a Very Bad Sign. Big looked dangerously close to a Blind Leap. Liam often wondered how Big got to be the Richest Man in America given that he was such a thick around women. He knew very little about the actual money-making machine of Big's empire and its workings – but he knew that it had something to do with food and farming. Farmers back home rarely held special talents in the 'field' of romance, and he guessed that it must be the same the world over. But one thing, at this moment, was sure. Big had the foot down and was heading for the turning marked Marriage on the Free-way of Love. It was Liam's responsibility to take the truck by the testicles and put on the brakes before he made a move they would both regret.

'I don't want to rush you, Lorna, but you are booked home on the four o'clock flight. Perhaps we had better move this meeting along?'

Lorna was delighted. She *loved* to pitch. And now, here she was, in America – the *home* of sales talk. She switched seamlessly from 'Seduction' to 'Sell' and gave it her all.

'Well, gentlemen. Cafferty Public Relations was founded in 1985 by myself . . .'

For a full fifteen minutes her audience of two's attention was imprisoned by the Special Mesmeric Voice that Lorna Cafferty used to aid Very Important Clients in parting with Very Large Fees for her services.

Her voice hummed and lah-de-dahed breathily over:

— The History of Cafferty Public Relations
   (featuring Lorna Herself)
— The Success of Cafferty Public Relations
   (featuring Lorna Herself)
— The USP (Unique Selling Point) of Cafferty Public
   Relations (Lorna Cafferty)
— Why Cafferty Public Relations is the Most
   Reliable PR Agency in Ireland (featuring Lorna
   Herself)
— The Client List of Cafferty Public Relations
   (Everyone) and finally,
— What Cafferty Public Relations Can Do For *You*!

By the time she had got this far, both Liam and Big
had their chins resting on their cupped palms, and were
in a kind of hypnotic trance. The lyrical tune of 'Caffff-
er-tee Publeek Relay-shunns' would lull them to sleep
for many nights to come.

Liam pinched himself out of her spell, just as she
began detailing how she was going to help Big. By
this time the man himself was beyond objecting. This
woman could have taken him to the ladies' room,
stripped him, put lipstick on him, then made a toga out
of the hand towel and asked him to parade through the
lobby of The Plaza and Big would have done it. Thankfully, it was simpler than that. Lorna had gathered every
bit of information on Big she could through a press
agency in New York. She knew about the Waterford
Crystal/Statue of Liberty plans, the Big Paddy Festival –
the way he was prepared to drench the world in tonnes

of money in order to be seen as Irish. Seven hundred and fifty thousand pounds should be a cinch. During the seven-hour flight Lorna had convoluted this joker's mad ideas about finding himself a wife into a plan that might convince him that giving her lots of money would be a good idea.

For Big's benefit, Lorna's plan was called 'A Project'. Then she gave the Project a Title. All Projects must have Titles if they are going to succeed. All Projects must have Titles if they are going to Convince the Client – one of the first rules of PR.

Lorna dropped the hypnotic tone and snapped into her Shoot! Brainstorming! Wake-Up! Voice.

The Project, she told them, was entitled 'Big Business in Ireland!' and worked on the Problem/Solution model.

Problem: Man of Big's status needs Colleen with Class.
Irish women with class don't answer ads in newspapers.

Solution: Establish Big as man of class.

'Hey – no problem there, honey – I got loadsa class!'
'Of course, I could see that *as soon* as I met you, Xavier . . .'

Lorna looked doubtfully at Big's glow-in-the-dark teeth and ageing, 80s porn-star haircut. 'But some people in Ireland are not quite as sensitive to –' she struggled to think of a way of putting it that didn't feature the words 'Yank' and 'bawdy' – 'the *cultural differences* between the Homeland and America.'

Big looked confused.

'You mean my wealth might frighten summa the good ones off?'

'*Exactly, Xavier* – you might, em, overpower them.'

Big liked that explanation. He checked his nails modestly and cocked his head coyly to one side.

'We-ell – I guess I am a Purr-itty Power-ful guy.'

Liam's irritation evaporated into interest. He had never seen Big played this well before. He was impressed.

Lorna moved in for the kill.

She leaned across to Big, giving her cleavage a full-frontal-lingerie-ad-pose-elbow-squeeze, holding his eyes in a look of blistering sincerity.

'Xavier – can I be frank?'

Big's eyes darted from chest to face. He squeaked a nervous 'He-umf', afraid to open his mouth in case one of her nipples leapt into it.

'A man of your stature – frankly, Xavier – your looks, your charm – should not need to, to – go *looking*? For a wife.'

She said it as if she were bitterly disappointed that this had never occurred to Big before. As if it were heartbreakingly sad that a man in his position had never been told this before.

'Women,' she said, as if she were Every Woman in the World Made into One, 'should be falling at your feet!'

'They are!' he insisted. 'Over here – over here they are, but they're . . . they're no good, Laura. They're no good for me.'

He started to well up. Liam anxiously checked his napkin for a linen-label, and handed it across to him.

'Xavier, Xavier, Xavier . . .' She reached across and took his hand in a motherly grip. Big blew his nose. The tears were streaming down his face.

'The Women of the *World*, Xavier. *That's* your market. *That's* what you deserve. If *you* want an Irish wife – then *we* will find you one.' She looked at Liam to consent and he nodded enthusiastically – this woman was really something else.

'But, Xavier?'

He looked at her bleary with grief and almost said 'Yes, Mammy.'

'You must let *them* come to *you*.'

He nodded.

'Promise?'

America's Biggest Billionaire smiled at Ireland's Most Skilled PR Queen like a Big Brave five-year-old child just after scraping his knee and said, 'Promise.'

For a few seconds, the three of them sat there in touchy-feely group-hug-type scenario before Lorna broke the Ashman-esque spell with a snappy, 'Right – let's get down to business.'

Big had had a corner of his soul carpeted with love. Lorna had won.

'What *we*' – use of plurals before deal is done. Works every time – 'need to do, Xavier, is create a presence for you in Ireland. A *name* for you. An *atmosphere* in which you can happily take your place as Ireland's Most Eligible Bachelor.'

The full pitch took about ten minutes. Lorna knew that Big's main business interest worldwide was in genetically modified farming and foods. Although Big was proud of his achievements (he had the world's first four-legged turkey under development in a research lab in Denver and was hopeful that by Thanksgiving 2005 they would be able to contribute something to American Family Culture by providing them with 'a leg each'), Lorna was able to persuade him that the Irish Public were slow to accept the progressive nature of GM Foods, not on *moral grounds*, of course (she could see that Big was *beyond reproach* on that score), but because they were all still sending their rosy-cheeked daughters out to milk their cows by hand in the beautiful rolling green hills of Kerry, etc., etc . . .

Lorna would commit herself (her tone implying at Great Personal Cost) to the Tireless Pursuit of finding Exciting New Business Interests in the Fast-Moving Celtic Tiger Culture of Europe's Fastest-Growing Economy in which Big could Invest His Capital. Thus making him the Primary Protagonist of a New – Vibrant – Booming – Ireland! Thus making him the Most Important Investor in Ireland. Thus making him a Benefactor of the Irish State *Itself*! Thus allowing him to Take His Place in the Annals of Irish History Alongside Glorious JFK! Thus Doing Justice to the Proud Memory of His Beloved Mother! And thus . . . *Thus!* . . . finally allowing him to wear the crown and take his Rightful Place on the Throne of that Mighty and Coveted title – the Most Eligible Bachelor in Ireland!

By the time she had finished, waiters had been dispatched to source more linen for the leaking mountain of emotion that was Big himself, and Liam was blown sideways with the sheer brilliance of Lorna's powerful backdraught of bullshit. It was all Lorna could do not to weep herself, for 'the most important part of the pitching process', as she was fond of telling her minions, 'was believing the bollocks for as long as it takes to secure the client'.

When Lorna walked back down the steps of The Plaza onto Central Park, Manhattan, New York, New York, in the US of A, Big was so tightly secured he was virtually screwed to the chair with excitement and almost had to be airlifted back to his office two blocks away.

The anticlimax hit when she realized that the scrawny middle-aged man holding open the limo door for her was not Ben, and that she was not going to be given a Send-Off anywhere near as revitalizing and enriching as the Welcome she had enjoyed earlier.

As the chicken-necked driver glided her mutely along the wide sky-scrapered streets of Manhattan, Lorna tried to console herself by computing the humungous bill she could charge to Big, not to mention the 'commission' she could demand from the Irish companies looking for Major American Investment. But the intensity of the last few hours and minor jet lag were conspiring to make her feel hollow in a nasty teenage way she recognized from before. Before the handbags and the highlights – the champagne and the clients. In the days before Lorna learned to pitch and party, when she was struggling to find a way of surviving in the world without being a mere appendage to her overpowering mother. Sylvia lived somewhere, here, in Manhattan but Lorna had never visited her. She had the address back home, on the back of a home-delivery pizza menu and, as far as she could remember, Sylvia Cafferty was on the Christmas-card list in the office. Lorna looked out at the towering landscape and realized that her mother probably lived in one of those high impressive buildings that watch over the citizens of New York like glamorous but forbidding parents.

A few minutes ago, Lorna had been taller than any of them, looking down as the world played maypole around the heel of her high Gucci mules. Now she was back down to right size – only smaller. She felt dwarfed by the towering hugeness of the New York landscape and seemed to take up only a tiny corner of the vast interior of the stretch limo she had so admirably filled only a few hours before.

She should have someone to tell about all her adventures, her triumph over Big. She should be going to her mother's apartment now for coffee and cake, astounding her with stories of billionaires and big lunches. She should have her own grey-haired Irish mammy to impress and make proud. Someone to tell her that her dress was cut too low, and her heels were too high. She should have a man in her life who would be ringing her mobile red raw; telling her to hurry home. Someone to make her want to heighten her neckline and lower her heels before she became a Sad Old Spice Girl with overly dyed hair, cradling the latest Fendi accessory as if it meant something. As if it were important.

The fact that Lorna felt disappointed that Ben hadn't been there to greet her at The Plaza made her feel worse again. How unbearably sad of her to have been looking forward to telling a stranger her news. She remembered her Welcome Romp, but it only depressed her further this time. A shallow self-insult which served only to remind Lorna of how truly lonely she had become.

When she arrived at the airport, Lorna went straight to the chemist and bought some over-the-counter sedatives for her journey.

She slept all the way back to Dublin, missing all the champagne and canapés in first class. Somehow, she didn't have the stomach for them any more.

Lorna knew she would have to be back on form tomorrow, bright and brisk to complete the task ahead of her. But in the anonymous atmosphere of this plane journey when she was neither home nor abroad, with no one significant either behind or ahead of her, Lorna felt safe to indulge herself in a final few hours of lonely self-pity.

PART THREE

THE POWER OF PR

17

The journey from JFK to Dublin was six hours long. When Liam had plenty of time on his hands, and absolutely nothing better to do, his mind allowed itself to indulge in the somewhat ill-advised, but sometimes unbearably tempting, Serious Young Writers' Daydream entitled My Interview with Melvyn Bragg. Liam opted for the Deluxe Transatlantic Full-Length version, which included full *South Bank Show* theme music and camera directions.

Location: Office/Library of Brilliant Young Irish Writer. (Note shelves lined with foreign edition titles and Whitbread award thrown carelessly on desk as paperweight.) Camera angle: Close-up of BYIW. He is smoking fags, looking Intense and Serious and Brilliant, but at the same time a bit uncomfortable with all the fuss. Note to cameraman: Occasional pan to back of Melvyn's head. Check hair.

MELVYN BRAGG: I'm sitting here in the home, if I can call it that, Liam *(huge show of teeth)*, of Liam O'Muiracheartigh, if I can call you Liam, Liam? *(More teeth.)*

Change of name from Murphy on early advice of agent. 'The most Irish name you can think of, darling – Irish is IN! And we are going to make you the-most-Irish Irish Writer on this planet. Anything more Irish than Murphy or McCabe that hasn't already been taken?'

LIAM O'MUIRACHEARTIGH: 'It's O'Muir-Hur-Thig, actually.'

One up for the Brilliant Young Irishman!

MELVYN BRAGG: I'm sorry – O'Muir-Hur-*Thig*. (*More teeth.*) Liam . . . ?

Liam nods sagely to indicate that Melvyn may indeed call him Liam.

Your first book, *A Fun Date With Sylvia Plath*, won the Whitbread. Your second, *Hedgehog Sex*, caused an uproar in the literary world when it failed to win the Booker. Salman Rushdie refused to chair the judging committee until the decision was, finally, reversed in your favour – a *first* for the world's most prestigious literary prize . . .

Liam shrugs as if he hadn't even noticed that he'd won – literary prizes mean that little to him and he hopes Mel doesn't want to see the prize itself, because he might have left it in some groupie's house after the party.

MELVYN BRAGG: You count among your admirers – and your friends – some of the most revered literary figures of our day. You are rumoured to be a hellraiser in the tradition of Behan and Thomas. In a recent interview on *this* programme, Seamus Heaney talked fondly about how you had opened his mind to the syntax and rhythms of modern language through the medium of rave music . . .

Liam smiles and shakes his head at the reminder of his night out with Famous Seamus at a rave in Wembly.

LIAM O'MUIRACHEARTIGH: *(Mumbles knowingly)* Yeah – Shay is a great guy.

MELVYN BRAGG: Your recent anthology of abstract and, some have said (and I count myself among them), *Revolutionary* and *Ground-Breaking* poems *The American New Man and His Skincare Regime* has influenced not only this generation but will, some would say (and I count myself among them), influence many generations of poets to come.

Liam is fidgeting and puffing on a fag as if bored and, frankly, modestly mortified by Melvyn's Obvious Adulation.

MELVYN BRAGG: You are only thirty-two, and yet you have already written *three* of the Most *Important* Serious Works of Our Time. Your eagerly awaited autobiography *Don't Call Me Joyce* is about to be published. Why that title, Liam? You've been hailed a genius by the Irish Literary Establishment – hell, the *World's* Literary Establishment already. Why *fight* it? Why *fight* that kind of praise?'

Liam leans back casually, and stubs the fag out on his Whitbread.

LIAM O'MUIRACHEARTIGH: 'Well, Melvyn – it's all just a load of old bollocks reall—'

'Ham or beef?'

Liam was woken from his moment of glory by a woman caked in twelve coats of bright orange foundation with her dyed black hair tied back in a green velvet scrunchie whose official title was Your Lovely Irish Air Hostess. However, her dry, dead-eye smile was one of a woman for whom there were too many years between her first answering the ad to 'Live a Life of Glamour in the Skies' and the weary forty-eight hours of trolley-wheeling she had just put in. A woman who had worn down many, many miles of logoed carpet in her time, been hopefully engaged, then let down by too many men in uniform, and dished out enough 'Hang Sang-wiches' to tired businessmen to own her own fleet of pigs. A woman who didn't give a shit whether Liam had ever, would ever, or was currently being interviewed in his head or otherwise by the Lord God Himself if he would just take the fecking sangwich and let her get her feet back into the Portable Foot Spa she kept in her curtain coffin at the top of this aisle.

Liam took the ham sandwich that was being thrust in his face and unwrapped it joylessly. The contrast between his as yet unachieved literary ambitions, and the reality of travelling economy from New York to Dublin, put a tin hat on the pit of depression that had been dug for him in the events of the past few days.

Rewind to the day before when Big had instructed Liam that he wanted him to go back to Ireland to 'Keep that Laura Caffrey doll in check. I wanna make sure she does a good job.'

When Liam had assured him that Lorna was more than capable of . . . Big had cut him off with one of his Ashman-learned 'I-am-hugging-you-with-my-eyes' looks (his therapist had recently told him that physical contact was not always a welcome form of communication with Europeans) and said, 'I TRUST you, Skip.'

Liam had not been back to Ireland in the three years since he'd moved to America for a whole host of very good reasons – Not Being a Famous Author being prime among them.

He had been so fraught at the thought of his trip home that the habitual ease with which he managed his daily skincare regime and wardrobe had been trip-switched into panic. Half an hour after he was supposed to have left his house, the courtesy car's engine was running and Liam was sitting on his bed surrounded with toiletries going, 'Scruffing lotion or exfoliating face scrub? Scruffing lotion or exfoliating face scrub?' He threw both in, and tried to console himself that at least he was travelling first class and it would be champagne and canapés all the way home. He was also slightly cheered by the thought that he could save the complimentary slippers and give them to his mother, which would probably impress her more than his (as yet fictional) Lifelong Friendship with Famous Seamus.

But, as often happens in life, Liam's indecision caused him to be downgraded – a unique experience in itself. Having arrived late for check-in, he had been told that first class had been overbooked (due to his Dublin destination being seemingly *awash* with money), and would he please accept the airline's heartfelt apologies and a voucher for a free flight as compensation. This voucher, however, did not entitle Liam to any special treatment from the Lovely Air Hostesses, nor indeed immunize him from the charmless, chaotic seat-swapping dance that inevitably takes place when a pregnant woman decides that she needs an aisle seat instead of a window and wants to be within water-breaking distance of the toilets. With the result that Liam found himself welded into the two-foot-square of space left him by the mother-to-be and a Large Man from Kansas who most certainly did *not* enjoy the same skincare regime of our budding author, and who was evidently unacquainted with recent advances in the cosmetic industry with regard to Underarm Deodorant for Men. Both Heavily Pregnant and Large Man glowered resentfully as Liam squelched into the seat between them, as if they had already earmarked it as extra elbow room for themselves which, as the flight progressed, Liam came to realize they both badly needed. Directly behind him was a small squabbly child, but not so small that he couldn't play 'Dislocate the Back of the Passenger in Front' with the soles of his new trainers.

Had Liam known he was going to be greeted at Dublin airport by a ceili band and an open-top bus full of fans with a banner hanging from its side saying 'BRINGING THE PULITZER BACK HOME TO IRELAND', he might have been better able to tolerate the 'Blurby-bleep-bleep – blurby-bleep, bleep, bleee-eeep' of the Nintendo handset that the brat's mother had given him when Liam finally *implored* her with an angry look to drug the child before he amputated its legs.

As it was, Liam's journey was filled with neither physical comfort, nor the mental release he was sometimes able to conjure up through fantasy. It was, he would recall, the most miserable six hours of his life. Stillorgan – Dublin – Ireland – Europe – the World could not possibly be any worse than the journey to get there had been.

18

Gloria walked up Grafton Street towards Henry's where she had agreed to meet Sam for lunch. She wasn't in the mood today. Gloria always felt that she had to be all right, on some level, whenever she saw Sam. And meetings with the bank these days rarely left her feeling all right. This afternoon's meeting had left her feeling considerably worse than all right.

'I'm sorry,' the nice girl in the navy uniform had kept saying to her, 'I'm sorry but you're heavily overdrawn, Ms O'Neill, and in view of that, we cannot sanction your request for a loan. I'm sorry.'

'But what about the business plan?'

Gloria had decided some weeks ago that she was not going to let Frank cheat her out of her future, however much he may have taken from her in the past. She had her solicitor working on a buyout plan for his half of the business, and had drawn up a business plan for the chain of Gaff salons she had always dreamed of. In actual fact, it was less of a dream these days than a necessity. The one salon was barely enough to support itself on its own. She needed to expand before she could consolidate it and pay Frank off. He *was* cheap, but she knew he wouldn't *come* cheap as the saying goes. Gloria needed half a million. It was a lot of money, but she knew that she could make it work. Three years' payback, maximum, on three salons. She had people ready to run them. She had a good track record of money coming in – but a bad one of late of money going out, thanks to Frank. Gloria had always enjoyed a good relationship with the bank. But as good news was always dished out by the manager, bad news was left to the likes of the little girleen in the navy suit who now looked across the laminate wood desk with a very worried face and a set of highlights trying to liven up a bored bob that looked like it could do with a bit of a wash.

'I'm sarry – but given your income record of late I'm afraid Mr Grisham can't sanction this loan. I'm sarry.'

Gloria was done arguing. This kid (for she looked like a teenager to Gloria, although they were probably around the same age) had obviously been programmed to say 'I'm sarry' no matter what Gloria threw at her. She was only doing her job. On the other hand, she'd have liked Grisham to have come down and told her himself, given all the business she had given him over the years. The cowardly shite. But the kid was a bit of a 'sarry'-looking specimen herself, and so Gloria picked her business plan up off the desk, left a relieved Drippy Sarry to get on with whatever bits of file-fiddling was her real job, and walked out of the bank and up along Grafton Street towards Neary's on Chatham Street.

Sam was waiting at a corner table. He was wearing a jacket with a Trembling Celtics On Tour T-shirt underneath it and a big warm smile. He looked like a man who was going on a date. Gloria sighed inwardly. The stuffy atmosphere of the pub and the failure she felt in the pit of her stomach meant that Sam's cuddly, cheerful, *hopeful* face just made her feel worse.

She ordered a gin and tonic and listened to him talk excitedly about his work. He had Warrior Wench, a girl rock group, flying in from Russia next week to record their new album in his studios, and The Trembling Celtics' bass guitarist had just had a baby girl. Gloria was briefly distracted from her problems as Sam enthusiastically described his visit to the hospital that morning. She wondered at how a man as childless and single as Sam could get so excited about the birth of somebody else's child. He was great. Really sweet. How the fuck had he ended up being Frank's closest friend?

'You look a bit down, chicken? Anything I can do? Anything you want to talk about?'

Shit. He'd noticed. If Frank found out about any of this, he'd be on to her like a shot.

Gloria ran her hand through her hair. In a poignant moment she realized she'd had no right to criticize Ms Sarry's greasy roots when her own were no great shakes by the feel of them.

'Oh, it's nothing. Just a bit tired, you know?'

Sam was having none of it.

'Gloria, I know something's wrong. You can tell me – I can't promise to help but . . .'

Gloria gave him a defiant look. It was slight, but enough to make Sam wither a bit. Still, he wouldn't be deterred.

'Look, Gloria. Let's get one thing straight. I won't go back to Frank with anything. I, of all people, have known him long enough to know what's he's like. Please? Trust me?'

Gloria's face softened. Light filtered through a stained-glass window behind Sam's head and threw a red glow scattered with hysterical dust mites across the top of his bald pate. Gloria smiled. She had always found bald heads kind of attractive. Perhaps it was because she was a hairdresser. Bald was easy. No trouble.

She told Sam about her plans for a chain of Gaff Hair Salons, her idea of replicating the personal, homely atmosphere of her mother's flat in Ballymun. The early days. Sam knew all about Gloria's background, but he asked her questions all that afternoon. He wanted to fill in the gaps. How had her father died? Where had he worked? An uncle of his had owned that factory, he told her. She went quiet then, and Sam knew she was thinking about how far away she was from it all now. Sitting in a pub having a casual drink with a man who was related to her father's old boss. Bosses and businessmen had seemed so foreign to her then. As if they were gods. Now they were a part of her life. Sam kept asking, and the more she drank – the more Gloria talked. About her sister and her many nieces and nephews. Her hopes for Shirley to go to college – to 'make the break'.

'Is that what you wanted?' he asked. 'To break away from Ballymun?'

'Well, yes . . . but no. Not from my family . . .'

Then she talked about how isolated she felt sometimes. How removed from her background, the comfort of her family circle, and how she felt as if this life, the salon, banks, the clients – somehow didn't feel like it belonged to her.

Sam rang his office from the men's loos and told them he wouldn't be back. While he was gone, Gloria rang the salon and told them the same.

At eight o'clock, Neary's was filling up with the evening crowd. Gloria was flushed and mossy with drink and Sam got a feeling in the pit of his belly that, if anything was going to happen, it could happen now. Tonight. He didn't know where to begin. He could lean across and try to kiss her. But that would be awkward and foolish. Not in public. They were too old. He could go back to the flat, and pounce on her. But that was too undignified – and if she didn't want it? Gloria had a good bit of drink taken and it might seem like he was taking advantage. Maybe he should just come right out with it. 'Gloria – I love you!' No. Too melodramatic. Not her style, and certainly not his. Sam's style was 'sit back and see what happens'. Not a proactive approach, but one which a very successful record producer mingling in a world of groupies and wannabes can afford to adopt. He had a fail-safe tactic for dealing with Hard-Bitten Husband Hunters (with which Dublin was rife) that involved just enough wrist limping to let them know he was unavailable, but not so much that wouldn't allow the occasional casual opportunist in a leather miniskirt to jump through the net. However, Gloria was different. Sam was in love with her and knew that if he stayed laid-back for too long, he'd fall into a kind of atrophied admiring sleep, and the most the object of his dreams would do was tuck him under a nice warm blanket and leave him there.

In the absence of his ability to alert her to his affections, or instigate any kind of hand-holding, face-touching, lip-locking scenario, Sam said, 'You know, Gloria, I'm looking for an investment opportunity at the moment, and I'd be more than happy to . . .'

The rest of the words crumbled in his mouth. He had said the wrong thing. Not just the wrong thing, but enough to make desiccated dog-shite of the positive feelings that had been consolidating their friendship over the last two meetings into the promise of something deeper.

Gloria O'Neill took nothing from nobody. She was self-made, self-sufficient and independent. Any offer of financial help from anyone that wasn't a bank or a building society or an independent investor smacked of the C-word. Charity. Not a popular concept to a girl from Ballymun who had proudly made her way through life with help from nobody. A girl who continued to support her family with pride, and her vile ex-husband with dignity. Gloria was a giver – not a taker. Sam knew all that. Fuck. He had just blurted out the worst insult he could possibly throw at her. Why had he said it? Why? Why? Why?

He thought of taking it all back and replacing it with: 'Sorry! I don't want to give you money! I just want a ride! A kiss! I love you!'

But he didn't. Sam Cohen just sat there shrugging like a bold, bald schoolboy knowing he's just flicked a spit ball at a teacher's tit and hoping she won't murder him stone dead.

'No thank you, Sam. I can manage.'

It was as good as murder to Sam. His moment was gone. He felt lucky when she pecked him coldly on the cheek and left the pub.

Gloria walked back to her empty flat, opened a bottle of wine and worried her way back into loneliness.

19

Sandy just did not *get* Maeve's big thing about this billionaire guy. The two of them were Getting Ready (Maeve never went anywhere without Getting Ready – that was half the fun – sometimes the *only* fun) to meet Maeve's brother Liam at the airport. It was his first trip home in years, and Maeve didn't seem to give a shit about anything except for getting at his boss.

'Don't you believe in love at first sight, Sand?'

'But you've never *met* him, Maeve. Hang on – you lunatic – you've never even feckin' *seen* him!'

'Have so.'

'Where?'

Maeve mumbled, 'Namagseen,' into her knees which were crunched up into her ample breasts as she went through her weekly toenail-polishing ritual.

'Where, Maeve? *Where* have you seen him? Out of denial and into the kitchen, please!'

'In a magazine, all right! M-A-G-A-Zine! That good enough for you? Fuck! Now look what you made me do – I'll have to start again.' Maeve pushed past Sandy and grabbed the remover and a handful of cotton wool from a nearby stool, dragging snowy shreds of it onto her mother's Good Carpet.

Sandy was worried because Maeve seemed to be taking all of this so seriously. Her friend had been really funny about Sandy following this whole thing through as a story. Almost as though Sandy was going to go after Big herself. Sandy knew, of course, that it was a ridiculous notion – not her style at all. But in truth, there was a worm of discomfort gnawing away at Sandy's conscience reminding her that, if she was going to make a success of this documentary, she was going to have to go at least part-way down the road to seducing the billionaire. While that was, of course, strictly in the interests of journalistic research, if Sandy had been honest with herself she would per-haps have realized that it was this deception that was at least partly responsible for her so desperately trying to persuade Maeve out of her rapidly increasing obsession with Mr Big.

'Anyway – I don't know what's making you so fucking judgemental about the whole thing, little Miss Colleen Redhead. You're no Virgin Mary yourself. Remember that gobshite video director you rode after *one* night? I *told* you you'd never hear from the slag again but Oh No! You went dribbling on about him for weeks like he was Mr Merchant Ivory!'

Sandy was almost in tears. She had never known Maeve to be so bitchy, but Sandy couldn't bear to fall out with her oldest friend. Ahem. Her *only* remaining friend in Dublin.

'I'm just worried about you, that's all. You just seem so het up about the whole thing, I'm just worried that you'll be, you know . . .'

'Let down? That's what you're trying to say, isn't it?'

'We-ell . . .' Sandy didn't want to upset Maeve any more than she already had, but it was her duty to be honest. 'Well – yes.'

'Look, Sandy.' Maeve balanced the open bottle of Purple Fury on the arm of her mother's Good Sofa and turned to face her friend. Sandy looked tearful and worried. Maeve melted.

'Ah – I'm sorry, pet. I know you're just worried about me, and I'm sorry I've been such a bitch about all this – it's just that . . .'

'. . . this one's *different*.'

'I know it sounds stupid – and you've heard it thousands of times before . . .'

'Certainly have.'

Maeve grabbed Sandy's hands and pleaded with her eyes.

'. . . no, *really*, Sandy. You know how sometimes you get a *feeling* about things?'

'Oh ye-aah! You mean like the time I thought Mr Video Man was going to be the One?'

'No – I'm serious about this, Sandy. I just have a feeling, an *instinct* – you know, like my life is about to change?'

Sandy grabbed the bottle of Purple Fury from the arm of the sofa where it was about to topple.

'The only thing that's going to change around here is the structure of your face if your mother sees those bits of varnish on her Good Carpet.'

In her earnestness, Maeve had scrunched her wet toenails into the shagpile and bits of fluff had coagulated to the Purple Fury.

'Shit! Sher-hi-hi-hit.' She mock-sobbed as Sandy started to gather up their beauty bits from the living room before Mrs Murphy came home and caught them.

Sandy continued her nagging in the car all the way to the airport.

'You know if you left home and got yourself a flat, instead of wishing that some man was going to come along and whisk you away – your life *would* change, Maeve. For the better – I mean, you'd have—'

'Just *drop* it, Sandy.' Maeve looked genuinely hurt behind her irritated squabbly voice. 'I don't expect you to understand, you haven't got a romantic bone in your body. Fuck-it, I don't even *care* that you don't understand. There is something about this man – I don't know what it is, and I know you think this is just one great big fantasy trip, and maybe it is – but I've got a feeling in the pit of my stomach that says this is Going to Happen. If it doesn't, well then, nothing ventured, etc. But one thing I do know, I can do without the lectures.'

'Yes, but I just—'

'Yes-but fucking nothing, Nolan. You know what

your problem is? You need a bloody husband yourself to have a go at so that you'll leave me *alone*.'

'I don't need a man to make me happy.'

'Oh-ho yes you do, girl! You just don't *know* it yet!'

Sandy didn't like the way the tables were turning on her. But she didn't mind a bit of a fight with Maeve. Cross words brought them closer together somehow. It made her feel like they were sisters. Like they could say what they wanted, but they would always love each other at the end of it.

'I am an independent woman.'

'You are in your hole. Look at the mess you made of your last job.'

'I moved on to better things.'

'By the skin of your teeth, girl – and probably only because the lecherous old goat you went to got a sniff of your gusset and wanted a piece.'

'Maeve! Don't be so disgusting!' There was a smile cracking on Sandy's face. She loved it when Maeve was outrageous. She said the things that Sandy thought, but was too afraid to say. 'He was a very nice old man.'

'My arse. There's no such thing. You go in to complain to some old goat after Randy Mac Rory gives you the sack and *bam!* He gives you your own radio show – just like that! My money's on his scrawny old claw looking to do a bit of pant-exploration at your next Christmas party. How can you be so naive?'

'It wasn't like that. What about my years of experience? Do you think they count for nothing?'

'In a plush media job in this town, girl? Frankly, *nada*. Look where he put you in the first place. Assistant to Randy Mac Roaring. Burial ground for bright young things – please!'

It was Sandy's turn to get irritated now.

'Well – that'll all change when I do this documentary piece about Mr Big Stuff. I'll race you to him and we'll see who gets him first, eh?'

Even as she said it, Sandy got an uncomfortable feeling, as if she was only half-joking. Maeve was an all-out man catcher, and, even in their teenage disco days, Sandy had never attempted to compete. If Maeve wanted someone, Sandy stepped aside and let her at it. Even played the Redhead Geek to Maeve's Sophisticated Goddess to better her best friend's chances. Sandy could make jokes about going after the same man because Maeve would never dream it would happen. Up until now, neither would Sandy. But that last quip had left a rotten taste in her mouth. The fact that Maeve responded with her usual hardy humour didn't make Sandy feel any better.

Maeve stuck her fag between her teeth and did a smoke-grimace as she wheeled the Astra into a space designed for a wheelbarrow in one go. Having matching toe and nail varnish did not preclude her from being an aggressive driver.

'You had better be joking, Sandy. I'd tear the eyes out of your head for this one.'

'I believe it, sista,' she said like she had said a

thousand times before. The difference this time was that she did.

⬭

Liam was delayed coming through. They had lost his luggage. The Lovely Irish Air Hostesses and the Lovely Irish Handling Staff had lost the carefully chosen collection of clothes and cosmetics he had selected to prove to the folks back home he was, if not Melvyn material, then at least a cool, funky Man of the Millennium. It felt like a bad omen, and Liam felt strangely lost without it.

The vision that bolted frantically towards Maeve and Sandy at the Arrivals gate in Dublin airport was therefore not the sauntering success story that they were both expecting. Instead of greeting his sister with a brotherly Good-to-see-ya hug, the first words out of Liam Murphy's mouth after years of absence were a verbal, panicked grasp for help.

'Do they sell Prescriptives in Dublin?' he all but yelped.

'I thought your skin had improved, you boily old bastard.'

Maeve knew her brother well enough not to expect, nor indeed *want*, a huggy-kissy reunion. She knew Liam was a bit of a scorpy bollocks – prone to self-indulgent dark moods, which he put down to an Artistic Temperament, but which his sister suspected were more connected to the Unfulfilled Physical Needs of a Warm-Blooded Irishman.

'You could get a blow job on the medical card – it's been that long,' she had said to him the last time he snapped at her about trying to muscle in on his boss romance-wise. He wasn't bad-looking, so she'd been told, but he was too self-absorbed and up himself to go out and get himself a girlfriend like a normal bloke. 'I'm waiting for Miss Right,' he would say. 'Someone Who *Understands* Me.' 'Well – you'll be waiting a bloody long time for that one, brother dear,' she had quipped and decided to let him get to it in his own time, which would probably be never – the big girl.

Sandy was not impressed. What an unbelievably arrogant way to greet his sister and his sister's friend after all these years! But then, what had she been expecting? To her own puzzlement, Sandy realized that she had been expecting . . . we-ll . . . *something*. Perhaps some kind of reassuring face from the past? She couldn't quite put her finger on it.

The three of them walked towards the car park. While Maeve was queuing to pay for her ticket at the pre-parking machine, Sandy and Liam stood in an awkward silence.

'So they lost your luggage?'

'So you want to marry Big?'

They said simultaneously.

Sandy was horrified.

So was Liam. What a blundering, stupid, stupid, *stupid* introduction to a girl he hadn't seen for years. A girl with glossy red hair tied back in that kind of tempting, tangly way he liked. A girl with pale, freckly, delicate skin and just enough no-make-up make-up to sharpen her soft, sensitive features. He tried to pretend he hadn't said it, and hoped that Sandy would play along.

'Yes, they lost my luggage.'

'Rea-ally?'

Sandy's tone was deeply sarcastic and she looked mad as a hellcat.

'Yes, and I had my new Armani suit in there and all my toiletries . . . that's why I asked Maeve about the Prescriptives . . . why I wanted to know if they sold them in Dublin . . . I like their stuff . . .'

'How *fasss-cinating*.'

Pouf! Big girl's blouse! Arrogant, smarmy-arsed, poufy, big girl's blouse fake! That's what he sounded like. First he'd offended her – now he was trying to convince her he was gay. Poor Maeve's never-had-a-girlfriend-brother, who had avoided coming home for years – why? Because he was waiting until he was a famous novelist? My arse, she thought. It's obvious. Because he didn't want to break the No Grandchildren news to his parents!

Maeve marched them off to the car before Liam was able to dig his hole any deeper.

Maeve suggested they go for a Japanese meal, but although Liam was dying for a plate of sushi, and was fascinated and intrigued that Japanese food had hit the land of fried breakfasts and a soggy-roast-in-a-pub-if-you-were-lucky he had left behind, he insisted, in the interests of appearing overtly masculine, that he was 'gagging for a pint'.

As a compromise Maeve, who was dressed up for somewhere more glam than a seedy local, dragged them to the lounge of The Morrison Hotel. As they took their seats among the tan suede (of both staff and furniture) and the hopeless tastefulness of their surroundings, Liam commented, he thought, innocuously, 'Wow. Dublin has really changed!'

That was Sandy's cue to blast him.

'Oh *what*? Like you think we're all still living here like muckers – a million years away from the civilized sushi-bar culture of New York? Still drinking our pints in scruffy pubs and singing rebel songs and—'

'Hey! Back off, you!' butted in Maeve. 'You've only been back a wet weekend from London yourself, and you've done nothing but complain about how Dublin Has Changed since you got here.'

Sandy withered, and Liam came to her rescue.

'No, I meant it's good. I like it. This place is as good as you'd get anywhere in Europe, and rightly so. Celtic Tiger and all that.'

'Oh – I don't know,' Sandy said, 'I still miss some of the old bits. You know, when I was in London, there was this great local Irish pub we used to go to, and on a Sunday they had a really fantastic session. Off the cuff, all these great traditional musicians used to come down and play. And yet here, in Dublin, I can't find anywhere like that. Oh Liam, everywhere's gone mad trendy, all chrome and cappuccinos. It's ironic.'

Liam nodded sagely.

'Yes, it seems a shame to turn our backs on tradition just when we're starting to—'

'Oi! Bord Fáilte Committee! Cut the Contemporary Ireland Essay,' barked Maeve, 'and lets have the beef on the Big Billionaire. Liam! What's the story?'

Maeve listened intently as Liam told her about the Mad PR, her plans to turn Big into an Irish Icon and the Big Party. Sandy laughed warmly at a couple of the ironic emphases he put in especially to impress her, and Liam was hopeful that he had . . . something. He wasn't sure what that something was, but it was better than his sister's friend thinking he was a complete eejit. He was sure now, having seen the hungry keenness in his sister's eyes, the look he recognized as the one that had got Maeve the widest flares in her school and the non-regulation Day-Glo socks, that she was the one behind Sandy's application. And that meant . . . what? Something. Something like she wasn't interested in Big herself which meant something, *something* for him? He wished he wasn't so jet-lagged and he might have been able to fill in the gaps. He settled for Sandy seeming like too intelligent a person to be mixed up with an ignorant gombeen like Big, even if she had a friendly beauty, an engaging smile and a warm laugh and fitted the Colleen Bill right down to the ground and then some.

'So when is he *over*? When can I *mee-eet* him?' Maeve wasn't interested in Liam's amusing Capote-style comments on the American Obsession With Ireland. She wanted Facts! Action!

'I don't know and you can't.'

Sandy, warmed by the half-pint and the bit of flirtatious banter with her friend's brother, suddenly blurted out, 'So, Liam – did you show Big my picture, then?'

Liam lost half a sip of beer down the front of his crispy white shirt. He studied the glass crossly, pretending it was the object's fault and said, 'Well – actually I didn't get the chance because ... er ... em ...'

'But I qualify for the party, yeah?'

'Well – I suppose I ...'

'Good!' She winked at Maeve – and pretended not to notice she didn't wink back.

'And I can bring a friend?'

'Well, I suppose I ...'

This was a turn that Liam had not expected. Nor Maeve, although she wasn't going to say anything. Sandy was, after all, her ticket to that party. Her Big chance. She knew about the documentary all right – but, given Sandy's prissy attitude up to now, she hadn't expected her to go about it with such – well – verve.

'That's settled, then.'

⬭

'It wasn't what she said – it was the *way* that she said it,' bitched Maeve to one of the girls in her office the next day.

It wasn't what she said – it was the *way* that she said it, thought Liam as he lay on the sofabed, looking up at the 'I'M SLIM AND I LOVE IT!' motivational poster that was on the wall of what had once been his old room, but was now Mammy Murphy's Weightwatchers Leader Office, and wondering why he gave a shit that his sister's friend wanted to marry a billionaire.

∙∙∙

What Maeve and Liam didn't know was the extent and commitment of Sandy's ambition to be an Important Investigative Journalist. One day, she dreamed of being a Serious Clever, standing in front of a camera in the forefront of some 'Terrible Scene of Carnage and Destruction' giving it loads of gravitas into a mike marked with the most coveted three letters in the universe of media wannabes – BBC. She knew she was a long way yet from a Kate Adie bob and an open-topped jeep with bullets whipping the air of some newly war-torn country. But damnit she was *done* dreaming! A shit-hot radio documentary could inch her ambition along a notch or two, and Sandy was going to use all the tools at her disposal to make it the best damn radio documentary about Marrying a Rich American that anyone had ever done. The tools she had were

    (a) A billionaire's PA
    (b) A billionaire's PA's sister
    (c) Feminine guile and cunning

She liked one, she loved the other and the third? Well, she hadn't had much cause to use it in the past, and she suspected it was a bit rusty, but she had been proud of the conviction with which it had come out in The Morrison that afternoon.

Maeve, Liam and the Whole World would know it was all a clever journalism scam when she exposed her hidden microphone during the wedding ceremony and left Big standing at the top of the aisle. She was sorry to be pissing on Maeve's fantasy, but she would make her a bridesmaid and she could always step in at the last minute to comfort the jilted groom. Liam, too, was kind of cute but then hey! She'd had her fill of Cute Men, and where had they got her? Not to Bosnia in regulation BBC combats, that's for sure.

No, Sandy was going to carry her plan through to the very end. Her career depended on it. Her pride depended on it. And her happiness? Sandy had too many plans to make to think about that one right now.

20

Lorna was on board the Great PR Wagon again, and whipping her minions, the Foxrock Fanny Fraternity and the Business Community of Dublin right into her herd. Money, she had come to realize, was a greater weapon than style, sass, culture, respectability and talent, and if there was one thing that Big had (and she was pretty sure it *was* only one thing) it was MONEY!

'Gerry. I have an American Investor who is interested in backing New Irish Business. That new restaurant you were thinking of opening? How does 0 per cent interest for the next five years sound to you?'

That was lunch for the rest of her life sorted.

'Donal. I have an American Investor who is interested in backing New Irish Business. Weren't you looking at a new retail outlet for Oakes Designer Wear? How does zero per cent interest for the next five years sound to you?'

One new wardrobe coming up.

'Pat. I have an American Investor who is interested in backing New Irish Business. Weren't you looking to expand the salon? How does zero per cent interest for the next five years sound to you?'

Facials and massages twice weekly from now on.

Lorna had saved the best till last. With the Glory of Success pumping through her veins, and a duty-free Gauloise dripping from the corner of her freshly scarlet-slashed lips, she stood up behind her desk to better enjoy the full I-Am-Bigger-And-Better-Than-You experience of her impending phone call to one Bridget Wilkin-Walkins.

'Bridge-jet – ' she used her sing-song hypnotic voice to draw the full pleasure out of the experience – 'Eeet's Lor-naa. Lor-naaa Caffer-teee.'

'Oh. Hullo, Lorna.' (Bridget was somewhat taken aback at Lorna calling her voluntarily at home. Given her disgraceful conduct of late and the shame of her sunken status as a Down-at-Heel Closet Lesbian.)

'Bridge-jet, I was wondering if you could help me with some-theeng?'

WW did not like the tone of Lorna's voice. It was the supremely confident tone of somebody with information which she did not have. She tried to get in a dig about the hiding in the hair-salon incident.

'Yes *of course*, Lorna. Is everything all right? I saw you in town there last week and—'

'I have a client – ' sod this, Lorna cut her off. Nothing, *nothing* Vile Bridget had to say would be allowed to piss on *this* six-inch killer Gina stiletto shoe – 'who has sanctioned me to donate Two Million Dollars to the

Irish National Gallery.' Lorna paused then to let the bomb drop – then *whoosh!* She went in for the kill.

'The thing is, Bridget, the Committee want *me* to come on board as his representative but you see, with all I have on at the moment, well, Bridget – I just don't *know* if I'm going to have the *time*.' Lorna whinged it out like it was a high-class problem – like not being able to choose between the foie gras and the truffle consommé, and *not* on the grounds of anything so cheap as price or fat-content.

In the circles that the Wilkin-Walkins moved in there was only one thing more prestigious than being invited to sit on the committee of a National Institution. And that was being too busy to take up the position.

'Well, Lorna – I don't know what to say. This is *marvel-hors*, of course, but I . . .'

But I . . . but I want to jump under a feckin' bus! Yes! Yes! Ya-hess! Vile Bridget was finally stumped for words.

I've won! I've won! I've won! Lorna thought. But she said, 'Oops – that's the mobile going again – Sheila? Sheila, honey – will you tell An Taoiseach to hold for me? Sorry, Bridget, I'm going to have to go. Bertie's at my back *again* – see you soon – bye now!'

After the glory of her victory in the WWWW (Wilkin-Walkin's World War – for on this day it *had* been Officially Declared), Lorna decided to celebrate with one of Kevin's magnificent head massages with a by-the-way blow-dry over in Gloria's Gaff. She hadn't spoken to Gloria since her return from New York, and figured that a bottle of Bollinger in the company of her new BF would be *madness* not to instigate.

However, Gloria was not in the mood to be led astray that afternoon.

Lorna was head-back-in-the-basin having her scalp deliciously mashed by the equally delicious Kevin, when Gloria, having finished her two thirty, came over.

Lorna strained up to have a look at her.

'Christ! You look awful! I hope it was worth it.'

Kevin hummed and kept on kneading. It was true. Gloria had been looking really washed out and pale of late. Even Kevin had volunteered to spark her up with a wash and blow that morning, but she had listlessly refused. He knew, all her staff knew, that the pressure of business was getting her down. None of them said anything, but they were all secretly afraid that the salon might close and they'd be out of a job. When the Ultimate Trooper Gloria O'Neill didn't have the strength or the motivation even to put on her Brave Face, they knew she was in real trouble.

'I've not been getting much sleep lately.'

'Sorry – I hope *he* was worth it!' Lorna was on that kind of high that was incapable of picking up the subtle nuances of other people's despair.

'No. I just haven't been getting much sleep.' Gloria looked slightly embarrassed, touched Lorna's shoulder and said, 'My three thirty's in. I'll see you later,' and gave Kevin the wink not to charge Lorna for today's session.

'Jesus,' Lorna whispered up to him, 'did I put my foot in it?'

'Kind of.'

'You mean that's not a Late-Night-With-a-Toy-Boy head she's got on her?'

'No,' he said. Kevin didn't like talking about Gloria out of turn, but Lorna looked like she gave a shit. Gloria was so bloody self-sufficient, she confided in nobody. Sure, she *gave out* about Frank all the time, but when she was in *real* trouble, she kept schtum. It was worrying. Frightening, even. One day she'd end up having a nervous breakie and it would be too late. Then they'd *all* be out of a job.

'She's been having a few problems lately.'

'What, not like anything . . . ?' Lorna grimaced and mouthed the word 'Medical'. She despised anything to do with sickness, and she put it all under the heading Messy Unpleasantness. She had begged for a general anaesthetic during her last smear test, and would have opted for euthanasia if she had ever had anything that couldn't be cured by antibiotics.

'No, no, nothing like that. Just Frank being an arsehole and, you know, just general money stuff.'

'Ahhh.'

Money. Was that all! She had conquered BWW this morning, and pulled in more favours than your average Italian/American wedding. If her friend was in the Bad Place, Lorna Cafferty was the one to pull her out.

Gloria was smoothing down her fifth Foxrock Fanny Regulation Beige Bob of the day with a smidgen of Smear Gloss, when a freshly blow-dried Lorna marched over and whispered in her ear.

'Kev's taking over your four thirty and five, and I'm taking you out for a drink. I'll be round the corner in Keogh's.'

Gloria was a bit put out, and glowered heavily at Kev.

'You had no right to do that.'

'I've no one else booked in for the day and –' he looked a bit sheepish – 'you look like you could use the afternoon off.'

Gloria caught sight of herself in the mirror behind reception and was horrified by the psychiatric head on her. The hair was piled up in a messy chignon that was more Germaine Greer than Julia Roberts and the pitiful make-up-less gawp on her face was that of a mother-of-ten with no-food-for-the-babby. Kev was right. She was not exactly an advertisement for Dublin's Most Glamorous Hair Salon.

Gloria rummaged in one of the juniors' handbags under the reception desk, and quickly threw on a bit of lipstick, then ran a brush through her grungy roots. She didn't want Lorna to see her looking like this. She'd shock a nun in this state, and although she liked her new friend well enough and trusted her – sort of – when Gloria got depressed like this, her pride turned into downright stubborn denial.

She needn't have worried. Lorna knew exactly where

she was coming from. There was a full bottle of bubbly on the table and two glasses when she got to Keogh's.

'I took the liberty,' Lorna said, nodding at them, 'to celebrate Our New Business Partnership.'

Gloria looked at her suspiciously.

'My New Big American Client has given me a five-million-pound budget to invest in New Irish Business, and a bit besides to Benefact some Arts. What was it you said you needed? Half a mill? Peanuts, babe!'

A look of horror spread across Gloria's face. She hardly knew this woman – and here she was treating her like some kind of charity . . .

'And before you whip into me with any of your Ballymun-pride charity shite – let me point out to you that this bottle of champs is *not yet open*. I am not *giving* this money away, Gloria. I'm going to have to go back to him with business plans, and year-on-year returns and the full nine yards. You show me you can make it work – or it doesn't happen.'

Gloria looked interested then, as Lorna knew she would. She wasn't Dublin's Most Successful PR Manager without knowing what carrot suited what donkey. Big, the foolish gob, needed nothing but Lorna's assurance of prestige and a rosy-cheeked virgin at the end of all this, but she knew that Gloria wouldn't take that route. She was too honest. Hardworking. She needed to feel like she had earned it. So Lorna would put a couple of hours into looking at her bits of paper, then give her the money at the end of it anyway.

'I haven't got the business plan with me now,' Gloria said in a small tired voice. 'It's in the flat . . .'

'Well – you go get it, girl, and if I like what I see, you're on for the backing. And hey,' she shouted after her as Gloria ran out the door, 'hurry up before this champers warms up – I'm *gasping!*'

Gloria found herself smiling – albeit on the inside.

⬭

The following morning Lorna was in at eight. She story-balled every business journalist with profiles of Big Fed-exed directly from his New York PR department, and sweet-talked every social columnist with details of Big's impending trip.

'The Party of a Lifetime, darling – no, *re-ally* – you have *no idea* how much money this man has and good-looking? Sure Pierce is only *trotting* after him! Elton? Sure don't be *talking*, darling, *of course* he'll fly in – EJ wouldn't miss this one for the *wor-ld!* Details have yet to be confirmed, darling – yes – yes, *exclusive* to you – oh *ab-sol-utely!* I'm telling you, darling get that' – depending on who she was talking to – Lorna always made mental notes of diarists' evening wear – very good politics – 'gorgeous sequinned jumpsuit/YSL gown/ Armani tux/little black dress I saw you in last time out of the closet and into the cleaners, honey. It's going to be the Event of the Millennium and it's going to be *soo-on!*'

The Chef's Table at top restaurant Gerry's Place was booked solid for the next fortnight with Cafferty Love-

Bomb Press Lunches, as the minions phoned and faxed and emailed until their little mitts were rubbed raw. Lorna even managed to fix up a radio interview with Ireland's Best-Loved DJ for Big to talk to the Listening Irish Public about his passion for All Things Irish, outrageously promising Randy Mac Rory that she would Redefine the Term Fellatio for him if he gave her this gig. She knew the badly jumpered midget would be too terrified *actually* to take her up on it and sure if he ever did, it would probably only take two minutes and it would be worth it.

It was *all* going to be, if she pulled this deal off, so, *so* worth it!

21

8.45 a.m.	Ms L. Laverty – Brazilian Wax plus legs
9.15 a.m.	Mrs Melanie Mufton – Stress Buster aromatherapy massage
10.00 a.m.	Mary Scanlan – electrolysis session (first)
10.45 a.m.	Francesca Dufée – mani and pedi

'No – I'm sorry, Flame honey, nothing before eleven today.'

Nylon ran his newly french-manicured thumb down the appointments book of BlueEriu, Dublin's most glamorous beauty salon and the Only Place in Ireland where you could get a full 'Brazilian', or 'Crack Wax' as Nylon rather crudely called it. Since Gloria's Gaff had started to look a bit shaky, and Lorna (before her New York triumph) had been teetering dangerously on the edge of becoming a Nobody, he had, reluctantly, sought gainful employment as a receptionist in 'Blue'. The first week had been fabulous. He had 'handbagged' over a hundred quids' worth of cosmetics, test-run two facials and blagged a full set of acrylic nails from Sharon by suggesting she 'could do with the practice'. In the last couple of days, though, since news of the Big Billionaire's impending trip, the place had gone mad. You couldn't get a facial this side of Longford, and BlueEriu was top of the list for most of the In the Know Crowd who were in the market for a rich husband.

'Nothing, babe. Really – *nothing*. I know! It's gone mad here! I don't know *what's* going on but my head's opened answering this shagging phone. *Whoops*, line two's off again. I'll stick you in for a Top-to-Toe at three. Yes, all right, honey . . . allergic to embryo – I'll tell her – no – I won't forget – bye now. BlueEriu – Sanctuary of Supreme Loveliness, how can I help you?'

When he'd finished, Sharon the beauty therapist was standing in front of him glowering like a frog with a grenade up her arse.

'What the *fuck* did you book Lynda Laverty in at that time for? Fanny at that time of the morning – *Jesus*, Nylon – and for *half an hour*! Are you joking? She's carpeted and creased like a baby rhino – it'll take me a good hour and fifteen!'

'That's what you're getting paid for, dolly,' he snapped bitchily before the next call came in. 'Hullo. BlueEriu – Put Your Face in our Fanny – Jesus – sorry. *Hands* . . .' He grimaced angrily at Sharon for putting him off his track.

'And fucking Mary Scanlan? My mate works out in the make-up room at Erin and she says her face is hairier than a hippy's armpit. I'll need a fucking pneumatic drill to get at those roots!'

'Oh Jesus, Lorna, thank God it's you!' Nylon put his hand over the receiver and waved Sharon away. 'Well, you'll just have to fucking *cope*, won't you! Now piss off and let me get on with my work!' He felt a small flush of pride at that last sentence. My Work. He had hardly noticed it but actually, that *was* what he was doing. Work. For the first time ever. It was kind of great.

'Sorry, Lorna – what can I do you for?'

'Nylon, listen, I know you're up to your eyes, but I've got a bit of a problem.'

'Booked out for Brazilians today, I'm afraid, Lorna, you'll just have to—'

'No, no – nothing like that. You know that big thick client of mine from Galway? Wallop? Paddy Wallop?'

'The guy that does the – *eurck* – incontinence jobbies?'

'That's the one. Well, seemingly he's coming up to town today and wants to meet me.'

'And you're too busy and you want me to put him off?'

'*Exactly*. Nylon, would you?'

'What's it worth?'

'A bottle of bubbly and my everlasting devotion.'

'Times two and you've got a deal.'

'I've told the girls to say I'll be in Blue at three – that's when he'll be in town, and I need you to pretend I'm tied up . . .'

'Shouldn't be hard.'

'No – *you know*, some sort of facial-gone-wrong, she'll-be-out-the-back-for-hours type thing. Just get *rid*!'

'Will do.'

'Nicely now, Nylon, remember he's a *client*. None of your "she-had-the-back-torn-off-her-last-night-and-she's -still-hungover nonsense".'

'I'll think of something, pet. Don't *worry* – Oh Merciful Hour of Jesus, will that fucking phone ever stop *ringing* – gotta go – Hello, BlueEriu, We Devote Ourselves to Your Delightfulness, how can I help you?'

Paddy Wallop pulled into the Brown Thomas car park at two fifteen. He knew he was early, but hoped to catch Lorna on her way into the beauty salon. He had tried calling her office, but the girl who answered said that Lorna was 'out and about' town all morning and had left her mobile behind in the office, but that he could probably catch her at three o'clock at her beauty salon, BlueEriu on South William Street.

Paddy had been trying to contact Lorna for weeks now – ever since he had read that terrible thing in the paper about her losing all that money. He wanted to help, but he knew (or rather he *thought*) that Lorna was a woman of great pride and integrity and would not take his money as either personal help or charity. (The idea of handing over three-quarters of a million as 'a token of love' as suggested to him by his friend and Romantic Advisor, François, was rejected with the requisite amount of horror one would expect from a Respectable Rural-Reared Roman Catholic Man.) Paddy had therefore concocted in his mind a plan which involved Lorna taking on exclusively the Global Public

Relations Contract for Wallop Medical Supplies World-wide – the advance for which would be seven hundred and fifty thousand pounds, then an annual fee negotiable after that. Paddy had convinced himself that it seemed a reasonable enough offer, but it was notwithstanding the fact that, to date, Lorna had achieved for him only one brief humiliation in the national press, and exactly nothing after that. This was something that bruised Paddy deeply, although he was loathe to admit Lorna's part in it. A few weeks previously he had seen the headline 'GO BRAZILIAN IN THE BLUE' – a full-page article in one of the Sundays giving a graphic descrip-tion of the salon's new Brazilian Wax treatment. Paddy failed to see how the brutal plucking of the entire female nether region was less offensive than the very real and essential service that he provided for people with actual medical conditions. The 'Brazilian' was certainly not essential, it didn't sound to him like a 'pampering-beauty-salon-type-experience' and unless one was suffering from pubic crabs, Paddy didn't really see the point of it at all. (His opinion was undoubtedly shared by the likes of Judge Mufton and Lynda Laverty's pet cat who were two of the first witnesses to the results of Blue's new service. The Judge declared his wife looked like a badly plucked pheasant, and threatened to hang her up by her CK G-string in the garage until it 'grew back'. Fifi took two firemen the best part of an afternoon to coax down from the guttering and back into the house, where she then sat mewing mournfully in the corner, refusing o eat her boiled liver and bacon dinner especially prepared by a distraught Lynda.)

To kill time, Paddy wandered around the bustling elegant interior of Brown Thomas. He found himself getting worryingly lost in a maze of Ladieswear and was most relieved when he found himself back in the relative androgyny of the Household department on the second floor. Paddy decided to use the opportunity to treat himself to 'one of them carpooch-ino machines' on the advice of Consultant Interiors Expert to the Rich (as she had rather ambitiously emblazoned on a faux gold plaque outside her house to attract business in the unlikely event of any other Important Notables moving to Bunkelly), Clara Fitzcronin.

The array of goods on display was too much for Paddy to comprehend (being as he was in a heightened state of Jitters at the prospect of impending proximity to the Great Love of His Life) and so he wandered to the nearest customer desk.

Behind it was an extremely friendly young woman who said, 'Hullo. I'm Róisín. How may I help you?'

Such was the warmth, the *sincerity*, of her manner, that Paddy's faith in Snooty Dublin Shop Assistants was temporarily restored.

'I'd like a coffee machine, please.'

'Oh – I'm sure we can manage that for you, sir . . .' she said, beaming brightly from her bosom to the sunny balls of her cheeks.

'Now if I can just take your name and address, sir?'

Paddy was a little taken aback.

'Is that necessary?'

Róisín laughed merrily.

'Oh *yes*, sir! We want to know *all* about you and your house so we can help you fulfil all of your home-making needs. After all, this should be the most *Important Shopping Experience of Your Life!*'

Now, Paddy had been to America. He'd been around the world, and shopped in a few places, but he'd never experienced anything like this.

He laughed nervously.

'It's only a coffee machine that I want. A cappuccino machine – one of those Italian ones.'

Róisín smiled so wide, Paddy thought she might offer to sell him her teeth.

'Oh, sir! There's no need to be quite that *modest* in your requests. Why, we have a *broad* selection of goods available in our service. All types of things. To suit all price ranges. We have beautiful bedlinen ... and if a whole cappuccino machine is too expensive, well then people can just settle for a single plate? Or two of a set of champagne flutes? Why, you'll have a full complement of dinner-ware in no time. You know?'

Paddy did not know and was certain now that this girl was smiling because she was, very possibly, insane.

'All I want is a cappuccino machine. Can you get one for me?'

Róisín was still smiling.

'Of course, sir. I'll tell you what. You fill out your details on this form and then – ' she looked around her conspiratorially, for the men in white coats, Paddy guessed – 'I'll take you around the shop *myself* and we can fill out the list *together*.'

Paddy took the form.

'Really, I don't want to fill out any list. All I want is a—'

Róisín winked at him knowingly, fondly even.

'Of course, I understand, sir. You want to wait until your affianced . . .'

Affianced? Forms? Lists? Paddy looked down at the sheet in his palm and read 'I DO. HELP US HELP *YOU* MAKE YOUR DREAMS COME TRUE!'

He looked behind Róisín's happy, Oh-So-Happy-for-You face and saw the same slogan etched on the white partition wall underneath two words emblazoned so big they seemed to fill the whole world. Two words which only a thundering eejit (or a man with his mind on Other Things) could have missed. WEDDING LIST.

He backed out, assuring the lovely Róisín he would be back with his fiancée the following day, almost toppling a display of Designer Mugs in his rush to get out.

The experience discombobulated Paddy somewhat. The Bleak Complex Poet who lurks behind the simple, laid-back exterior of every Galway man was hip to the terrible irony of it all and giving it loads of Oh Woe Is Me and If Onlys. But the positive thinking Paddy, the man who had – albeit out of Quiet Desperation – picked up *Carpet Your Soul With Love* by 'Love Advisor to the

Rich and Famous' Dr D. Ashman at an airport bookshop after his last trip to America, chose to see his brief encounter with acute mortification as a Possible Sign. Perhaps, one day, he *would* be in Brown Thomas? With his beloved Lorna? Fingering bedlinen? Colour-co-ordinating mugs? Ruminating over the good and bad points of various cappuccino machines? Why not? Stranger things had happened. Here comes the bride, all dressed in ... Paddy put a lid on it and reverted back to the modest domain of the Galway man If Onlys before he lost the run of himself. Positive thinking was all very well and good as long as it didn't force you into doing something you might regret afterwards. Like declaring your intentions to a woman who was way out of your league and making a Big Thick of yourself into the bargain.

Wallop arrived at BlueEriu at exactly five minutes to three and looked in. There were glass shelves lined with cosmetic concoctions. At least he presumed them to be cosmetic, but nothing would surprise him of a place that was able to bewitch women into parting with good money to have the Godgiven 'protection-fur' ripped out by its roots. Every available surface was shimmery blue glass, and lit up from behind with eerily cold strip lighting. It did not look like the sort of place where a man might walk in on his own enquiring about the whereabouts of a woman to whom he was not betrothed. Behind the desk, to the left of the door, sat a kind of a 'crea-thure'. Paddy could not tell from peering through the clear glass 'B' in the largely smoked window if it was a man or a woman, but 'it' kind of had the mark of one of those Parisian types that wore lipstick and were overly interested in men's bottoms.

Paddy decided that, under the circumstances, it was probably best to stay where he was, so he stood around outside, hopping from foot to foot and rubbing his hands in nervous anticipation. In a few minutes, Lorna would come along, and they would 'accidentally' bump into each other. Then, after she had been into the salon and had her he-didn't-want-to-think-about-it treatment, Paddy would meet her back here and whisk her off for a slap-up cream tea in The Shelbourne Hotel on Stephen's Green. They did scones and cakes there that came on tiered platters and all manner of interesting teas – Earl Grey, Darjeeling, even that yellow camomile stuff. Would Lorna drink camomile, he wondered. Maybe with a slice of lemon? She seemed like the sort of woman who looked after her figure. Sure, she needed a bit of fattening up. Looking after. He'd talk her into a scone just this once. Show her he was the sort of man who wasn't fussy about a few extra pounds. Make her relax a bit with herself.

The facts that Paddy's daydream had distracted him from were:

(a) Lorna had not eaten a scone, cake, or in fact any dairy product since 1981, and would not dream of ever indulging in anything so pedestrian and dull as a cream tea, in The Shelbourne Hotel or otherwise. Her street cred would be in ruins at the mere suggestion.

(b) Lorna was, at present, on the other side of the

city being wooed by a bevy of estate agents who were pitching for her impending purchase of the property in which Big would hold his Inaugural Irish Party, and would not be showing up for an appointment which, in fact, had never existed in the first place.

(c) Paddy Wallop, due to his impressive physique, was a conspicuous and all-round Obvious Lurker.

(d) There was a guard watching him with great and grave interest from the opposite side of the street. (After the 'GO BRAZILIAN AT THE BLUE' headline, a group of young men had taken to gathering around outside the salon and ambushing exiting clients with verbal assaults such as 'Give-us-a-goo-at-yer-gee-missis!')

At ten past three, there was still no sign of Lorna, and Paddy was shuffling and checking his watch. He began to spin it around and around on his wrist, his eyes darting nervously up and down the street. Once or twice, he peered in through the 'B' in the window to check that she hadn't slipped in there without him noticing. He started to mutter – a habit not unknown amongst men who live on their own in a big house in the middle of nowhere, but not one likely to impress a young Guard who had just come off a long stint on traffic duty, and was only longing to 'apprehend' a stalker or potential serial killer so he could be a hero and appear on the TV show *Crimeline*.

Paddy stood at the door, his hand pushing in and pulling back as he tried to decide whether to go in. As he did, a statuesque redhead pushed past him with a loud, and not entirely polite, '*Ex-cuse me!*' and Paddy found himself inside, having been caught up in the backdraught of her mighty door-swing.

'You're late, Flame,' the 'crea-thure' said.

'Fifteen fucking minutes – big deal!' the redhead said.

'Is there a problem here, sir?' said Guard Collins – who had rushed across the road when he saw the Conspicuous Lurker follow the Gorgeous Redhead into the salon.

'Well – *actually*, Guard – yes there is.' Nylon was a sucker for men in uniform, and the Big Farmery Type standing behind Flame looked like he'd know how to Nail a Dublin Queen to Her Cross and say a decade over her lost soul into the bargain!

'I've got two manis and a facial waiting, and a lady out back in tears with a strip of wax stuck to her butt and not one therapist left with the courage to pull.'

Guard Collins looked at the apparition behind the desk, at the glowering redhead and the Gormless Stalker who suddenly looked the less threatening of the three.

'I don't suppose you fancy having a go? Or is that a job for the Firemen?'

Nylon then turned his attention to Wallop.

'Mr Wallop?' he asked.

Paddy nodded speechlessly.

'I'm afraid Ms Cafferty is going to be tied up for some time' – Paddy fought against the image of His Loved One lying on a cold slab with a strip of wax glued to her Unmentionables – 'but she specifically asked me to apologize on her behalf and said she would call you in the morning. Flame?'

'Listen here, you filth—'

'You can sit and wait for that one, sweetheart. You need *us* more than we need *you* today! Guard – if there's nothing else – you're clogging up our delicately set air-conditioning system with your testosterone so – nice and all as it is – if you don't mind?'

Guard Collins and Paddy made a speedy exit and walked in opposite directions down South William Street, both despairing in their own quiet ways.

Flame took her seat with reluctant obedience and started to flick through last month's *Image* magazine for evidence of her importance in their social pages.

Nylon – well, he hadn't had this much fun in ages. Flushed with the magnitude of his own efficiency, he decided that he was beginning to enjoy this whole work thing.

He might even consider taking it up for a living.

22

Liam, for all he had been impressed with Lorna's pitching technique, was sceptical about her ability to pull this whole thing off. Despite her sass and savvy, Liam felt pretty sure that Lorna did not *fully* understand the magnitude of either Big's ego, his outrageous wealth, or his ability to surround even the simplest of tasks with a circus of people.

Undoubtedly, the star of Big's circus – the person who wore the crown and the tutu – was Sugar.

When Liam called the office to get dispensation to stay in a hotel (and away from the Weightwatchers posters, 'My son's home!' hysteria of his mother, and endless harassment by Maeve), he was told that Big's Personal Lifestyle Advisor, Sugar, was on his way to make sure that 'Mr Big's Integrity of Image' was being preserved – especially with regard to 'the purchase of an Irish home that suits both his needs and best displays his wealth and good taste'.

Sugar was employed to make sure that Big was seen to be a Man With Taste That Befitted His Position.

Xavier had no taste – that was undisputed.

The problem was that Sugar, according to Liam at least, had no taste either.

To Big's credit, he often chose to ignore Sugar's advice that 'pink is *in* this season', or 'pleated shirts are *the* latest business wear' or, alarmingly, last summer that 'the sarong is the *new* trouser'. Big had his work clothes custom-made by the Donegal tailors Magee and stuck steadfastedly to Irish linen / cotton-mix shirts (although he did own a large collection of alarming sport-slacks which Sugar, to *his* credit, was longing to burn or bury).

However, when it came to Homes and Interiors, Entertaining and Image, Sugar's word was law. Another thing that never came into question was Sugar's absolute devotion to Big. This was the man that had hauled Mammy Big out of the kitchen and onto a chaise longue, teaching her how to run a home in the manner of a Rich American Socialite as opposed to a pot-boiling aul' one. He had introduced her to the best hairdressers – transmogrified her wardrobe and her face through haute couture and surgery. Mammy Big had spent the last ten years of her life valiumed up to the eyeballs with boredom, listening to Songs From Home on her Bang and Olufsen and dreaming about the days when she was allowed to cook herself a decent pile of spuds in *her own* kitchen. But she had mixed with Kennedys and died in Valentino – that was the important thing. Out of loyalty, Big had kept Sugar on. He was one of the Big family and as such was fiercely protective of Xavier and deeply suspicious of fly-by-nights like Liam and 'This Cafferty person? Who *is* she? Have I ever *heard* of her? Is she *related* to Rose K.?' Rose Kennedy had been Sugar's Mistress before Mammy Big and a Close Personal Friend. The name Kennedy was 'Irish' in the only palatable sense of the word. Anything else was just muck and potatoes.

That Sugar had taken such an active interest in the whole Image for Ireland thing was good news for Big, but bad news for Liam. There would be no bitching or piss-taking over the next few weeks. It would be all work, work, work.

Standing a squat four foot eleven with bleached blond hair and wearing his 'signature' white kaftan over matching cotton pants, the man himself did not look unlike a sugar cube. As he pushed his trolley into Arrivals, Liam could barely see his head above the Louis Vuitton mountain that seemed to be wheeling through by itself.

'Fucking economy' were the first words he uttered as Liam hopped around the disembodied trolley catching and reinstating bricks of tumbling Louis V.

'Did you not travel Business?' Liam bit his tongue, but it was too late. As Big's unofficial 'Auntie', Sugar was the only person in the organization who went out of his way *not* to actively waste Big's money. ('Couture,' he often insisted, 'is *never* a waste of money. Junior secretaries lunching at The Plaza *is!*')

The trolley came to a dead halt and anyone watching might have wondered at the young man listening nervously to a pile of bags as if they were talking to him.

'Now – before you even open your mouth, you nasty

little free-loading bog-boy – you listen to me and you listen *good*. *I* am in charge of this gig – not *you* – and who's this Cafferty *nobody* person whom you appear to have magicked up out of nowhere?'

'I'm sorry, Sugar, I—'

'Booking yourself first-fucking-class to Ireland – I checked – I checked – oh yess! *First-fucking-class* from America to Dublin, you jumped-up little fag, who the fuck do you think you are and hey! I suppose you'll be wanting to stay in a hotel next . . .' Sugar was given to bouts of extreme verbal abuse, largely due to chagrin at the fact that he was in charge of *nothing* except for Big's (albeit large) collection of boxer shorts and had managed to get to fifty-odd without ever so much as peeking outside of his closet door – hence 'fag' and 'queer' being his favoured terms of abuse. Today, however, Liam was to be subjected to the verbal rigours resultant of a seven-hour economy flight with his Long-Flight Prozac Supply trapped in the luggage hold. Screwing up his face into a spiteful gurn, Sugar squeaked out in a mincy, bitchy voice, *'Oh excuse me, sir . . . I'm afraid we're all booked up at The Royal Hotel Important for Fancy Young Secretaries . . . perhaps you can call back later and we'll see if we can find you a suite for five hundred dollars a night, sir!'* Sugar started to wheel the trolley blind at high speed, fuelled by the power of what was rapidly turning from turbo-annoyance into a psychotic episode. 'Christ, you little faggots make me sick! You little turds, with your fancy words and your smarmy suits – you're only out for one thing! Xavier's money! His money! That's all you ever think about!'

'Xavier said—'

The trolley came to a speedy halt, a falling vanity case almost decapitating the head of a small child who was innocently passing.

'WHAT? What did you say?'

'I said, Mr Big—'

'You did NOT! You called *him* by his first name. How DARE you! How DARE you call him that! You don't even *know* him! You are NOTHING! Do you understand? N-O-T-H-I-N-G! Spell it, Big Brain Bog Boy!'

And so it went on. All the way to the taxi rank. All the way out of the airport, through Drumcondra, Phibsborough (to the delighted amusement of the taxi driver who kept fuelling Sugar with incendiary questions like 'Where did ya get tha' dress, wha'?'), down Parnell Square and O'Connell Street until, *finally*, by the time they got to Lorna's office in Temple Bar, the Prozac they had scrabbled through his cases to find had kicked in, and Sugar had run out of vitriol – for the time being at least.

Liam prayed that Sugar would like Lorna. She was no bowl-of-fruit herself, but he could not bear the thought of going through the whole drama with Sugar alone.

Once again, he had underestimated the Archduchess of Public Relations.

Lorna, on hearing of Sugar's impending arrival, had

sloughed through Big's cuttings again – and there it was: 'Pictured in the Manhattan Penthouse of Xavier Big Is Interior Designer Sugar Duprés.' A six-page, glossy, full-colour interiors feature in *Harper's Bazaar*. All she needed.

As soon as the buzzer went, the minions were sent downstairs on luggage patrol. Lorna perched herself on the edge of the desk, and as soon as the blond munchkin walked in the door, she held out her hand in a dramatic point.

'There. He. Is.'

Sugar looked around confused.

'Stop! I want you all to look. Girls?' (Three sets of pretty minion eyes looked at her with the dull exhaustion of those who had heard-it-all-before.) 'Liam?' She wagged her finger to the beat. 'There. He. Is. Do you see him? I want you all to have a Good Long Look.' The atmosphere was afloat with anticipation. Even Sugar was silenced.

'There . . . *there* is the man who decorated that apartment that I have been *talking about for months.*' Then she hopped down from the desk, her eyes moist with admiration and respect.

'Girls. This – *this* man is the one I have been talking about. Haven't I been saying If Only I Could Meet That Man? That – no *this* – ' and Lorna waved her hands across in a dramatic ringmaster's sweep – 'is the sort of person, the kind of *brimming* creative spirit that I Can Work With!' She took a step towards him. 'You still don't know, do you? You still don't know Who You Are. The Manhattan Penthouse of Xavier Big . . .'

'*Harpers and Queen*, May 1998.'

Sugar was grinning so wide that tooth nudged ear.

Lorna marched towards him and took his hand in both of hers.

'Mr Duprés, I am so – pleased seems so small a word, can I say honoured? Can I?'

Sugar shrugged, barely hiding his euphoric delight.

'Well, it is. It is an honour to meet you. Welcome, welcome, Cead Mile welcomes to Ireland.'

Lorna had won again.

In the next hour, the three of them got down to it. Rifling through the details of castles and stately homes for Big to buy and for Sugar to decorate.

'I see open fires!' he exclaimed.

'Absolutely!' agreed Lorna.

'I see . . . I see . . . acres of gardens lit up by night!' he cooed.

'Oh yes – *ye-ess!*' orgasmed Lorna in agreement.

They settled on Ballynafiddy Castle in Galway. A beautiful eighteenth-century castle that had been restored lovingly and sensitively to its former glory. Liam left the two blondes as New Best Friends.

'Now, Sugar – I am going to take you out for lunch. On *me*.'

'I *like* this woman. You see, Skip? Not everyone in the world eats on *expenses*!'

Little did he know.

'I've taken the liberty of drawing up a list for the party, Sugar. Music, food, marquees – that sort of thing, and I can run through the guest list with you too. And, Sugar?' She touched his arm with blistering sincerity. 'Nothing – *nothing* – gets done without *your* approval.'

'Sounds like you have it pretty much under control, Lorna – seems like I won't have to do much more than maybe tweak things round a tweensy-weensy bit?'

Little did *she* know!

Liam walked out onto the streets of Temple Bar feeling like he could breathe again. Dublin looked so different. When he had left Ireland for London almost ten years ago, this area had been a run-down badland, full of empty warehouses and rubbish-strewn alleyways with resident lurkers. Now it was a mix of contemporary and cobblestones; the warehouses converted into trendy apartments – probably inhabited by young men like him. He realized, with a kind of bleak reality, that he had nowhere to go and nothing to do. Dublin was a place where you shouldn't need to make plans. It was a city that had always run on the rules of parochialism. A place where socializing started when you bumped into people you knew and the evening just went from there. If you were at a loose end you would take your paper into a pub, order a pint and sure enough, an old school friend or work mate would drop in and join you for one. But suddenly, this place felt unfamiliar to him. Not like the Dublin he had left behind. Even the architecture and the pubs were different. What was it Sandy had said? 'All chrome and cappuccinos'.

He wandered around Temple Bar, and, when he started to feel like too much of a tourist, Liam found himself gravitating towards a place which, to him, represented the zenith of his lonely despair – a bus stop on Dame Street where he could join a vehicle full of pensioners who were also on their way out to Stillorgan, and back home for a nice cup of afternoon tea.

How sad – how *pathetic* his life had become.

23

Gloria had tried to get Frank to meet somewhere neutral, but he was having none of it.

'You can come around to the house tomorrow morning. I'm a busy man, Gloria, I don't have time to be running about after you.'

Gloria knew there was no use arguing with him. She needed Frank to sign this legal agreement entitling him to half of the earnings of Gloria's Gaff on South Anne Street, and no more. She hoped that he wouldn't suss she was planning to expand. He was a crafty bastard, and if he didn't sign this – she was stuffed. Under the current agreement as managing director, he could take half of everything, which meant that the new venture backed by Lorna and her American financier would be a complete waste of time. Frank was cute enough to want to meet her on his own turf. She just hoped he wouldn't make her grovel. Gloria didn't give good grovel. But in this instance, she hoped she wouldn't be driven to it. There was a lot riding on him signing this piece of paper.

She took a deep breath as she stood outside the two-storey sea-view luxury apartment block in Sandymount and rang the bell.

'Frum hup.' A muffled voice that sounded like it could be female came through the intercom, then the door buzzed open.

A creature with a horribly bulbous and deformed face opened the door to Frank's apartment. She looked as if, perhaps, in another universe she might have once been a fashion model, but today her face resembled a pile of badly peeled potatoes.

'Thwaglot are flu sglaring ah?' Flame said through a mouth full to bursting with her new outsized tongue. One eye had disappeared under a swollen, puffy bag of flesh, and the other glared out angrily through its spiked lashes. It was *very Clockwork Orange*, and if Gloria hadn't been so comforted to see the disarrangement of the face of a young woman who so dearly deserved a few days of disfigurement, she might have been scared.

Frank appeared behind the gory apparition. He was wearing a black suit with all the trimmings – tie, cufflinks, the works – and had a new goatee which, to Gloria's trained eye, looked like it had been filled in with mascara. He was also wearing a pair of sunglasses. Indoors. In his own house. He was styled in the image of Lucifer, and Gloria knew him well enough to know that the new image was designed for her benefit. To intimidate and frighten her. He looked ridiculous, but Gloria knew enough never to underestimate her ex-husband. The satanic garb may not have had quite the

Sunken Cheekbone menace he was aiming for, but it was a sign of his intent – and the David Bowie As Satan look was rarely a good sign.

He nodded his head towards Flame.

'She had a facial yesterday and was allergic to one of the products. Fucking goat's embryo or something. She forgot to tell them—'

'I fwucking fold flat flick Gylon!'

They looked at her bewildered.

'I fwucking fold him! I fwucking fwid!!!'

Frank looked back at Gloria.

'We're going to sue anyway. Don't worry, love, it'll be back to normal by tomorrow,' and he touched her arm.

'Oh Fwuck og!' and four pounds of red curls bounced into the bedroom, slamming the door behind them.

Frank gave Gloria an apologetic smile. He was embarrassed, Gloria knew, that his arm-dolly wasn't looking her best. He always made a point of being affectionate towards Flame when Gloria was around. Probably because they both knew, on some level, that part of him, with his own exclusive brand of selfish dysfunction, was still in love with his ex. His wardrobe, along with his demonstrative touching of Flame, was, in part at least, defensiveness. But Gloria still knew not to let her guard down.

'So what's this piece of paper you want me to sign, then?'

Gloria didn't know whether to play it up or down. If

she played it down – pretended it was nothing important – then Frank might get suspicious and start looking around for the small print. If he as much as suspected there was more to be had, he'd start rummaging around her business with the vigour of a rat running through Egon Ronay's garbage. On the other hand, if she played it up, as if it was really important, he might get thick with her. Refuse to sign for no good reason except to annoy her. Gloria decided to opt for the latter. She was able to handle a fighting, truculent Frank better than a cute, crafty one. Gloria was a What You See Is What You Get merchant. She liked to be able to see the blows before they landed.

'It's a formality, Frank, but it *has* to be signed.'

'Saying *what*, exactly?'

'Saying nothing you don't know already. That you own 50 per cent of the business in South Anne Street, and that's that.'

'What is it you're saying, that I've been taking more than my share?'

'No, Frank, I'm not saying that, it's just that . . .'

Frank may have been a lying, cheating, lazy, coke-snorting, glove-puppet-fucking loser, but he still had his pride. He was no scrounge!

'I'm no fucking scrounge, Gloria. I worked *hard* for that money. That business is as much mine as yours.'

O Sweet Merciful Mother of Christ, save me from going over there and turning that lying scumbag's testicles inside out on themselves, thought Gloria. The lousy bastard was the living embodiment of scrounge, and no man ever more deserved to have his manhood whipped through a Moulinex than Frank Doyle.

'I know that, Frank. I know. It's just a bit of paper, y'know? Just to make things formal.'

Then something happened. Frank still had the dark glasses on and was standing square in front of her like he was blocking her from coming any further into his space. But Gloria could sense something in the way you do once you have been married to someone, when you feel you know them better than they know themselves. Even when you don't. Even when you are just second-guessing love; when you imagine an intimacy that is unspoken, sometimes even though it isn't there at all.

'I'm tired, Frank. I don't want to fight.'

Frank was shaking slightly. She could see his hands quiver as they reached up to take off his glasses. He rubbed his eyes and his body slackened. Gloria felt sure that he would do this thing for her. That despite everything, or perhaps because of it, Frank was ready to take one small step in her direction.

He held his hand out and Gloria handed him the document.

He looked down at it, kneading his temple with his free hand.

Gloria adjusted her handbag on her shoulder and rubbed the top of the arm that held it. She was trying not to look as nervous as she felt. She couldn't let Frank see how important this was. How much she *needed* him to sign.

After a few seconds, still looking down at the paper, he said, 'I'll look into it.'

Gloria's stomach tumbled over on itself.

'Frank – it's just a formal—'

He looked up at her and she could see rage bubbling through the red exhaustion of his eyes.

'I said – I'll fucking look into it, o-*kay*?'

There was no point in challenging him further. She'd lost. Whatever shred of loyalty she had been hoping for, whatever bit of admiration or love she thought she held in her armoury against him, was gone. Gloria realized in that moment that she had been telling the truth. She was tired and she didn't want to fight.

'All right, Frank. We'll leave it to the solicitors, then.'

Frank nodded and looked away again. He couldn't hold her eye. For all of this, Gloria still knew he was afraid of her. Everyone knew what Frank was. The suits and the spending were fooling nobody except, and only sometimes, himself. Everyone went along with him, his flashy mates, his dealer, Flame, the girls at the agency. They did that because, ultimately, they didn't give a shit. His lifestyle helped Frank to fool himself, but when your life's a sham, a lie, sometimes fooling yourself is the only thing that keeps you going. When Frank looked into the honest face of his ex-wife, he saw all that he was reflected back at him. He knew that somewhere, underneath it all, Gloria saw something that was worth believing in. That was why he had married her, because of who he had wanted to be. Gloria, in her fighting, in her working, in her honest, genuine ways was everything he had ever hoped for in himself. When his lies had got beyond his own control, Frank had left her. He had to. Now he had to fight her every step of the way to keep that lie alive. To make it real.

Gloria knew that if Frank had just signed that paper, he would be losing – not the grand business opportunity that he didn't know existed, but the lie about who he was. Without the lies, Frank Doyle had nothing left. Without them he couldn't survive.

As Gloria left Frank's apartment she felt finally beaten. Frank had broken her heart long ago and while the wound had far from healed, it had at least been sewn together with tiny threads of hope. His refusal to help her in even this one thing had unpicked the final chance she thought she had.

For all that, Gloria didn't even feel like she could hate him. Perhaps that was the worst thing of all. For today, at least, Gloria O'Neill's fighting spirit had flown.

24

This whole Billionaire Documentary Programme thing could *not* have been going any better. Sandy had received a call the day before from the producer of the *Rory Mac Rory Show* tipping her off that Lorna Cafferty had arranged an interview with this Big Shot American Wife Hunter. Was it the same guy she was doing the documentary on and would she like to sit in? Sandy put in a call to Maeve to check if Liam, as Big's assistant, would be going along to the broadcast. She figured it would give her an opportunity to grill him about Big without raising suspicion. Get a few insights about him that might help her. The *Rory Mac Rory* team had been asked to pretend Sandy was still working on the show to preserve her undercover status. If Liam knew this was all a ruse, he might go on the turn and deny Sandy access to her Big introduction.

'Can I come – please, please, plea-ase!' crooned Maeve down the phone.

'No, Maeve. Liam's coming because he is Big's PA, but the producer said maximum two people.'

'I can't believe you are taking this all so seriously, Sand.'

'What do you mean?'

Sandy wanted to get Maeve off the phone quickly, but she felt as if there was something coming that couldn't be rushed.

'Well – this whole Mr Big thing. I kind of got the impression the other day in The Morrison that you were – well . . .'

'What are you talking about, Maeve?'

Sandy started to feel nervous and she didn't really know why. She kept her voice light and slightly irritated, but was conscious at the deliberateness of it.

'Look – I know you would never do anything to hurt me, Sandy, and I know that you would never go after the same guy as me . . .'

'Too right, you've got terrible taste . . .'

'It's just that, well . . . I suppose I'm kind of scared. Scared that he'll like you better than he'll like me . . .' Maeve's voice sounded small and vulnerable – as if she really was worried.

'Don't be ridiculous, Maeve. No man has ever chosen me over you—'

'I knew it! I *knew* it! I was right!'

Shit! Sandy hadn't seen that one coming. Christ, but Maeve could be a manipulative bitch at times. Her voice sounded triumphant and angry. Not a good combination.

'I knew you were after him. "Sandy Nolan Fools

American Billionaire to the Altar." That's it, isn't it? Your Big Chance documentary. And who am I in all this, eh? Where do I fit into this cunning little plan? Fucking bridesmaid, is it?'

Sandy should have known better. Maeve was her oldest friend and could read her with the speed and accuracy of a cheap women's magazine. Sandy had two choices now. Come clean and lose out on her first real crack at solo success. Or lie.

'Actually, Maeve, you *couldn't* be more wrong.'

'Oh really?' Her voice was heavy with hurt and sarcasm.

'Yes, really! As a matter of fact, I was going to make you the focus of the documentary. I didn't tell you before now because I didn't want you acting up. I knew you'd ham it up. You're such a drama queen.'

Maeve was silenced. She had been sure she was right, but if there was one thing that Sandy Nolan wasn't, it was a liar.

'Sorry.'

'So you should be!' Sandy's face was grimacing with the effort of maintaining her horrible deception, doubling the strain by trying to keep her voice light and flippant.

'I'll call you later.'

'Right. Can I go and do my job now?

'Sure . . . Oh – and Maeve?' Sandy added, just before they hung up. 'Not a word to Liam, yeah?'

'Schtum – I promise.'

'We have to keep him believing I am genuinely interested in netting Big – otherwise it's no intro, no party, no go.'

'Gotcha and hey, Sandy?'

'What?'

'It's great all this undercover work, isn't it?'

'How so?'

'All this subterfuge – lying – *kind of fun!*'

'Yeah,' said Sandy flatly, 'it's great all right.'

When she put the phone down, Sandy rested her head in her hands and breathed through some justifications in her head. There was no way this documentary could be about Maeve. It would dilute the whole thing. Sandy had to be at the centre of it, otherwise it would lose that first-person heavy-duty undercover edge. Maeve would make it too light and frivolous. She would wriggle out of it somehow. She still had a few weeks. After all, if she really thought about it, this was just a game to Maeve. Marrying a rich American, the great girlie drama of it all. But it was Sandy's career. And that was far too important to have jeopardized by Maeve's silliness. It might undermine the No Make-Up Hairy Clever reputation she was determined to carve out for herself.

Liam was quite happy and excited, actually, to be out at the ENB studios. Or rather, that was the Ashman version. The real version, the *true* version, was that he was pathetically grateful to be not eating a 300-calorie

Weightwatcher meal, with his increasingly doting mother asking him *again* if he had *really* once seen Rose Kennedy *in the flesh* getting out of a limo and being wheeled into Tiffany's. He was also happy to be enjoying this afternoon without the company of the Lorna/Sugar double act. A new and not-very-beautiful alliance that had been forged between Ireland and America, and one which had resounding sound effects taking the form of false hee-haw bouts of laughter and a constant stream of camp humming.

'Hummmmmmmm. Lorna – Tartan or Prince of Wales for the dining room?'

'Hummmmmmmm. Tartan! Prince of Wales, darling? This is *Ireland*!'

'You're right!'

All together now . . . 'Hee-haw-hee-haw-hee-haw.'

Liam had been demoted to the position of minion over the last few days by a delighted Sugar who had convinced himself, with the aid of Lorna, that he was Finally in Charge of Something Important. Without back-up from Big, Liam was in no position to object. Besides, he had nothing else to do each day except munch low-cal snacks and watch *Altogether Now!* with his mother in the afternoon, and even Slow Death By Sugar was better than that. So Liam had been answering phones, booking builders for Ballynafiddy, calling in fabric swatches for the New Themed Traditional Irish Decoration Extravaganza Sugar was planning for this listed historic house, and generally wearing a path to the cappuccino shop across the road – an hourly errand he welcomed as it got him out of the oestrogen-charged offices of Cafferty PR.

Liam had also been looking forward to seeing Sandy again. Since he had heard that Mr Big was to be interviewed on the show he (still believed) she worked on, he had become almost certain that her reluctant entry into his Wildcats and Colleens file had been some sort of scam. Perhaps it wasn't Maeve who had put her up to it at all. Perhaps it had all been an 'act'. She was investigating Big for her job or something. Anyway, he was looking forward to seeing her, and there was the germ of an idea forming in his mind that perhaps the two of them might continue the bit of flirtatious banter they'd started in The Morrison.

Sandy was looking great. She knew it too. She had just felt, that morning, like getting herself done right up to the nines. As she did, whenever she made the slightest effort, Sandy Nolan had managed to hit a ten.

'The Look' today was a new one. If Clarissa von Biscuit (pronounced Bis-cay), renowned social columnist and all-round Irish Fashion Baroness, were trying to define it she would have described it as 'No-Make-Up-Hairy-Clever-Goes-to-Hollywood'. Smart, but glamorous. Intelligent, but stylish. Clever – but with hair in all the right places (i.e. on head. No moles, no armpits, no tash, and *definitely* tidy but basically still intact 'downstairs').

The wardrobe was London – but nothing that would cause offence. Understated Ladylike as opposed to Psychiatric Fashion Victim. Knee-length Agnès B skirt, beige; black Smedley polo, cashmere; fishnet Wolford's; Hobbs' mules, not hobbly high but not blue-stocking flat either. The make-up was No Make-Up, its only compromise to fashion being a good dribbly dab of Oatmeal lip gloss that made Sandy look like she could snog a camel without touching tongues. And the hair? Darlings! The hair was, *of course*, the Julia Roberts' Tendrils – and the sight of them sent a headline to Liam's 'something' story shooting straight from his testicles up to his head. The headline was 'I Love My Sister's Best Friend Sandy' and the story was 'Brilliant Alcoholic Novelist Meets Stunning Redhaired Journalist and They Both Live Happily Ever After in a Caravan on the Athlone Bypass'. (The story itself needed work, he realized – but the headline was definitely a winner!)

Sandy swept into the studio as if she were in charge, which she had told Liam she kind of was, and the others had told her they would cover for her.

Rory was just finishing up the last item. Hairy Mary had followed Sandy's lead, and had just done a review of a recently published edition of Sylvia Plath's diaries.

'Well, Mary, that was very interesting. Our Sylvia certainly sounds like she was a bit of a handful there . . .'

'Thank you, Rory.' (The few weeks back on Children's TV had put manners on her.)

'. . . and we'll finish off with a track from one of my fave bands – here's Dr Hook and the Medicine Show with "Sylvia's Mother Says".'

Rory gave the thumbs-up to check the phone line where Big was holding, and the technician turned to

Liam to see if he wanted to talk to him for a few seconds while Doctor Hook was playing out. Liam declined rather too vigorously with a shake of his head, and the musically discerning production team fell into a solemn, shamed silence as they often did when Rory made them play one of his Fave Tunes.

'Now, I have a man here on the phone who is looking for an Irish wife. Is that right, Xavier?'

Rory deliberately omitted to mention that Big was one of Irish America's Most Successful Businessmen, as Lorna had told him. He didn't like people richer than him fishing in what he considered to be *his* pond. His attempt to do a sneaky put-down was quashed as soon as Big made his opening address.

'Cé chaoi bhfuil tú, Ruaidhre?'

It had taken Big twelve hours with a retired Professor of Celtic Languages from Harvard to learn how to say 'How are you, Rory?' in Irish, but, to his credit, he said it to such a standard that it sounded, certainly to Rory's untrained and panic-stricken ear, as if there were plenty more where that came from. Rory went straight into Americans Are Lovely Overdrive.

'So, Xavier, I believe you are One of Irish America's Most Successful Businessmen – a Billionaire, no less. Goodness me – that must be a very interesting job!'

The interview took an upturn after that.

'Well – I sure am, Roor-ee –' it was how he pronounced it anyway – 'but you know what? I am still Irish and proud of it.'

Rory was still nervous that this fucking mental

American might revert back to *As Gaeilge* and start talking about the Struggle or the Famine or some other incendiary topic that might blow his ratings out of the water. So he let him rattle on about his mammy and his Big Paddy Festival and his aborted attempt to have the Statue of Liberty remade in Waterford Crystal. Once Big got started, there was no stopping him. He forgot he was on the radio and started to chat away as if Rory were his New Best Friend. He talked about how he longed to meet a Modest Irish Colleen like his mother and shower her with all the love, attention and diamonds that a man of his stature could afford. He was a man of simple tastes, he assured the nation, and would love to meet an untouched Celtic country girl with red hair and quiet unaffected ways. (Wouldn't we all, thought Rory, giving that bint Sandy a sideways sneer.) Big also talked about how the voice of that Great Irish Singer Ber-nard Heffer-naan could move him to tears. He seemed astonished that Rory had never heard of him, and offered to send him a copy of his latest single, 'O Sweet Mother Ireland' – *'It's a beau-tiful track, Roor-ee. It was written about my own mother – not by Ber-nard, he hadn't the honour of meeting her, although I'm sure they'd have got on. No, it was written by'* – Liam tensed visibly and prayed – *'a Good Friend, and, Roor-ee – guess what? Hey – I'm comin' over!'*

Oh fucking marvellous, thought Rory, looking at the clock. He had to wind this nutter down now, he was already four minutes over on the item.

'Great, Xavier – well, it's been lovely talking to you – thanks for calling and now—'

'Yeah – we're having a Great Big Party down there in a place called Gal-way? In an old castle? I bought it? I haven't seen it yet, but it sure sounds great! Really old? Big gardens 'n' all?'

'Well, that really is super, Xavier – and now we have to . . .' Rory gave the cut-him-off neck slice to the production suite, but Barry, the new guy, had his head buried in a sausage roll and missed it. Sandy gave Liam a little smile, and he thought his heart would explode.

'Hey! Maybe you could come down and do the music? You being a top DJ an' all? I'll make it worth your while – Oh man! I gotta go, my therapist just arrived – all right – ALL RIGHT! – gimme a minute! It's been really great talking to you, Roor-ee – I mean it. I'll see you when I come home and hey! Make "Sweet Mother Ireland" a hit over there for us, willya? It sure would mean a lot to the Irish folks over here. Bye now!'

Rory did not like being referred to as a DJ.

DJs played records and he was much more than that. He was a Celebrity. But money was money, and he would get his agent to call Lorna and negotiate an outrageous fee for Big's party gig. And besides, Lorna Cafferty had promised him that blow job.

Sandy asked Liam if he wanted to pop to the ENB canteen for a quick lunch.

Now that he had become aware of his feelings for Sandy, Liam found himself treating this casual eating experience with the seriousness of a First Date. It was, of course, out-of-the-*question* to actually *ask* Sandy out on a date, for all sorts of reasons. Primary among them being that Liam would need *at least* a couple of months ruminating over where and when, and torturing himself about how-he-wasn't-worthy, and what he would do if she said no, and fantasizing about what might happen if she said yes, and generally working himself into a state over the whole thing. Who knows, if he worked it hard enough – he might be able to knock a couple of half-decent love poems out of the whole thing without having to go through the torment of the actual dating itself. After all, there was nothing like a bit of unrequited love to get the old creative juices back up to speed.

Besides, Liam, despite his attraction towards the self-flagellating Yeatsian approach to romance (keep-coming-at-her till she kicks you down, then write a 'pome' about it), was essentially a Modern Young Man, and tended towards the Take No Chances Method of Courting. This involves just loping around in the general vicinity of your loved one, being neither one thing nor the other, as regularly as you can over as long a period of time as possible. Then all you have to do is wait for her to either (a) get really drunk one night and lunge at you because you happen to be there, or (b) read a wimmin's magazine article on 'Why Friends Make the Best Lovers' and decide to come after you herself. Once she starts turning up to meet you in little more than a bra and knickers and learns to stone cherries with her tongue to impress you, then you *know* it's safe to make a move.

However, Liam was going back to America in a couple of weeks and it would be churlish of him not to turn this opportunity to impress Sandy with his urbanity. So, as they arrived in the sprawling Formica greyness of the unlovely prefab that housed the ENB canteen, he searched around for a corner table-for-two, preferably one with a linen tablecloth and candle. In the absence of same, he eventually had to settle for one near the window that offered a little natural light and wasn't strewn with empty yoghurt pots and polystyrene cups laced with fag holes or butts floating around in a half-inch of cold coffee, but not before expressing his genuine disgust at the overall 'lack of ambience'.

Liam pulled Sandy's chair out for her, puffing slightly at the fact that there were crisp crumbs on her seat and a dribble of old mayonnaise on the table.

'This is disgraceful!' he exclaimed, grabbing a listless young kid with a dishcloth in his hand and making him remove the crumbs with a limp swipe. Sandy was mortified.

Once he had complained about the fact that the canteen was self-service, Liam insisted that Sandy stay where she was, and he would bring her food down to her.

'Now – what would you like?' he said in the grandiose manner of a man with money in his pocket and a Little Lady to spend it on.

Sandy wished she hadn't asked him. Jesus – America had really got to him. What a pain-in-the-arse fusspot!

'Anything – something light.'

'Rightio – a light lunch. Vegetarian? Any allergies?'

She had work to do this afternoon. Why the fuck was he making such a big deal out of this?

'No – *anything* – really.'

With no guidelines, Liam stood for ages looking at the curled sandwiches and grey/brown slop on offer under the plastic counter. A large Woman in Plastic Cap and Navy Tabard came to assist Liam in deciding on his selection. Except it wasn't just an ordinary selection any more. In the last few minutes, the 'light lunch' which Liam would bring back to Sandy had become the Most Important Decision of His Life.

'Yes?' said Doreen, who was five minutes over on her shift, and anxious to get home and have a right good go at her corns, which were killing her.

'Do you have something light? Nothing fancy – just something like, *sa-aay*, a nice goat's cheese and char-grilled pepper salad?'

'No.'

'Hummmmmm. Right. Something green, then – how about avocado? With perhaps a little rocket?'

'No.'

Doreen had been Candid Camera'd a couple of years beforehand – hence her reluctance to use one of the many colourful expressions of discontent that were currently rampaging around under the plastic hat.

'No avocado?'

'No.'

'No crab?'

'No salad.'

No salad! This was a disaster! What was a 'light lunch' if it wasn't salad?

But the vengeance of Doreen's unpaid overtime on her weary corns had just begun.

'We've got chicken curry –' she spooned some brown slush around in Stainless Steel Basin One – 'beef stew –' ditto brown slush in Stainless Steel Basin Two (she had long given up trying to pretend it deserved the title boeuf bourguignon) – 'then we've got sausages, a few eggs' – Liam's stomach turned as she saw five eggs swimming slowly towards each other in warm grease like a gang of warring amoebas – 'and the chips, I'm afraid, sir, are finished for the day.'

By the sarcastic look that Doreen had swiped across her face, Liam guessed, correctly, that there would be no point in him asking her to see if she couldn't whip out back and get Chef to drum him up a lightly cooked mushroom omelette with fresh herbs, shitake or otherwise.

He wandered, hopefully, down to the basket of Prepared Sandwiches. Cheese and pickle or ham and cheese. The plain cheese sandwich had a single lettuce leaf squelched against the polystyrene wrapper, so he went for that.

In the meantime, Sandy was frantic. She had a load of phone calls to make, and had to edit down that morning's Big interview. This lunch was her chance to have a good chat with Liam about Big, and talk about the whole Irish-American thing – otherwise she'd have been long gone. What was he *doing* over there? Preparing the bloody thing himself! (Oh, little did she know how he would have wished it.) Bloody fussy nancy was probably looking for de-caff this and low-fat that. Typical American codology. He really was a right jumped-up fairy – with his Prescriptives for Men and his making people wipe tables for him. Who the hell did he think he was? God had no right to make Liam Murphy as cute as he did. He should have set the girls straight by matching his outsides to his insides with a pinched-up ugly-old-lady face and a proclivity for spandex tops – because that's what he was *really* like. Sandy was annoyed with herself for checking out Liam's Levi-clad buttocks at the food counter. She must have been out of the game too long if she fancied an idiot like him.

Twenty minutes later, Liam came back with two sandwiches and two bottles of water. Sandy, by this time, was *famished* and would have *inhaled* a plate of Doreen's Best Beef Stew with chips. When Sandy was hungry she needed hot food and when she didn't get it she got irritable. Being already *highly* irritated by waiting *half an hour* for this *halfwit* to score her a *cheese sangwich*, she was instantly onto Phase Two on her Irritation Monitor which read as Downright Aggression. She snatched the sandwich and tore into it with an enthusiasm that filled Liam with a temporary (*very* temporary) delight.

When she had devoured half of it, she noticed Liam

staring at her with what her grandmother used to describe as 'sheep's eyes'. Sandy hated people watching her eat. She was a fast, messy eater and one of the few things she had enjoyed about living alone was that she could dribble and scoop and burp and swipe and chaw and chew as loudly and as sloppily as she liked without some finicky, hygiene-obsessed bloke giving her googly looks across a table. Liam was at this point, naturally enough, wondering if she could attack a mere cheese sandwich with such . . . such *passion*, such . . . such *vigour* – what on earth must she be like in bed? Sandy, however, felt as if she were being judged, and decided to put him in his place.

'You were a right mean little prick earlier.'

Liam, his reverie having been so rudely interrupted, looked around to see who she could possibly be addressing.

'Yes – YOU – Mr Lovely Skin 2000! I said you were a right mean little prick, shaking your head and making faces when Big was being interviewed. I saw you . . .'

It was him! She was talking to him! And she was being . . . being . . . *horrible*!

'You wouldn't even talk to him before he went on air. I thought that was really rotten of you – not to give him any moral support. Really small and mean and . . .'

Liam went into a kind of trembly shock. A few hours ago he would never have let *any* girl talk to him like that – and he'd met a few humdingers in his time. But this was Sandy. After he'd gone and fallen in love with her! And bought her a *sandwich* and everything!

'. . . petty. Really petty and mean of you. I don't know why either. I mean, I thought Xavier sounded like a lovely guy – down to earth, really nice. In fact, I can't wait to—'

'Excuse me.'

Liam had gone pale. He got up from the table and walked out of the canteen. His legs buckled under him as he searched for the little room marked FIR he had seen on the way in. When he got there, he sat down in a cubicle and he did something that he had not done since he was a small boy. Something which shocked him to the very core of his being. Something which made him feel sick and shaky and very, very alone in the world. Liam Murphy cried.

With some kind of terrible truth he realized that this wasn't a game any more. He realized that he had reached a place where he had always wanted to be and yet he didn't want to be there at all. Sandy Nolan had been spiteful to him, and he hadn't wanted to fight back. Worse, he hadn't been *able*. She could say and do what she liked, and it wouldn't make any difference to how he felt about her. He felt weakened. By the living in America, by the not being able to write – but most of all, by his feelings for Sandy. Although they were new and they had come out of nowhere they were like *bam!* Pull the lid down on the No Pride Coffin and throw away the key.

He'd get on with it. He knew that. He'd go down to Ballynafiddy and Big would either fancy/marry Sandy or not. He would go back to New York, to his loft, and his wardrobe, and all of it. But it wouldn't be the same without the dreaming. And somehow, Liam knew, his dreaming days were over. Anything that Liam wanted, he dreamed about. He had hoped to dream about Sandy, to make her part of the whole fake world of what he wanted, his ideal of the man he might one day turn into, the life he always hoped he might have. The ferocity with which she had shown him how little she thought of him had cut those dreams off at the pass. All that was left in the place where his fantasies had lived was a black hole of grim reality.

Sandy Nolan had swiped the dreams, which Liam had so carefully placed under his feet, away.

25

Lorna had hoped to be able to get away with *something*.

Of course, she would have put together the best possible party for Big anyway. Of course she would have. It was her job. She was good at it. She took pride in her work. She was a great party organizer. The best.

However, she had not been planning to hit quite the level of Extravaganza/National Event/Party of the Century that Sugar had in mind. But she had to keep the Mother Superior of Camp happy, especially if she was going to keep him distracted from all of the behind-the-scenes business dealings she was doing. And *especially* as there would be no adding 15 per cent onto the costs of catering, DJing, etc. In fact, Sugar did not see why anyone should be paid at all. When it came to spending Big's money he was as tight as a mouse's ear.

'I mean, this is Xavier *Big* we are talking about here, Lorna! One of the most High Profile Men in America. It's an *honour* to be serving him.'

Lorna would nod grimly in agreement, shake her head at the Disgraceful Realities of the Consumer Age in which we live, complain at how good, old-fashioned Irish Hospitality was, sadly, 'a thing of the past' and then get Sugar to sign off on ten grand's worth of canapés.

By the second week, Lorna was beginning to feel like they were joined at the hip. Sugar worked thirteen-hour days, and when they were finished, he insisted they eat and 'hang out' together. Working with him was one thing, but Lorna did not think she could take another night listening to Rose Kennedy anecdotes. It was time to call in the heavy artillery.

'Nylon,' she said from the virtually strange comfort of her own home where she had barely been for the past ten days, 'I need you.'

Nylon took some convincing, which surprised her. Entertaining an American Queen was just the sort of lazy, highly paid gig he liked – but he seemed reluctant to give up his new job in BlueEriu.

'What's my job description?' he asked.

'Getting him off my back.'

'Sorry – I am currently Receptionist and Hostess at Dublin's Most Exclusive Beauty Emporium, I couldn't possibly move for less than, say, Public Relations Executive and three fifty a week.'

'Cash?'

'Certainly.'

'Done.'

Nylon was briefed that his new boss was locked in the closet, and there was to be no feather or leather flaunting. She needn't have worried.

'I've unlocked more doors than you've popped champagne corks, dearie. Leave him to me.'

The two of them were instant buddies. What with Nylon's newfound work ethic he responded delightedly to the whole bossy Mother Superior thing. 'Nail me to that desk,' he said on Day One, 'and *punish* me with work!' Sugar was impressed.

When Sugar came in on Day Two with his exhausted eyes badly disguised with concealer Nylon took him aside.

'No-no-no,' he said, digging in his bag. '*Too* obvious.' Sugar's horror on being caught wearing make-up was immediately amended as Nylon whipped out his YSL Touch Éclait and proceeded to do the *best* cover-up job on his boss's bags.

Sugar's delight at finding another 'straight' man who saw *nothing* wrong with wearing a little concealer and lip gloss meant that Lorna was, for the time being at least, off the hook.

On her first day of freedom, Lorna called Gloria and the two women arranged to go shopping.

They met outside the main entrance of Brown Thomas on Grafton Street, and the doorman doffed his cap to the two women on their way in. Lorna, delighted to be away from the office, was full of confidence and glamour and ready to go to war with her credit card.

Gloria, on the other hand, looked like shite.

'You look like shite,' said Lorna.

'I'm not really in the mood today, Lorna. Can we not

just go down to the basement and have coffee?' Lorna was already marching through Menswear and making for her very own Stairway to Heaven – Ladies' Designer.

'No way. The party starts *now*, Gloria – there are thousands of frocks in our vicinity, and we're not leaving till we've tried on a fair portion of them. Besides, what kind of a friend would I be if I let you go another ten minutes looking like Woman Without a Wardrobe.'

'Am I *that* bad?'

Lorna stopped at the bottom of the stairs and looked at her.

'Well – the shirt could do with a rub of the iron, but mostly, you look like you've had the devil himself hanging off the end of your face all night. What's the matter?'

Gloria's face crumpled and she started to cry. Lorna took her arm.

'It's that prick again, isn't it? Oh come on, Glor, you can tell me about it over one quick coffee, then, I don't give a shit what he's done this time – you're coming up those stairs for the Gucci Cure.'

Gloria told Lorna about her attempts to get Frank to sign the agreement. Lorna promised to 'get my solicitor onto it tomorrow', but with her record in Unreliable Accountants, she didn't hold out much hope. However, she was grateful to have somebody she could let it all out with. Somebody she could trust. Lorna had a hard-nosed glam-queen image, but somehow that made Gloria feel closer to her. As if they were both misunderstood.

'The main thing is, Gloria – he is OUT of your life.

Cheesing it up *somewhere else* with that ghastly orange-haired baggage – oh bollocks.'

Lorna's phone rang.

'Won't be a sec . . . Hullo? No, I needed to speak to Sam himself. I've an important "do" happening down in Galway next week and I was hoping he might be able to fix up The Trembling Celtics for me? No – I know they're booked for the next year . . . yes I know that . . . Oh *Jesus*! Just tell him I called and get him to call me back a.s.a.p. Yes, Lorna Cafferty. No! Caff-er-ty. Tee! Right. Good-*bye*. Christ. Fucking rock-chick groupie secretaries. I've been trying to get hold of that bastard all week. Sorry, Glor, what were we saying?'

'Is that Sam Cohen? The record producer?'

'The very man. Why? Do you know him?'

'Yes he's a . . .' and Gloria found herself struggling for a word to describe the part that Sam played in her life. He had called her last night, and she had snapped down the phone at him. He had seemed well meaning and upset that Frank was being difficult, but at the end of the day Gloria knew where Sam's loyalty lay.

She settled for 'friend'.

'Oh Gloria – this is *great*! Is there any way you could persuade him down to Ballynafiddy with you next weekend and by-the-way bring the Biggest Rock Act in Irish History with him?'

Gloria was sorry that she had said anything, but Lorna had been so kind to her that she agreed, not to ask herself, but to let Lorna use her name as an influential contact.

Even though Lorna was asking Sam for the impossible, and he had no reason to do her any favours, especially after the way she had spoken to him last night, Gloria had the strangest feeling that Sam would say yes.

⬭

Sam rang the bell to Frank's apartment. He was nervous as hell and he didn't know why. That morning he had persuaded Gloria's solicitor to fax him a copy of the agreement she needed signed, and he wasn't leaving here until he had Frank's paw-mark on the bottom of it. As he was waiting for a reply, the Redhead emerged from the front door in a cloud of powdery scent.

Sam Cohen may have been small, and he may have been bald, but he was one of the most powerful men in this town and a veritable babe-magnet for ambitious young models who were keeping their options open in case they ever got it into their heads to become the next Madonna.

Flame practically doffed him on the head with her cleavage.

'Hi, Sam.' Then she just stood there pouting and wriggling about in her dress *thanking God* that her face was back to normal and *cursing Him* for not making Sam arrive a few minutes earlier when she could have answered the door in her Invisible Glossy G-string and bra.

'Hi, Flame,' he said with minimum politeness and pushed past her into the building.

'Little bald fuck,' she muttered after him.

Flame had bigger fish to fry. She had heard that Lorna Cafferty was organizing this American Billionaire gig. She knew better than to go knocking on *her* door, given that she was all chummy with that bitch Gloria these days. She had phoned that ignorant little shit Louis in New York and given him a right roasting. He told her that there was some kid from Big's office over in Dublin who might give her a way in. Flame was determined. If she had to blow off half the United States of America, she was *going* to that party.

Frank was still in bed when Sam rapped on the door and called through, 'It's only me – Sam.'

Frank answered the door naked, with Mr Aussie clamped to the end of his flute.

'Da-daaaa!'

Frank had not imagined Sam would be particularly impressed, or overly amused to the point of hospitalization, but he had not expected his old mate to take quite such a po-faced attitude to his amusing little intro.

'Get dressed, Frank. I want to talk to you.'

'Yeah-yeah.' Frank turned and wobbled his hairy naked buttocks in a brief jokey gesture before wandering over to the fridge and grabbing a bottle of tonic.

'*Whoops*, tonic – on its own, Jeeves? At this time? Why, sir, I believe it is gone midday and is therefore the Cocktail Hour Chez Doyle . . .' He grabbed two glasses from a shelf overhead and turned sideways to give Sam a view of Mr Aussie in profile. 'Reach into the cupboard there, Sam, and get out the gin, there's a good man.'

Sam got the bottle, and grabbed Frank's dressing gown from the sofa on his way over.

'I won't have one and here – ' he thrust the robe at him – 'put this on.'

'Woooah! What's up with Mr Baldy-Locks today?'

They had that sort of friendship. The sort of friendship where they could wander about with cuddly toys on the end of their mickeys and drink beer for breakfast and talk about getting it up or not getting it up without worrying about what the other bloke thought of them. They were more brothers than friends, although Frank was the one who took primary advantage of their level of intimacy. He was the one who did the crazy things and Sam was the one who bailed him out. Frank was the one who started the fights and Sam the one who forgave. Frank was the one who was needy – needing money; needing help; needing reassurance. Sam was the one who always paid.

But today, for the first time in their lives, Sam needed something. He needed Frank to sign this piece of paper, and leave Gloria alone. He needed Frank to know that he was in love with his ex-wife and give him his blessing to go after her.

'Put it on, Frank.'

Frank plucked the toy from his groin, threw it aside, put on the gown, poured himself a drink and they both sat down at the kitchen table. Frank rubbed his forehead.

'My head's fucked today.'

'I need you to sign this thing for Gloria.'

Frank looked over at Sam's face. He had a pen clicked open in his hand and was holding it out to him. He pushed the papers from Gloria over towards Frank. His jaw was shivering.

'What the fuck is this?'

Frank's voice was angry, but already it held a hint of disappointed betrayal.

'I need you to sign it for me, Frank. I've never asked you for anything – I just want you to do this thing for me.'

'For you? You *need*? What the fuck ... did *she* put you up to this ... ?'

'No, Frank. Gloria didn't—'

'Gloria? So what is this crap – *fucking* Gloria? That nobody little slag, I—'

'Don't talk about her like that, Frank.'

'No!' He stood up and walked across the floor as if he was afraid to be any nearer to Sam in case he lost control of himself.

'No. Fuck YOU, Sam! What the hell is this? You're *my* friend! How fucking *dare* you let yourself be *manipulated* by that jumped-up common slag ...'

Sam wasn't really aware of what he was doing. One second he was in the chair trying to reason in his own mind ways of making this all work without compromising his friendship with Frank, the next he was standing over a groaning pile of naked flesh and towelling robe holding a sore fist.

For a split second Sam considered picking him up, then he realized that his desire to do so was just a stupid reflex. That was what his friendship with Frank had become over the years. A reflex. He hadn't actually liked the guy, in all honesty, for a long time. So he hadn't succeeded in getting Frank to sign Gloria's papers, but perhaps punching his lights out was a step in the right direction.

The tide was out and Sam walked part-way home along Sandymount beach. He realized that Gloria had been right to keep him at arm's length. Her rejection of him, her suspicions, were not about her not trusting him. They were about Sam not having been sure.

But Sam Cohen was sure now. One hundred per cent sure about what he wanted.

All he had to do now was figure out a way of getting it.

PART FOUR

THE BiG EVENT - WEDDiNG OR WAKE?

26

Xavier Big did not do things by halves. One of the reasons why he travelled so seldom was that, essentially, Big was a home boy and did not like to leave behind the little comforts and the people in his life that gave him security and a sense of belonging. And so – he brought them all with him.

The detailed list which Liam had been requested to submit to the Customs and VIP Security unit on call that day therefore went as follows:

Mr Xavier Big – *American Tycoon*
Mr Chuck Jordan – *Chief of Security*
Ref: Above (team of five bodyguards – names to come)
Dr David Ashman – *Professor of Love Carpeting*
Mr Carter Strange – *Dr David Ashman's Personal
   Assistant*
Mr Bernard Heffernan – *Entertainer*
Mr 'Friendly' Patterson – *Mr Bernard Heffernan's friend
   and associate*
Dr Franz Sherlock – *Cryogenics expert*
Ref: Above (team of five technicians – names to come)

(Mammy Big had been cryogenically frozen and while Xavier had finally come to terms with the fact that she was no longer – strictly speaking – alive, he still had enormous difficulty describing her as Actually Dead. The freezing process was a halfway measure in his gradual Emotional Journey to Acceptance as he was able to think of her being, while not in the fullest of health, at least as still 'Fresh'.)

Mrs Ita Big – *plus freeze container*
Miss Dolly Grumble – *manicurist*
Mr Bert Grumble – *barber and hair stylist*

. . . and on and on times several dozen.

It took almost an hour to check them all through Customs, and Hairy, who was travelling with his drinking associate Friendly, almost got sent home. The journey had been declared a 'Dry Trip' by Big, and lack of alcohol manifested itself badly in our erstwhile crooner. Friendly had lived up to his name a little *too* admirably with regard to what he referred to as the 'Air Hostages' (a term which had caused some discomfort amongst Chuck and his crew) but was also anxious to sample the delights to be found in the nearest hostelry by the time they hit the ground. Suffice to say that being asked to 'settle down' and 'queue in an orderly fashion' were not instructions that sat well on the shoulders of either Hairy or Friendly and cross words were exchanged. Big himself was unaware of all this, as he had been immediately whisked into a Private Hospitality Suite being as he was both Enormously Important and Highly Emotional at Coming Home.

Liam, too, was highly emotional, but not in a good way.

Sugar and Nylon had travelled down some days earlier to prepare Ballynafiddy for its master's inaugural visit, and Lorna had 'bags to pack!' and 'legs to wax!' and 'people to see!' The implication being 'Deal with it, squirt – you're the PA.'

Therefore, the whole Big Entourage Arrival at Airport Project had been left in Liam's hands. Maeve had offered to take a couple of days' holiday from work to help, but he was having none of it. The last thing he needed was his younger sister standing at Arrivals in some class of a disgraceful outfit trying to hit it off with his boss.

He needn't have worried. Maeve in a bikini with a big banner saying MARRY ME, BIG BOY would have caused no notice with the bedlam that was currently ensuing.

For the past two days, Liam had found himself being stalked by a very tall woman with long red hair. If he hadn't been so (a) upset about Sandy (b) gutted at the shallow disappointment that was his life and (c) *not* looking forward to the coming circus with such acute anxiety, he may have been flattered by such a good-looking (almost model-material, actually) female taking such an active interest in his movements. She had tried to pick him up in the cappuccino bar next to Lorna's office the day before, but his level of obsessive self-pity had precluded him from taking her up on her 'generous offer' and just resulted in a buttock-clenching blushing embarrassment that did not bode well for Liam's hopes of ever having sex again.

Now here she was again today, at the airport, sitting in the coffee bar behind him, nursing a bottle of water and staring intently in his direction. Once he had realized who she was, Liam was steadfast in his not looking, although he had hardly recognized her, as Flame had traded in the usual high-glam image for a simple sprig print dress, bare legs and no-make-up make-up. However, Flame's Julia Roberts effort did nothing for Liam but remind him how miserable he was over Sandy. And he did not have time to be thinking about that right now.

Right now, Liam Murphy had a more immediate and pressing problem.

That problem was the one hundred or so Textbook Irish Colleens who had formed a solid scrum around the Arrivals ramp.

Along the front row, holding aloft a banner emblazoned with the words CEAD MILE FAILTÉ, MR M'aaOR, was a gang of women in Traditional Irish Dancing costumes. Of varying heights and ages ranging from fifteen to fifty, they were fully bedecked in green velvet triangular skirted frocks with felt Celtic symbols and gold trim. They were the ones that had their mothers with them. The break-away Riverdance Rebels took up the row behind them, and were distinguishable by the sporting way in which they had crammed eighteen years' worth of hearty country dinners into Lycra bodysuits with little swing dance-skirts on top. They bravely jostled for position in the second row behind the Traditionalists, some of whom had been waiting there since the night before, and were Going Nowhere.

On their own, and even given the sign, they could have been the Kerry Branch of the Michael Flatley Fan Club on a day out were it not for the third row who Liam, in his own mind, had already labelled the Mercenary Milkmaid Contingent. These were obviously women who had taken Big's radio interview to heart, and had kippered themselves up to look like Irish-American Wet-Dream Colleens. A veritable *mountain* of red hair suggested that there wasn't a box of hair dye left in a chemist on the whole island. These women had pulled out all the stops. GONE were the Imported Italian Heels. GONE were the Miss Selfridge boob tubes. GONE was any sign of fake fur, sequins, Lycra. GONE the great designers Gucci, Treacy, Rocha, Keogh. Gone! Gone! Gone! It was as if that most modern of phenomena, the Celtic Tigress, had devoured herself and this shawly red-haired rabble were setting the hard-won notion of Irish Fashion back one hundred years.

If the Baroness of Irish Fashion Media, Clarissa von Biscuit, had been there, she'd have called Brown Thomas for an emergency delivery of Fendi baguette bags and run amongst them with a Mac lipstick and a phial of Lancôme Micro Paillettes glitter.

Liam, alas, was not feeling that resourceful, and had he had the benefit of Baroness Biscuit's expertise to hand, he might have felt more confident about loosening up this pond of ever-thickening oestrogen jam before his Lord and Master drowned in it on his way through Arrivals.

As the sliding doors slid back, Liam spotted Chuck

standing at the security desk mumbling into his earpiece looking *very* FBI in a dark suit and glasses and rather *too* obviously like the bodyguard of an Important American Notable. Just as Liam was panicking about the impending Rosy-Cheek Riot that was sure to happen, the Tall Redhead appeared, as if by osmosis, at his side. She grabbed his arm with a sharp bony hand, and motioned Liam masterfully to an empty square foot at the edge of the Arrivals ramp, then in an authoritative (and frankly dominatrix) whisper said, 'They don't know what he looks like – follow my lead.'

Before Liam had the chance to say 'Leggoa my arm, you mad bitch.' Flame had thrown herself forward into Big's Personal Space and was loudly pronouncing 'Eric! Darling! How was Milan? Don't mind this lot, they're waiting for some American to arrive.'

Liam would have assumed, at this stage, that Chuck and his chums would have had her wrestled to the ground in an arm-lock and the Guards called to carry her away. But Chuck was one step ahead and had himself been wondering how they were going to get Big through the mash of females waiting for him. In all likelihood, Big would have waved, the women would have cooed, and that would have been that. But this was exactly the kind of dramatic subterfuge that affirmed Chuck's need to think of himself as a man in a job which meant that he Diced With Death on a Daily Basis and made him feel less bad about his (even more) macho friends who worked in NYPD thinking he was a nancy.

'You saved our bacon, missy,' said Chuck as they got

outside to where Big's hired limo was waiting. 'Yessir, missy, that sure could have been a tricky situation right there and you sure as hell saved us.'

Yeah – like what, Liam thought, American Billionaire Crushed Underfoot by Irish Dancing Shoes? Visiting Dignitary Suffocated in a Fog of Floris? Liam might have enjoyed a few more short seconds of Cynical Overview, if he had not had the job of organizing this vast entourage through Customs and into a series of minibuses and limos without compromising the growing queue of irate taxi drivers whose rank had been blocked for the past hour and a half.

And so it was while Liam was overseeing the insertion of Mammy Big's frozen body into an especially customized meat transportation lorry that Flame was able to slide seamlessly into the back of their hired limousine.

For the first few minutes, Big didn't even notice his glamorous gatecrasher. From behind the smokescreen windows that so often separated this important man from the rest of the world, he drank in his first view of Ireland.

As the men in white paper suits carried the metal coffin out of the airport terminal, Big's eyes filled with tears. Almost inaudibly, he whispered the words that, underneath it all, were what this trip was all about, 'We're home, Mammy. I've taken you home.'

27

There was no way that Sandy was going up to that party without Maeve. Maeve had sat and watched while she rang Lorna Cafferty and asked if she could bring an assistant. Sandy felt a bit of a failure having to blow her cover by ringing the PR Queen and telling her she was doing a story on Big, but since Liam had stormed out of the ENB canteen, she knew there was no other way she was going to get there.

The two girls were in Maeve's bedroom, packing the last of her wardrobe into a large suitcase.

'I still don't understand your whole thing about this guy, Maeve, I mean, joking aside—'

'You fancy my brother.'

Maeve was pissed off with Sandy always shifting the focus on to her. She had a funny feeling about this American and she just wanted to run with it. If Sandy was going to hound her over it, well – two could play at that game.

'Wha-at!'

'You do – I saw you checking out his arse at the airport – you fancy him.'

'I do NOT!'

'*Oh Liam, everywhere's gone mad trendy . . . it's so ironic* I heard you – trying to impress him with all that pseudo-clever-chicky-I-lived-in-London bollocks. You were giving him the once-over.'

Sandy was bright red. Furious, but kind-of-speechless at the same time.

'As a matter of fact quite the *reverse* is true!'

'*Quite the reverse is true.* You fibbing fairy – you fancy him and that's that and frankly – I think it's disgusting!' (She didn't really, but Maeve hadn't had this much fun in ages. She had only thrown it out as a stupid red herring, but now it looked like it was true. This was great!)

'I don't even like him.'

'Oh no – of course you don't. You hate his guts . . .'

'Well, as a matter of fact—'

'Ah yeah . . . he's a stuck-up pseudo who thinks he's something really special with his Prescriptives for Men and his Looking Down His Nose at Americans even though he lives there.'

Sandy was surprised at Maeve putting her brother down like that because, usually, she was fiercely loyal but she had to admit she was right.

'Yes, and his—'

'God, Sandy, you are *such* a *cliché*. All that I-Hate-Him-But-I-Love-Him-Really stuff. Straight out of Hollywood. You fancy him you do, you do, you do – admit it and be done!'

'I do not fancy Liam.'

'Do.'

'Don't.'

'Do fancy my brother – do, do, do!'

'Don't!'

'Do.'

'Don't.'

All the way down the stairs, into the car, out past Heuston and onto the road for THE WEST.

Before Mullingar they pulled into a service station for lunch and drew a temporary truce while Sandy went to the toilets to freshen up.

While she was applying a smidgen of Invisible Lip Gloss, Sandy caught her own eye in the mirror and something occurred to her. Why was she doing this? For her career obviously, but really? She wasn't interested in Big, beyond getting a good story out of him – and Liam? Did she like him more than she was letting on? She looked at all of her cosmetics spread out on the Formica shelf in front of her, the careful tendrily way she had put up her hair that morning. Why? What was the point of it all if not to have a bit of fun, enjoy herself. Flirt, flit about the place looking pretty. Perhaps she was taking all this too seriously. Maybe Maeve was right – perhaps she did have a pole up her hole, and should loosen up a bit and take life a bit more as it came? The truth was that Sandy was afraid to let go. Afraid that if she let herself relax and allowed her Inner Disco to take over, she wouldn't know where she might end up. At least if she kept focused on her work, Sandy believed she could keep control of where she was going. If she let some fly-by-night Yank-brother-of-her-best-friend get in, she would end up getting hurt. Especially one as cute as Liam. He was sure to be trouble. But somehow, as she saw her not-quite-thirty face looking back at her in the mirror, she felt like it didn't quite fit. It was round and pretty, not sharp and angular like a proper Hairy Clever's face should be. Sandy did not look as serious as she felt, and it had always disappointed her. She felt as if her pretty party girl looks let her down in a way. They were unrepresentative of her ambition to be Taken Seriously as a Great Journalist. For one moment, Sandy allowed herself to imagine what her face, framed in feathery red hair, with its small, delicately etched features, and its open friendly eyes, might lead her into if she just let it be. Into the arms of a billionaire businessman? Or his assistant?

She snapped herself out of the daydream with a reminder that she did not want the first, and that she had blown the second one good and proper only a few days beforehand.

Then she marched back out to her oldest friend to defend herself in the good fight against fancying her brother.

28

Gloria had not wanted to go down to the party at Ballynafiddy, but Lorna had called around to her the day before and insisted.

'You'll enjoy it. Champagne on tap, darling – and you know what these Americans are like – it'll be oysters for breakfast, dinner and tea. No expense spared.'

Gloria was not a big fan of oysters, and was not feeling in the most glamorous of spaces. Two days locked in her flat with the phone off the hook, a bottle of gin and the TV for company was all she felt fit for.

'Can you not just do the deal for me, Lorna? Do I *really* need to meet this Big guy myself?'

'Yes you do, honey. Strictly speaking, I could do the deal without you, but a pretty face behind the cheque never hurts, and besides – he's looking for a wife. If you get that scraggy head of yours sorted out before Saturday, you could be in with a chance.'

Gloria wouldn't even stoop so low as to reply to that one. She knew, or rather she hoped, that Lorna was joking. Interest levels in that department had hit an all-time low.

'But what about the salon?'

'Stuff the salon, Gloria. Two days without you won't kill them, and anyway, from what I have seen of you lately, you've been neither useful nor decorative in that salon for weeks. You need the break – I insist. A few days queening it up with me will do you the world of good and besides – ' it hurt Lorna to say it – 'I could do with the support myself. To tell you the truth, I'm a bit out of my depth with this one.'

Gloria put her listening face on, but Lorna didn't have the time or the inclination to expand.

'Will you come?'

Gloria caught the barely discernible look of anxiety behind Lorna's heavily made-up facade, and conceded.

But now that they were on the train to Galway, Lorna looked at her friend's drawn face staring motion-less out at the grey mist of the Irish countryside, and began to regret her choice of travelling companion. Lorna's life depended on being a sparkling, splendid hostess for the next two days, and the wet weekend sitting opposite her was contributing nothing to her party mood. As it was, Lorna was fast running out of laughs herself, and Gloria was beginning to look like middle-aged-misery made flesh. At this rate the two of them would be alighting at Athlone and flinging themselves in the Shannon.

Lorna decided to get on with it, and snapped open her mobile to pick up her messages. She wished she hadn't bothered. There were seven – *seven*, no less – messages from that wretched Wallop, urging her to call him back as he had some 'urgent business' he wished to 'discuss' with her. Yeah, she thought, a new Outsize Range on his revolting incontinence pants, no doubt. Lorna was not up to it today. She had enough to do keeping this nut Big happy, and dealing with the string of misery sitting opposite her, without her other clients chasing her down. Determinedly, she picked up and dialled Paddy's home number, knowing he would be at work and hoping his machine was switched on. The signal on the train was atrocious, and the voice on Wallop's machine kept breaking up. Lorna thought carefully about what she was going to say. She had to be firm, but not put him off. Whatever happened, he was still a valuable client. She hoped the message would get through okay.

'Paddy, this is Lorna Cafferty. I am working down in Ballynafiddy Castle on a very hard and taxing assignment for a new client, an American Billionaire, Mr Big, who's urgently in search of a wife. *All* my clients keep harassing me with persistent phone calls! My mobile seems to have broken down, so there is no danger of your getting hold of me this week in any case. Please God this hellish account will rescue me from this tax thing and we can meet for lunch soon.'

Gloria looked over at her briefly as she was talking. When Lorna hung up she said, 'Sorry – I'm not exactly a dream date.'

Right. That was it. Lorna was going to get Gloria to

bond with her Inner Disco if it killed her. She would start by flinging a sparkler into the black bin of depression that Gloria was so determinedly inhabiting.

'Oh – I meant to say "Thanks".'

'What for?'

'For putting the word in with Sam Cohen.'

Gloria shrugged and turned to look out the window again. Ooops. Touched a nerve there, thought Lorna. Let's jiggle it around a bit and see what happens.

'Yes, as soon as I mentioned your name, he was all Three-Bags-Full-Ms Cafferty – problem solved.'

A barely audible 'Good' was her only reply.

'He whipped those lads straight off their tour and it was Trembling Celtics – Galway, here we come.'

Silence.

'Great band, though.' Dramatic pause. 'Marvellous. Don't you think?'

Gloria shrugged and raised an eyebrow, keeping her eyes firmly peeled on a passing flock of sheep.

'Still, couldn't have done it without you.'

Nothing.

'And Sam, eh? Lovely bloke – he went as pink as a peeled prawn when I told him you might be coming down.'

Lorna left a gap for Gloria to reply, but she was giving nothing away.

'In *fact*, he said he might come down himself. Keep the lads company and all that. Seemed quite keen, actually.'

There was the slightest hint of colour moving up

from Gloria's neck, and Lorna could have sworn she saw her jaw move slightly. This was fun. She had two whole hours to make her crack. Lorna almost hoped Gloria would hold out for a bit longer. Prolong the game.

'He's quite cute, actually. Thought I might have a pop at him myself, but then – I'll be very busy, you know, organizing the party and all . . .'

Gloria blinked a couple of times, but still wouldn't turn her head to face Lorna.

'Anyway, I don't think he'd be interested in me. I rather got the impression that there was another attraction *luring* him down.'

Gloria's face was set in a look of positive rage at this point. Goody, thought Lorna, she's wound up as tight as Brad Pitt's arse in a prison shower.

'Really,' was the best she could respond.

'Oh yes.'

Gloria turned to face her, and her eyes were sparking with her verge-of-tears glower.

'And *what* would that be?'

Lorna looked around as if someone might be listening and leaned forward.

'We-ell – and don't quote me on this – but *I've* heard that he rather fancies Nylon. Sam Cohen *is* gay, isn't he?'

It was a nasty trick, but then when you are Dealing With Denial you are entitled to break the rules, and sometimes the most *wicked* of manipulations are the only hammers strong enough to break down the wall.

Gloria looked fit to burst, but Lorna was not a faint-hearted friend, and kept going.

'Is he not – gay – then?'

Gloria searched the face across from her for a few seconds. Lorna's high-eyebrowed expression was swiped with the blinking innocence of a woman who is obviously lying. Gloria's face melted, finally, into a wide smile. The first of the day, and the first real smile for several weeks.

'*No*, Lorna. Sam Cohen is *not* gay.'

'Care to expand on that?'

'No.' But she was still smiling.

'Offer evidence to the Court of Catholic Heterosexuality in the case of Sam Cohen vs Gloria O'Neill?'

'No. Thank you!'

'Sure now?'

'Positive.'

And that was all that was said about that. But it had been enough to break the spell, and for the rest of the journey Gloria joined in happily with Lorna's excited babbling, and even helped devise a Joint Three-Day Wardrobe Plan. By the time they reached the tiny station of Bunkelly, county Galway, Gloria was, if not entirely at one with her Inner Disco, at least slightly more available for the sometimes tricky business of living.

29

It was a bit of a crush in the back of Baldy Brannigan's limo. An ex-showband man himself, Baldy and the three Brannigan Brothers had moved into the luxury transport hire business some years ago when things had gone very quiet on the Scene for them. And it was on the wisdom of that decision that Baldy was musing as he picked up the first batch of clients from this Big American Party they had been hired to collect at Dublin Airport. He'd had them all in the back at one time or another. Elvis (actually – it had been Engelbert Humperdink – but Baldy had got such a fright-of-joy initially that he had not ever been prepared to let go of the story), Tom Jones, The Diamond (Neil), and The Trembling Celtics (he'd had to turn them down to do this job. They were nice lads – not like that shower the Dirty Filthy Animals who had proved to be *just that* – dropping Tayto crumbs and mauling their mollies all over his nice leather upholstery). It had been a passing face which had looked awfully like an old partner of his – Bernard Heffernan ('Hairy', they used to call him) – which had put Baldy in mind of a kind-of-a-sadness that he was up-front-driving instead of in-the-back-lounging. And it was in this melancholic state of déjà vu that he began the four-hour drive from Dublin to Ballynafiddy, Bunkelly, county Galway.

This is only significant insofar as Irish drivers are usually a genial and talkative class of person – guaranteed to break up an awkward silence with a joke or a political argument or two. After three hours in a car with one, it would be all you could do not to invite them for a spot of tea the other end – or at the very least, furnish them with the additional price of a pint for their trouble. But on this occasion, given the quiet thoughtfulness of their driver's mood, the passengers in the back of 'Ireland's Most Exclusive VIP State of the Art Limousine Luxury Model Transportation System' (Baldy's nephew was training as a copywriter) were thrown back on their own devices.

Conversation-wise, their devices were proving to be limited.

For starters, it was crowded in there. After all Liam's efforts to the contrary, Our Hero was berating himself for managing to turn what should have been an easy and straightforward task into a Class A Bag of Bollocks. He had decided that, actually, fucking things up was a special talent of his. He should make a career out of it – write a book, *Liam Murphy's* Carpet Your Soul With Shite. *Chapter One: How to Underachieve in the Career You Have Always Wanted. Chapter Two: How to Royally Piss Off the Only Woman You Will Ever Love. (Lifetime Supply Of*

Boiling Self-hatred Guaranteed; Suicide Within Six Months or Your Money Back.)

The slight lessening of leg room in the limo was, granted, Liam's fault, but then he hadn't banked on the Tall Redhead, who took up more than her fair share of space, what with her additional piece of luggage – the Cloud of Obvious Intent that was crackling through the atmosphere like a Hooker at Mass. It was all that himself and Chuck could do to avert their eyes from the No Pants Scenario that happened every time Flame crossed and uncrossed her legs, which she did frequently with the ravenous grace of a hunting tigress.

Ovary Spotting was not one of Liam's Subjects of Choice in the Great University of Life, but poor Chuck, with all his talent and ambition in that area, was straining himself back, on a twice-minutely basis, from making an unsightly and animalistic lunge in the presence of his boss.

Flame's unsavoury display put Liam, strangely, in mind of an expression that his mother used to use during his sister Maeve's Spandex Pants and Sequinned Boob Tube phase in her mid-teens. 'Tuck Yourself Away' Mammy Murphy used to say.

It was exactly how Liam felt. Liam gazed out of the window and felt like just curling himself up into a little ball. He wanted to be back in his loft apartment, in his bed, rolled up tight under the duvet. Thousands of miles away from all of this, from his family, Maeve and her insane ideas about men, his mother and her Weightwatcher dinners. From this wretched raining country, with its stupid pseudo-trendy bars that he didn't recognize, and its mad blonde PR women. Normally, Liam could cope with the craziness of his working life. Somehow, it was so far away from what he wanted, from what he hoped for himself, that it offered him a distraction, an excuse for not doing anything with his life. It was as if Liam had been living in a state of suspension and now he had come crashing down into the failure of his own life with a flat thud. At least when he had been 'trapped' in a job he had been able to live out the drama of 'not being able to return home'. In the last week or so, all of that had been turned on its head. He had fallen in love, and he was back home anyway – everyone around him not seeming to notice that he had been away for ten years. The ordered little cocoon he had wound around himself was unravelling. Liam wanted to tuck himself back under the warm blanket of his illusions again. He wanted to be back on *The South Bank Show* with Melvyn, he wanted to waste away the few hours of this journey thinking up his Desert Island Discs, his Whitbread wardrobe, 101 interesting things to do with a Pulitzer. But he couldn't. The finality of his failure seemed to have brought him to a level of reality that Liam did not like. He was in a limousine travelling to a castle in Galway with a Girl With No Pants, a Brain-Dead Bodyguard and a Billionaire. Life was stranger than fiction, he realized – if he could only get close enough to it to find out what happens in the end.

As Liam pondered on these profundities, and Chuck tried to calculate the number of points scored by the

New York Yankees in the last five years (to avoid the No Pants Scenario escalating into a Nasty Unpleasantness beyond his control), Xavier Big was lounging in a glorious reverie of his own entitled 'Being Home'. It had taken David Ashman almost three years to recarpet Big's soul in the emotional equivalent of something resembling linoleum with a few very expensive hand-woven rugs scattered about. But now, as Big drove through the land of his childhood holidays, the land of open fires and turf bogs, the land of scraggy aunties with no teeth and warm hearts, the land of tea and brown bread in neighbours' houses and making hay with cousins – the land that his newly millionaired father had refused to visit after Big was ten on the grounds of 'begrudgery and bad memories' – it was as if the billionaire's soul was sprouting a lush carpet of the greenest, moistest, freshest, most comforting green, green grass of home.

The brittle blonde wives of his past, the money, the struggle to be the Best – the Biggest – the Most Be-Billioned Billionaire all faded into insignificance. Finally, this was what he had always wanted. The Statue of Liberty/Waterford Crystal Project, the Big Paddy Festival, 'O Sweet Mother Ireland' – the ice box in the modified meat truck which was lumbering behind the limo – he saw them all for what they were. Mere trappings. Quite suddenly, Xavier Big didn't care about the Irish assistant, the linen hankies or even, so much, finding himself an Irish wife. He was here – *here* – in Good Old Irish Ireland. And it made him feel that he didn't need all those other things to make him the one thing that he now realized he had always been, right from the start.

A fully paid-up, fully qualified, fully functioning Irish-man.

30

Saturday afternoon was a busy time for Festy Pointer in the shop, although the word 'busy' as experienced in this seven-by-five-foot square of Rural Ireland was not really an apt qualification for the word as described in the *Concise Oxford Dictionary*. And Festy, who often filled his quiet hours there studying said tome (in order to reverse his beloved wife Bridie's opinion of him as a 'Thick No-Good Gobshite'), should have known that when he used it to describe his morning to Clara Fitzcronin as she came in looking for a tin of curry sauce with which to liven up her husband's otherwise ordinary chicken dinner.

'Very busy, Clara.' (Had Ireland not freed itself from the merciless regime of its oppressor, and had they been present to witness the lackadaisical casualness and ease with which he had managed to serve all of his five customers that morning, Oxford University Press might have sued under Trade Description at Festy's bare-faced cheek in appending an already misused adjective with 'very'. Alternatively they might have launched a Bunkelly edition, in which 'Very busy' was given to mean: 'Removing one's behind from the seat of one's chair more than two times during any given four-hour period.')

'Did ye hear about yer man the American buying Ballynafiddy?'

'Aye.'

Festy didn't look up from the book. If you gave Clara Fitzcronin one iota of eye contact, she'd be there all day talking, and would have the ears peeled off of him.

'I hear it's *great gas* up at the castle. Seemingly, there's a big party starting tonight, and they've some blondie little Yank Loo-lah up there decorating the place.'

'Is that right?' Festy mumbled. 'Beryl. Noun. *A transparent pale green blue, or yellow mineral . . .*' Jesus, and he'd thought it was a woman's name. Wait till he told Bridie about that one! (In reality Festy's poor wife was being driven demented by her husband's constant quoting of words at her but the more she called him a Thick Gobshite, the harder he sought to use words which he thought would impress her. Last night he had told her she looked nice by saying that her new hair colour 'beneficently complimented' her 'general demeanour'.)

'That's it now and our Colm is up there at the moment. He got a call from the oyster farm in Clifden saying that this little American decorator lad had ordered a ton of shells, and was looking to concrete them into the wall of the hall or something. Oh d'you-know-now I'd *love* to get up there and have a look at what he's done to the place. These Americans have great style, you know. I'd say it will be *only fabulous!*'

Festy remained unmoved and stuck with the reading. '. . . *sometimes used as a gemstone.*' Perhaps he'd try and buy one for Bridie – a ring or a bracelet or something, with one of them in it. Then she'd say 'That's a lovely stone – what is it?' And he'd say 'What, that little thing there – sure that's a *beryl.*' And she'd say . . .

'Festy – come quick – your mother's at it again!' Bridie bellowed into the door of the shop, and disappeared out again as quick as she almost didn't come in.

Mammy Pointer was out the front wobbling at the top of a kitchen stool, strapping her chum Attracta Slattery to a lamppost outside the priest's house. Although Attracta was standing on top of Festy's paint-splattered stepladder, the addition of a broom handle inserted into the sleeves of Attracta's Good Wool Coat helped lend authenticity to the Crucifixion tableau. In any case, Mammy Pointer had thought of that, and had a long white sheet which she planned to drape over the ladder to give the effect of her friend being suspended in mid-air. The sky-blue tablecloth she had secured to her head with a Barbie tiara belonging to her granddaughter suggested that she herself was planning to play the part of the BVM (Blessed Virgin Mary) weeping at the foot of the cross. They hadn't gone for the Lego/thorn crown or the ketchup stigmatas today. There hadn't been time. Attracta Slattery was eighty-six, and Dominica Pointer was two years older. Both had been diagnosed by local doctors as suffering from 'nerves' on certain occasions over the years when they had displayed a religious fervour over and above the daily Mass attendance and twice-yearly pilgrimages that were customary in this area amongst women of their age. As individuals, the occasional midnight break-in to the church for a sneak round of the Stations of the Cross was manageable. But when they got together, there was no reasoning with them at all.

Father Donnelly was pleading;

'*Plee-ase*, Mrs Pointer – do you not remember what happened the last time?'

A crowd of school children had stopped to check out Mrs Slattery's gathered and voluminous underwear, and while that was not enough to cause undue excitement, in her disgusted rush to chase them away, Dominica Pointer had fractured her hip, and ended up having to get a replacement which, in the end, had doubled her lively-ability and made her twice as unstoppable.

'I'm grand now, Father, thanks!'

She had it covered this time. Attracta was wearing navy slacks procured from her son, and, in any case, Dominica planned to strap her friend's feet together with bailer twine. Between the trousers and the twine, and with her grey hair tied back – make no mistake but Attracta Slattery was going to make as convincing a JC as had ever been seen in the townland of Bunkelly, in the parish of Kilbunion, in the county of Galway this century.

'Please,' begged Father Donnelly, 'I'll have to call the Guards if you don't stop this madness at once!'

The words 'guards' and 'madness' did nothing but strengthen their martyr's resolve. While Father Donnelly was undoubtedly, in his own modest way, one of God's Good Foot Soldiers, he was far down the pecking chain from the Great General Himself whom they believed was about to pass through their humble homeland.

'THE POPE IS COMING!' Attracta exclaimed from her perch.

'*What?*' Father Donnelly, Festy, Bridie and Clara all cried in unison.

Dominica exhaled a deep disappointed sigh, shook her head mournfully and looked at the group as if they knew *nothing* about *anything* at all. Virgin Mary/Barbie veil aside, Dominica Pointer was one of the most formidable mammies in Kilbunion. When she looked at you as if you knew *nothing* about *anything* at all – it was all you could do not to believe her.

'Catríona Regan called from Claretown, she said there's a bunch of vehicles just after driving past her house that's a match for the Pope *Himself's* Convoy.'

Catríona Regan was a competitive aul' biddy who had tortured her Rival Religious from the neighbouring townland with stories of her Visionary Devotions during the Pope's last visit in '81. The two old ladies had missed the Pilgrim's Bus and, in the dark days before mobile phones, had been unable to contact either of their sons for lifts. They had watched it on the telly, but it wasn't the same. Their failure to make it to Knock that year had undoubtedly contributed to the subsequent escalation in their eccentric devotional activities.

'It's the American!' said Clara, in a voice resonant with the opinion that this was *even better* than the Pope.

The group looked around.

'From the *Rory Mac Rory Show*! The Big Yank that bought Ballynafiddy! He's having a party there! Tonight!'

Festy looked hopefully at his mother – as if she might take a blind bit of notice of that flibbertigibbet-of-a-woman, Clara Fitzcronin.

'There you are, Mammy, see? It was a mistake anyone could have made – now will you let Mrs Slattery down off the cross?'

'Please, Mrs Pointer.' Father Donnelly bravely took up the rear.

The five faces looked up.

'I'm not coming down.' Even from this angle, they could see the tight set of Attracta Slattery's mouth indicated that she meant it.

'You'll catch your death,' hollered the Good Padre.

'So what if I do!' she cried. 'Isn't it better to die in the manner of the Lord Himself than above in that house with an English whore!' Nanny Slattery had recently had to endure her grandson's pregnant girlfriend moving into the house. It had not had the best effect on her mental health, and, given the Situation at home, there was a very real danger that this incident could turn kamikaze.

'I'm not going back to the hospital!'

Such was the level of Paddy Wallop's self-absorbed depression since his aborted attempt to meet Lorna

Cafferty in Dublin that he barely noticed the Local Priest attempting to evict Nanny Slattery from the lamppost outside his house as he drove past on his way home from the factory.

He had left several messages for Lorna in her office and on her mobile, but got no reply. Paddy was beginning to feel that either she was a very bad PR agent, or that she didn't like him. Not didn't like him as in – Didn't Want to Marry Him Just at the Moment. But didn't like him as in – Thought He Was a Thick-Headed Nyuck From the Country Whom She Could Do Without.

This bleak realization had left Paddy feeling listless and without his usual enthusiasm for life. Why, only yesterday he had waved aside his designer's drawing for a new multicoloured plastic covering for the range, as if it were nothing new. All his friends were noticing how depressed their beloved Paddy had become, but attempts to cheer him up with pot plants (Clara Fitzcronin), big bacony dinners (housekeeper Marjorie) and emails of naked French fashion models (François) had gone virtually unnoticed.

As Paddy turned into the drive of Wallop Mansion, a huge convoy of cars thundered past. Paddy wouldn't have noticed them at all, only for the enormous meat truck which had two speakers strapped to its roof belting out an old recording of 'I'll Take You Home Again, Kathleen'. It had been one of his own mother's favourites, but Paddy did not stop to question what might be the purpose of this strange vehicle, or what it was doing driving through the small, sleepy townland of Bunkelly.

When Paddy got into his house, he automatically clicked on his answering machine for messages. By this time, he had come to expect nothing except for news from the factory, and the odd call from François inviting him over. He wandered over to the microwave to see what offering Marjorie had left in there for his tea, but as he went to open the door, Paddy Wallop stopped in his tracks and started to shake. The voice on his machine was her. It was small, and hysterical and the line was crackling. But it was undoubtedly her – Lorna. Lorna Cafferty! The Great Love of His Life! Between the hissing and the crackling he was only able to make out a few words. But they were enough.

'Paddy . . . Lorna Cafferty . . . down in Ballynafiddy Castle . . . hard . . . tax . . . Mr Big . . . wife . . . harassing . . . persistent . . . broken down . . . danger . . . getting hold of me . . . Please God . . . hellish. . . . rescue me . . . soon.'

A mighty tidal wave of testosterone pumped up from the size twelve feet across and around the broad solid chest and right up through the six foot three it took to get to the top of Paddy Wallop's by now Deranged with Braveheart Loyalty head.

Everything fell into place. The newspaper articles. Clara Fiztcronin talking about the Yank who had bought Ballynafiddy. The mad convoy that had just passed his house. Lorna's tax scandal. In seconds, he had woven it all into a story. Lorna had needed money, and had applied to that billionaire's ad. He had come over here, Lorna had changed her mind and now she was like-as-not trapped in the back of that meat truck en route to Ballynafiddy to endure who knows what kind of humiliation and abuse. Paddy couldn't hate her leading on the American. She was desperate. The foolish, foolish, darling wee girleen. And now *this*! The cry for help. His small lamb bleating in the darkness at the mercy of some monstrous American wolf.

This was Paddy's Big Chance.

He threw off his overalls, and grabbed the first thing to hand – one of the snazzy Armani suits and shirts that François had made him buy on his last trip to Paris, and which was still in its bag by the front door.

Paddy threw it on and rushed straight out to the Merc.

He only hoped he could get to his One True Love in time.

31

The vehicle carrying the body of Mammy Big was a hastily customized meat transportation truck with MCHALE'S SAUSAGES emblazoned on the side. Ambrose McHale had been persuaded to take on this strange commission with a fee large enough for him not to cock as much as an eyebrow when the request had been passed down from Big's office. *'Music. I want music – the great music of Ireland – to herald my mother's return to the Homeland.'* Hence, a State of the Art Sound System had been fitted by McHale's brother-in-law (a part-time Fine Gael campaigner) to the top of Ambrose's meat transport truck. So far the inhabitants on the Dublin–Galway route had been treated to Daniel O'Donnell's *Greatest Hits* (Dublin to Maynooth), *John McCormack Sings Percy French* (Kilcock to Killbeggan), *Johnny McEvoy Live at the Galty-more* (Moate to Ballinasloe) and Val Doonican featuring 'I'll Take You Home Again, Kathleen' which had carried through the glorious country air from Athenry to Bunkelly where it had finally – to Ambrose's eternal relief – seized up.

Had Ambrose known that with their tinted windows up, the lucky inhabitants of the sound-proofed cruising limo couldn't hear a shred of noise other than the sound of their own breathing and the occasional uncomfortable squeak of hot thigh on leather from Flame, he might not have bothered attending to the musical repertoire of Ireland's Greatest quite so vigilantly.

However, Vigilant Bothering had been *very* much on the agenda at the castle itself as Sugar had travelled down a week beforehand to oversee the decor of the 'outdated and *ghastly* piece of gothic' that was to be his boss's new Irish home.

'Look – *look* – at these curtains!' he had said, fingering the full-length antique red velvet drapes. 'Dirt, dirt – *dirt* everywhere! They'll have to go. Trash, trash – *trash the lot*! And the upholstery!' He belted the ornate chaise with a crumbling cushion and a puff of eighteenth-century dust billowed across the front of his sparkling white kaftan. 'Urgh. This place is *filthy* and just *look* at this fabric. Fleur-de-lis – so *80s*! That *hound* Lorna told me not to order a scrap before I saw the state of the place and she was wrong, wrong, *wrong*! I want Ralph Lauren Country Collection and I want it *now*! Nylon? Get on to that wretched little Dublin shop – what's it called?'

'Brown Thomas,' mumbled Nylon.

'Them! Get on to Bran Thorns and tell them we want *everything* in tartan they've got – *ev-ery-thang* – do you hear me? Plates, cushions, mugs, rugs – the lot. Then ring Saks, Fifth Avenue, and tell them to ship me every *scrap* of Ralph's collection left in stock. Tell them to put it on my account . . .' Sugar looked like he was fit to blow, but he was clearly enjoying the challenge. Nylon was impressed beyond words. He had never seen such acute campology – and displayed with such style, such *commitment*. This guy really *was* the Queen of Queens. 'It'll take *kilometres* of linen to get this place up to even the most *basic* standard and we've only got a week – oh and sweetheart' – for after a week of running around after him in a state of permanent awe, Nylon really was just that – 'those Waterford people Xavier likes – the people that make the glasses? They're here, aren't they?'

Nylon nodded.

'Good – tell them we'll need two hundred of everything they've got.'

Nylon stood shell-shocked at the magnitude of all he had to do.

'Well – don't just stand there, sweetie – get on with it! I've got to load these staple guns and see if I can't do something *interesting* with these *hideous* drapes. Now, what *will* we do with this dreary hall?'

Less than one week later, the place was transformed. Gone were the dusty old curtains and the moth-eaten rugs. Every antique sofa and chair had been mercilessly punctured and re-covered with a million shots from Sugar's turbo-charged staple gun. Throw cushions in every shape and style of tartan were arranged symmetrically on every sit-downable surface. Nylon's hands were *raw* from rubbing down mahogany antiques ('*If*

319

this were home I'd have that dresser sanded down and distressed – but alas – we simply haven't the time'), and one lucky carpet man in Dublin had quadrupled his annual turnover by getting every male person that he knew to come down to Galway and help him fit all seventeen bedrooms in rose-pink shagpile. There were flowers in the hall, flowers in the bedrooms, flowers in the toilets, the scullery, the kitchen, the living rooms, the drawing rooms, the study and library. There were flowers everywhere. 'If in doubt – Arrange It!' was one of Sugar's decorating mottos, along with 'If it smells – Trash It!' and 'If it's old – Bury It!'

Sugar and Nylon had worked twenty-four-seven, and by the time Big's convoy hit the Galway border, the workmen had more or less finished and the interior of one of Ireland's oldest and grandest residences had been transformed from quirky-gothic into something that better reached the hygienic and homogeneous standards of an American hotel.

As Lorna and Gloria arrived, the two men were scrubbed, manicured, dressed to kill and standing in the front hall admiring Sugar's pièce de résistance – the Oyster-Embedded Chimney Breast.

'What the hell happened *there*?' Lorna exclaimed when she saw the mollusc-infested wall. 'It looks like there's something *growing* on it!'

Sugar had spent half a day up to his armpits with sand and cement mix creating this masterpiece. He was not impressed.

'*That*,' he said, looking at Lorna as if he had never

seen anything quite so common and ignorant in his whole life, 'is an Interior Sculpture Piece Celebrating the Oyster as an Icon of Love. It's supposed to be Ironic – but then, I wouldn't expect you to understand that.'

The idea – no – the *irony* of an American Closet Queen who took Interior Decorating as seriously as he did explaining the concept of same to an Irishwoman for whom wit was a way of life stopped Lorna short of flattering her way out of a potentially explosive situation. She could not laugh out loud at Sugar, but she *could* ignore him – and she did.

'Nylon – could you show Gloria up to her room? I've to go outside now and check on the marquee and the caterers. Has the sound equipment arrived yet?'

Nylon stood between Sugar and Lorna, not knowing which way to turn for the best.

'I don't know.'

'You don't know? And why not?'

'I don't know I . . .'

To be honest, Nylon had got into the whole slave/ master thing. He had been following quick-fire instructions all week, and working his balls off. He couldn't quite remember how to stand up for himself any more.

'You were *supposed* to be down here setting things up for me?'

'I've been helping Sugar.'

Sugar was disgusted at the way this Uppity Cow was addressing what he now saw as His Property.

Lorna was furious at the way that Nylon had been kidnapped out of her servitude.

Sugar looked at Lorna. Lorna looked at Sugar. It was a stand-off. Lorna broke it.

'Well! I suppose I'll just have to go out there and sort it out *myself!*'

As an afterthought she looked at Gloria who was feeling as spare as a bacon toastie at a bar mitzvah.

'I'm sorry, Glor. I'll be a couple of hours *at least –*' she flicked an angry stare at Nylon – 'I'll come straight up to your room later and we'll get ready together, yeah?'

⬭

Gloria unpacked her bag and looked at the collection of evening wear and smart daywear that Lorna had made her buy on their Great Shopping Expedition. Dashed across the bed like a pile of gaudy corpses, they looked so much brighter, so much sparklier – so much more *alive* than she felt. She wished that she had enough energy to think of an excuse to leave at this early stage. Perhaps if she hid herself up here, Lorna would become distracted with all her organizing and forget to come back for her. Some how, Gloria knew that wasn't going to happen. Some way, somehow, she was going to have to get herself tarted up and go downstairs to schmooze this American who wanted to back her business – even though, with Frank tripping her up all the way, it almost certainly wouldn't happen now. Still, she thought, checking her watch, it was early yet, and there was a brand-new big TV in the corner (*Decorator's note: 'A bedroom with no television! What kind of a country is this?'*) that could perhaps take her mind off things for a few hours. Gloria stripped and reached for her new silk dressing gown – the one thing she did not regret buying on Lorna's advice. *'It'll be handy for all those glum nights in in front of the telly you so enjoy.'* She smiled when she thought of her. Gloria wondered how in the hell her friend kept going. She admired Lorna's constant flow of steam, and wished, especially at times like these, that she could be more like her.

She wandered over to the window and looked out over the manicured gardens. Beyond them the rolling landscape seemed to go on for ever. A row of tall yew trees yearned towards the sky and, ironically, they reminded her of home. The aggressive concrete of the tower blocks, defying gravity – grasping for the sky.

Her contemplative mood was broken as she saw a limousine pull up in the drive. Out of it stepped three men – she could only see the back of them – and a set of model legs emerged from the low interior in a sluttish, confident slide, followed by a body which she recognized all too well.

Gloria groaned.

That fucker Frank had followed her here. He must have got wind of her plans and come down to muscle in. She was just getting ready to pack as there was a gentle tap on the door.

She didn't even bother answering, but a few seconds later the door opened anyway.

'Gloria? Are you in here?'

It was Sam. Brilliant. This was all she needed right

now. Frank had probably sent him to find her. Flame was probably already sharpening her nails on the edge of a glass of brandy waiting for some delightfully smug torturous foursome scenario. Three against one – well, they could all just . . .

'*Fuck off!*'

'Hey, Gloria? I just came up to say—'

'Well, you can just take a slide back down those bannisters on that slippery bald head of yours and I hope you fuck it into smithereens on the flagstones.'

She was standing in front of him, a great boiling bundle of Ballymun brimstone. Sam didn't know what was wrong with her, but he hardly cared because, for all her wrath, standing there with a suggestion of breast shrugging itself out of the purple paisley gown, she *looked gorgeous.*

'Okay, okay – I'll see you downstairs.'

'You will in your *ARSE*, you *slithery, little, two-faced TOAD!*' Gloria screamed as she chased the Small But Extremely Important Record Producer out of her room, slamming the door behind him.

Sam was more confused than upset. He had already decided that it was high time Gloria O'Neill was taken in hand and he was the man to do it. If he could, at a squat five foot two, attract any number of determined music groupies – and then be man enough to turn them down on the grounds of decency – then he was more than able for the towering inferno of confusion and sharp-shoulder-chips that was Gloria. Now, however, was not the time. He had to settle his Trembling Celtic lads into their gig, and get his head round the whole Frank/Money/Gloria's Gaff situation before he went in with the flowers and the 'I love you' routine.

No, this was not the time – but Sam was confident that his moment was only around the next corner.

32

Paddy Wallop arrived at the gates of Ballynafiddy just as Big's car was drawing up to the house. He had waited behind until he saw the crowd gathering at the door of the castle before snailing up the crunchy gravel.

He needn't have worried about the accusations of trespassing. Anyone who drove a Merc as swanky and new as his would be entitled to drive into any castle grounds they liked around here without attracting notice. If he had been behind the wheel of a tractor – as Festy's brother had been some months beforehand, looking for a couple of mislaid sheep – it would have been a very different matter.

However, after Lorna's desperate message, Paddy had launched himself into full James Bond mode, and was lamenting the lack of a black bally-clava and a climber's rope flung over the shoulder as he swerved the Merc silently in half-behind the high hedge that ran along the edge of the castle lawn. He got out of the car, and stood peering through a hole in the foliage. From the big black limousine emerged a large blond man with a jutting-out jaw and hands the size of car batteries (Paddy hoped that wasn't him – he was no wimp himself, but Blondie looked like a real killer), a thin, ferrety-looking lad (no problem there) and finally a tall, well-dressed man who, even to Paddy's untrained eye, was clearly a looker in that American, groomed, film-star way.

Paddy's stomach dropped as he instinctively knew that was the Big Billionaire. Good-looking, well dressed, loaded with money. A million times better than him. How could he hope to compete? Perhaps he was wrong to have come here at all? Perhaps Big *was* the one that Lorna wanted. Determinedly he remembered her message: '*Big . . . harassing . . . persistent . . . broken down . . . danger*'. He knew it was wrong, but Paddy felt warmed by the memory of his loved one's pleading. He had to proceed. He *had* to find Lorna.

He saw two womanly legs slide out of the limo, and for a second, he thought it was her. Imagine his disgust, his *horror* therefore, when Paddy Wallop's eyes were assaulted with what the porn mags call 'A Right Eyeful' of this languid redhead's uncovered unmentionables – right there! In broad daylight! In Kilbunion! In Galway! In Holycatholicireland! The significance of this Unmerciful Display took a few minutes to sink in, but when it did, Paddy's heroic intent was strengthened all the more. Clearly this woman was a prostitute. Probably some poor girl from Dublin's Inner City who was trying to feed her children. Big had not, after all, kidnapped Lorna with the intention of marrying her (an action that *any* man might be driven to take – she was that adorable).

Big's intentions were surely far more sinister than he had thought – hence the terrified message. No, this reprobate, this . . . this . . . *Brute* was clearly forming some sort of harem for himself. White slave trade! Paddy had read about it in magazines – Lorna could be carted off to Cuba – or Los Angeles – or some *awful* place and kept in a small concrete cubicle where men would come and pay ten dollars to have her . . .

Paddy stopped it right there. It didn't bear thinking about. He *had* to save her – and he had to do it NOW!

But first he had to find her.

Desperately Paddy Wallop looked around him. There was a huge tent going up in the field behind the castle, and to its left a stage with rigging and scaffolding for the concert. Paddy strained his eyes up across the stonework of the castle itself. She was like as not already in there. Trapped! Imprisoned! In a tower! Then Paddy looked up and he saw her. Or rather, he saw a woman who *might* have been Lorna – was *possibly* Lorna – was *probably* Lorna – standing at one of the front windows on the first floor. Paddy saw the edge of a purple gown flicker out of sight just as he noticed the redheaded prostitute walking through the door of the castle. Lorna was watching them all arrive too. What must have been going through her mind? Seeing this monster bring another poor victim into this house. What fear – what *dread* – was going through her pretty blonde head as she must be imagining some kind of dreadful scenario involving the two women. Some kind of a filthy, depraved sexual act involving . . .

No! he mustn't think about that now. He had to leap in and save her. And before you could say 'Plastic Pants', Paddy had leapt over the shrubs and scaled the scaffolding at the back of the castle which had been left by Sugar's troupe of sweaty window cleaners the day before.

⬭

As the two girls finally arrived at Ballynafiddy, Maeve pulled the car in to the side of the castle gates and turned the engine off.

'What's up?' Sandy was puzzled. It had taken them the best part of four hours to get to Galway with a major bickering session as Sandy had got them lost. They had booked into a nearby B & B, showered, changed, and made up at double speed as Maeve had been all het up about getting there in plenty of time for the party.

Now she had stopped the car, and was breathing heavily like a woman on the wrong side of a nervous breakdown.

'I don't want to go in,' said Maeve.

'What? Oh don't be so stupid!'

Sandy was getting seriously impatient now. Maeve had stuck to her guns over this stupid game and that put her in the awful position of having to rethink how she was going to angle the documentary. She certainly couldn't go in all guns blazing, tits out and red curls flouncing as originally planned – not without incurring the wrath of Maeve. In any case – now that the nice

Undercover Documentary theory had turned into an Actual Operation Seduce Billionaire reality – Sandy wasn't sure she felt up to it. I mean – how do you seduce and then string along a man anyway? Especially one you are not remotely interested in. Really – there must be an easier way to Kosovo than this. To make it worse, Maeve had been prodding the radio equipment in her bag all the way down saying 'G'wan. Interview me, then.' The reminder she had lied, and then her own inability even to follow the lie through properly, was making her super-tetchy. Now Princess Maeve was changing her mind again!

Then Maeve turned her head and looked her straight in the face. Sandy was shocked. She hadn't seen such a tearful and frightened expression on Maeve's face since they were children, and the bold brunette hadn't wanted to face her father after being caught smoking in school.

'No, Sandy. I mean it. I'm scared. What if he doesn't like me? What if, after all this, he—'

'Maeve – what in the hell has got into you? This is just a bit of fun.'

Maeve closed her eyes, and cut her off.

'No, Sandy. I know you don't understand, but it's not just that to me. This is important. It . . . it *feels* important somehow.'

Much as Sandy wanted to wave Maeve aside, something in the dribbly blueness of her friend's eyes indicated that she should give her some space. Maeve was so seldom serious, and if Sandy thought she was being stupid, that was one thing. But obviously she was upset and, despite it all, Sandy loved her, so she kept her mouth shut.

'Maybe all of this has just been my most stupid idea to date. I don't know. I mean, I have all of these stupid dreams and notions, then right up to the last minute I think they're going to work, then, you know? I get let down and . . .'

She was right. Maeve had flunked fashion design at college. She had been to New York, and lasted two months doing bar work before finally escaping back home. She had done acting classes, dance classes, singing classes – and none had revealed the humungous talent she was so certain would lead her on the path to fame and fortune. She had picked up at parties, gone home with and slept with almost all of Ireland's Most Eligible Bachelors – holding onto the firm belief that her dreamed-about foot-sweeping happily-ever-after ending was only a ride away. Maeve kept getting knocked down, but she always dusted herself back up into the fray of life. She always believed that one day her life was going to be sparkly and happy and Hollywood. Everyone always laughed at her hare-brained schemes, even her best friend Sandy. *Especially* her best friend Sandy, she realized, as they sat there in the quiet car about to cross the threshold to the Party of the Decade. Sandy knew that it was that brave heart of Maeve's that made her as lovable as she was. Maeve had an enthusiasm and a belief in life, and love, and romance and dreams-come-true that Sandy didn't have. She had had it once, when they were young, when she had headed off to London with her big bagful of hopes and promises to herself. But then, when they hadn't happened, she had grown bitter and ambitious instead of trusting and ever-hopeful like good-old-Maeve.

'. . . and, the thing is, Sandy – I just don't know if I can take another knock. I just don't think I can—'

'Start the car, Maeve.'

'No, I said—'

'Start the car.'

'You're not listening, I said—'

'No, Maeve – *you're* not listening. I said *start* the car. We are going to that party.'

'But I—'

'No buts, Maeve. We are going to that party, and you are going to hook up with Big, and he is going to sweep you off your feet, and you are going to live in a big fuck-off house in America, and I am going to come and visit you twice a year and shop in Tiffany's and lunch in The Plaza because you are Gorgeous and you are Clever and It's What You Want and You Deserve It.'

Maeve looked at her, gobsmacked.

'So start this *fucking* car and get us *up* to that house and let's start schmoozing and partying and making those dreams come true, girl!'

Sandy's mind was made up. About the documentary, about Maeve, about everything. Stuff the career – stick Aul' Fella and his poncy kiss-arse organization and all who sank in it. Tonight belonged to her friend Maeve and her crazy dreams. Sandy's own dream would have to wait. It was built on lies and ambition and greed anyway – and sooner or later dreams that are made of shite turn to shite. Maeve's dream to marry Big was the little-girl fantasy of sugar and spice. Sandy knew Maeve well enough to know that it was pure, for all it might have seemed to the contrary – and in that sense, it at least *deserved* to come true.

By the time Paddy had levered his considerable frame away from the scaffolding and onto the foot-wide ledge that ran along the front of the castle, he was beginning to feel that perhaps he had been a little hasty in his decision to mount the walls in favour of, say, sneaking in the back door, or climbing in one of the ground-floor windows (which seemed to be calling at him from below, saying 'Ye big hairy gobshite up there teetering when you could have climbed through one of us in a minute!')

There were a number of good reasons, he now realized, why clambering up the side of this castle had been a bad idea. Number one was the profusion of seagull shite under the feet of his leather-soled tread-free Italian loafers, *not* the first choice of footwear for your safety-conscious climber. Number two – a house interior of this type offers any number of hiding oneself behind pillars/in cupboards/under-stairs opportunities. Clinging to the second-floor window ledge in an Armani suit, with his arse to the wind, Paddy was starting to get a feeling of . . . well . . . *exposure*, visually in that he could be easily seen, and frankly, nippy-windwise in the trouser department. Number three – and most importantly – was his concern that perhaps a woman, in the delicate emotional state which Lorna must surely be in by now, might not react favourably to a man's face suddenly appearing at her bedroom window with the cocktail of anxiety and fear which Paddy felt certain was currently inhabiting his face. And it was indeed this third concern that was borne out in the instant that he thought it.

Swiftly turning from her fight with Sam in a dramatic 'All Men Are Bastards' demi-turn, the very last thing that Gloria O'Neill expected to see was a strange man, his eyes boggling out of his head and his mouth strained back in a distorted voiceless scream, his arms out-stretched and hugging the window surround swinging from her window. She let out a scream that would castrate a cat and would have run howling from the room itself – if she hadn't wanted Sam, her ex-husband, her ex-husband's tart and all the sundry pricks who were surely by now gathered in the Great Hall of Ballynafiddy to see her in her dressing gown. Her alternative involved slapping the window with the nearest object, which – happily for Paddy – was a silk chemise, to indicate her heartfelt desire that this intruder would go away.

But Paddy, as his persistent love for Lorna had proven, had nothing if not staying power. He was not, granted, in the most comfortable of positions, but his options were limited. It was down or in. Of the two 'in' was the more favourable, but in the meantime he was clinging on. He had of course noticed, at this stage, that the woman who was currently whipping the window with her nightie was not his beloved Lorna. Disappointment was a word which Paddy would normally have associated with the Experience of Not Seeing Lorna When One Was Expecting to. But frankly, given his aborted attempts of late, it was a feeling to which he was rapidly becoming inured. In any case, under his current circumstances, any creature with the combined intelligence and manual ability to open a window would do. There was a curious pigeon lurking to his left. He didn't care who was in there any more; Lorna, Mad Nightie-Wielding Woman, Queen Elizabeth Herself, Attila the Hun. At this stage it didn't matter – just so long as they opened the fucking window! Please!

Gloria eventually stopped and stood with her hands on her hips surveying the situation. Who was this man? What did he want? On both counts, she drew a blank. He could be a burglar, or a peeping Tom (albeit a very adventurous one), or an escaped lunatic. Thinking about it, in the mood she was in, Gloria could handle just about any man right now. She was that mad anyway that tearing the head off a man – *any* man – did not seem like an impossible task. In fact, the more she thought about it, the more attractive a task it seemed. At least, this way, she might get to vent her rage by 'defending herself against an intruder', rather than 'make a complete show of herself' by getting into a fist fight with Frank in front of a whole bunch of people.

The angry grimace that she gave Paddy as Gloria lifted the sash window made him think that perhaps he was safer staying where he was. However, she at least deserved an explanation, and Paddy always found that when women were angry, politeness was always a gentleman's best defence.

'Good afternoon, miss. I'm terribly sorry if I startled you.'

Gloria stood looking at him, her arms folded, resting her mouth on a clenched fist.

'I was concerned about the welfare of a friend of mine who I thought was . . . em . . .'

'I've opened the window now, either you come in or I'm closing it again.'

Paddy stepped gingerly inside, and sighed with relief as the full, flat soles of his loafers hit the carpet.

Gloria, the killer instinct suddenly melted out of her in the face of this man's sheepishness, said, 'Well? Go on, then – get out!'

'Do you not want me to explain—'

'Go on – move! Vamoose – out!'

Paddy took a few steps towards the bedroom door, but as he reached it he realized that he did not want to go through it. He needed to sit down for a minute and recover from his recent adventure. He needed to gather himself back together again and decide what was the best thing to do next. It had been the lack of planning earlier that had landed him in this strange woman's bedroom with concrete dust on his knees and seagull shite on his shoes.

'I was just wondering if I might—'

'Are you still here? What did I say?'

Gloria released one of her crossed arms to point Paddy towards the exit.

'Out! Out! Out!'

The headmistress tone of her voice suddenly made Paddy feel small and weak. He wanted to cry. It had all gone wrong – horribly, *horribly* wrong. The wedding list girl at Brown Thomas. The humiliation in that terrible beauty salon. And now – *this!* His chance to rescue Lorna – this chance to prove what a big man he was, and here he was. Weak as a Kitten, not man enough for any of it. How could he hope to be with a woman like Lorna when he was such a . . . such a . . . *wimp!*

He looked at Gloria and his eyes blinked and blistered with the shock of tears that were welling up. Like all Good Galway Men, Paddy didn't 'do' crying. Not officially, anyway. So he held one hand up and pinched his middle finger and thumb across his two eyes as if he were just rubbing away an eyelash. Gloria recognized the action as one she had seen many's the time at a Ballymun funeral. She softened.

'I can't go down there,' he said in a tiny voice.

'Why not?' she asked, quietly this time.

'Because I'm afraid,' the large man said, 'I'm afraid of who might be down there.'

Gloria knew exactly how he felt.

'I'll tell you what,' she said, pulling her gown tightly around her waist and double knotting it, 'you sit down there for a few minutes and I'll see if I can't find us something in the minibar.'

And with that, the large, strange, country man sat down on the edge of the four-poster, and Gloria didn't get to watch the TV.

Although she would have been loathe to admit it, Gloria was kind of glad of the company.

33

When Maeve and Sandy arrived at the castle, Big and his entourage were already in the Great Hall. Surprisingly, the first thing the two girls noticed when they walked in the door was not the handsome figure of America's Biggest Billionaire, nor indeed the awkward shuffling of his (cute assistant) Liam. No. The first thing that assaulted them as they walked through the ornate oak doors of this historic monument was the terrible, *terrible* smell.

'Jesus,' Maeve whispered into her friend's back (for by now Sandy had very much taken the assertive party-girl lead), 'do you get a whiff of underwashed festering gusset or is it just me?'

Sandy smiled at the gathered party and whispered through clenched teeth over her shoulder and out of the side of her mouth, 'Someone's a bit challenged in the undergarment hygiene department all right. My money's on the tall, tarty redhead down there. Say nothing – just keep smiling.'

'Oh God – she's *gorgeous!*' said Maeve. 'He'll *never* look at me.'

'Course he will – now shuddup' – for already her nostrils were starting to seal with the stench – 'and keep smiling.'

'Good afternoon,' said Sandy, holding her hand out to Mr Big, 'I'm Sandy Nolan . . .'

Mr Big was instantly charmed. Another redhead! Was there *no end* to the gorgeous women in this country? This was gonna be one helluva night!

Maeve shuffled forward with a sharp instructional pinch on the arm from her friend.

'. . . and *this* –' Sandy spread her hands in the manner of a game-show hostess showing off this week's prizes – 'is my friend Maeve. Thank you *so* much for inviting us down.'

The dark-haired one was no great shakes, but Big took her hand politely before turning his attention back to Redhead Number Two.

Redhead Number One was not impressed. Big had been quiet enough on the drive down, but then, the Goon and the Geek were their travelling companions – so he was hardly going to make a move in front of them. Besides, Flame felt confident that she had struck just the right balance between innocence and sensuality with her Catholic Virgin Who *Whoops!* Forgot to Put Her Pants on This Morning ensemble. Little did she know, as she seductively played with the hem of her skirt, with the suggestion of warming her bare buttocks on the heat of the Great Hall Fire, what a desperate impression she was making. For her nose job last year had all but killed Flame's sense of smell. Not usually a problem, as she simply purchased the most fashionable perfumes available at the time and hoped for the best. But on this occasion, a sense of smell would have been essential in avoiding the social faux pas in which she was currently taking the leading role. Sugar had simply *presumed* that the oyster farm from whom he had purchased the shells, which were currently embedded into the chimney-breast walls, would have bleached, boiled and generally extinguished any trace of their original inhabitants. Sadly for all concerned, they had neglected to do so. Once the fire was lit, the stench of rotting fish was almost unbearable. Flame with her No Pants advert and persistent fire/skirt flapping was, unbeknownst to herself, getting the blame.

Big, not being a country man himself, and therefore someone for whom bad smells might be tolerated more easily, suggested that they all retire to the library. He didn't know where it was, but there was sure to be one in here somewhere. He made his First Lady choice clear by taking Sandy's hand and leading her through the candlelit corridor.

Flame sneered in their wake and went into the bathroom to sharpen her claws and possibly revise the whole pants thing with a fishnet CK G-string she had in her purse. Sugar, who had been horrified out of speech as his mind had finally computed the fishy stench/oyster connection, went to make a skull-squashing phone call to the farm in Clifden, with Nylon dutifully clicked to heel.

That left Liam and Maeve, alone, in the Great Hall of Ballynafiddy.

Brother and sister looked at each other.

There is a moment in adulthood when you look at one of your siblings and you realize, 'They are me.'

No, they are *actually* me, as in twins. More of a realization that while friends and partners can leave you, and families will sometimes separate and move on, your brother is *always* your brother and your sister is *always* your sister. Blood being thicker than water and all that.

The two of them looked at each other's dark hair, sallow complexions and into each other's blue eyes and they realized, somehow, that in this moment, they were all the other had left.

'I'm in love with Sandy.'

'I've made a fool of myself again.'

They both spoke simultaneously – then added almost immediately:

'No, you haven't' – Liam.

'Well, tell her, then' – Maeve.

Their voices echoed across the empty hall and the hollow sound made both of them feel alone but together.

'Fuck this!' said Maeve, realizing that if the best she could do was be standing here with her gobshite brother, then she really was scraping the bottom of the barrel.

'Bollocks!' said Liam, realizing that he really *was* a gobshite if the best he could drum up woman-wise was a mad sister and a Weightwatching mammy.

'I'm going out the back to see if one of the Trembling Celtics will ride me before the party,' Maeve announced, drilling her heels into the flagstones as she went. Blood may be thicker than champagne, but fuck it, champagne tasted better!

Right, Liam thought, if Maeve can do it – well, then – so can I!

He wasn't entirely sure what it was that he was planning to do (certainly not ride one of The Trembling Celtics in any case), but inspired by his sister's vim, he went in search of the library.

Lorna was bush-whacked, knackered – all out of steam. In the past couple of hours she had overseen a marquee erection; taken delivery of 1,000 Waterford Crystal glasses ('*Who the fuck ordered these? – all right – all right – put them out back!*'); scored an ounce for a shaking drummer; calmed an egotistical DJ in the *worst* jumper she had ever seen in her *life*; attempted to eject a scraggy group of raving gate-crashers led by a pleading Scooter ('*Remember me, missis – I wash your hair in Gloria's*') before finally finding white pinnies for them all and putting them to work in catering; sound-tested a state-of-the-art sound system; turned away a Bouncy Castle ('*Who the fuck ordered this? – No, no – I don't care – take it*

AWAY!'); briefed twelve bouncers with their lists (*'If they're not on your list – they're not in – but obviously if it's fucking Elton John. . . . use your heads.'*)

Her Manolo's were in shreds from walking them across grass and gravel, and she was just about ready to *die* for a hot bath and a glass of giggly with her good friend Gloria.

What Lorna was just about *not* ready to die for was the presence of Ireland's Largest Supplier of Incontinence Pants sitting enjoying a can of Fanta on the edge of the bed which housed the contents of her and Gloria's joint weekend wardrobe.

But just about die was just exactly what Lorna did.

Where in the name of God she got the energy to whistle up a charming PR smile and a, 'Hullo, Paddy. What a *nice* surprise!' she does not know to This Day.

By this time, of course, Gloria had explained the whole thing to Paddy. Lorna hadn't been kidnapped, there was no harem/white-slave scenario – and if there was, Gloria, by the cut of her head earlier, would have had no problem dispersing same. The two of them were therefore looking relaxed and cosy by the time Lorna and her crazed feet entered the scene.

Paddy had been telling Gloria all about his feelings for Lorna. Between Gloria being Lorna's best friend, and her saying he was a nice guy (despite getting off on such a bad foot), and assuring him that he was in with a chance, and – well – the relief of just getting the whole thing off his chest, Paddy had temporarily forgotten that the Woman Herself was actually in the vicinity. His shock, therefore, at the immediate proximity of the goddess whom he had been chasing, and yearning for, and waiting for months by the phone to merely speak to, nearly finished him off altogether. He leapt up from the side of the bed, sending a healthy slurp of Fanta flying across the cream, sequinned shift which Lorna had been planning on wearing that evening.

'Oh Jesus – I'm sorry – I'm a big – here . . .' and he grabbed a hundred-pound pair of pure silk Janet Reger camiknickers and began to mop frantically.

'It'll brush off – don't worry, Paddy,' said Gloria, a little *too* casually for Lorna's liking.

Paddy, still holding her expensive undergarment in his heavy fist, said, 'Jesus, I'm awful sorry, Lorna, you gave me a fright there, well, I suppose not a fright really, I just wasn't expecting to see you and . . .'

Lorna could have let him carry on rambling in a state of acute mortification, but he was a client – so she put him out of his misery.

'That's all right, Paddy,' she said coldly, although by the set of her gob it was more than clear that, actually, it *wasn't* all right. It wasn't all right *at all*!

Paddy started to back out of the room.

'Well, and so I'll leave you ladies to it . . .'

'I told Paddy he should stay for the party tonight,' Gloria said with more than an appropriate level of glee, 'that's all right, isn't it, Lorna? Good-looking guy like him shouldn't be on his own here in the arse end of nowhere when there's all these chicks up from Dublin – isn't that right, Paddy, wha'?'

Paddy applied a stuck-on smile, but even he could tell that Gloria was going over the top.

'Indeed,' was Lorna's curt reply.

'Rightio, Paddy, then, that's settled. You run off home and get changed and we'll see you downstairs in the library about nine, eh? See if we can't fix you up.'

Paddy nearly fell backwards out the door with Gloria's audacious attitude. He went home, and spent the next two hours on the phone to François in Paris trying to decide what to wear. He did so because he loved Lorna still – but he did not do it with a song in his heart. For this evening, after the Day That Had Been in It, Paddy Wallop did not hold out much hope.

Had he heard the conversation immediately after he left the room, Paddy might not have come back at all that evening. In fact, he might not have ever left his house again.

'What the *hell* was that?'

Lorna squalled at Gloria. The hairdresser was unfazed. Now it was her turn to sit back and turn up the gas.

'What was what?' She blinked innocently.

'Paddy the Pants – in this room! *Here*, for fuck's sake – coming to the party! All that!'

'Nothing. Just thought he was a nice guy, that's all. Kind of sexy too – in that sort of hairy, grumpy country way. Hmmmm.' Gloria licked her lips lasciviously.

'Don't be disgusting. He makes incontinence pants – anyway, how do *you* know him?'

'Just met him this afternoon, actually. We bumped into each other.' She smiled sweetly, but didn't let on about the window and the screaming.

'Well – what the fuck was he doing in here?'

'He was looking for you – actually.' She said it with a 'shame' tint to her voice. In her experience, women were always more interested in men if their friends fancied them.

'I knew it! Can't leave it alone – any of them. They will *hound* me to the grave, my frigging clients. Wondering why I'm down here putting in all these hours for Big instead of trying to flog his wretched plastic undergarments. Honestly – what the *fuck* does he expect me to do? Turn down a big money job and devote myself entirely to him?'

'Well – I do think he was hoping for something like that – yes,' said Gloria quietly.

'What! You are fucking *joking*! The CHEEK of him. You mean, he came in here and told you I wasn't doing a good job for him – well, now that's IT! I've had it up to here with the lot of them. Up – to – HERE! HERE! HERE!' and she sliced her hands across her head repeatedly like a madwoman playing charades.

'Lorna, sit down and relax a minute, will you?'

Lorna was marching by now. She really HAD had enough. She felt as if she hadn't had a minute to herself for ever. Between the mobile on twenty-four-hour call, and keeping the minions happy, chasing around after press, juggling clients' needs, booking caterers, taking charge of the seven-day-a-week Happy-Charming Fest that the world expected of her. Oh sure, she got to party, but it was always someone else's party; always someone else's product; always someone else's life. All her life Lorna had lived in a vacuum of one drama to the next – and when there wasn't a drama, there was nothing. Her short friendship with Gloria was the closest thing she had to real life. Lorna didn't think she could live through one more wild party. This was the greatest event she had ever organized, but for Lorna Cafferty it felt like the party was over, and poor Paddy was the Party-Pooper.

'No I will *not* fucking sit down – I am going to find that Ignorant Culchie and tell him just what—'

'Lorna – he's in love with you.'

Not the most subtle of approaches, but it worked.

Lorna stopped pacing and started sitting.

'Sorry?'

'Paddy Wallop is *in love* with you!'

'Don't be daft.'

'Lorna – I'm serious.' Gloria was smiling – as if it wasn't such a bad thing. 'He told me – that's why he came down here. To look for you.'

'You mean . . . ?'

'In L-O-V-E with you.' And she pressed gently onto her friend's chest with her forefinger. Gloria hadn't known Lorna long, but she had never seen her like this. Her head was down looking at her knees and the long blonde bob was forming a still curtain either side of her face. She was embarrassed. *Actually* embarrassed.

'He can't be . . . I . . .'

'He's been trying to contact you for weeks. He wants to sort this whole tax bill thing out for you he read about in the papers, but you've been avoiding him.'

'Well, I couldn't possibility take money for—'

'Lorna. The guy has been paying you God knows how many grand a year to get publicity for a product which it is not possible to get publicity for. Why do you think he's been doing that, eh?'

Lorna looked at Gloria sideways up through her eyebrows like a shy schoolgirl who'd just been asked a difficult question during a telling-off.

'Because he's stupid?'

'*He-llo?* I don't think so, Lorna. Dirty Great Mercedes? Degree in Medicine? Built own business from scratch? Worldwide customer base? Armani suits?'

'Armani?'

'Ye-hess!'

'I didn't notice.'

'Well, then – *you're* a bit thick, aren't you?'

'And you say he came here looking for me? Well, I mean, what was he expecting – what did he want if it wasn't . . . ?'

'Lorna . . .' Gloria was surprised at how quickly Lorna had gone from being brittle and hard to soft and squidgy. But then, they were very alike in some ways. Under the harsh fishnets and Prada suits of every tough modern girl lies the froth and femininity of their mother's romantic heroines.

'. . . he is *stone mad* about you. He actually told me that he wants to *marry* you, for God's Sake. And he *meant* it.'

It was a lot of things really. The exhaustion of the last few weeks – the strain of her financial disasters; holding the business together; the pounding of her blistered feet; the daily pressure of having to be nice to people *all* the time; the yearly pressure of coming to Christmas and realizing that she was alone again; driving around the city where her mother lived in a limousine and not being able to share it with her. But mostly it was the tender way that Gloria looked at her when she said the word 'marry'. Lorna had never thought about marriage. Not really. At least not in relation to *herself*. It just wasn't an idea that had seemed worth entertaining. The Young Woman's Ideal of Romance had left her years ago, along with the few short relationships she had had in her twenties. The ones where she had been brave enough to hope. The idea that someone – *anyone* – wanted to marry her, and that it wasn't some sort of a sick joke, reached down into that place where Lorna kept her secrets and touched them so sharply that Ireland's Most Successful PR Queen suddenly burst into tears.

For two hours, they sat like that. Lorna crying and Gloria laughing, then Gloria crying and Lorna laughing, then both of them laughing and Lorna crying again. Had David Ashman not been sculpting his goatee into the shape of a heart, he would doubtless have been impressed with the level of Love-Carpeting that was going on in the very next room.

By eight o'clock, Lorna was almost back to normal. Although, it would have to be said, it was a softer and, some would say, slightly more normal 'normal' than it had been before.

'Jesus – look at the time! We'd better get ready . . .'

The two women put in one hard hour of pumicing, powdering and perfuming, and by the time they were ready to make their grand entrance to the library, they could have knocked an army of twenty-year-old fashion models off their pretty little perches.

'You all right, love?' said Gloria as she linked her New Best Friend at the top of the Grand Staircase.

'Sure am,' said Lorna.

And for the first time in as long as she could remember, Lorna Cafferty realized that she meant it.

34

Outside, the party was in full swing. Elton hadn't turned up ('*Yet! – Boys – yet!*') but Lorna's black-bow-tied troupe had already let a good one hundred of Ireland's most committed partygoers and social climbers through the gates of Ballynafiddy.

Rory Mac Rory's Roadshow was in full swing.

Despite the fact that he was a National Celebrity and, as such, shouldn't *really* have been Dirtying His Hands and Compromising His Image (arguments which were put forward in negotiations by his Acidic Agent to procure him the Highest Possible Fee), the Man With the Mad Jumpers was enjoying himself. 'Randy Mac's' pretty new assistant Clodagh had hit her Touch-up Toleration Threshold on the way down in the car, alighting speedily and without notice during a brief traffic stoppage in the town of Athlone, in time to catch the last train back home to Dublin, the safety of her boyfriend and the Saturday job section of the *Irish Times*. And while Rory was a little lacking on the technical side these days, help had been acquired from a spindly little

DJ/hairdresser calling himself 'Scooter' who had volunteered his services after Rory's agent made an announcement for help over the mike, which, eventually, they had both got working.

Rory was having a ball, Dishing the Discs *'This is one of my Fave Raves from the Swinging 70s – remember this one, folks? Ih-hits "Ser-wur-heet Caroline" by the Master of Music Himself – Mr Neillo Diamondo!'*

After Mud's *'70s Boogie Tune – "Tiger Feet!"'* (which Lorna had adopted as Her Song of the Night after thinking they were singing *'Tired Feet'*), Scooter announced his price for doing the actual table-turning. It was to choose every other record himself, and Rory Mac, not wishing to share one single penny of his fee with this spiky-fringed little guttie, agreed.

The ensuing mix of You-Spent-the-Last-Twenty-Years-Trying-to-Forget-Them-80s-One-Hit-Wonders and Bad-Neighbours-Hammering-Shelves-at-3-a.m.-Rave-Tracks was nothing if not eclectic.

However, a film-maker (and there were several there – although they were mostly of the Hairy-Clever-Looking-for-Money variety as opposed to the Glossy-Oscar-Looking-for-a-Ride variety) might have found it an apt soundtrack for the Great Festival of Romance that was taking place in the Parish of Kilbunion, county Galway, Ireland, that balmy, summer evening.

THE GREAT FESTIVAL OF ROMANCE

LOVE AMONG THE CANAPÉS

1. CATERING TENT IN GROUNDS OF HISTORIC IRISH CASTLE.

Soundtrack: Moby's 'Bodyrock' (Scooter). Sound F.X.: bang – walloping of pots and pans. Lots of people, men shouting.

Story so far: Judge's wife, the voluptuous MELANIE MUFTON, *has come away for the weekend in search of fun and distraction from the philandering cruelty of her husband,* JUDGE 'MUFF', *as his mistress has now taken to calling him. On seeing all of the beautiful, svelte creatures swanning around this elegant soirée,* MELANIE *has become disheartened at the general Grumble-weedy Frumpiness of her own appearance, and has gone looking for the one place where she always knows she will find solace and comfort. A fridge. We find her alone and desolate tearing the lid off a catering-size tub of Häagen-Dazs in the supplies tent.*

Meanwhile, bodyguard CHUCK, *due to the profusion of bouncers employed by the party organizers, finds himself with no work for the evening. The beer in Ireland being very much stronger than it is at home,* CHUCK *is already in a state of Acute Inebriation when we find him staggering across the lawn in the general direction of Nowhere in Particular. Due to experiences earlier in the day, he is sporting a crazed head and a hard-on that could ride a cow from the next field.* CHUCK *stumbles into the catering tent clearly in search of Something. He passes a trestle table and grabs a canapé, stuffing it unceremoniously, almost unaware of himself, into his mouth.*

CHEF: Gerraway outta tha' an' geh dem mushrooms inta dem dere vol au-vents! Gerraway outta tha' ya greedy gobshite.

CHUCK: Fuck off!

Spying the fridge through a gap in the supplies-tent curtain, CHUCK *makes his way haphazardly towards it, the kitchen workers avoiding his substantial, menacing frame.* MELANIE *turns around and sees* CHUCK's *heaving frame lurching towards her. (Close-up* CHUCK*) Chuck raises an eyebrow which twitches uncertainly across his vast forehead in* MELANIE's *general direction. (Close-up* MELANIE*) Clearly in a state of some flux,* CHUCK *delivers the line which he always says to the ladies on occasions such as these.*

CHUCK: You look like a woman who's 'Been to Brazil!'

For the first time in his life this line actually works, as MELANIE, *only too obviously, knows exactly what it means. (Close-up* CHUCK. *Close-up* MELANIE*)*

MELANIE: And back again – Big Boy!

CHUCK *then picks* MELANIE *up in his vast arms and carries her into the catering tent. Clearing the staff out with a loud roar, he then flings her down on the trestle table (Director's note: a platter of mushroom vol-au-vents could go crashing to the ground in slow motion here?), and makes mad passionate love to her among the canapés.*

CUT TO . . .

OFF-DUTY CARPET FITTING

2. INTERIOR. POWDER ROOM INSIDE HISTORIC IRISH CASTLE

Soundtrack: 'Uptown Girl' by Billy Joel (Rory). Sound F.X.: loud sobbing and roaring through a toilet-cubicle door. Tinkle of bottle against glass.

Background: ex-Miss Ireland LYNDA LAVERTY *is trapped in a toilet. After being publicly humiliated by Ireland's Most Popular Talk-Radio Host over the microphone in front of society glitterati ('Oh I see the Bouncy Castle's arrived – No. It's my OLD friend Lynda Laverty!') she has taken refuge in the ladies' bathroom with a bottle of gin for comfort. Now, with mascara streaming down her once-beautiful face, and a false lash dangerously spiking the side of her eye,* LYNDA *is unable to find the door handle to get out. She is in a state of obvious inebriation and emotional distress.*

Meanwhile, Love Doctor DAVID ASHMAN *is on his way up to his room in the castle to reapply some eau-de-cologne and check on his new heart-shaped goatee. It been almost two hours since he has viewed himself in a mirror, and he is anxious to check that he still exists and is looking as good as he did when he started out. Unable to find the key for his room, and sensing that the castle itself is empty, he sneaks into the ladies' powder room on the ground floor. Once inside he hears wailing from inside the cubicle.*

LYNDA: Lemme how-ow-ow-ow-out. Am stuckinna toileh and no-ho-ho-ho-ho-body cares abo-how-how-how-out m-he-he-he-heeeeeeeee!

DR ASHMAN: Are you all right in there?

   LYNDA *stops and there is a dead silence as she realizes that there is actually somebody outside the door. (Cut to interior of cubicle:* LYNDA *blinking: she is in shock)*

DR ASHMAN: I said, is there anybody in there?

LYNDA: *(Pause)* No?

DR ASHMAN *looks at himself in the mirror, brushes an eyelash off his cheek, smooths his hands over his goatee, then opens the cubicle door, indicating that it has been unlocked all along.* ASHMAN *looks at* LYNDA. *(Close-up* LYNDA: *blinking, confused. Director's note: false eyelash frees itself from eyeball and flickers down her cheek)* LYNDA *looks at* ASHMAN. *(Close-up* ASHMAN) *(Director's note: Face conveys look of intense interest, indicating male character's sexual attraction to vulnerable, needy women.)*

LYNDA: Who-isseauw?

DR ASHMAN: I *(dramatic pause)* am the Doctor of Love.

CUT TO . . .

The library of Ballynafiddy where Paddy Wallop has just arrived. He is standing awkwardly in a group which consists Of Mr Big, Bridget Wilkin-Walkins and her husband, Mr Tom Wilkin-Walkins, the clever biochemistry, scientist-type person who just happens to be working on an Outreach experimental farming project for Mr Big's GM company. Bridget, being as resourceful and subtle a social climber as ever there was one, had managed to wangle an invite via Big's American PR office without going through the Cafferty channels. And oh – Oh! – *how* she was looking forward to seeing her dear – *dear* friend Lorna again! The Wilkin-Walkins duo, operating from within the perfect exclusivity of their Happily-Married Unit as they did, failed to notice the growing levels of discomfort in their conversation companions.

Big had been made to take the pledge to be a pioneer at the age of eleven by his mammy. In America, not drinking was not a problem. Not even, at a push, if you were Irish. Xavier managed fine on Perrier and Prozac and, happily for him, he was important and powerful enough for his disinterest in drink neither to be noticed nor commented upon by the people he met the world over. However, not drinking was quite simply *not* an option at this Celebratory Extravaganza. Put bluntly, when it came to occasions such as these, drinking was the Point. Despite his insistence to the contrary, Big had found himself almost being wrestled to the ground by a friendly young barman called Jack, who hadn't the least interest in the fact that Big was clearly Too Important to Be Bullied, and had been 'Ah gwan there'd' into two pints of plain and a whiskey chaser. Frankly, Big already had the demi-sway of the semi-pissed, was having trouble focusing properly and, worryingly, was starting to feel a bit ... well ... cross and irritable. He didn't know it, but Xavier Big was about a half one away from Full-On Aggressive Drunkenness.

Pioneer Number Two may have been clutching a Fanta, but he was equally as discombobulated. Paddy Wallop was *frantic* with nerves. The Armani was drenched in sweat – and he too was irritable. Irritable that he was standing here, like a prick, talking to these *eejits* – and all he had to look forward to was Lorna coming down the stairs and finally blowing him out for ever. At least while she was in Dublin, or locked (albeit in his imagination) in some grand castle, she was trapped in a life that was far away from him. He could dream, and wonder and want. *This*, standing here, waiting for her to come down the stairs and reject him was purgatory of the first order. He cursed Gloria for putting him through it, although she was clearly a nice woman and trying to do her best. However, Lorna's Final Word was a reality that Paddy didn't feel ready or able for.

But however hysterical were the two men's inner monologues, they had no choice but to be led through the skilled level of social chit-chat on offer by the Charming and Undeniable Beigeness of the Perfect Marrieds.

Currently on the agenda was the Four-Legged Turkey Research Project which Big's GM company was funding. Tom was waving his hands about in an uncharacteristic display of enthusiasm for his own work in modifying a cow to produce human breast milk. Big was humming general agreement – despite the fact that he was, strangely, longing for somebody to say something he could disagree with so that he would have the opportunity to punch them. And in the meantime, Bridget's skilled and social third eye was on turbo-swivel waiting for Lorna to come in and 'catch' her.

Paddy found the whole conversation absolutely disgusting, for all sorts of Law-of-Nature-type reasons. Being a medical man himself, and not entirely ignorant of the necessary rigours of research, etc., he could have easily swept in and flattened the pair of them verbally.

However, given that he was Big's guest, and this Tom-person had a lovely beige wife, something which he didn't have, Paddy just kept quiet.

'Here she is!'

Bridget put every tooth in her head on full show with her widest, brightest, most fancy-seeing-you-here smile. Lorna was here – and linking that hairdresser woman. *Linking* her. Like a great big linking lesbian. Oh, this was fantastic. This was *better* than she could have *ever* hoped for!

'Lorna! Darling! And your . . . *friend* . . . Gertie!'

'Gloria.' Ms O'Neill made her complete disinterest in the WW contingent clear by taking the exit before the introductions were complete.

'I'll leave you to it,' she said to Lorna, giving Paddy an encouraging smile as she sashayed out the french windows. Big looked after her with a level of drink-induced Lascivious Want that was new to the lifetime teetotaller – a strange feeling, but not entirely unwelcome, it would have to be said.

Lorna stood next to Paddy. She was so *ready* for this it hurt.

Very gently, she put her hand down and brushed a tiny fist into the cup of Paddy Wallop's large palm. The hairs on his arms pricked the Armani wool so hard, he thought they might puncture the fabric.

'So-ooo, Lorna? Another fab-ulous party?' Bridget cooed.

She waited for Lorna's reaction. How did you get here? How do you know Big? I see you're wearing that dress *ag-ain*? Something – anything. Bridget was ready for her. All she needed was a starting point. Something to get her teeth into.

Lorna just smiled and said, 'Thank you.'

Bridget tried again.

'So your friend Gloria? Seems like a *sw-eet* sort of person and, I believe, quite well-known in her chosen, em, *trade*.'

Bridget said the word 'trade' in the same disgusted and puzzled tone as a gentlewoman who has been forced, by circumstance, to use the word 'penis'.

'And how very *praag-matic* of you to bring your hairdresser down with you. Although, I suppose one reaches a certain age and . . .'

Lorna had not looked at Paddy at all yet. Her hand was just sitting there. In his. Not doing anything in particular. Just forming this warm little ball in his palm. He did not know what to do with himself. Should he curl his fingers around it in an obvious holding action? But perhaps it had just fallen in there by accident. Perhaps she hadn't meant for him to . . .

'Actually, Gloria came down here as our guest. My fiancé has a house very near here.'

Paddy's heart sank as low as any man's heart had ever sunk – Jesus, what a fool he'd been!

Then Lorna looked up at Paddy's face and gave him a kind of soft pleading smile – the kind of look he recognized from that day when he caught her in the field.

'Don't you, darling?'

Paddy's heart all but shot out through his chest and bounced off the rosewood panelling that lined the library walls.

Paddy wasn't sure of much in that moment. He wasn't sure if Lorna was joking or not, or if he had heard her right, or if this was all just part of some weird tricky social game that her fancy social Dublin set were into. But Paddy Wallop was sure of one thing. And that was, if he was ever going to win Lorna Cafferty's heart, fair and square, he was going to have to be up to her. He was going to have to be suave, and cool, and smart and adventurous, and he was going to have to be *able* for the sophisticated juggling circus that she lived in.

Big had been standing there thinking. Thinking in that roundabout, delayed-reaction way that drunk people do. Seemingly, apropos of nothing – he lurched his eyes in Lorna's general direction and said, 'Am payin' you to fand me a woman an' I want *that* one . . .' and he waved his whiskey glass in the direction of the doors out of which Gloria was long gone.

Paddy had had enough by now. With his free hand he pointed at Tom Wilkin-Walkins and said in a voice, so assured, so confident, so goddamn high and mighty that he barely recognized himself, 'I think it's a *disgrace* what you're doing with them cows.' He pointed at Bridget Wilkin-Walkins and he said, 'And at *your* age you should know better than to put a woman down in front of her man.' And he pointed at Xavier Big and said, 'Thank you very much for your hospitality but frankly, Lorna doesn't *need* your money and is far above finding wives for any man – any man, that is, except for me. Now if you'll excuse us – I think we'll be off now. Ready, darling?' And with that, Paddy Wallop curled his palm tightly around Lorna's delicate little hand and gave it a firm – and it would have to be said quite deliciously *masterful* – squeeze.

As they walked out the door, leaving a congregation of gobsmacked mouths behind them, Lorna gave one last look around the grounds at the Most Important Party of Her Life and decided that – yes! – she was more than ready to leave it all behind.

35

Flame had re-applied the warpaint and was ready for round two. *No man* – especially not a filthy-rich American one – had better *dare* resist her. Clearly, she hadn't been trying hard enough in the limo – or the other two goons had put him off. But one thing was clear. Within the next hour she was going to have that American bastard tied so tight into her gusset that he wouldn't be able to *breathe* another woman's name!

She punctured holes in grass and gravel until finally the only place left to check was the castle itself. She was in luck. With no Lorna to torture, the Wilkin-Walkins had just left, and Big was on his own in the library. This was going to be a cinch.

Flame walked in with her best catwalk wiggle – squeezing her buttocks together under the flimsy dress till they were dancing like two rats in a sack. She shut the french doors behind her. She did a Paris turn at the door, smiled, pouted – then *catwalked*-two-three, *turned*-two-three, *catwalked*-two-three over to the chaise long. Before Big knew it there was a five-foot-eleven redhaired model pawing her pedicured toes across the newly Ralph Laurened upholstery looking like she was in serious danger of 'accidentally losing' a nipple.

Flame looked at Big. Big looked at Flame. Flame licked her lips and gave him her best front-cover sultry 'Take Me' look. Big stiffened. Flame arched. Big grinned. Flame let out a little 'hummf' moan. Big took a step forward. Flame – *whoops!* – lost that nipple. Big – a little unsteadily – took another step forward. Flame – *ooh there it is!* – found said nipple and began to twist with tip of french-polished nails. Big took another step forward.

Big tripped over foot stool.

Library door opened and Sam Cohen walked in.

The last two events were *not* on Flame's agenda.

'Sorry – I was just looking for— Shit, man! Are you all right?'

Sam rushed over to help Big to his feet, and could feel Flame's eyes boring hot spikes into the back of his head.

'He's *fine*,' she said sharply – anxious to get back to the whole high-class porn film sequence of events. 'You can *go* now.'

Big lumbered to his feet, and a little whiskey gremlin whispered through his mind-fog and reminded him who the magnificent redhead was. Sadly, the gremlin didn't stretch to brain/mouth co-ordination and he blurted out, 'Hey – you're the one that *smells* bad!'

At that precise moment, having done a quick round of the grounds, Gloria came in to check up on Lorna and Paddy. She marched straight into Big's line of vision, and with his sharpened sense of vision he stretched his arms towards Gloria and shouted, 'Thass the one I want! – C'mere . . .'

With that last announcement, Big lurched forward on both feet simultaneously and fell, head first, over the foot stool once again.

Gloria and Sam barely had time to take Big by both elbows and lift him, when the fiery dervish that had been nipple-tweaking on the chaise, enraged by Big's earlier pronouncement regarding her unsanitary hygiene levels, came spinning across the room.

'You fucking sla-aag!' she screamed at Gloria. 'You fucking ruin everything – I'm going to . . .'

She did not get the chance to finish the sentence, because she was not halfway through it when she felt the firm grip of Sam Cohen's small hand on the back of her neck in a paralysing grip.

'If you were as dangerous as you look, Flame – we'd be scared. Now get out of my sight.'

And he led her, by the neck, out of the room and deposited her on the patio, locking the door behind her.

'Now you,' he said, pointing at Gloria, 'are owed an apology.'

What the hell was this? If Sam thought that just by kicking Flame out Gloria was going to get on to some great big 'Thank You, Mr Cohen' trip, he was very much mistaken.

'If you think that just by kicking Flame out you're going to get—'

'I don't want anything, Gloria. I just want you to listen to me. For a change, eh? Just listen?'

Gloria didn't have much fight left in her, but what she did have left, she was more than willing to put into fighting Frank and Flame and Sam Cohen.

She sat down on the chaise.

'Where's Frank, then?'

That's what she was expecting. That Sam was going to whizz Frank in for some kind of an apology game. Manipulate her into some kind of a scheme that involved her giving him money and him shitting all over her. She'd been here before.

'What?'

'Frank, Frank? You know? Your Oldest Friend? Where is he? Come on, then, wheel him in for your Big Apology scene. *Sorry* for ripping you off, Gloria. *Sorry* for being a shitty husband, Gloria. *Sorry* for not managing your business properly, Gloria. I'll do better this time, Gloria – I promise. Then you do the He's a Gobshite But He's All Right Really routine. Well, *come on*. Get on with it. I don't have all night – let's get it over and done with.'

Gloria was feeling rather pleased with herself. She'd got them sussed all right. Coming down here after her with all their Big Bloke Clever Dickery. She knew what it was all about. She was going to get fucked anyway, but at least she had let them know that *she* knew it was coming.

Sam was shocked – but then, deep down he must

have known what she thought of him. She'd been through a lot. The anger was justified.

'Frank's not here, Gloria.'

He sat down next to her.

'What do you mean, he's not here? What about . . .'

'Flame? I don't know –' Sam shrugged and shook his head and held his hands up in the air, in a real puzzled Jewish-guy way that made Gloria believe him – 'just looking for a rich guy, I guess?'

'So what was all that about an apology?'

'It's *me*, Gloria. *I* have to apologize.'

Sam turned his head away from her face and faced the floor. He really just wanted to grab her by the shoulders and seduce her into the kiss that he had waited over ten years to give her. The kiss that had always made him walk away from her – the kiss that had only ever allowed him to be half her friend because he was always afraid of wanting so much more. It was that bit more than he had ever felt he could give her until now. But Hollywood Feet-Sweeping physical gestures were not Sam Cohen's thing. He was an important man, but when something mattered to him as much as Gloria did, he remembered he was small and bald – and small, bald men didn't generally Give Good Feet-Sweeping. He would have to apologize first and feet-sweep later. If he was lucky.

'Gloria – this isn't easy but I feel I must let you know that, over the years, I have always remained loyal to Frank, and in many ways, in that way, as such, it has meant that our friendsh—'

Gloria didn't want to wait. She knew what he was

going to say. Sam had come down here without Frank. He hadn't betrayed her – and that was enough. Maybe it was the whole Lorna/Paddy thing, or the influence of this mad American, or the shocked look on Flame's face, or being away from the salon for a few days; or maybe it was the evening light playing across the bald pate of this little man's head and the shy way he was stuttering out his words – but Gloria O'Neill just grabbed the moment, and, without thinking, she took Sam's face in her hands, held it, looked at it, smiled and said 'Shut up' – then launched into the longest, loveliest, lushest kiss that either of them had experienced in their entire lives.

When they had finished, and were still flushed with the glory, the relief, the outrageous fantasticness of kissing a person whom you have wanted to kiss for ages, a head of tinted brown hair set slightly askew from its usual state of perfection emerged from the back of the chaise long and, underneath it, the undoubtedly green face of Mr Big said, 'Hi fthink hime going to be shick!'

36

Maeve had been successful in her endeavour to procure
the lead singer of The Trembling Celtics. Although, it
would have to be said, the blasé way in which she had
approached it was not born out of an innocence, but
rather the certain knowledge that engaging a pop star in
the promise of a no-strings ride immediately before a
public performance would *not* be much of a challenge in
itself.

All the same, Sandy felt terrible. She had escaped
from Big's clutches as soon as she could, but by the time
she had got back out into the hall, Maeve and Liam
were gone. She didn't mind about him so much, but she
felt awful about going off with Maeve's Big Dreamboat.
The way he had dismissed her best friend, after Sandy
had built her up into believing IT was going to happen,
had left the redhead feeling terrible.

Sandy had instinctively known that the Rock Stars'
Camp would be a good place to start, and cursory
investigations had revealed that someone fitting Maeve's
description had indeed been seen going into the lead

singer's trailer. Sandy sat by a nearby tree and waited. If Maeve's stories about rock stars were true – this wouldn't take long.

⬭

While Sandy was sitting, Liam was wandering.

When he and Maeve had made their exit from the Grand Hall, Liam had a Great Fire of Action raging in his belly. He was going to go to Big and HANDIN-HISNOTICE! He was going to grab Sandy and SWEEP-HEROFFHERFEET! He was going to stay in Ireland and write a BRILLIANT NOVEL!

But after an hour of walking around the party looking for someone to start off this whole Action Movie with, Liam's great intentions had kind of . . . well . . . *dissipated*. What if Big got cross when he handed in his notice? What if Sandy told him to piss off? What if he got writer's block? What if he couldn't get his skincare products in Ireland? What if . . . what if . . . what if . . . ? Liam's internal whingeing was really starting to bore him.

Walking around looking at other people having a good time; other people being DJs; other people being in rock bands; other people living lives and having fun and – well – just *doing* stuff, made Liam realize that *not* doing stuff, or rather stuff that he wanted to do, had become a way of life for him.

He *wanted* to do something about it of course, but perhaps it had become just too much of a habit at this stage. Dreams were just about all he was good at.

371

Turning them into reality was just too hard. It was as if Liam was stuck in a buried bunker underneath his own life; the TV that contained his dreams was busted and above him was all the success and love he ever wanted – but he was just too much of a wimp to climb out and get it.

As his motivation to find Big and Sandy took a nosedive, Liam went in search of Maeve. Maybe he'd get to meet a rock star who was Doing Something with his life. Wouldn't that be a *big treat* for him.

He was almost on top of the Trembling Celtics' trailer and about to knock on the door when Sandy, who had been wistfully watching Maeve's brother's bottom walk across the field and thinking about her friend's claim that she fancied him, called out, 'Don't go in!'

Liam gave a little start accompanied by a squeal – which he knew made him look like a girl. That's what he was. A girl. A daisy. A fairy in waiting. Waiting for what? Some handsome princess to come charging through and pick him up on a white horse? He wandered over to Sandy and stood there like a tit. Looking at her. A stupid prat. Not even able to muster up a few smart words for himself to impress the woman he had fallen head over heels in love with. He didn't even have the nous to be nervous. What was the point? Nothing was going to happen anyway.

'You look a bit down,' she said. Her voice sounded sweet. He had been expecting some nasty quip.

'Yeah, well.' Oh Christ. It had started – the voices

that had plagued his teenage years. Yes – here it was!
He-Man vs Wimp Hour in Liam Murphy's head.

SYLVESTER STALLONE: Yeah well . . . yeah well . . .
yeah well – WHAT? Smarten yourself up, man. Here
she is practically crawling out of the sprig-print dress,
all tousled and lip glossed, and you're too much of a
GIRL to do anything about it. G'wan – be a man –
give it to her!

WOODY ALLEN: But . . . but . . . suppose she doesn't
like me? Suppose she recoils from my advances?
Suppose she doesn't kiss me back? Suppose she smells
those Cheesy Pringles I ate earlier? Suppose I trip on
wet grass on my way over and break my nose and
bang her head against the tree?

Sandy butted in on the two-voices-one-man conversation she had a funny feeling might be going on.

'Are you going to come and sit down or are you just
going to stand there – staring?'

Oh God! She had noticed him staring! She knew he
liked her!

Sandy was doing nothing. Just sitting there – smiling
at him. She didn't *look* like she would rip his throat out
if he went to kiss her. In fact, the way she had shrugged
the dress over one shoulder and not bothered readjusting
it suggested that a bit of breast-manhandling wouldn't
be entirely out of the question. However, Liam had
whipped himself up into such a frenzy of mortified
desire, that he actually thought he might burst into tears.
The realization that he was about ten seconds away

from a dribbly display that would surely horrify any woman started to put manners on his emotions. The He-Man stepped in to save him.

SLY: Look. You're a grown man. Okay – so you're a bit on the sensitive side. But some women like that – and look at her. She's a fucking Goddess. If you don't whip in there and drop the hand, some other bastard's going to come along and nab her. Maybe even tonight – sure the place is crawling with them. G'wan, man. Take a chance. If you're not in – you can't win!

And that was how it happened. It wasn't easy. Liam did indeed slide on a piece of wet grass on his way over, but he kept going. Thirty seconds later, he had launched himself into her – and to his eternal delight, Sandy Nolan – Goddess, Colleen, Wildcat – was kissing him back.

Big time.

By the time Maeve came out of the trailer her best friend and her brother were all but hammer and tongs at each other. She didn't have the manners to wait for them to 'finish' because, by the cut of them, they were only just getting started.

She stood over them and gave Liam's buttocks a little kick.

'Hey! *Inside* is the place for that kind of malarkey. Preferably a bed.'

The two of them came up for air, and they were smiling like a couple of bold young wans, which in reality was really all that they were. Maeve was happy for them, but she was still blistering from Big's rejection.

'Didn't seem to bother you – *groupie*,' said Liam good-heartedly.

'Ah – we didn't do anything in the end. Just helped him polish off a half of Jack Daniel's. We had a nice chat.'

'Muryaa!' said Sandy.

'Don't care if you don't believe me. Anyway – they're on in a few minutes so he chucked me out and this is a *lovely* display to be faced with in my state of romantic desperation.'

Maeve said it jokingly, but New Love had sharpened the young couple's ears to the genuineness of her disappointment.

Liam and Sandy got up, and the three of them walked towards the castle.

Halfway across the field, Liam stopped and made an announcement.

'I'm going to hand in my notice!' he said, 'Right now! Fuck it, I am staying here.'

'What will you do?' said Maeve.

'I dunno – copywriting again? Write a book? Certainly keep your best friend here supplied with Vintage Murphy Saliva . . .'

'Urgh! Don't be disgusting.'

'Could be a full-time job,' quipped Sandy.

They found Big standing outside the library doors, getting a bit of fresh air. The drink – he had decided – did *not* agree with him. His mother had been right, he realized, not for the first time. He felt awful, and kind of depressed. This was his party, but he didn't know anyone at it. Everyone was just drinking and talking to each other. His tie and jacket were off, and above his open shirt there was a carpet of thick black hair. He looked groggy and rough – just how Maeve liked 'em. A shiver of desire ran through her, then a pebble of disappointment dropped in her stomach as she realized that she was Never Going to Get her billionaire. She held back and let Liam and Sandy walk forward. She hoped Liam would be quick, so that she could concentrate on getting maggoty drunk for the rest of the night.

Big was delighted when he saw Liam come towards him. A friend! And he had that cute redhead with him. That friend of his sister's – this was more like it. The night was looking up.

'Xavier,' he said.

That was okay. This was a party, after all. First-name terms were in order – especially if he was going to introduce him to . . .

'I want to hand my notice in. I've decided to stay in Ireland with my –' he looked at Sandy in an almost unbearably cutesy way and took her hand – 'girlfriend here.'

Big was not impressed. He was not impressed At All!

'But I . . .'

'I'm sorry, Xavier – my mind's made up. I've really enjoyed working with you but—'

The Big Man blew.

'You *cannot* leave my company. You *cannot* do this to *meee*! You are Under Contract to my company for another five years and nobody – NOBODY – resigns from my employ unless they are . . . unless they are . . . unless they are fired. And yes! You are FIRED! I fire you!'

Liam stood there shocked, but it wasn't enough for Big.

'And what's more – I am DISGUSTED at the way you have behaved this evening. You know very well what tonight was all about – and here you are – being with a . . . with a . . . with a . . . WOMAN yourself when it was supposed to be MY night. MY party. MY woman . . . Who paid for all this is what I want to know. ME! ME! ME! That's who! And so furthermore . . . GET OUT. All of you! Get off my land and out of my house NOW!'

Liam and Sandy stood there, stuck to the spot with horror at the boiling red-faced vision that was spitting acid in their faces.

But something had happened to Maeve Murphy of Brennan Road, Stillorgan. That little pebble of pride that had dropped earlier when Big had rejected her grew inside her, and fuelled by the indignation of her Irish Pride had grown into a red-hot volcano of fearsome, untamable proportions. No one – NO ONE got to cross her family *or* her friends and got away with it. How Dare He! Horror that she could have displayed any interest in this man, and loyalty to Liam, Sandy and the Basic Ethics of Irish Party Hospitality drove Maeve Murphy forward into Big's Personal Space.

Before he knew it, Xavier Big had a dark-haired wildcat with poison shimmering out of her emerald-green eyes poking him in the chest.

'HOW DARE YOU SPEAK TO PEOPLE LIKE THAT! Who the FUCK do you think you are – coming over here with your Big Shot American Bollocks speaking down to Good Irish Citizens as if You Were *Somebody*? Well, let me tell *you* something, Mr I've Got Billions and I'm *So* Important, we don't GIVE A SHIT over here about your Smart-Arse Ego! As far as I – WE – are concerned – you can Take Your Money and you can Shove It Up Your Hole – because it doesn't mean SHITE if you haven't got the decency to show people Good Manners and Respect!'

Then Maeve Murphy *threw* her handbag over her shoulder, *snapped* him one last Killer Tigress glower and *marched* across the gravel with a high-heeled-catwalk-wiggle that would have put Poor Flame to shame. The other two lovebirds pottered after her, arm in arm.

Little did all three know what had happened to Mr Big in that moment.

No one, in his whole life, had ever put him in his place like that; spoken to him with such shoot-from-the-hip honesty, such forcefulness, such discipline, such passion. No one, that is, since his dead mammy had died.

Mr Big had fallen head-over-heels. With the Real Thing this time, a Proper Irish Woman just like his mother.

He went inside his New Irish Home and up to his

four-poster bedroom. He got showered and changed. As he was leaving, Mr Big checked himself in the mirror and gave his reflection a Big Billionaire Hollywood wink.

Now, as a Fully Fledged Irish Charmer, he was going to go back down to that party and – finally – Get His Gal!

EPILOGUE

Celtic Tigress

World-renowned fashion pundit and 'Friend to the Stars' Clarissa von Biscuit brings you this week's hottest gossip on the Social Scene from Dublin & New York.

Wedding Belles!

Irish-American society was positively sizzling this week as news came that the final guest list for American tycoon Xavier Big's impending wedding to our very own Maeve Murphy of Brennan Road, Stillorgan, county Dublin, was about to be released. Although a relative newcomer to New York society, this raven-haired colleen has proven to be a gem in our crown and has already been christened the 'New Jackie' by Big's ex-fashion advisor, Mr Sugar Duprés, who has now taken on the role of Xavier's Right-Hand Man (although he doesn't look like he plays with the right hand to me – if you know what I mean!) Yours truly is naturally waiting for the familiar plop of gold card on carpet. Xavier and his new wife intend to honeymoon here in Ireland in the recently purchased Ballynafiddy Castle where Big held his introductory party to Irish society last year, and at which the couple first met. Word is, we'll be seeing a lot more of America's Biggest Billionaire before the year is out!

Incontinence!

One name which will most certainly not be included on the list is that of Incontinence King, Mr Paddy Wallop of Bunkelly, county Galway. After his 'run-in' with Xavier last year (some say it was over the heart of your friend and mine, the Lovely Lorna Cafferty – I say it was sour grapes over the title Ireland's Most Eligible Bachelor which our Paddy wins hands down every time), he is sure to be off the list. Of the Wallop/Cafferty Day Itself, I can report little because I was sunning myself in The Villa at the time, but I did hear that the bride's mother – the unforgettable (alas!) Sylvia Cafferty – made a guest appearance. Seemingly mother and daughter were reunited as Paddy flew in Ireland's First Lady of Divorce as a 'surprise' for his bride. And for those vultures among you who delight in a bit of spark-flying – I regret to say that the word is there was none. Not a dry eye in the house, apparently, the theme of the day being Slobbery Sentiment. In any case Paddy and Lorna looked well recovered when I bumped into the recently returned honeymooners at the Galway Races last week. Lorna (who is currently taking time out from her PR business to oversee the redecoration of her new home, Wallop Mansion) was sporting a delightful cream suit by Irish design duo Oakes, in whose business she is rumoured to be a 'sleeping partner'. In deference to her recent nuptials, I shan't make a quip about that phrase, but one does wonder how she managed to pull together such an impressive new-business portfolio given her financial disaster last year.

Exposure!

Another resourceful lady is the delightful Gloria O'Neill, who this week officially opened her new chain of nationwide Gaff salons at a charming party at her new home with Husband Numero Duo in

Waiting, Sam Cohen. When asked about his predecessor's recent move to South America with one of his young models, Mr Cohen declined to comment. Rumour has it that 'Bad Frank' (as he was named after his exposure in the whole Underage Model Scandal) was paid off his half of Gloria's business interests before the new salons could be opened. Watch out, Frank! I've heard the girleen's daddy is a big man, mad as hell, and carrying an air ticket with Gloria's name on the cheque!

Books!

I don't normally go to book launches – the crowd is altogether too Hairy and Clever for me. All those dull women in sensible shoes, and what with the warm weather upon us – I just wasn't ready for all that unsightly armpit hair. But this young lad-a-buck's offering was plonked on my desk and, as I was popping stateside for my annual Tiffany Trawl, I took a chance on it as a long-haul read. Set in New York and Ireland, it's a charming tale of how an aspiring young writer wins the heart of a beautiful young red-haired journalist. Now, I shan't pretend to know my Sartre from my Sandals, but *A Dream Date With Sylvia's Plaits* is a wonderful, light-hearted love story that certainly brought a tear to these weary old eyes!

Nameless!

Speaking of weary old eyes, an eminent judge (shan't name names – old-fashioned form of fur handwarmer popular in the 50s – plus word for very heavy weight) was sitting in front of me on the plane. I happened to overhear him telling someone that he had taken a sabbatical to go to America to look for his missing wife, who shall remain nameless (large round fruit, popular in third-rate restaurants as starter – plus name of drug widely used by today's youngsters). Seemingly name-of-fruit left Judge fur-handwarmer for a large, blond American man whom she met at a party last

summer and hasn't been seen since. Fur-handwarmer said that all she took with her was a leather biker jacket belonging to their son and a large supply of leg wax which she had, strangely, been stocking up on.

Cheap and Nasty!

Now here's a cautionary tale for all those young mollies out there looking to seek fame and fortune abroad. Who remembers Flame? International Supermodel? I don't think so! Who did I spy spraying the Good Ladies of New York with an unfortunate confection called Midnight Seduction at the front door of Macy's last week? None Other Than! I gave her agent a quick tinkle just to check, and he confirmed that she had indeed been dropped by the agency and didn't know where she was. I told him about the perfume spraying and his comment was 'Cheap and nasty is, as cheap and nasty does.' Straight-talking Americans – I love them!

Decorating!

Flicking through the New York edition of *Homes of the Rich and Famous* last week, who did I spy but our very own Seamus O'Shaughnessy (know to the more Socially Eclectic among us as that avid partygoer – Nylon). It seems that our stocking-namesaked friend has well and truly 'made it' as a Decorator to the Stars. Having single-handedly refurbished our own historic Ballynafiddy Castle, Nylon took the chance and moved stateside, and was featured lounging in the LA home of a 'famous friend' who 'wished to remain anonymous'. No surprises there! If the photos were anything to go by, Nylon has also picked up an American Tan Dernier along the way, which would suggest more time spent poolside than inside hemming curtains!

Peel and Squeal!

Which puts me in mind of the new sign outside one of my fave beauty spots, BlueEriu, warning fans of the national craze for the Brazilian – Do Not Try This at Home. Seemingly many of Dublin 4's finest have been exposed as cheapskates after unfortunate home-waxing accidents have landed them in casualty. I'm not in the business of naming names, but a Well-Known Television Presenter of a Certain Age and a One-Time Children's Television Presenter (for whom, frankly, the need of a good waxing would come as no surprise to any of us!) have all passed through the hands of the nursing team at Vincent's – one of whom says she has become so proficient at the whole peel and squeal process, she is thinking of taking it up full time. Ladies! Please! Show a little decorum! Bald may be beautiful – but not at the price of a lady's dignity!

Beige!

And dignity is one thing that this lady has in buckets. What about Bridget Wilkin-Walkins's wardrobe at the trial of her husband Tom! While the wife of the man who had been dubbed the Mad Professor for those hideous experiments on cows – which we all know enough about now thank-you-very-much! – listened to his sentence yesterday, she bravely faced the press in that most difficult of ensembles – the Beige Suit. God, how I admire that woman! She may have lost her job, her place on the board of several National Institutions, that gorgeous house in Dalkey, her husband and, lets-face-it, her Standing in Society, but she will always – always – have a place on Clarissa von Biscuit's list of Ireland's Best-Dressed Ladies!

Carpets!

As a fashion doyenne, I have always believed that the tidy appearance of people's outsides is a reflection of their inner lives. In other words, appearances aren't deceptive! And my 'theory' was verified when

famous American Psychologist Dr David Ashman gave his inaugural lecture at the new Institute of Inner Being in Rathmines. All participants, lecturers and students alike, were wearing a 'uniform' of the most magnificent slate-grey suit and white shirt, the ties logoed with the Love Carpet that has become an emblem of Dr Ashman's new movement which is sweeping the world. Chief among his advocates here is Ireland's Premier Beauty Queen and, and I'm sure she won't mind me saying this, is looking more splendid than ever, having lost four stone in weight. Luscious Lynda Laverty 'converted' to the Love-Carpeting Program last year and told me when I commented on her svelte new image, 'You have to learn to carpet your own soul with love before you can carpet anyone else's.' True words from a woman whose 'feisty' reputation indicates she knows a thing or two about such matters! I have heard the dirty word 'cult' being used to describe this most worthy of causes, but take it from me – any organization that advocates such magnificent use of tailoring cannot possibly be a bad thing! All donations can be made through the institute itself and I know where I shall be putting my Christmas charity money this year.

Jumpers!

And if best-dressed is high on your list, you'll be interested to hear that our own Rory Mac Rory is launching a range of jumpers. 'Oh no!' I hear you cry – but really, Rory's not as daft as he looks. He has gone into business with a trendy young club DJ. Former hairdresser 'Scooter' is the design talent behind the new contemporary range of dance-knitwear which he has called 'Raving Randy'. Not my scene, but I'm sure the youngsters will love it!

Word of Warning!

Now, you all know me. I am always the very soul of discretion, especially when it comes to affairs of the heart, and especially when it comes to my own activities in that department. But in the public interest I have a duty to stay silent no longer. I will spare you the details, but suffice to say if you are approached by a powerful older man in the media, one with pointy-bushy eyebrows and drilling blue eyes, who offers you fame and fortune in exchange for a rummage in your bottom drawer – just say no! I shan't be drawn further on the matter in the interests of legal action and good Christian Decency – but ladies – consider yourselves Warned!

Hair!

And speaking of Media Affairs – did anyone see Sandy Nolan's documentary last week on Prozac Addiction in Dublin 2? Very enlightening! I know that dear Sandy's heart is in the right place with her reports on all those serious things like Poverty and Underfunding and Drug Abuse – but really, as one of quite the most pretty girls on television she has a responsibility to us viewers to ditch those dreary khaki overalls and put a bit of colour onto our screens! Pink is 'in' again this summer, dear! Perhaps if you livened up your wardrobe a bit, cynical old birds like me might start to Give a Shit!

Opera!

Before coming back to complete his sell-out dates in Ireland, Hairy Heffernan embarks on his nationwide tour of the UK this week with Baldy Brannigan and the Brothers on their 'Come Home, Sweet Mother Ireland' Tour. Our country-loving cousins over the water (and we all have them, darlings – like it or not!) had better watch out for the boys in Blackpool, Bristol and Weatherby, where they will be performing their US hit 'O Sweet Mother Ireland'. It's not exactly opera, darlings, but it's good to see the old boy back again. There's hope for us all!